Neiko's Five Land Adventure

A.K. Taylor

Soaring Eagle Books
Publishing Division of Soaring Eagle Publications LLC
1670 Chester Road
White Plains, GA 30678
www.soaringeaglebooks.org

This is a work of fiction. Names, characters, places and incidents either are the product of the author's imagination or are used fictitiously, and any resemblance to any actual persons, living or dead, events, or locales is entirely coincidental.
This book was printed in the United States of America.

ISBN 13- 978-1-943326-01-3
ISBN 10- 1-943326-01-0
LCCN- 2010932887

Edited by Ken Kane
Cover Design by Mallory Rock
Illustrated by A.K. Taylor

For other works and to contact the author visit:
www.backwoodsauthor.com

Neiko's Five Land Adventure

Map of Hawote/Georgia

Map of Qari

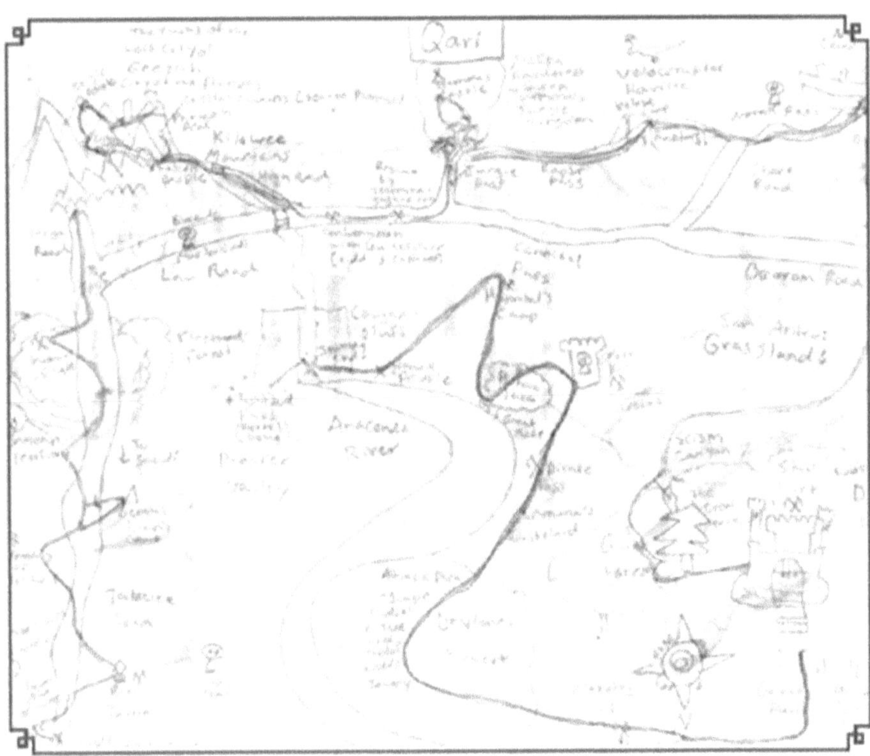

- CHAPTER 1 -

THERE WAS A GIRL who lived in Loganville, Georgia. You would probably believe she was the average teenage girl, but she wasn't. She was extremely shy and quiet, but she had many friends that were outside acquaintances and Indian peers from the hidden land of Hawote, which coexisted with the state. The inhabitants of Hawote had lives similar to hers in how they lived double lives. She went to school just like most ordinary people, but there were things that separated her from the norm, and no one knew about these things, not even her parents because of a rigid code of secrecy in Hawote.

Most of the normal world knew her name to be Amanda Kathrine Hawk, but in her other life she was Captain Neiko Kidd. All the years of her life were spent in living this double life, and she juggled it pretty well; no one suspected, not her close friend Jennifer who lived in Rome or her even close cousin Jessica because she did well in keeping the secret. In both worlds she was the same in looks. She was a fairly short, eighteen-year-old girl with long, black hair, green eyes, and a slim, muscular build. In some ways she was more mature for her age, but in other ways she was not.

Her immaturity came from still playing with toys. She did this because she had trouble letting go of her childhood as well as being able to immerse herself into the imaginary world in an uncanny way. This was an escape from her stressful double life. Other reasons may have been about teen rebellion, losing some of her childhood to being a warrior, and she was a nerd at heart. Because of this double life, she did not do normal the things that teenagers like to do, and for the most part, normal teenage activities bored her, except for going hunting, fishing or camping with her Indian friends or her family. Neiko's friends understood her in this area of her life, but Neiko's parents, especially her mom, was not happy about her playing with toys at this age. Her mom constantly got onto her about this. Neiko's tribal friends more supportive in the matter since she had lost part of her childhood to war and since they knew the truth.

In the world of Amanda Hawk, she was a high school senior who was ready to bust out in the grown world and attend college. She made As in school and had many friends; she dealt with the pains all people had to deal with in school. She didn't go places very much with her outside acquaintances, but she mostly hung out with her Indian peers and stayed close to her family. She was in the high school band where she dealt with most of these pains, but managed to play the French horn without any additional headache. Amanda had a peaceful home life, and she lived close to most of her relatives. She attended church regularly and played for the church. All of this masked her other life.

This other life was much more turbulent; the world of Captain Neiko Kidd was not so peaceful. She was the commanding officer of the Desert Storm Falcons, an organization of woodland warriors, and she was a friend with most of the other tribes who were on the same side. The surname "Kidd" was coined by one of her friends as a joke since she was known as "Neiko the Kid" due to her young age and for some coincidental relations of her heroic deeds in how they vexed their enemies were somewhat likened those of the legendary privateer William Kidd. The name stuck. People in Hawote usually didn't have last names.

Neiko, as well as the others, was in constant gridlock with the Crackedskulls, a band of bloodthirsty savages ruled by Raven and Bloodhawk, who were even worse than their followers. Neiko was always a thorn in their side; she always ruined their plans of conquest of the Desert Storm Falcons. She even liberated the ones that were conquered and made them fight their oppressors. On top of all this, she was also a skilled warrior and an expert leader to the tribes; she fought along with them and trained the young. She was fluent in each of the languages of the tribes, so she had constant relations with each tribe. As one would think, the Crackedskulls despised Neiko, and this was true except at the top of the ladder.

Most would believe Raven and Bloodhawk would be the ones to hate her most, but just as much as she was a pain, she was beautiful. Bloodhawk, Raven's son, was hopelessly in love with her; Raven approved his choice, but Neiko hated the Crackedskull with every ounce of her being. Many times in battle, Crackedskull warriors were ordered to capture her, and every attempt failed. Other times they sent their best men to kidnap her, but they failed as well. Neiko always made it home in time for dinner; she would always tell her mom and dad she had been strolling in the woods when she was really having a battle or a secret meeting. This constant threat of Crackedskull attack was the main reason why Neiko could not participate in normal teenage activities with outsiders since the Crackedskulls could camouflage themselves just like the other inhabitants of Hawote to attack. No one from her family knew that these people existed.

Prior to her life in Loganville, she lived in heavily wooded areas; this is also when she discovered her tribal roots at a very young age, but she now lived in a subdivision with barely any trees. Woods were across the main road to the left of her house, but she was not permitted to enter them, so most of her fighting time was cut short. School was also taking up the rest of her time, so she only got to hear the stories and plan the next move. Meetings were hard to schedule due to the visibility and her busy schedule. She had to set them up when she had time; she had to find a fairly concealed areas, which were few. She could use her room when her parents were not home, so meetings were short these days. When things were boring, she read a book, played video games, played with her animals, went somewhere, or she played with her toys, which consisted of: the Attack Pack, a group of animals and people that were brought together by hardships, the Skull Bearers, who were part of the Imperial army of Ramses, the archenemy. In these crazy times the story begins.

"Oh, yeah, that'll be great! I'll be there in a few minutes," Neiko said into the phone, talking to her cousin Jessica with enthusiasm. "What do you want me to bring? Killer Instinct, Donkey Kong, which one? Three? Okay, anything else? The Attack Pack, any bad guys? Ramses and who else? Osiris, Menes, and five others, okay see ya, bye!" she said and she hung up the phone. Jessica, Neiko's nine-year-old cousin, had arranged for her to spend the night with her, and Neiko's parents agreed. After she got everything packed, she then remembered the meeting scheduled for that afternoon. "Oh crap! I better tell Monganata right away that I ain't able to come," she said thinking out loud. She looked under her bed and pulled out the phone she uses to call her tribal friends, which her mom knew nothing about. She pulled back her Fireball Island board game and pulled out the phone and dialed the numbers to reach Monganata; his phone began to ring. "C'mon pick up! Oh, I hope he hasn't left yet," Neiko whispered hopefully.

The phone was picked up and a woman answered, "Hello!?"

"Hello, Windsong, it's me Neiko. Is Mongie still there? I need to speak with him right away, it's urgent."

"Yes, he is. You just caught him," said Windsong, Monganata's sweet wife. Then she asked, "Neiko, how are you? Is everything all right? I'm terribly worried about you."

"Yeah, everything's fine, and there's no need to worry, there's no big crisis going on," replied Neiko reassuringly.

"That's good," she said relieved. "Oh, here's Mongie. Take care, you hear?"

"I will," said Neiko smiling as she heard the rustle of the phone in the background when Windsong handed the phone to Monganata, the leader of the Chang Battlehawks who was also Neiko's mentor.

"Hello?" asked Monganata.

"Hey, Mongie, it's me Neiko. I was just calling to tell you that I'm not coming to the meeting this afternoon."

"Well, thanks for telling me, but why did you change your mind on such short notice, especially since this meeting was very important?"

"I know. My cousin called me, and she wanted me to spend the night with her and help her out. You know she's having such a hard time, and I have so much fun with her. Everything was planned just a few minutes ago."

"I understand completely, but you know the Grand High Mohican won't be very happy about this. Oh, and by the way, Sigma had a surprise for you at this meeting. You need to stop with the teenage rebellious streak and skipping meetings so you can get the scoop on the latest battles and all." Sigma was the chief of the Scraah Wareagles.

"I know. What surprise did Sigma have for me? I'm eager to know!"

"I'm sure you do, but if I tell you, then it won't be a surprise."

"Aw, you ol' party pooper. Did you say the Grand High Mohican was coming too?!" The Grand High Mohican was the chief of the Mohican- Sparra, a conglomerate tribe made up of two smaller tribes, who was named Francesco. This was the only chieftain that Neiko had problems with. Everyone always wondered why he had such a strange name for an Indian chieftain and was often razzed about it with Neiko being among them.

"Yes."

"Awww, I didn't ask that goat-sniffing oaf to come to this meeting, and man, I hate that guy."

"I know—" before he could finish, Neiko interrupted.

"I hate him more than Raven and Bloodhawk put together! And if he comes to meetings for the next fifty years, then I'll skip all of 'em!"

"Now, now, that's not the way to be."

"But still—" before she could finish a red Camaro drove up and her mom called and said,

"They're here! Do you have everything packed?" her mom asked.

Neiko answered, "Yeah, just about. I still need to put my shoes on!"

"Well, hurry up!" she called out.

"Mongie, gotta go. Meet me at the big oak tomorrow at 6:30 sharp and tell me what happens."

"Alright, have fun," Monganata said, then hung up.

Neiko did the same, and she threw the phone under the bed, tossed Fireball Island in its original spot, and made a lot of noise doing so.

"What's going on in there?" her mom asked.

Neiko remembered she couldn't find Ramses, and she replied, "I was—um, trying to find Ramses, and I can't find him. Have you seen him?"

"Who?!" her mom asked, confused.

"He's the guy with silver armor, red eyes, and a purple cape. I left him on the bed yesterday, and now I can't find him."

"I don't remember seeing him," she replied.

"Well, darn. I guess this will have to do, but I could've swore—"

Neiko mused as she kicked her foot under the bed in a disgusted manner, but she stubbed her toe on something.

"Owww! What in blazes—" she said, then lifted the bed skirt and looked what stubbed her toe. There lay Ramses on his back staring blankly into the box springs with his dagger in his left hand, which was raised to stab some unknown victim. His purple cape was draped to his right on the floor. She picked him up and looked to make sure nothing was missing and said, "There you are, Monster Gas, I wondered where you went to—Mom I found him! No need to send the search party."

"Okay," she replied.

Neiko took the dagger out of the archvillain's hand and put it in the sheath in his belt and fixed his cape, and gave him the once over. Even though he was just a toy, Ramses was sinister-looking. From the top of his head to his feet, he was the most elaborately colored and complicated to describe. The majority of him was black and silver, with blue and red stuck in random places. Every inch of him was covered in armor except his eyes, which were two pools of red fury. His chest to his lower torso was covered in silver. On his shoulder blades he had two silver wing-like plates flaring out in both directions. His arms were covered in black with red stripes on his wrists. He had a red spike on each elbow and blue plates just below the elbow on the outside of each arm. He had a silver hand guard on each hand and underneath these were black gloves. On the back of the upper part of the arms, there was a dull silver section and another on the outside part of the arm. His legs were black up to his kneecaps that had a large, skull knee guards with spikes, and the rest of his legs were silver. His face was silver across his nose, cheeks, and forehead. In the center of his forehead he had two black horns trimmed in silver pointing up and just clearing the top of the head and his silver pharaoh's headdress which flared from both his shoulders to both sides of his head. He had a black plate protecting his mouth and chin, and it had a silver stripe down the middle. The temples were black and separated by a wide, silver stripe. His feet were covered with heavy, armored shoes Even though his armor was just plastic, the shiny, silver paint that covered most of him made him look metallic. His eyes had a frozen glare of hate and one that would scare Satan himself. The sinister belt he wore around his waist had two sheaths that held his sword and dagger.

The sword had a long and slender blade with a slanted tip and sharp point to one side; it was like a razor the rest of the way. It had a long handle; the sword was so long that it almost touched the floor when it was sheathed while he was standing.

The dagger was much shorter than the sword, and it had a curved blade and a sharp point at the end. These weapons were sheathed on the backside of Ramses' waist. His magnificent weapons were nothing more than dull, red plastic that was not painted.

Neiko found nothing missing for the second time, and she threw him in her overnight bag with his friends and foes, and threw her clothes on top of him and zipped the bag. Neiko slipped on her shoes, just as her cousin ran into the bedroom.

"Hey, Adnama, I missed you," said Jessica happily.

"Hey. Well, Acissej, are you ready for some fun?" "Yeah!" she said.

"Alright, let's go!"

Both of them ran from the room into the living room where Neiko hugged her parents, then they dashed to the car and climbed in. The car backed down the driveway and started down the road.

- CHAPTER 2 -

WHILE THE CAR WAS LEAVING, Raven and Bloodhawk watched from the woods.

"What's going on?" asked Bloodhawk.

"It looks like Neiko is missing another meeting," replied Raven, his father.

"That's good, but why is she missing so many?" he asked.

"I don't know, but I'm sure Francesco will have the honor in telling us. A rebellious streak would be my first guess."

"When is he going to come? I'm getting sick of waiting on that poor excuse for a man—I'm ready to plan and take action now!"

"Patience, my son. You'll get the chance. Besides, we need to know their plans, and the meeting has just started," said Raven, smiling at his impatient son.

"You're right. But I'm so tired of watching Neiko go free. I'm so anxious to get her, bring her to the castle, and make her my queen. I would love the opportunity of kidnapping her myself."

"Of course you do, but you couldn't possibly sneak into that neighborhood without being seen or causing panic among the neighbors. Then the Seven Tribes would be on you like flies on day old carrion. You wouldn't want that would you?"

"No, I could just shanghai her from her cousin's house tonight when it's dark, when she is sleeping."

"Now, you know that won't work either because you can't fit in that house, you would be seen, panic will spread, and you may be caught and made into a circus attraction. Besides, you don't know how long she will stay up. She stayed up just about all night once, remember? Bloodhawk, use your head like I taught you. You must not let your heart overpower your head. Just think, in a matter of months she will be in college and then getting her will be a snap. No one will know what happened, and it will be too late. College will separate her from everyone, and you can find the opportunity, and she will be yours."

"Well maybe, but then she may be even more of a nuisance if she has too much time on her hands when college starts. So if I grab her now, then that'll be all she wrote. Then she would be out of the way and be mine at the same time."

"Very good, that's the way. Both have their drawbacks and advantages, and you nailed them both, I'm proud. You know, you're right. We do need to get her out of the way so we can conquer the Seven Tribes, but she needs to be safe; not in our custody till after we win. But at the same time be where she will be easy to retrieve, and be out of the way. But I have no idea how to do all of those at the same time."

"Father, I don't believe we can do *all* of them at the same time; we may have to give a little, but we can think of something that can put her out of commission. Her safety will be assured, but if we do decide to take her, then she won't be too badly missed."

Raven cocked his head in a questioning manner, looked at him blankly, and asked, "What are you getting at?"

"Well, like—um, if we made her look like a traitor, then her friends won't miss her if she disappears suddenly. And they will think she ran away because she couldn't stand the heat. Only we will know she is innocent, and we don't have to worry about any suspicions or rescues; she will be out of the way, safe, and our helpless prisoner. When we win, they will never see her again and never know what happened or what hit them."

Raven rubbed his hands together and smiled devilishly. "Oh, I get it. Try to ruin her reputation so that no one will believe her if something happens or if she finds out one of our secrets, and at the right time, get her. Good thinking, but there are a few problems with this."

"Like what?" he asked frustrated.

"First, there will be few to believe that she would be capable of treachery; for those who are convinced, these believers will meddle, find the truth, and clear her name. Second, *if* we do take her, then her parents will be missing her. Also, people will discover that we are responsible and make a war to rescue her. You have the right idea of making tension between Neiko and her friends, but we need to take it a step further. We need to think of something to make tension with *everybody*. This includes her parents as well."

"How will we make her guilty of treason in front of her parents? Eighteen-year-olds don't sell important documents to enemy countries of the U.S."

Raven laughed. "No, no. Not treason. We need to make a different approach."

"Like what?! Treason is the most terrible crime I could think of. Should we try murder?"

"No. There is no need for a crime. All we need is something small and simple, but at the same time extremely damaging to reputation, mood, and friendships."

"What are you suggesting?"

"I'm not sure yet, but it will come to me, and when it does, we will start to plan."

"Goodie, I can't wait," laughed Bloodhawk cruelly.

Francesco came in running and complaining. "Crazy bunch of heathens! I can't believe they didn't plan anything. Who needs that wretch anyway?" he said moodily. "I'm terribly sorry, your majesties, but the meeting ran late thanks to Monganata and his stupid wife."

Ignoring the rest, Bloodhawk and Raven thought of the same idea and pointed at each other and said in unison, "Crazy, that's it!"

Francesco didn't have a clue and asked, "What is it?"

Raven chuckled and looked at him and said, "Francesco, you're a genius!"

"I still don't understand. What's so great about a crazy bunch of heathens?" he asked, frustrated. Francesco was a slender man, not very tall, with black hair and blue eyes. He was the Grand High Mohican, and he was wearing the traditional headdress of falcon feathers and a robe of rabbit fur. He always had a weakling appearance and an annoying high-pitched voice. His weakness was one hundred times more obvious when he was lined up with the massive monarchs.

Raven stood nine feet from head to toe and had an enormous build. His armor was titanium scale mail made from professional Crackedskull craftsmanship. His breastplate was made from silver and gold-colored titanium discs that overlapped each other to form a solid surface. The armor on his arms and legs was made of gold-colored titanium. His helmet was the most exquisite. The part in the back was gold titanium fixed with eagle feathers. The part around his eyes had outstretched wings of a bird of prey in a swoop that was elaborately colored in gold, silver, and white titanium. The part covering his nose was the hooked titanium beak that was colored as the beak of an eagle, and the remainder of his face was bare. His hands were bare, except at the end of his fingers where there were gold titanium finger guards that had retractable gold titanium claws.

Bloodhawk was much larger than his father, standing at eleven feet and having a build four times larger than his father was; he was also the largest in his entire bloodline. His armor was made exactly like Raven's except it was colored black and silver. These two were not like any normal men; they were mostly human, but partly bird. Both had feet of eagles complete with talons that remained unarmored. Their eyes were like an eagle's in looks; they could see like an eagle in the day and like an owl at night. Both of them possessed a pair of wings. Raven had a wingspan of fifteen and a half feet and colored with beautiful white plumage. Bloodhawk had solid black wing plumage and an eighteen and three quarter foot wingspan.

Raven told the Grand High Mohican, who was actually a Crackedskull, about the plot against Neiko.

Francesco's mood changed. "So that's the plan and where does 'crazy' come in?" he asked, perplexed.

"Aaah, that's the part we build on. If we can ever make Neiko seem she is suffering from lunacy, then most of our plans will go into effect, and the Seven Tribes will fall," replied Raven.

"So, then what? What happens to Neiko? Even if no one listens to her, she is still a walking time bomb ready to explode and a constant threat even then!" Francesco said in a worried way.

"Don't get so excited. Once she is having problems with her family and friends and trying to make everyone believe her, then we will step in and *remove* her. Then we will wage full war on the Tribes, and it will be finally over," replied Raven.

Francesco smiled evilly and rubbed his hands together. "So you mean you'll off her? That sounds nice."

Bloodhawk stood up and glared at him with hate. Francesco scrunched back in fright, and Bloodhawk fanned his fingers and his claws shot out of his finger guards. The already terrified man covered his head with his arms and curled into a ball. Bloodhawk raised his hand ready to swipe, and Raven threw his hand up. "No! Don't. We have no need for this. We will not harm Neiko; we will take her away and by then no one will really miss her. She will no longer be a threat to you once we have her. Then we will take care of the rest."

Francesco uncurled himself, shaking. "Alright, but h-h-how do we take care of her before the opportune time? I mean, she will give me headaches till then, and she will still have access to the army even then! What if she finds something out, like me being a Crackedskull? I mean, if it is proven, then I will lose my position, and your plans of conquest and my espionage will be shot."

Raven scratched his chin. "Well, I can't do anything about the headaches she will give you, but you can handle the rest yourself except the abduction part."

"But how? How can I deny her from the army? By the way, who will be the kidnappers, and how will you keep it under wraps?" he asked, confused.

"Francesco, Francesco. Have you forgotten your power? You have the power to disband her against anyone's say-so, even Monganata's. But, you must have full evidence of her phony lunacy so that no one has a just argument. The rest is to be taken care of by you. That's your job. Keep us informed of the progress of our plan, and the next strategic moves are also your job. As for the kidnapping, I don't know who will do that job. As for further planning, we will keep you informed of any changes."

Before Francesco could say anything, Bloodhawk stood up. "I'll do it! I'll be the one who will kidnap her! This is a one-shot deal and no room for mistakes. She is no match for me, and I won't fail. I won't leave until she is my prisoner! Besides, I've been waiting for the chance to get my hands on her!"

Raven rubbed his chin and thought. "Alright, my son. That is a splendid idea, and a very good point. You get your chance. We will have to plan later on when and how you will move in with no problems from anyone, especially that thorn in your side Monchiska—that pain in the butt."

Monchiska was the son of Sigma and Puma from the Scraah tribe and one of Neiko's best friends.

Bloodhawk bared his teeth menacingly. "If anyone gets in my way from claiming my bride to be, then I will bathe them in their own blood!"

Francesco shuddered and felt a little sorry for anyone who crossed the path of this eleven-foot, angry Crackedskull prince; he hated it when his temper flared up and when he made death threats. He finally broke the silence saying, "Well, um—uh...sorry to bother you two, but...um, I was thinking, um—"

"Come on, spit it out, Francesco! Stop doddering!" Raven snapped with a tone that was so sharp and whip-like that he jumped.

"Well, what are we exactly going to use to make Neiko look like a lunatic? I mean, we need something that everyone knows about, especially her parents—and how are we going to find it?" he managed to ask fighting the knot in his throat.

Raven stopped and thought and thought. "I can't think of anything. What do you have in mind?"

"I don't know. I haven't the slightest idea, but there has to be something—"

"Well, find it. That will be your second job."

"What if she gets in my hair and—"

"Do what you have to do to throw her off and get to work—NOW! If you do find something, then contact me as soon as possible. Then we will plan what to do next; in the meantime, be patient. You have a lot of work to do. Try to keep Neiko under control. She will give you many pains, so be prepared."

Francesco bowed to them and turned to leave, and Bloodhawk called after him in a harsh warning, "Neiko better not be harmed or have even a scratch, or I'll make you my scratching post!"

He shuddered as he left the woods near the road and hearing the blood-curdling warning. Many thoughts went through his mind of all the work that must be done, and all of Bloodhawk's curses and threats that he had hanging over his head. He knew he must keep his cool and work fast, too. He had to keep the world from falling around him, since there was a small strand of string keeping the wrath of the Crackedskull monarchs and the chieftains from the Seven Tribes from consuming him. Neiko was one of these chieftains, and she was slicing at this strand. *Oh, if only I could clap my hands and Neiko be gone and married to Bloodhawk, then this nightmare would be over, or just easier to cope with,* he thought. He walked into his home and breathed a long sigh of relief. *Home sweet home,* he thought then shuddered because Bloodhawk's threat began to ring in his ears.

"I'm so tired," he muttered. Without changing out of the robe, he flopped on the bed and fell asleep instantly.

- CHAPTER 3 -

NEIKO JUMPED OUT OF the car and danced around upon arriving from her cousin's. Then she turned and waved good-bye to her uncle, aunt, and cousin as they pulled out. Her mother greeted her as she entered the house. She told her of all the events, and then said, "I need to put this stuff up."

"Alright, honey," she said, smiling.

Neiko entered her room, threw her bag on the bed, and looked at the clock on her nightstand; it read: *4:30 p.m.*

Plenty of time, she thought. She put everything where it was supposed to go, and she hung up the clothes her mom had thrown on her bed. The last thing she did was put up her toys. The last toy she got out was Ramses. She held him by his left foot and positioned him to face her. She stuck her tongue at him, giggled, and stuffed him in the fortress which was inside her closet.

After she finished all of her chores, she looked at her watch. "Only five o'clock? Man, I did all that in thirty measly minutes?" she grumbled. "Oh, well, I guess I'll just have to play Killer Instinct till about six, then go meet Mongie at the oak."

At six she turned off her game and went into the living room, she told her mom that she was going outside for a while, and then she asked, "When's supper going to be ready?"

"In about an hour," her mom said.

Oh good, one full hour. That's all the time I need, Neiko mused to herself.

Neiko reached the oak fifteen minutes early, but Monganata was already there waiting. Neiko looked at him and then at her watch. "You're early. What's up?"

"Not much. Nothing was happening at home, and Windsong had to run errands, so I came early. You're pretty early yourself. So why are you early?"

"Well, kinda the same thing, I guess. I finished my chores, then I played video games for an hour, and then I came out here to get some air."

So what happened at the meeting?"

"Actually, you didn't miss anything. It was a *very* boring meeting. No one planned anything, no Crackedskull advancements, and nothing really important was discussed, except a weapon theft— nothing alarming or anything that you would be interested in. Mainly the rest was listening to the Grand High Mohican talk the entire time. Oh, yeah, Sigma was so disappointed you didn't come. He told me to tell you he won't accept any more rain checks on that surprise. He said he will drag you to the next meeting kicking and screaming if he has to, and Puma said she would help." Puma was Sigma's wife.

Neiko chuckled. "He said that, huh?" she asked, smiling. "Well, I guess I will be coming to the next meeting, or you will have to save me from the terrible Sigma and Puma. Well, about that theft, who were the conspirators, and did they catch 'em?"

Monganata smiled. "I guess I will, and yeah, they did catch them. They were two Crow twins: Rasputin and Napoleon. They stole three pikes and four tomahawks. We managed to catch them at Yahweh's Ridge. We arrested them, put the weapons in the armories and put them away. They were also charged with other thefts as well."

Neiko whistled. "Man, they're regular pros then, huh? Boy, I wished I coulda helped you bust 'em. Oh, by the way, are they fans o' Bloodhawk and Raven? If they are, I would like to go tell their mommies and give 'em a good thrashing. Besides, ain't the Crows our friends now?"

"Well, no one knows for sure if they are tied in with the Crackedskulls or not. The Crows are our friends except that secret society the Black Hand, who Calling Wolf, the Crow chief, has tried to banish or disband."

Neiko whistled. "Really? I didn't think Calling Wolf would actually turn someone out even if they didn't fly right."

Monganata sighed. "That bunch has done more than just steal weapons, Neiko. They have sent him threats and attempts on Calling Wolf's life, and they have sent threats to various tribes. They even did the despicable act of kidnapping Calling Wolf's family, and holding them for ransom, saying: *If you don't leave, we will kill them.* I helped him save his family from spear point. I stung the gang, and Calling Wolf hasn't had too many threats since. There hasn't been too much activity from them except weapon thefts."

"Wow, are you sure they're not affiliated with the Crackedskulls? I mean they seem like some of Raven's company. When did you have the run in with this gang, and who's the big enchilada?"

"Gosh, Neiko, no one has asked me about that in a while. Well, there has never been any evidence of them working for Raven, and I put them in their place about twenty-five years ago. The Black Hand had two ringleaders and their names were Quick Death and Night Crawler. I'm not real sure they are still alive, and if they are, they haven't really done anything rash in a long time. Sometimes I wonder if I'll hear from them again someday."

"How did you know those two punks were from that gang? Are there any other secret societies in any of the other tribes?"

"Well, I could tell from their actions; like when they spit in Monchiska's face when he asked them a simple question. I checked their left arm because they have a specific mark on their left arm, and they both had it along with that violent, rash behavior of theirs which is typical of a Hand member."

"What does the mark look like?" asked Neiko. "So I know if I ever see it."

"Well, um—" mused Monganata, rubbing his chin as he gathered his thoughts. "It's a Black Hand holding a dagger covered in blood, and the dagger has a cobra handle; the cobra has a hood and an open mouth ready to strike. The mark is usually located on the upper arm on the outside, like under where a short sleeve shirt would cover it. Sometimes it's on the inside of the lower arm where only a good, trained eye could see it. As for any other lethal societies, there may be a few, but they're not as bad as the Black Hand except for the Crackedskulls that is," replied Monganata.

"Man, has Calling Wolf had any more problems from them, and why were they trying to run him off or kill him?" asked Neiko, confused.

"No," Monganata replied and went on to explain, "The only problems he has are from armed robberies or hijackings, and no one usually gets hurt. As for the rest of your question, I'm not really sure. The best way I can answer it is by saying they're like the Ku Klux Klan. They usually attack in disguise, so no one will suspect them, and they have a lot of codes and mysterious rules that they follow. But, I don't really know anything about them. Now they are almost obsolete, and I'm glad because I hated it when I met Night Crawler. I had a duel with him; I took his left eye and slashed him several times in the face and once in the neck with my knife. He gave me this." Monganata pulled up his sleeve showing a long, ugly scar. "He gave me this with his knife. After I almost killed him, he ran away, and I haven't heard from him or his brother since."

"If you had a rematch with that creep, I bet you would kick his butt," said Neiko, smiling.

"Really? Gosh, that was long ago. Even then, I was in my thirties, and they were only in their late teens or early twenties. Now I'm a fifty-year-old and a little too old for that type of combat and heroic stuff."

"Gee, you don't look fifty, you look pretty good for an *old* guy, besides you barely have any gray, and you probably got those from me," said Neiko kindly.

Monganata smiled warmly. "Well, you know how to flatter me and make me feel better. I appreciate the compliment." Monganata was a tall man with a stout build and in excellent shape for a fifty-year-old. He had long, black hair with two wide stripes of gray in the front. His skin was tan and he had large black eyes. He had a somewhat aged appearance with lots of energy and stamina.

They laughed together a few minutes, and Neiko's mother called for dinner. They said their goodbyes and went their separate ways.

- CHAPTER 4 -

FRANCESCO WAS SUDDENLY AWAKENED by a knock at his door. "Who could that be?" he grumbled to himself. He stomped down the stairs and opened the door.

Wolfgang, a Scraah messenger, stood there smiling. Wolfgang was a young, cheerful twenty-year-old who was always sent to deliver important messages for Sigma to other chieftains. "Good morning, sir. I came at Sigma's command to inform you of the meeting scheduled for the twenty-fifth. He said you must attend," Wolfgang said in his casual, polite manner.

"What's so good about this morning? And look what time it is! You interrupted my beauty sleep. I'm so tired of these stupid meetings," Francesco snapped angrily.

"Well, I apologize, sir, but Sigma wanted me to inform you at once. And, it's eight o'clock—it's kinda late. Well then, I must be on my way. Good day, sir."

As Wolfgang walked away, Francesco spat in his path. He slammed the door as he walked inside. In his tired, angry frenzy, he remembered his instructions from the Crackedskull chieftains. "Oh, what am I gonna use to nail that annoying Desert Storm Falcon? I can't think of *anything*. Rocks? No that's stupid... Sticks? No, no, no. Argh! I can't think of anything to make her look insane, but at first talking rocks sounded good, but that's too dumb. I need something more practical, close to home, and something Neiko sees on a regular basis, but it still sounds like rocks. Weapons chasing her? No! I give up," he said as he kicked a small toy across the floor that belonged to Monganata's small grandson.

"Owww! Stupid toys! I have them all in my house thanks to Monganata and his little, bratty grandson—" An idea came into his mind and interrupted his tirade. "Toys! That's it! No one would ever believe in a toy coming to life, and no one would expect it! Francesco, you're a genius! Which one, though? She has so many— dinosaurs, men, mutants, strange, changing creatures. Dinosaurs and creatures chasing her?! No, men sound much more reliable. Most of those men look so strange. Should I use one or many? One should be enough. Who should I use—Rahzar? No. Coldstone, Mace, Axe, Tusk—no. What I need is a leader—a Pharaoh. There are five of them: Osiris, Re, Tut, Menes, but what is the other one's name? I know it starts with R. He is extremely special; I'll use him, I suppose. What *is* his name? Oh well, I suppose it'll come to me; meanwhile, I'll need to go to Neiko's and find that little man, so Raven can plan what to do next. I hope he has magic to bring toys to life."

Francesco walked casually from his home to Neiko's neighborhood. He cautiously looked around for any signs of anyone. There were no warriors around. Neiko and her mom walked to their car and left. As they were leaving, he ducked behind a tree and waited till they were far down the road. He left his hiding place and cautiously approached the house. He listened.

No one was home. He searched for the spare key and found it on top of the porch light. He unlocked the door and quickly sneaked into Neiko's room and went straight to the closet. As soon as he found the box that contained her toys, he dug wildly for the one he wanted but found nothing. "I found everybody but that one I want. Where does she keep him? I'd better hurry before she gets back! I hope they went to the grocery store," he said to himself. He began to put the others back. He accidentally bumped the fortress, and it fell onto the floor spilling all of its treasure and the toy he was searching for. "There you are," he said gratefully. "But now I have to clean up the rest of this mess, whoever you are." He picked up the rest of the mess and set it just as it was. He took a minute to look at the pictures in the room. On the bulletin board there was a picture of his booty, and at the bottom it said: *Ramses the Dark Pharaoh*. He looked at the toy doubtfully and thought a minute. "So your name is Ramses, huh? Well, that sounds about right. You are my ticket to getting rid of Captain Neiko Kidd for good. Just looking at you is enough to make anyone go mad. We are going to see Raven who may be able to bring you to life. Alright, let's go."

Ramses did nothing but stare back with his icy stare. Francesco stuffed him in his bag and left the house to go to Raven's fortress.

Francesco arrived at the fortress within thirty minutes. As he approached the door, a guard noticed him coming and asked, "Who goes there?"

"It's just me—Francesco. I wish to speak with Raven ASAP. I have something important for him."

"Alright, you may proceed," he said gruffly.

Francesco entered the door and was greeted by a servant, and Francesco told him exactly what he told the guard. "I will tell him you are here, and I will admit you as soon as I can," replied the servant. Within a few minutes the servant returned and said, "He will speak with you now, sir."

That didn't take very long, he thought to himself. He took a deep breath to relieve the lump in his throat and entered the throne room.

"I didn't expect you back so soon, Francesco. What do you have for me? Is Neiko already getting to you?" He asked jeeringly.

"No, I came because I have the thing we will use to frame Neiko. I hope we can pull it off."

"Well, let me see it. What do we have anyway?"

"I have a toy."

"A *toy*? Is that the best you can come up with? Is it one of Monganata's grandson's toys? Now I can tell you did a rush job. Francesco, you're useless!"

"You won't say that when you see him; he is magnificent and perfect for the job. It is one of *Neiko's* toys," he said proudly.

"Him? So you're saying it is a man? How did you get him? What is his name? Let me see," Raven said holding out his hand and curiosity in his voice.

"Okay, meet Ramses the Dark Pharaoh," he said triumphantly as he pulled him out of his bag.

Raven took him and laid him in his massive hand. He looked him over and said, "He's perfect and scary enough. I've never seen anything like this in my entire life. Where did she find something like this?"

"I have no idea. I found out about him by eavesdropping on conversations. I found out a little about his personality. He doesn't sound too nice."

"Are you sure he is an enemy? And what else did you find out about him? Tell me everything you know."

"Well, judging from his name and title, he sounds like a villain and a special one at that. All I know is he picks on this group called the Attack Pack and is the slayer of a whole lot of people. He is also obsessed in trying to marry this girl named Lydia. He is very sore at this guy named Sandstorm because he married Lydia when she was betrothed to him—and what's more—Saracens and Pharaohs do not get along. Also he is supposed to be the first-born son of this Pharaoh named Osiris. He has three brothers named Menes, Tut, and Re."

"Tell me more about these Pharaohs and Saracens. And judging by the title *Dark Pharaoh*, Ramses doesn't actually seem like his so-called brothers and father."

"I know. The Saracens are a group of people with traits similar to those of the Seven Tribes in doing good deeds, and there are two types: Qarian and Saudian. Both are descendants of this Saracen named Saladin, who is a predecessor to Sandstorm, the guy I mentioned earlier. The Pharaohs are descendants from a Pharaoh named Rumi, and are the killers of the Saracens. Rumi and his son Xerxes killed Saladin in a battle. Later when Sandstorm was a small boy the Pharaohs and their henchmen, the Skull Bearers, came and murdered all of the Saracens except Sandstorm. Sandstorm's homeland, Amir, was wiped out. His father, Omar, was crucified; his mother, Persephone, was tortured to death along with all of his siblings. Sandstorm already knew the enemy; he watched the devastation and sought after them immediately. During this time he met Lydia—I forget when, and then there you are."

"Ramses sounds like a natural terror, doesn't he? And the others sound pretty awful as well. I believe you made a great choice. Where do the others in the Attack Pack come from?"

"I'm not really sure, but Ramses has something to do with it; I'm not sure how. I remember her saying something like the rest were from Etowah, and they were two groups, the Predacons and Maximals—I think the Maximals were animal-like and the Predacons were insect-like; both had some types of hybrid creatures of some sort. They joined Sandstorm to find the killer of their tribes, and these two groups were close friends. So Sandstorm is the leader of the Attack Pack—I think, and they live to fight the Pharaohs and their many allies. That's all I know except that Sandstorm's father was Saudian Saracen and his mother was Qarian."

"So he is both types in one. I'm wondering how does a Dark Pharaoh differ from a plain one from Qari? Surly there must be something."

"You're probably right, but I'm not very sure about that. Do you have enough power to bring him to life?"

"Hmmm, I think so, but I've never done this before. I'm not sure how much is necessary, and from what you told me about Ramses, we need to be careful. I would hate for something to go wrong—are you *sure* you've told me everything? I'm not so sure that I have to make him chase Neiko around the room. Instead, I have a better idea. Before I show you, think and tell me anything you may have forgotten."

Francesco thought and thought. "Oh yeah. The Pharaohs are also equipped with magic. The Saracens too."

"Well, what about *Dark Pharaoh* magic? Is it more powerful than any other magic, or is it just different?"

"It's just probably different—nothing to worry about."

"Are you *sure*? You're not holding out are you?"

"No, that's everything I know."

"I can't believe Neiko could create something like this—he is even meaner than I am. Do you suppose this is his original name and character?"

"No, probably not."

"Now I want you to hold him, and when I say go, I want you to tap him with this nail," said Raven as he handed the nail and Ramses to Francesco.

Raven brought the Eye of Mohica out and the talisman shone with green light. "Go."

Francesco tapped him.

Pop!

"Nothing happened. I guess it didn't work."

"I didn't cast the spell yet. I wanted you to hear the difference." Raven took the round glowing stone and began to chant into a language he could not understand. The Eye changed from green to red to blue. Francesco shivered at the sight. Magic made him uneasy. "Now tap him," Raven said in a strange voice. Francesco shuddered and obeyed.

Clang!

The sound of metal on metal startled him, and he dropped Ramses. When he hit the floor, the sound of plastic echoed in the hall. Francesco looked at him in a frightened manner. "H-h-how did you d-do th-that?" Francesco stammered. "I mean, for one second he's plastic, then metal, then plastic again. That scared me to death."

"You couldn't possibly understand. It's too complicated to describe. You were scared? Just think how Neiko will feel when this happens when she plays with him. I can do much more than just making his armor clang."

Francesco looked at him with eyes as big as saucers. "You can do *more*? What are you trying to do—give her a heart attack? What else can you do?"

Raven chuckled. "Don't worry. Neiko's heart is strong. Well, who will believe his armor clanged when he and Sandstorm were fighting? Neiko would tell everyone, and they would be convinced she is crazy. When I'm through, Neiko will be without a reputation. There you have it. You came up with a very good idea, and you picked the arch-villain and someone you wouldn't want alive. Good work. I will surprise you with what else I can do."

"Well, thanks, but what if her parents have her put in a loony bin? How will you be able to seize her? I still think it's a bit much."

"Oh, don't wuss out on me now. It would be worse if he chased her around the room. Besides, we would have no problems then. As for threat, Bloodhawk will swipe her before that happens. You, my friend, must act like you don't know the plan, and help prove her false lunacy. Now, return Ramses to his home as soon as you can, and hang on for the ride. Prepare for the unexpected. I will inform Bloodhawk about the plan, and I will keep you informed. Now go."

"I won't suffer from Neiko so badly since I know where the plan will lead to."

"Well, good. You should be proud. Good luck."

"You, too. See ya."

Francesco left feeling good and lightly laden. *I can now rest easier*, he thought.

- CHAPTER 5 -

NEIKO AND HER MOM RETURNED from the grocery store two hours later. "Amanda, help me get out the groceries and put them away," said her mom.

"Okay," Neiko replied casually, but she had a feeling of uncertainty.

"Is something wrong?"

"Uh—no, why?"

"I was just wondering. You sounded strange for a second there."

"I'm feeling a little tired. Grocery shopping always wears me out," Neiko said in a casual manner.

"I know what you mean."

After she finished putting away the groceries, she went around checking the house. *I feel that someone's been here,* she thought to herself, but she did not want to mention it to her mom. She found nothing suspicious in the rest of the house, so she went to her room. She checked the DSF files and logs, but nothing was missing. All of her other belongings were intact, and then she went to check the closet. "What's behind door number three?" she asked and pulled back the doors. All of her toys were in place. "Let's see if Monster Gas is still at home." She looked in the fortress, and Ramses was there. "Well, everything's still here, but I felt like somebody was here. Funny. I'll call Mongie and see if the meeting's still on." She pulled out the phone and dialed the numbers.

"Hello?" came Mongie's voice.

"Hey, Mongie, it's me Neiko. I was calling to see if the meeting is still on."

"Yes it is. Don't tell me you're playing hooky again. Sigma told me he isn't taking any more rain checks on his surprise for you."

"Relax, will ya? I'm not skipping; I am making sure it isn't cancelled or nothing."

"Well, okay. Just checking. Nothing's been changed, so I'll see you there?"

"Yep. I'll be at the oak in a jiffy."

"Alright, everyone, the meeting is now in session," Xartna said to get the meeting underway. Everyone stopped their conversations and quickly sat down. "I'm glad everyone made it, and Captain Kidd is here with us. I'm so glad you could make it." Xartna was a wiry but strong man, and he had long, black hair and green eyes. His light tan skin, like that of his identical twin brother Aquila, shone in the sun. He was a member of Neiko's tribe and served in the chieftain council.

"No problemo," she replied in a Spanish accent. Laughter and applause filled the air.

"Well, thanks for the laugh, Neiko, now down to business. Item one, what is the report the scouts have found on the Crackedskulls?"

"Nothing, sir, the Sparra Scouts said the Crackedskulls are not mobilizing, and they aren't doing anything," replied Wolverine, the Sparra lieutenant.

Everything was presented in twenty minutes. "Boy, that was a short meeting," Neiko said.

"I know," Monganata replied, "This was the shortest one all year, and they all really have been quite boring, and no debates have been brought up. Sometimes I wonder what Raven is up to."

"Why haven't we adjourned yet? We covered everything from A to Z. What else is there?"

Xartna approached the stand. "Sorry, everyone, for the delay, but Sigma has a few additional words to say. Give him your undivided attention."

Sigma approached the stand. Sigma was a large, brawny man with long, shiny black hair. He had extremely dark skin and chocolate brown eyes that were filled with kindness. He was Monchiska's father and the chief of the Scraah Wareagles. "Thank you everyone for being patient; this won't take but a few minutes of your time, but I assure you it is worthwhile. I would like to ask Captain Kidd to come forward please."

Silence filled the air. Neiko eyed the others like a student caught talking in class. She slowly arose and approached the front. Francesco eyed her contemptuously. Once Neiko came to the front, Sigma told her to face the audience.

"Well everyone, I have something I wish to present to our loyal friend Captain Neiko Kidd," Sigma replied as he pulled out a wrapped object out of his pocket, and Neiko eyed it unknowingly. "Now, on behalf of all of the chieftains and all of the Seven Tribes of the Land of Hawote, I ask you Captain Neiko Kidd, to accept a new title and responsibility. We grant you the position of Admiral of the Desert Storm Falcons. Do you accept?"

Neiko's eyes filled up with tears and she blinked. "Well, shoot yeah, I accept."

Immediately the crowd shouted and clapped. Sigma handed her the object, and she unwrapped it. The object was a badge. It had a bird's foot—which was the symbol of the DSF—three bars, and *Admiral Neiko Kidd* engraved on it. "This is the badge you will wear to show your new rank. This has three bars instead of two to show you are admiral and not captain. Congratulations."

Sigma pinned the badge on her shirt, and hugged her. Puma, Windsong, and Monganata followed suit. Wolverine gave her high five. The crowd began to chant. "Speech! Speech!"

Neiko stepped up to the podium. "Alright, I'll give you a speech. Thank you everyone for this honor, and thank you, Sigma, for embarrassing the daylights out of me."

The crowd laughed.

"Well, I really appreciate this, and I feel honored in being the first and only admiral in history of the DSF. This decoration is really magnificent. I can see that y'all had plenty of planning time out of all the times I've played hooky, and I'm surprised you picked me after that same reason."

The crowd laughed.

Sigma shouted, "You're the best woman for the job."

Neiko laughed. "Well, who will be captain? We have a vacancy, and it's a very important rank, so who do you have in line?"

"That I left for the admiral to decide. It's your call, unless you want us to do it," Sigma replied.

"Well, I'm getting all important now. I've always had this person in mind just in case I was ever captured. An officer has to have this in mind, so he'll be our new captain."

"And who gets this honor, Admiral?" Sigma asked.

"Aquila, stand up and look beautiful." Aquila, Xartna's twin brother who was a good trustworthy warrior, stood up and looked at Neiko shocked. Neiko went on, "As you all know, Aquila is my most trusted friend, a good officer, and trustworthy. Do you have any objections, and do you accept, Aquila?"

"I accept," Aquila announced boldly. No one objected; everyone cheered and gave him slaps on the back.

"Meeting's adjourned, let's all go home," Neiko replied.

Everyone shouted and Neiko found herself in the mob. Francesco left the yard, and burned with anger, dread, and disbelief. "This is not good, and I must tell Raven immediately!"

– Chapter 6 –

R AVEN! THANK GOODNESS I found you! I have terrible news!" exclaimed Francesco in between gasps.

"Already? What is it this time? It seems trouble has been brewing around you lately," Raven said, annoyed.

"You—don't—understand. It—happened—at the—meeting," he gasped.

Raven turned and faced him. "Is it Neiko? What did she do now? Did she skip? Was she disbanded?"

Francesco gulped and breathed in. "No—worse."

"Did you run a marathon? You sound like you ran twenty miles to get here. When did the meeting end?"

"Yes, I did run. The meeting was over ten minutes ago. I left as soon as it ended because what I have to say is so bad it couldn't wait another minute," he said breathing steadily.

"Ten minutes?! You got here just about as fast as we fly— that's a record for you. If it's that bad, you had better tell me. Does it put a dent in our plan?"

"You bet it does. Neiko wasn't demoted; she was *promoted!*"

Raven looked at him doubtfully. "Promoted?! Are you trying to put a fast one on me so you have an excuse to complain?"

Francesco shook his head. "No, I swear!"

Raven put his hand on his hip. "Alright, what rank is it?"

He swallowed deeply. "Admiral of the Desert Storm Falcons."

Raven was so angry he slammed his fist on the table. "That's impossible! Who's responsible? I can't believe this!"

"Er...um—well, they all are, but Sigma was the one who presented it to the rest of the Indians," Francesco said as he cringed at the sight of Raven's anger.

"A thousand curses on all of them! I *will* get even! When I'm finished, Admiral Kidd will never see the dawn of battle against me because I will destroy her life, and she will be my son's wife! They will never see their precious Admiral again! The DSF won't have an officer, and they will be the first to die!"

"Um, that's another—problem." He said weakly.

"Problem?!" Raven thundered. "What now?!"

"They have a new captain; Neiko chose Aquila for the job."

Raven grabbed a nearby chair and threw it against the wall with all of his strength. The chair smashed into splinters upon the impact, and it made a terrible racket that echoed through the hall. Bloodhawk ran in upon hearing the racket, and he just returned from his errand.

"Father, are you alright?" asked Bloodhawk, startled and confused.

Raven raised his hands in the air. "Yeah, I'm just peachy," he snapped sarcastically.

Bloodhawk looked at Francesco concerned. "What happened?"

Francesco told him everything that happened from beginning to end.

Bloodhawk shook his head shocked. "Well, this is just great. What will we do now? We can't do anything till he calms down."

Francesco glanced at Raven. "That's *if* he calms down. I say we go on with the plan. It's foolproof even if Neiko is an admiral. If we play our cards right, she won't be one long. Then she will become a queen—an even higher rank."

Bloodhawk rubbed his hands together and smiled deviously. "I agree, but he is the one who is responsible for bringing Ramses to life or whatever it's called; we can't do it without him. Aquila a captain? Who would've thought it? Also it is an excellent choice, even though he won't do as good o' job as Neiko. All he needs is experience, and he will easily grow into it. But I'm not really concerned about him."

"I know, but your father is in no shape to do anything right now."

Bloodhawk glanced at his storming father. "We will be able to get things done, if he would calm down and stop breaking things. Anyway, if he doesn't stop in five minutes, I'll take matters into my own hands. I'll bring Ramses to life myself; it couldn't possibly be that hard; besides, I know enough magic—" said Bloodhawk loud enough where his father could hear.

"I heard that!" Raven boomed. "You stupid, illiterate teenager, you couldn't possibly do that yourself! You think you know everything! You couldn't bring your dead dog back to life. What makes you think you can bring a toy to life? You can't do without me, and you know it!"

"Yes father. And I'm not a teenager; I'm 21 years old—"

"And you're still my son, and you barely have any magical knowledge." Bloodhawk winked at Francesco signaling him to say something about beginning the plan. "Well, do you want to begin the plan now?" he asked.

Raven spun around. "Yes, no more planning. It's time to go on with the show. I'll get the Eye, and we'll sit and wait till the time she plays with her toys," he said then he left the room.

Bloodhawk looked at Francesco mischievously. "Works every time.

Now, in a matter of time, I will finally have my queen!"

Francesco smiled. "Yes, Neiko will be out of my hair. Boy, I wished that worked on my dad."

He shrugged. "It only works when he's mad. Most of the time he catches on, but he was so mad this time that he didn't even suspect. Besides, I think he was ready to pull the pin from the grenade."

"Neiko will be lost in the explosion, and no one will know what happened."

They laughed devilishly, and hugged each other.

Raven appeared. "Alright, let's get to work."

Francesco smiled. "I want front row seats for this show, and victory is evident."

Raven smiled. "Until there is a meeting, or you're needed on stage."

"I'll be ready," he said cruelly.

- CHAPTER 7 -

AFTER THE MEETING, MANY people stayed and mingled for a while. Neiko and a handful of chieftains were discussing various topics.

"I wonder where the GHM went to in such a hurry. I wonder if he had another engagement to keep," mused Neiko.

"I don't really know, Neiko. He's been doing that a lot lately—he's just probably has a lot on his mind," Xartna replied.

"Well, I don't know—he seems like he's up to something, and I'm not really sure it's good, nor am I sure he's planning on our annual victory ceremony," Neiko said as she twisted her hair around her forefinger.

"Pah, poppycock! He may be moody, but he's as trustworthy as they come. No more talk about him; so, how is your cousin?"

"Okay I guess. She seemed fine to me, and she didn't mention anything negative going on between her parents since they've been having marital problems, so I guess everything's fine."

"Well, good—oh, well, I need to get home and so does everyone else for that matter. Well, see ya!"

"Come on you sleazy Pharaoh, give me your best shot!" shouted Sandstorm at Ramses in challenge.

"You will die, Saracen dog, for insulting me! Eat lightning!" he shouted back and he threw imaginary bolts of lightning at Sandstorm, but he missed.

"Ha! Missed! You couldn't hit the broad side of a barn, and you need to get your eyes checked, Ramsneeze!"

"Amanda, what are you doing? Why are you making so much racket? Melissa's trying to sleep and that wasn't very nice," asked Neiko's mom as she walked to the doorway of her room. "Are you playing with your toys again?" she asked sharply.

"Yeah—Oh, sorry, mom. I kinda got carried away because I'm playing with the Attack Pack," said Neiko.

"Well, okay, but you need to clean up this pig sty of yours. What have I told you about people your age playing with toys?" she asked sharply.

"Just a minute. I've got to the best part, and then I'll clean it up," she said, ignoring the comment about her age.

"Well, alright. Just get it done, and don't make too much noise," she said and left.

"Alright, now, where was I? Oh, yeah—" Neiko thought and resumed playing.

"You Pharaohs are all alike; hotheads with a poor aim, and Dark Pharaohs take the icing on the cake, you—" before he could finish, Ramses hit him with a lightning bolt and sent him crashing to the ground from his flying carpet. Sandstorm groaned and looked up, and saw Ramses standing over him with his sword drawn. "You were saying? Well, now I'll teach you respect, farewell, Duststorm!" he raised his sword ready to stab, and Sandstorm gulped.

"Stop right there, Chrome Dome!" cried a voice, and Ramses spun around. Phoenix, the new Pack leader who was a wolf-eagle, swooped down, slammed into him, and sent him flying. Ramses flew through the air and hit the wall.

Clang!

Neiko was so startled she dropped Phoenix on the floor, and looked and listened; waiting for her mom to yell at her. Her mom said nothing. Then she heard the noise of her mom trying to find a pan.

"I can't believe she didn't hear that," she mused. "I can't believe this!" Neiko looked at him and swallowed hard. She walked over to where he lay and picked him up and looked at him. She flicked him a couple times. "Plastic. This is sooo weird. Hold on, plastic don't clang—metal does—how could—no, no, no! There ain't no way—never mind. I'll just clean this room and forget about the rest of what I planned, which is the boring stuff anyway." Neiko picked up each toy and tossed them in the box one by one, and listened for any noises. She threw in all of them, except Ramses and she did an over shoulder toss. She missed the box, and he bounced off.

"Owww!" said an angry voice. Neiko jumped and looked around horrified. She got on her hands and knees and studied him closely.

"Did you say 'Ow'?" she asked curiously. Ramses said nothing and stared blankly into space. Neiko shook her head. "I can't comprehend this! Here I am talking to a *toy*, and he just said 'Ow'? What's going on? I'll tell mom about this and see if anything else happens. Well, here goes nothing—hey wait, I'll wait till dinner."

"Amanda, dinner!"

- CHAPTER 8 -

WELL, HERE GOES NOTHING," said Neiko as she walked down the hall. She was trying to measure up what to say to her mother about what happened. She sat down at the table and waited for her mom to hand her dinner. They prayed, and after they finished, Neiko began eating.

"I wonder where your daddy is," her mom said, trying to break the silence.

"I don't know, probably got held up at LP again," Neiko replied with a mouth full of cabbage.

"Is there something on your mind? You're awfully quiet."

"Yeah, um—did you hear anything strange—like in my room... like metal hitting the wall or something?"

"No, why?"

"I was just wondering because a couple of strange things happened a few minutes ago."

"Like what?"

"Well—like...um—I was playing with Ramses, and when he hit the wall he clanged, and then I tried to ring him in the toy box; I missed, and he hit the side and said 'Ow'."

"Who is Ramses?"

"One of my toys—the guy with the shiny armor."

"Amanda," she groaned in an aggravated manner, then said gently, "Oh—yeah—well... that's nice, dear."

"Mom, I ain't makin' this up. It really happened."

"That's really using your imagination. Did this happen during a battle?"

"No! This wasn't pretend—this was real. Like in real life," Neiko stammered.

"Oh, well, that's a really nice joke—"

"I'm not joking—and I haven't even laughed about it. If I was joking, then I would be laughing my head off."

"Has he ever done this before?"

"No."

"Did he come with any special real-life sounds or anything?"

"No, he was just a plain toy. I've had him for a long time, and I've played with him a million times, and it's never happened before—never mind, let's talk about something else."

Raven, Bloodhawk, and Francesco laughed about their first feats as they gazed into the Eye. "Her mom doesn't even believe her. Look at the disgust on her face!" laughed Francesco.

"It's working like a charm; it won't take too much more of this, and Neiko will be out of commission soon and very vulnerable," Raven replied.

"How much longer?" asked Bloodhawk.

"Not much longer. Probably two more will do it. Francesco, prepare to kick her out if anything is mentioned to the Tribes about it," Raven said.

"Oh, don't worry, I'm ready for that. I can't wait till then," Francesco sneered.

"The best part is that she doesn't even suspect. And when she does, it'll be too late," Bloodhawk said with glee.

"You're absolutely right, son. Now be patient. We can't make any mistakes, I'll let you know when the time is right. Now, Francesco, go and be ready for the next step: expel Admiral Kidd!" Raven said in a sinister manner.

"With pleasure," Francesco said with a devious smile.

- CHAPTER 9 -

AFTER SUPPER, NEIKO WENT into her bedroom and shut the door. She thought and thought about what happened with Ramses and about what happened at dinner. "I can't believe she didn't believe me."

Neiko muttered under her breath. "Oh well, it's probably nothing—but still... " The phone rang and interrupted her thoughts.

"Amanda, telephone!" her mom called. "Who is it?" Neiko asked.

"Jessica! Don't talk long," said her mom handing her the phone.

"Olleh?" Neiko said into the phone.

"Olleh, how are you?" asked Jessica.

"Okay, I guess, boy, I got something to tell you, and it's really weird."

"Really! What?"

"Um, well, I was playing with the Attack Pack and Ramses did some weird stuff, like one time he clanged and later he said 'Ow'."

47

"Really? Cool! I was wondering if your mom will let me spend the night with you. Will you go ask your mom?"

"Say, hold on a sec, will ya?" Neiko put the phone down and ran into the living room and asked, "Mom, can Acissej spend the night tonight?"

"I don't care," she said.

Neiko ran back into her room and picked up the phone. "Mom said s'ti yako, so you can come on over!"

"Alright! What time do you want me to come over?"

"Hmm, well it's six now, so you can come around seven thirty, okay?"

"Why seven thirty?" she asked.

"Well, you need to get packed, and I have to um, go outside and, um, see Tweety's grave a minute, okay?"

"Well, okay, see you then!"

"Okay, bye!" then she hung up. "Well, I can't tell her I have a meeting with the Seven Tribes!"

- CHAPTER 10 -

QUIET, EVERYONE LET'S GET down to business," Xartna ordered. "Alright, Monchiska, will you pray for us before we start?"

Monchiska prayed, and when he finished, everyone was seated.

"I have some alarming news, but it has nothing to do with the Crackedskulls, I'm afraid. The Black Antler Tribe has lost their land to the Georgians in which they will make new homes for the Outsiders. They are asking us to find them a new place to live and with another tribe if need be," Xartna said with a sigh. "Well, I needed to bring this to your attention, and are there any suggestions?"

A great hubbub broke out, and disbelief was seen on every Indian's face, even Neiko's.

Pike, the comedian of the Seven Tribes from the Scraah tribe, stood up and said, "The Antlers have never had this problem before.

How did they lose all 500 acres of their territory? Didn't those old folks with the help of the Black Antler donations help in keeping their land?"

Xartna said, "That's very true. That's the reason why they were able to stand out this long. But a wealthy landlord went to a Georgian Chief and pleaded to raise the taxes on that land and everything on it. Therefore, the taxes were so high that it exceeded the donations of the tribe and the amount the old couple had. So they were forced to sell. The Antler Tribe tried to wait it out, but the clearing for the subdivision began to take place right after purchase. The clearing crew got dangerously close to the tribe itself, and they were forced to leave. Chief Pronghorn phoned me last night and said he had no idea what to do next, so I told him I would talk to everyone about this and see what we could do." Everyone began talking at once, and a few stood up.

Pike yelled, "That's not fair! That Outside Worlder Chief needs to tangle with a few Indians before taking their land!"

White Fang, Pike's brother, who was the opposite of Pike in being quiet and reserved, stood up and said, "He's right, it's not right!"

Many others stood up and angry shouts rang out from the entire crowd.

Xartna shouted, "Everyone, please, calm down!" No one listened, and the hubbub grew louder. Xartna sat down and shook his head.

Neiko stood up took a deep breath and shouted, "Everybody, shut up!" Everyone stopped and listened a moment, and tried to figure out who said it. Neiko cleared her throat, "Alright, thanks. Xartna has more to say, so will you do me a favor and sit down and be quiet?" Everyone sat down and waited till Xartna came to his perch.

"Well, thanks, everyone. We need to be concentrating on the needs of the Antler Tribe and not making war with the Outsiders. Does anyone have any suggestions on where they can stay?"

Nighthawk, a tracker from the Falcon tribe who was one of Neiko's right hand men, stood up and asked, "How many people are in the Antler Tribe?"

"Five hundred to one thousand people," Wolfgang, the Scraah messenger, replied.

"That rules out the Death Mountain Territory, it can only hold about 400 people," Nighthawk said, disappointed.

Neiko stood up, "What about the Etowah Territory? Surely that's big enough till it's wrecked."

"Good idea! I don't think we have to worry about it being wrecked because the Outsiders don't like to live near a river like that because it floods. What do you think, Xartna?" cried Nighthawk.

"I agree to that, but what will we do about their families till we can get them moved? We will let some of our men help them move," Xartna replied.

Puma stood. "We'll open up our homes to them till their new land is ready, and I'll open my home to Chief Pronghorn and his family." Many agreed with this idea, and everyone of the Antler members had a place to stay.

Xartna was pleased with the decision and said, "Well, I will notify the Chief tomorrow. Now is there anything anyone has to say that may have to do with the Crackedskulls?"

Neiko stood up and said, "I think I do, sir."

- CHAPTER 11 -

WELL, NEIKO, TELL US about it," Xartna said taken aback.

"I was playing with my toys awhile ago, and one of them did strange things like clanging when he hit the wall, and he hit my toy box and said 'Ow'," Neiko replied.

"Neiko, this is no time for you to share any of your Attack Pack adventures," Xartna scolded.

"It's not a game! I mean, this happened for real. I tried to ring him in the toy box and he said 'Ow'. Doesn't that sound a little unusual to you? I mean, toys don't talk," Neiko sputtered.

"Well, yes, but I—well, where do you think the Crackedskulls come in?"

"I think Raven has something to do with it," Neiko trumpeted.

"Why do you think that?" Xartna asked.

"Well, doesn't he have a history of making strange things happen or bringing stuff to life?" Neiko asked.

"Well, yes, but it was only sticks and rocks, and they chased the armory keepers and treasurers around the room while the Crackedskulls made off with some documents. Besides, I don't believe he is capable of bringing a toy to life. Which toy was it?"

"Ramses," Neiko said annoyed.

"The King of Egypt?" asked Francesco jeeringly.

"No, the Dark Pharaoh of Qari," Neiko snapped angrily.

"Oh, you mean the evil twin of Ramesses II?" Francesco sneered.

"No! He's not even related to him nor is he Egyptian!" Neiko thundered back.

"Enough, you two. Now, Neiko, did he chase you around the room?" Xartna questioned.

"No," Neiko said honestly.

"Why do you think he picked him? What do you think he could profit from this?" asked Xartna.

"I don't know the answer to question two, but I think he picked Ramses because he is the meanest and scariest of all of my bad guys," Neiko replied.

"Good point, but do you think this is a test run for another sinister plot?" Xartna asked worried.

Neiko shrugged and said, "I don't know."

I have to stop this before our plans are shot!, thought Francesco. He stood up and said, "Xartna, do we have to listen to this lunacy? There is no proof Raven is behind this, and he is not capable of bringing toys to life!"

Xartna was taken completely off guard. "Now look, Grand High, every incident must be brought to our attention—"

Before he could finish, Francesco pointed at Neiko and said, "Do we have to listen to unreasonable accusations? All of this is unproven and why would he use *toys*? I mean, this is insanity!"

Neiko put her hands on her hips and asked angrily, "Are you calling me crazy?"

"Yes! That is *exactly* what I'm saying!" Francesco thundered back.

"I'll show you crazy!" Neiko said as she pushed up her sleeves in a fighting manner. "How do you know what Raven is capable of? You don't even have magical knowledge unless you're his lapdog selling us out. C'mon and fight, you yellow-belly Raven lover!"

"This is insane! First you call me a traitor and accuse me of espionage, and now you want to end this dispute in violence? These are the actions of a complete lunatic!" Francesco said in defense.

Neiko was so angry that she stormed up and socked him in the nose. The force of the blow caused him to topple to the ground; Francesco grabbed his nose with one hand and staggered to his feet. The entire crowd was silent, taken aback by what happened.

Neiko put her fists on her hips and looked triumphant. "Well, how do you like lunatic, Crackedskull worshipper?"

"Owwww, you will pay for this, you little witch!" Francesco thundered. "Oh, it's bleeding!" he said with a miserable whine. A crimson trickle of blood ran of both nostrils and started dripping on the ground.

Neiko rolled her eyes and shook her head. "Wuss." Neiko looked around at everyone's startled faces. "What?" Neiko asked.

Puma handed him a handkerchief to stop the bleeding. He placed it on his nose and leaned his head forward.

Xartna had had enough. "Stop it! Both of you! There will be no name calling or accusations made without just cause, and this is a meeting ground, not a battlefield!"

"Alright, Admiral Neiko Kidd, from this day forth, is officially disbanded!" Francesco thundered.

The entire crowd began to murmur.

Xartna looked at Francesco horrified. "No, Grand High, this is not necessary, there isn't even just cause—"

Francesco took away the handkerchief revealing his bloody nose. "You don't call *this* just cause?" he asked as he pointed to his nose then replaced the handkerchief.

"Well…" Xartna began.

"There is plenty of just cause! My nose and all this Ramses talk are enough! My decision is *final!*" Francesco shouted, interrupting him.

Monganata approached him and put his hand on his shoulder. "Disbandment is a little harsh, Grand High. I just think she's under stress and needs a small vacation. Summer vacation is in two weeks. She can get back to doing her duties."

"Yeah, she will be on vacation, alright, *permanently!*" Francesco snapped. "Now, if you'll excuse me, I need to get home—I have unfinished business to take care of." Francesco pushed Monganata out of the way.

Everyone watched him leave and shook their heads.

Monganata sighed. "Well, there's no talking with the man when he's that mad."

"I didn't mean to get so mad, but he's been picking at me all evening. I do have a lot on my mind. I'm sorry," Neiko apologized.

Xartna smiled. "Well, I know. Mongie and I will do everything we can to get you back in." Then he rubbed his chin. "Hmmm, well it seems to me he got you riled intentionally, but I'm not sure why."

Monganata nodded. "You're right. I know he hasn't been too fond of you, Neiko, but tonight put the icing on the cake. No harm done, but there has been something suspicious going on for a long time, and I think we're close. Xartna and I will check more on this and this Ramses business. So hang on."

Xartna nodded. "Well, I'll talk to Sigma on helping us out. We are the only three that will work on it, and we'll keep it under wraps. Just hang on, Neiko. We'll fix this, so kick back for a while. It won't hurt."

"Okay, I will. Xartna, will you adjourn the meeting? I need to get home. My cousin will be here in ten minutes," Neiko said.

"Sure thing. Neiko, you take care, and lie low, hear? I'll keep you informed," Xartna said patting her shoulder. "Alright, everyone, the meeting is adjourned!"

– CHAPTER 12 –

ON HER WAY HOME NEIKO kept thinking about what happened at the meeting. "Well, I'll wait for two weeks and see if they come up with anything. If they don't, I'll do a little of investigating of my own. What are you hiding, Francesco? Whatever it is, I'll find out," Neiko murmured to herself.

Neiko made it to her house, and her cousin's car pulled up into the yard. Neiko walked over to help Jessica get all of her things into her house.

Noticing the expression on Neiko's face, she asked, "What's wrong?"

"Nothing, I've just got a lot in my mind, that's all," Neiko replied casually.

"Emoc no, Adnama, s'tel og yalp htiw eht Attack Pack," Jessica said in Greyhawk.

"Yako, Acissej. So, you've been working on your Greyhawk?" Greyhawk was the language of Neiko's tribe. The Falcons discovered it as backward English after English speaking settlers introduced English to all tribes.

"Yep," she replied.

A few hours passed, and Neiko and Jessica decided to get a snack.

After they finished, they stayed and played with her sister Melissa, who was almost a year old. "I need to use the restroom, but I'll meet you in your room, and let's play video games," Jessica said.

"Alright, fine with me," Neiko replied. Neiko walked into her bedroom and put her finger on the light switch. Before she flicked it on, she noticed a red light out of the corner of her eye. Neiko looked a little closer seeing that they were two little eyes glowing, and she remembered that was where Ramses had been lying. She turned on the lights and saw him staring into space. She walked over and tapped him—plastic. She walked back and turned the lights off, and his eyes glowed like two tiny hot coals. Neiko turned the lights on.

The toilet flushed.

She turned the lights off—nothing. Then she put the lights on just before Jessica opened the door. *Good one, Raven*, Neiko thought. "So what do you want to play?" asked Neiko trying to get her mind off what happened.

"Let's play Donkey Kong 3," Jessica said, and after she did, Neiko felt a chill ran up her spine, and the back of her neck began to prickle. She had the terrible feeling that someone or something was in the room with them watching her. The chill intensified and she shuddered as goosebumps appeared on her arms. Neiko wrapped her arms around herself, and she rubbed her hands on her arms to get rid of the gooseflesh. "Are you okay?" asked Jessica.

"Yeah, I'm okay, just had a chill, that's all," Neiko replied casually. The chill ceased but the feeling didn't. *Obviously she doesn't feel that we're being watched, and I better not mention it because she is scared of the dark, and she wouldn't go to sleep if I did*, Neiko thought to herself. "Well, let's play, shall we? We don't have all night," Neiko said trying to sound cheerful and trying to hide the terrible fear in her soul.

A few hours passed, and Jessica wanted to play with the Attack Pack again. Neiko made Air Hammer say, "Things will get worse if Ramses showed up." After she said that, the feeling of being watched almost tripled, and Jessica made Ramses show up, and Neiko made Sonar say in his Transylvanian type dialect, "Oh no, it's the mean, ugly Chrome Pharaoh."

As soon as she said that, chills shot through her body and she dropped Sonar. "Uh, Jessica, I'm ready to go to bed, I'm tired," Neiko replied, shaking.

"Okay, but you were fine a minute ago," she said, and she noticed the fear in Neiko's eyes. "Are you sure you're okay?"

"Uh—yeah, I'm just...um—well—a little nervous about my Civics test Monday, and I'm really tired. I now just realized it, so can we go to bed?" Neiko fibbed.

"Well, okay, if you say so, Adnama," Jessica said.

Neiko got into the bed and pulled the covers over her head, but she could feel the invisible intruder's eyes staring at her through the covers. She shuddered and fell asleep.

- CHAPTER 13 -

TWO WEEKS PASSED, AND she graduated from high school; nothing else strange happened. There were no more visits from the silent watcher. Neiko hadn't heard from anyone about the secret investigation. "I haven't heard anything from Xartna in two weeks. I'll ask him and see if he found anything," Neiko mused. Neiko dialed the numbers and waited for three rings, nothing. "Luckily my parents aren't home," Neiko thought out loud, then the phone rang the fourth time, and Xartna picked up.

"Hello?" he asked.

"Hey, pal, what's up? Haven't heard from you in two weeks. Are you leaving me out in the cold?" Neiko asked, teasing.

"Hello, Neiko, how are you? Has anything else happened?"

"Oh, yeah. Two weeks ago when Jessica came over—oh you won't believe this—Ramses' eyes glowed in the dark, and I had the creepy feeling that someone was in my room watching me, but there was no one there."

"My goodness! Do you think a Crackedskull might have been in the room with y'all?"

"No, it didn't feel like a Crackedskull at all. It was so—different, and I had chills like crazy, and check this out—every time I said Ramses or anything about him, the feeling got worse."

"My, my. Raven came up with a good one, didn't he? I think he did that to scare you and throw us off. I wouldn't worry too much about that."

"You're probably right. Have you found any dirt on Raven or the Grand High Mohican?"

"Nope, not a shred of evidence to help your case. We have searched everywhere, but now I believe we have to call it quits for the time being. If we find something, we'll let you know, alright?"

"Yeah sure..." as soon as she said that, she saw a Crackedskull messenger crossing her yard! "Well, Xartna, I've got a prowler in my yard; call ya right back, bye!"

Neiko hung up and ran to the corner of her room and grabbed her fighting stick. She sprinted to the back door and looked out of the window. The Crackedskull was directly in her range and only one hundred yards away. She opened the back door and shouted "Hey, you!"

The Crackedskull spun around with surprise, and fear gripped him when he saw Neiko charging at him with lightning speed. He turned to run, but she hit him with a flying tackle, sending him crashing to the ground. Neiko got up and stood ready, and the Crackedskull got up and stared at her angrily.

"You meddling Indian! I'll cut you to pieces for messing with me! No one messes with Dingeye and gets away with it!" he snapped as he pulled out his dagger.

"Ooooh, give me your best shot, loser!" Neiko challenged.

Dingeye lunged at her, but Neiko sidestepped, spun around and hit him in the back of the head with her stick. He landed on the ground facedown, got up with grass and dirt in his mouth. He spat the grit out. Before he had time to strike again, Neiko hit him in the hand and sent the dagger flying, and Dingeye yelled with pain. He turned and dove for it. Just before he could reach it, Neiko kicked it out of reach. Dingeye tackled Neiko and sent her crashing to the ground. They wrestled in a tangle of arms and legs, but Neiko managed to get her right arm free and she dealt him a hard punch in the eye, sending him toppling backward. Neiko got up quickly and kicked him in the chin; Dingeye landed hard on his back.

Seeing he was outmatched, he retreated the way he came. Neiko looked around and picked up her stick and his dagger. "Thanks for the souvenir," she said as she slipped the dagger in her pocket, but something in the corner of her eye caught her attention. In the spot where Dingeye fell, there lay an envelope. Neiko picked it up and examined it finding the Crackedskull insignia. "Hmm, I wonder who this is to, and he was heading toward the Grand High's house," Neiko mused. Neiko opened the envelope and unfolded the paper inside.

Francesco,

I wish to schedule a meeting as soon as possible to work on phase two of the plan. I want to commend you on your great performance at the meeting, and the outstanding work of keeping all of our information safe from those meddling Indians. Write me as soon as possible on when you wish to meet with me.

Sincerely,

Raven

"Aha! I just hit pay dirt. So there is a plot against me, and I just found who the traitor is—it's addressed to the GHM! So that means one thing—*he's* the traitor! Well, I'll call Xartna back now," Neiko mused.

Neiko walked into her room and pressed redial; Xartna immediately picked up the phone.

"Neiko, thank goodness you called. Well, what about that prowler?"

"Oh, it was nothing, um, it was just one of my neighbors, I didn't recognize him at first," she said covering up what she found out.

"Oh, that's good. I'm glad it wasn't a big emergency."

"Sorry to break it up, but gotta go."

"Well, okay, call me if you find anything about your case or if anything else strange happens, and I'll keep you posted. Hope to see you soon, Neiko, bye."

Neiko hung up and put the phone back under the bed, and thought about everything she just found out. *Busted!* Neiko thought gleefully. "Well, now I know what Raven meant about the 'performance at the meeting,' but I wonder what 'phase two' is. I have to handle this myself, and I want the pleasure myself especially after all the rotten things he's done to me. I wonder what else he's hiding and why does he hate the Seven Tribes so much? But now I know why he wants me out of the way. I can't mention anything about this letter to anybody because he will say I wrote it to frame him and to get my revenge. Well, I'd like to get a little revenge. I want to do something rotten to him, and at the same time stir up something so that the Tribes will be alerted; that rules out practical jokes— but I wonder what would happen if Raven got mad at him? That's it! I'll write a letter to Raven with my personal touch of insults—which I have wanted to do for a long time—and put Francesco's name on it!"

Neiko went to her computer and typed a letter that read:

Raven,

Didn't you know that your mom was the big fat hen that lays rotten eggs? Of course that's what you hatched out of and you're afraid to admit it! You won't fight the Seven Tribes since they can smell you coming because of your foul stench, and you are just an overgrown yellow-bellied stuffed turkey! You are so stupid that you thought Salmonella was the name of your next-door neighbor, and your type of company because they are bacteria like you. As for the meeting, I wouldn't be caught dead in that dump you live in, so go choke on a chicken bone and die, you big fat ugly toad! Thanks for the compliments because you know that I'm smarter than a pinhead like you! Oh, by the way, tell your overgrown pothead son to cut off the Mary Jane and go suck on the rotten egg he hatched out of after he kisses a dead dog. I think you're feather-brained phase two is a stupid idea, and I can't believe I listened to two stupid retards like you! So good riddance you loonies!

Sincerely,

Francesco

P.S. Go to Jenny Craig and lose a million pounds, birdbrain!!!

Neiko looked at her handiwork and giggled. "Boy, he'll be in so much trouble when Raven sees this."

Neiko looked at the clock, 5:00 p.m. "My parents will be home in two hours. I have plenty of time to pull off the delivery. Now all I gotta do is print this out, call Raven, and put this in Francesco's mailbox for the messenger. Oh boy, this will be fun! Good thing I know Raven's number, and he doesn't have a caller ID." Neiko pulled out the phone and dialed the numbers to Raven's fortress.

- Chapter 14 -

ELLO?" ASKED A SERVANT AT Raven's fortress.

"Oh, hello, it's me Francesco. I need to speak to Raven, please," Neiko said in Francesco's voice.

"I'm sorry, sir, but Raven doesn't wish to be disturbed—can I take a message?" he asked before Neiko could say anything. Neiko could hear Raven in the background.

"Who is it?" he asked harshly.

"It's Francesco, Majesty," replied the servant.

"Give it to me," he snapped. "Hello?"

Neiko's mind started racing. "Oh, hello, I didn't mean to disturb you, I was just about to give a message with the servant—"

"Out with it!" Raven snapped coldly.

"I was calling to tell you that I received your letter, and I'm leaving my reply in my mailbox. I want a messenger to pick it up at six thirty," Neiko replied in her disguised voice.

"Alright, I'll have a messenger run by. So when do you wish to meet?"

"Um, I need to go run errands, and I haven't got time to talk; the meeting time is written in the letter. Bye!" Neiko hung up sighing with relief. "Boy, that was close. I wished I could just have told the servant about the letter. Boy, doesn't old Grand High have such awful company. Well, I'll run this by Francesco's house, and wait and see if the messenger gets it."

Neiko placed the letter in Francesco's mailbox and waited behind a bush. At exactly six thirty, a shadow came and took the letter. Neiko sniggered and waited till the Crackedskull disappeared. "Well, mission accomplished. Too bad I can't see Raven's face when he reads the letter and the look on Francesco's face when Raven raises Cain."

Taken by curiosity, Neiko tiptoed, peeped into his window, and saw him typing away on his computer, totally oblivious to what she's up to. "I'll make a point to visit his house and see if I can find anything I can use as info when he's not at home," Neiko thought to herself. Neiko touched the light on her watch to check the time which read: 6:45. Neiko noiselessly slipped down his driveway and quickly ran home. When she got home, she erased the letter from the computer, hid Dingeye's dagger and Raven's letter to Francesco under the phone that was under the bed, went to the computer, and started playing games. Her parents came in the door and started mumbling so she wouldn't hear.

Finally her mom called her, "Amanda, come here. We need to talk to you," she said in a worried manner.

Astonished at her tone, Neiko ran down the hall, and when she came into the living room, she asked, "What's up?"

"Amanda, me and your dad have been very worried about you. We went and talked with Dr. Macintosh, and he wants to see you tomorrow," she replied.

"Who's that?!" Neiko asked.

"A psychiatrist," she explained.

"What for? What's this about? Why?"

"We told him about the things you have been talking about what happened with Ramses and about you refusing to lay down the toys. He wants you to bring him with you tomorrow," she said.

"What time?"

"At one o'clock," she replied.

"Okay, well, I need to give T-bird some food, and I'm ready for bed, so good night," she said curtly. Neiko put the seed in T-bird's feeder and covered her cage up. "Thanks a lot, Raven!" she spat indignantly. T-bird, Neiko's cockatiel, squawked. Neiko turned around and her parents stood in her doorway shocked. Neiko avoided their eyes and stared at the floor.

They went on to bed and Neiko shut her door. Neiko waited till she could hear her parents snoring, then she turned off her main light. Then she turned on her lamp beside her bed. She noiselessly pulled out her secret phone and called Xartna.

"Hello?" asked Xartna asked sleepily.

"Hello, it's me Neiko, I've got something I want to tell you," said Neiko sadly.

"Neiko, do you have any idea what time it is? It's midnight!" Xartna scolded.

"I know, I'm sorry, but this couldn't wait another minute," she said fighting back the tears.

"You don't sound happy, what's wrong?"

"My parents are sending me to a shrink tomorrow."

"About what?"

"The Ramses business, and he even wants me to *bring* Ramses tomorrow."

"Oh, no! This is terrible! Do you want the Seven Tribes to know about this?"

"Yes, please. Well, I'll let you go, bye." Neiko hung up and put the phone in its original spot. Neiko slipped into bed, covered herself, and cried herself to sleep.

CHAPTER 15

H AVE A SEAT," SAID Dr. Macintosh, as he ushered Neiko in. Neiko sat down in the large chair in front of his desk. Macintosh had on a shirt and tie, and his ID tag was clipped onto his white shirt. He was a short, middle-aged man with thick glasses, bald with a ring of curly gray hair around the rest of his head "Did you bring Whatshisname?" he asked.

"Yes," Neiko said dryly. He took Ramses in his hands and looked at him closely. After he finished looking at him, he set him on the desk. "What is his name again?" he asked.

"Ramses," she replied.

"Ramses," he repeated softly, nodding. "Tell me everything about him."

"Well, um, he's the worst and meanest guy that ever lived in the history of Qari, Saudi, Iduas, Occorom, and Tiawuk. He's also the Dark Pharaoh, and the slayer of many people and beasts alike. He's in love with Lydia, and he wants to destroy the Attack Pack. He is living as an ordinary Pharaoh of Qari as the first-born son of Osiris. He's using this as a cover, and he stole the birthright of Menes. That's it."

"What is a Dark Pharaoh exactly?"

"A pharaoh that is immortal, more powerful, and meaner than a regular one. Ramses is the only one."

He picked up Ramses and pointed at his chest. "Is this his skin?"

"No, that's his armor. He is completely covered with armor, and nobody has ever seen his face."

"I see, and have you any idea what he may look like underneath or where he came from?"

"Nope, never thought of it."

"Tell me more of the Attack Pack and his relationship with Lydia."

"Well, the Attack Pack is basically a group of beasts and people that live together with one thing in common, Ramses wrecked their life, and they want to bring him down. Well, Lydia, let's see. First of all he watched her be born, and fell in love with her instantly. When she was a year old, her mom, Nefari, died of a bad disease, so Ajax, her father, raised her. Ramses came and started seeing her when she was twenty-five, but later Ajax found out that he was a Pharaoh; he broke them up and promised her to someone else. Ramses got ticked off and murdered Ajax and kidnapped Lydia. Cheetor, her adopted cheetah cub, came home from a hunt and found Ajax dead, and his mom missing. He went to look for her. She stayed with him for one hundred thousand years, but Phoenix came, saved her, and married her. Ramses was so mad, he tried to kill him; he thought he was dead, and he took her again. She stayed with him another one thousand years. Silverbolt came, rescued her, and married her too, but this time he was able to let a king named Ajax take her in, and he changed her age so he was able to hide her before he disappeared. Many years went by and Ramses showed up, but he didn't know it's the same Lydia, and Ajax didn't realize he's the guy Silverbolt warned him about. Lydia thought he was someone else, so she fell in love and Ajax betrothed her to him, but Sandstorm showed that he's evil, and he married her. Then the Attack Pack members started coming, including Phoenix, and they fought against him trying to save them, keep Lydia safe, and save the world."

"I see. What a bedtime story, and you have quite an imagination. I see that Ramses is a very bad person and violent. Do you really believe he said 'Ow' and all of that other stuff? Oh yes, who on earth is Raven?"

"Yeah, I believe it, because it really happened! Raven is, um, my imaginary friend. I got mad at him because he forgot my graduation present," Neiko fibbed.

"I see. Excuse me for a moment; I must get myself a cup of coffee." Macintosh got up and when he left the room, Neiko scowled.

"This is a waste of my time, and he doesn't believe a word I'm saying," Neiko muttered angrily. Then in her anger she kicked the trash can and the trash scattered all over the floor. "Oops," she said as she cleaned up the mess and finished just before Macintosh walked in.

"Well, let's get back to work shall we?"

Joy, she thought sarcastically. Macintosh asked her many more questions about her imaginary world of the Attack Pack. Finally he called her mom to the office, but they stepped outside just out of earshot. Neiko picked up Ramses and rubbed his breastplate.

"Yeah, just what I was thinking," she said to her silent companion, but suddenly, the creepy feeling and her invisible visitor came accompanied by the chills. She laid him down on the desk as the doctor and her mom came in, and her chilling visitor left.

"Well, all Amanda needs is a stress-free environment for a few months. I must admit she has quite an imagination. We will have to work on her putting down her toys a little at a time. I'll schedule a session next month to see her progress, good day, Mrs. Hawk. Amanda, you may leave now," he said gently.

"Can I take Ramses home?" Neiko asked. "Yes of course," he said.

"Good, we can leave now. I didn't think the meeting would ever end.

Stress-free environment, my eye! I'll put down my toys when I'm good and ready! I'm perfectly fine except for Raven is screwing up my life. I need to search Francesco's house soon. I guess I'll see when there's a meeting, and I'll see about doing so; I can't say anything about this creepy feeling, Neiko pondered as she walked to the car to go home.

CHAPTER 16

NEIKO GOT UP THE NEXT morning feeling chipper. "Okay, I'll call Xartna, and see when there's a meeting. Good thing my mom is gone to the clinic for Melissa's shots." Neiko pulled out the phone and called Xartna.

"Hello, Neiko, how did the session go yesterday?" he asked.

"Okay, I guess. He wanted me to tell him everything from A to Z about Ramses, the Attack Pack and everything. He even asked who Raven was because my parents overheard me say something about him in anger, so he asked. My parents are trying to make me stop playing with the Pack."

"Oh no. What did you say about Raven? I hate to hear that about your made up adventures because they always sound so exciting."

"Oh, I just made up some crap like he was my imaginary friend, and I was mad because he forgot my graduation present. He bought it."

Xartna chuckled. "Well, that was a close one. Did the shrink tell you if you're crazy or not?"

"Well, he said for me to have a stress-free environment for a few months. He wants to have a session soon to check progress, and I'm perfectly fine. Gosh, I was so mad."

"Gracious, what a drag. I haven't said anything to the Tribes about it because there's a meeting tonight at eight, and I'll tell them at the meeting. Is there anything else you need me to know or anything you need at the moment?"

"No thanks, not right at the moment, but if anything interesting comes up at the meeting, please let me know."

"Sure thing, call me later—about ten, okay?"

"Sure, no problem—gotta go, my mom's home, bye!" Neiko hung up, put the phone under the bed, turned on Killer Instinct, and started playing. Her mom came in, checked to see what she was doing, and walked to the kitchen to fix her sister's lunch.

Neiko was playing Riptor on the hardest setting and just barely beat Jago. "Oh, great, here comes Cinder. Eat floor, Ramses Gas! Oh you like that? Aw, darn," she said at the game. Ramses Gas was an offensive smoke screen that Ramses used to elude the Attack Pack. The Attack Pack used it as well as "Monster Gas" as insults to annoy Ramses, and so Neiko also used them as an everyday expressions though no one understood what it meant.

"Amanda! That wasn't very nice!" scolded her mom.

"Well, you know I get into my games," she replied smiling.

"I know. I don't want to hear anything about Ramses or his gas, and remember what the doctor said you should think about Ramses as little as possible, and this is about the tenth time I've heard you say something about him in three days! Just try harder," she scolded and walked into the living room. Neiko looked at her clock and saw it was only three o'clock. Neiko played video games till supper, which was at six. Neiko took her time eating till seven, and at seven thirty she told her mom she was going walking, and went to Francesco's house.

Neiko arrived about seven fifty and cautiously approached his house. She peered in his bay window and saw he hadn't left yet. *I wonder why he hadn't left yet; he'll be late*, Neiko thought. Francesco started going toward the door, but the phone rang. He ran and picked up the phone.

"What now?" he grumbled. He picked it up. "Grand High Mohican here and what do you want?" he snapped with a scowl on his face. Neiko listened and watched. His face changed into fear. "Oh, Raven! I'm sorry. I thought you were an Indian. I need to hurry because there's a meeting— "

Before he could finish, he had to pull the phone from his ear because Raven was so angry he was yelling.

We have liftoff and the crowd goes wild, Neiko thought as she covered her mouth and giggled.

"It's not like that at all, Raven! Hello? Hello?" Francesco laid down the receiver slowly, with shock written all over his face. "What is he so mad about? I'll definitely go to Raven's after the meeting." Francesco ran from the door to go to the meeting while Neiko hid behind a bush.

"The fireworks are going, and he'll be dead meat when he visits Raven," Neiko mused as she laughed. Neiko went from her hiding place to make sure the coast was clear. She sneaked up to his door and looked for a spare key for quite a while in many possible places, nothing.

"Well, that's just peachy," Neiko grumbled and slammed her fist in his rock-faced wall, but something hit her on top of the head and clattered on the porch. "Wo! What in the world?" she asked, rubbing her head. She looked down and one of the small rocks came out of the wall. She inspected the wall and found where the rock was supposed to go. In the hole was the key. "Bingo! Thank you, Great Spirit!" Neiko said as she unlocked the door; then she replaced the key in its place with the rock. Neiko opened the door and walked inside.

The house was one story with only two bedrooms and was cluttered. Neiko walked into the kitchen. Looking on the table, she found it covered with books of Ancient Egypt and books on hieroglyphs. She flipped through the books and found only notes on dead pharaohs, relics, and temples. Neiko found pages of his own hieroglyph-coded writings that had been translated. "Good grief! I had no idea he was a nut on Egypt, and he has a shipload of notes on Ramesses II the Great. I don't find him all that interesting. He's sort of a mean guy. I can't believe this guy; he even has pictures and sketches of him everywhere, and he probably knows more about him than the museum! Well, on with the search."

Neiko searched the house and went into his bedroom last. He had more posters of Egypt on his wall, and she found plaques and certificates everywhere, along with newspaper clippings of his past feats. Neiko read them closely, but nothing was suspicious. "Well, this trip is a bummer so far, oh yeah—his computer! Why didn't I think of that earlier?" She facepalmed herself. "Oh, well, here goes nothing."

Neiko started up the computer and waited till the desktop showed. Several icons showed along with the usual ones. "Hmm, Egyptian History, Hieroglyph Decoding, and Classified Info. Well, let's see what's in Decoding."

The window came up, and Neiko scrolled down and skimmed the screens, nothing. "I'm not interested in history, so I'll check Classified. The screen came up but it read: *Need password to proceed.*

"Aww, man! I'll see if I can crack it, but I must think like him, so I'll try 'I hate Neiko.'"

Access denied.

"Raven rules."

Access denied.

"The Seven Tribes suck."

Access denied.

Neiko thought and thought tapping her forehead with the palm of her hand saying, "Think, Neiko, think! Egypt!" Neiko typed it in, but with the same result. "Darn! I thought this would be easy—darn Ramses Gas! Wait a minute! I think I know! 'Ramesses the Great!' I'll try this and see."

Neiko typed it in and access was allowed!

"Finally! I hope the info in here is worth the headache. Good password. I would've never thought of it, if I hadn't look at that stuff earlier, I would've never guessed. He must have a thing for this guy because he is all over his house. He's even the password to his secret stuff. He needs to visit Dr. Macintosh for going wild over an ancient crackpot like some kind of a groupie!" Neiko slowly read the screen, which started back in 1960.

"I am a young, ambitious Crackedskull with a taste for adventure, and Raven has treated me well. Now he has a great task for me. Become a chieftain, live under cover, and give the secrets and plans to him . . ."

"Holy smokes! I hit the honey pot! So this is where he keeps the information about Crackedskull plans and his past, and he's not just working for the Crackedskulls, he *is* a Crackedskull! Well, I'll see what else is in here, and get a printout." Neiko read down the screen and found all of the secrets given to Raven and past plots that have been thwarted. "Golly, I can really nail him to the wall with this! Wait, what's this?"

Neiko scrolled down the screen and it read:

May 5, 1999 Plan Alpha

Take Ramses to Raven and see if he can use him to destroy Neiko's reputation. I will disband her ASAP. Phase two: Wait for further instructions and signal Bloodhawk.

"Aha! Gotcha! So that's why Ramses is doing strange things. Phase two will be underway when ol' sourpuss finds out about the shrink and tells Raven. I still don't know what phase two is—oh well. I'll print this out, and I'll need to make like Tom and cruise."

Neiko printed the files, shut down the computer, put everything back the way it was, and left for home.

– CHAPTER 17 –

A S SOON AS THE meeting was over, Francesco ran to Raven's fortress, fearful of what may have happened to disrupt the plan. He got through all of the security and came into the throne room. He was only greeted by scowls of hate from Raven and Bloodhawk. Raven stood up and glared at him and said, "You have a lot of nerve to show up here after what you said to me!"

"I said I was sorry! I really—actually thought you were an Indian because they have been calling me all day! I..."

"This is not about Indians! I'm surprised you want to come to meet with me in my dump, and I haven't choked on a chicken bone yet!" he snapped.

Bloodhawk stood up and shouted, shaking his huge fists. "You say I smoke marijuana, and I don't take drugs! You even told me to suck on a rotten egg, in which I hatched out of, after kissing a dead dog!"

Francesco looked at them horrified. "What?! I never said anything like that! What are you talking about?"

"You know *exactly* what we're talking about! Don't play dumb with me because I'm not a retard, pinhead, or a birdbrain! Do you actually think I need to lose a million pounds, know-it-all?" Raven shouted, boiling.

"You even say that kidnapping Neiko is a stupid, featherbrained idea! You said this in your reply to the letter dad wrote you even after he complimented you!" Bloodhawk stormed.

"What letter? I didn't get a letter from you!" Francesco stammered.

Raven stood up. "Liar! You called me and told me to send a messenger to pick this letter up in your mailbox at exactly six thirty! Take back your letter and eat it, and you better leave the room for my fist because I'll ram it into your stomach and break your spine, you little pipsqueak!" Raven wadded it up and threw it hitting him in the head.

Francesco picked up the letter, unwadded it, and read it. After he finished, his mouth flew open and his eyes were wide with disbelief.

"I-I didn't write this! I never called you or received a letter!"

Raven scowled. "That was your voice on the phone, you ungrateful little toad, and it was set up just perfectly by your style! Explain that, smarty breeches!"

"I was on the computer the entire day working on an Egyptian project, like I said, I never got a letter, and I would not be ungrateful toward you for any reason."

"If you didn't do it, then who did?" asked Bloodhawk.

"Dingeye! Get your butt in here *now*!" Raven shouted, and it echoed through the halls.

Dingeye ran in the room scared and covered with bruises where Neiko had hit him.

"You called, Majesty?" Dingeye asked.

"Did you *really* get that letter to Francesco and why do you have bruises?" Raven asked as he stood over him. "Don't lie to me."

"The truth is—no. An Indian attacked me, and I fled. I thought I had it, but I discovered I had lost it, so I lied to you. Forgive me," he pleaded.

"So where is the letter now, hmm?"

"I guess she got it, I'm sorry I failed; I tried to defend myself, but she was too tough. I threatened her, but she got the best of me."

"She? What did *she* look like?"

"Short, long black hair, green eyes—"

Bloodhawk stood up. "What Indian looks like that and can do impressions well?"

"Admiral Kidd!" Francesco, Raven, and Bloodhawk said in unison.

"You mean you were seen, and you lost the letter?" Raven asked.

"*And* you threatened her?" Bloodhawk snapped.

"Aye, and I'm sorry, my prince, I had no idea it was her, forgive me!" Dingeye pleaded.

"Never mind. Now all we need to do is *fix* the mistake," Raven mused.

Francesco scowled. "Great. Now she has proof that I'm working for you, and if she goes to the Tribes about this—I'm finished! Oh, by the way, Neiko visited a shrink the other day, and she has to stay in a stress-free environment with another session in another month or so."

"Well, *finally* good news! Now everything is going our way except for Neiko finding out the truth, but she is playing right into our hands. Did Xartna say anything about you at the meeting or any suspicions?" Raven asked.

"No, but he did say something about a secret mission to uncover a traitor and clear Neiko from 'my dangerous wrath,' and Neiko hasn't told anyone what she found; it seems like she's handling it herself," Francesco answered. "I don't think she'll stop there! She may search for more proof, and then she may tell everyone about it!" Francesco said in a high pitched shriek.

Raven put his hands on his hips. "Did you take steps to make sure that no one knows our secrets, *especially* Neiko? Answer me!"

"Yes! They're all in my computer and guarded with a secret password that no one would ever know or even think of."

"Well, relax, will ya? Now all we have to do is silence her by going on with phase two, right? Still, the time to make the move is quite difficult. What if she doesn't come outside—we can't possibly afford another slip up or wait till whenever, argh!" Raven growled with disgust.

"Well, her parents are going on a trip in two weeks on a Friday, and she didn't want to go, so she will be left all alone for an entire day!" Francesco replied gleefully.

Bloodhawk stomped his foot as an idea popped in his head. "I've got it! We'll wait till dark that day. If she's not outside, then we send a few men to flush her out while father and I wait in hiding. We'll fly in, swoop, and she will be ours!"

Raven smiled. "Very good thinking. There are no kinks in the plan and there is no one to stop us this time! She will not think that letter prank was so funny when she is our captive!"

Francesco sneered. "She'll think twice before she messes with Crackedskulls, and soon she will be one herself after she becomes our prisoner of war!" They all celebrated and laughed as the rest of the plan was laid out!

- CHAPTER 18 -

A FEW DAYS AFTER NEIKO'S great discovery, Jessica called and wanted her to spend the night with her. "You want me to bring the entire Attack Pack, Skull Bearers, and everything? Well, okay. I'll be there in about thirty minutes!" Neiko said and she pushed the button to hang up the cordless phone. "We'll make sure everyone is still in the toy bag because my sister demolished my room!" Neiko mumbled. Neiko dragged them all out and put them all back, but two were missing. "Well, that's just great! I can't find Ramses or Quickstrike. I know Melissa didn't take them because I watched her the whole time, and she put them back on the floor. I remember putting them in the bag, and they were on top—I remember exactly."

Quickstrike was an Attack Pack member who was a scorpion with a cobra tail.

Neiko searched her closet and under her bed, nothing. "Well, I guess, this'll have to do. That really bothers me—they couldn't have just *walked* off, or I guess Raven stole them to make it look like they ran off. Nobody has to know, so I'll just say they went on vacation." Neiko hopped in her car and drove to her cousin's house.

Neiko arrived at Jessica's house, and the first thing they did was go exploring. Neiko was teaching her the secrets of being an Indian, but not letting her know she was one. Neiko always passed it off as being imaginary even though the Tribes mingled and worked with the rest of the known world; no one really knew who they really were because they hid their Indian identities. They stopped under a shady spot near a creek and began to talk. "You know, that was really weird when that lady asked if you were an Indian. I mean, you look kind of like one. I remember when you dressed up you looked like a real one," Jessica said.

Taken off guard, Neiko said, "Well, some people think that because I think I have some in my blood, but I'm not a full-blooded Cherokee or whatever." Neiko was truthful, but she didn't lead on about the Indians of Hawote; she kept on the subject of tribes that moved into Hawote thousands of years ago that were not the original Hawoteyan tribes such as the Cherokee.

"Oh, I see. Well, I always wondered why you were so fearless and all." "I'm not totally fearless, but most things I come across everyday don't scare me. Unknown things are a little different, like I would be afraid of a T-rex, velociraptor, or a fifty-foot anaconda."

"Me too. Well, it's getting dark, and I'm ready to play with the toys now," Jessica said. They arrived at the house thirty minutes later, and they dragged out the entire group. Jessica looked for Ramses and saw he wasn't there. "Where's old Chrome Shnoz?"

"I don't know—I couldn't find him anywhere. What's weird is I remember where I put him, but he wasn't there, so I guess that means some scary man by my window stole him. What's really weird is Quickstrike is missing too."

"Really? Oh well, I guess Ramses went on vacation and took lunch," Jessica said, laughing.

"Yuck! Scorpion with a cobra tail doesn't sound very tasty," Neiko replied.

The next day, Neiko returned home and her mom had gone somewhere, but there was no note. "Hmm, I guess she had something last minute at the church, so I'll just chill out and play Killer Instinct."

About ten minutes later the front door opened, but she didn't call to see if she was home, so Neiko called her. "Hey Ma! Where'd you go?"

No answer.

"Yo! Ma! Hellooo!"

No answer.

"Well, be that way," Neiko grumbled to herself, but then she heard heavy footsteps down the carpeted hall. "Gosh, Mom, what did you do? Eat the church out of house and home? I heard Baptists eat, but this is ridiculous. It sounds like you put on about 500 pounds! You know I'm just joking! Remember when Pastor Parks says stuff about Baptists love to eat?"

Still no answer.

"Man, what's with the silent treatment? Indians What's the matter, Ramses steal your tongue and have it for dinner? Sheesh." Neiko resumed her game, but something was wrong. Neiko put it on pause and noticed she didn't hear Melissa. "Yo, Ma, what's up with Mel? Is she sick? If so, I need to know, or did he get her tongue and have it for dessert? Did you notice I mentioned Ramses twice, and I'm not supposed to because Mr. Shrink said so, right? Are you going to get on to me or what? Helloooo!"

Neiko had shut her door and she could see a shadow in the crack on the bottom. Neiko stood up and walked to the door; the knob started to turn and the door flew open, and there stood Ramses in full height!

Neiko was so overtaken with fear and surprise that her legs gave way, and she toppled on the floor. Every detail of him matched the toy exactly except for where paint may have chipped off. There were no chips or scratches. His armor shone like a brand new chrome bumper; it glistened in the sunlight that entered the room. His helmet looked more like a pharaoh's headdress than the toy and there were skull clasps holding the purple cape on his shoulders. He stood six feet eight, had a massive build and one could gather he weighed 400 pounds of pure muscle; even in the day, his red eyes glowed like two smoldering coals, hot and hard in their stare. His dagger was drawn. It was not red plastic, but gleaming, razor-sharp steel.

As Neiko scrambled and flattened herself against her nightstand, some things clattered in the floor. Neiko was so terrified she could hardly breathe, gasping to get air through the knot in her throat and chest. Neiko couldn't stop her body from shaking. Suddenly, he raised his dagger. Neiko scrunched up waiting for the sting, but it landed in the nightstand above her head, and Neiko shuddered. She uncurled herself and stared back at him with shock. On his dagger was a three-inch cockroach, which he flicked off and stepped on with his heavy foot. Looking back, he stared at her with his hard gaze that shifted into a soft expression; he sheathed his dagger in the hilt on the backside of his waist beside his long slender sword, and he fixed his long purple cape.

"Stop that! I'm not going to kill you," he said gruffly.

Neiko scrambled to her feet. "S-sure, like I was supposed to know that! People just don't walk into people's houses with daggers unless they want to kill somebody!" she snapped. Neiko recovered her bravery and slapped her forehead with her palm three times. "Snap out of it, Neiko! This is just another one of Raven's tricks! Okay, Mr. Crackedskull, listen, you go tell Raven that this ain't funny anymore. I'm sick and tired of this Ramses stuff! That was really cute when he stole one of my favorite toys, and sends you into my house dressed up in chrome armor—which you probably ripped off from someone's car—to drive me nuts! Why doesn't he just send his son to kidnap me and force me to marry him, huh? Send the whole Crackedskull army for all I care, I'm game! Anything but this retarded, two-bit, cheesy scheme! Oh yeah, and tell him to send me back Ramses without a scratch, or I'll visit it back on him with a whole hoard of stinkbombs!"

Ramses stared at her, puzzled and amazed at her composure. "What are you talking about? I'm not a Crackedskull. I *am* Ramses! I know all about Raven and Crackedskulls, and I am in Hawote at last! I am a part of no one's scheme, and I serve no one, Neiko."

"Oh, that's real cute! Every Crackedskull knows my name! Stop with the act, okay? Since you seem to be on drugs or PCP or some crap like that I'll remind you, oh, before I do, let me set this straight. Ramses does *not* exist! He's a *toy*, a child's plaything, and a figment of my imagination. In other words, he's made up! End of story! All Crackedskulls serve Raven, the king of the Crackedskulls, who are enemies of all Indians in the land of Hawote. Just in case you forgot, me Indian, you Crackedskull," she swiveled her finger between the to of them, "which we're enemies, and you better go before I make you eat floor!"

"Maybe I didn't explain myself clearly enough, Neiko. It seems *you* don't understand. I *do* exist, and you are in my presence. I know of your little playtime with your cousin Jessica and about the little toy that looks like me. But the truth is I live! I am more than imaginary; I am reality, Desert Storm Falcon!"

"Now we're kind of getting somewhere. At least you got my tribe right! Not bad for a junky. I suppose after this fiasco, the entire Crackedskull army will know of the five-inch tall Pharaoh in chrome, who is a cold blooded killer that was formed in the mind of Neiko. The only real pharaohs who went by that name died years ago and they even spelled their name R-A-M-E-S-S-E-S, and they pronounced the 'E'. They spelled their name differently than the made up one which was R-A-M-S-E-S, and my cousin named her Betta fighting fish after the made up one. So stop—I'm sick of hearing it! My mom sent me to a shrink because Raven did something to make him say 'Ow'!"

"Amusing, sweetie. Well, it seems I haven't gotten through to you, and I shall. I will prove it to you. I really felt that! I was sleeping and dreaming when a voice summoned me. I felt myself flying through the air, and I hit something. The pain went through my helmet and I cried out. You heard me. You know of me being in the dark. Two times something hit me, but you know of one, I gather. As for your deceased Egyptian pharaohs with a name kind of like mine, I know of them. Especially the second one, but he was too soft. By the way, was it you that summoned me?"

"No, wrong number. I wouldn't summon the likes of a dope head like you! Sweetie? Man, you *are* drunk, and when Raven and Bloodhawk find out, you will become their scratching post. You won't be anything but a greasy spot on the floor, and your armor of chrome won't save you. As for your little experiences, I don't need to know about your LSD trips, okay? You're cruisin' for a bruisin', pal. So go back to your friends, loser, in the woods across the road and head northwest to your home, Crackedskull country. Raven probably wants you, so get lost, scidattle, shoo, outa here!"

Ramses just laughed. "I will go for now, but I will return. I have a surprise for you when I do. You *will* believe me, and—never mind. I'll let you find out when I come. Ha ha, ha!" He turned, ran down the hall, and disappeared. Then the front door opened.

"Already?!" Neiko asked in despair.

"Amanda, I'm home!" her mom said. Melissa was crying, and Neiko sighed with relief.

CHAPTER 19

THAT NIGHT NEIKO THOUGHT about what happened that afternoon and couldn't get it out of her mind. Something just didn't add up. How did he know anything about her playtime with her cousin? Who did he think he was coming into her house saying he's Ramses, dressing like him, scaring her to death and making threats? All of these things ran through her mind even at dinner to the extent she didn't talk. She just stared at her plate and fiddled with the noodles because her mom had cooked spaghetti for dinner.

"Is everything alright? What's on your mind? Amanda!" her mom had to raise her voice to get her attention.

"Huh? Oh, uh—what did you say?" Neiko asked in a daze. "I didn't hear you."

"She asked if everything is alright," her dad said gruffly.

"Yeah, everything's fine. I was just thinking about what movie I wanted to watch. Sorry. Can I be excused?" she asked.

Neiko walked into her bedroom, trying to find a movie to stop thinking about the intruder. "Hmm, not something that reminds me of Ramses, no action, violence—something funny, *Liar Liar*? No, it's got a curse like thing—*Cowboy Way*, *Ace Ventura*, or *Hot Shots! Part Deux*. Well, they all sound good—I know! I'll watch them all! Okay, I'll watch *Hot Shots* first."

Neiko watched and laughed and put in Ace Ventura next. When it was over, Neiko reached for the last movie, but suddenly her blanket moved! Startled, she dropped the movie, froze, and stared at the blanket. It moved again and this time something hissed like a snake and grunted. Thinking there was a snake in her bed, she grabbed her machete, unsheathed it, and yanked back the blanket. She held it up to make the kill, but she stopped because there was Quickstrike!

He had the attack stance of an ordinary scorpion and he had his cobra tail hissing and ready to strike. The tail's jaws were open and venom dropped from its fangs. He was only the size of the toy. His body was only four inches from the claw, and his tail was six inches. His tail was mostly brown except for the green bands on the head and hood on top of the cobra, which spread from its red eyes. He had a golden and green body with two brown sections on his sides with a large green band down the middle of them. His head was golden with a green band coming from behind each eye and coming together on his nose. He had two small red eyes and eight orange legs. He had a brown upper part of his arms to his elbows; the rest of his arms were golden, and he had two wide green bands on the tops and bottoms of his claws and two slim ones in the middle of his claws.

"Don't move or you're dead, monster!" he threatened.

"What now? Look, Quickstrike, I won't hurt you, and I'm not a monster!"

"Oh yeah? Prove it. Drop the sword. How do you know my name? Did your pal Ramses tell you?" he said in defense.

"Okay, I'm putting down the machete nice and slow." Neiko laid it down gently and put her hands up. "Ramses? I haven't even

seen him. I know your name because you are one of my toys, and you belong to the Attack Pack."

Quickstrike settled down somewhat. "Whaddya you mean *toy*? I'm just as real as you are!"

Neiko scratched her head. "That's what that creepy dope head said earlier. Will you let me show you something? I have something I want to explain." Neiko got her toy bag and dumped them all on the bed. Quickstrike turned around and looked closely.

"Wow, you weren't lying." He scurried over and tapped Cheetor and saw he wasn't alive; he tried to talk to Buzzclaw, Sonar, and Scarem, but they said nothing. "How is this? I remember they were my size, and I was bigger, but they were alive—"

Neiko sighed. "Well, you *were* just like them, and I played with you, and that's what I meant by toy. I went to my cousin's yesterday, and I tried to find you and Ramses, but y'all disappeared. That's right, old Chromy was a toy too. Can I touch you?" Neiko walked over and felt of his tail. Real scales, and it wasn't jointed plastic, but a real snake. She rubbed his back and claws. Real scorpion armor. "Wow! This is too weird! How come you're real and no one else is?"

"I don't know, but I'll tell you this and see if it makes sense to you. We were having a battle against Ramses for the Eye. He dropped it, and I ran after him. He went into this cave, and I followed him. Right when I grabbed his ankle with my claws, he said 'Hawote.' Then there was this light, and I was in this strange place. It was dark, and I crawled out, but there was no sign of Ramses. I've been in your room since then, but I went out, and I came in when you were eating."

Neiko's eyes were wide. "He said 'Hawote'? That's where you are now! That's the name of my land! So that means he's in Hawote! Oh man! So he got away. You haven't seen him since! So, in that case he'll only be five-inches tall. I can just kick him, and he'll kiss my wall if he tries to start anything with me!"

"Well, I heard this lady say something about a 'Georgia.' Where's that?" asked Quickstrike.

"Well, see—um, Hawote and Georgia are kind of the same place. Hawote is a part of Georgia. Georgia is a part of a place called the U.S. Hawote actually coexists with the entire U.S.,Canada, and Mexico. Canada and Mexico are other Outsider countries. Outsiders are anyone who are not Indians. Where you are now is only a small piece of Hawote. It's the woodlands and rural areas that belong to

Indians in our tribal territories—my tribe's territory is further east, but my parents moved out here in the middle of Crackedskull territory because of my dad's job change. Most Outsiders live in cities and towns, but a few unknowingly live in our tribal territories. I am an Indian, not like what most people think. Most think of Indian as a Cherokee, Comanche, or something like that, and that is American Indian and not one of the original Hawoteyan tribes. Hawoteyan Indians are Scraahs, Monte Carlos, or Desert Storm Falcons like me. Georgians, or we call 'em Outsiders, don't know we exist because we hide our Indian identities. We use their types of names, and we work and live like they do, sort of. My Georgian name is Amanda Hawk, and my Falcon name is Neiko Kidd. I'm the admiral or the supreme commander of the warrior forces of my tribe. Indians don't have mortal kings, only spiritual. We worship the Great Spirit and his son, but the outsiders call 'em God and Jesus. I have to be careful and not call God Great Spirit or Yahweh at church or people'll look at me weird. There are some other Outsiders who use the name Yahweh. The Crackedskulls, our enemies, have kings, and they live like the Pharaohs of Qari in trying to destroy the Indians, and Prince Bloodhawk wants me to be his queen, yuck! His father, Raven, is the supreme leader of the Crackedskulls and likes his son's choice. There are seven Indian tribes that form an allegiance including mine to liberate and protect other tribes from the Crackedskulls, kind of like the Attack Pack."

"Wow! Are your parents Indians? We follow them too. Interesting."

"Nope—well sort of. They are by blood, but they don't know about their heritage since the Outsiders have ruined them, so they don't even know they are," Neiko replied then paused. "Really? Wow!" she said in response in finding they worshipped the same deities.

"How did you find you are one and not your parents?"

"Well, when I was little, we lived in a small town, and we moved near a river. It was on a steep hill, and that was Falcon land—

of course we didn't know that. I went exploring in the territory one day when I was young and met them. I was accepted as one of their lost ones, and I came to find out my ideas were like theirs, and I also found out from them that my parents were long lost Desert Storm Falcons too. Then I realized I was supposed to be already part of the tribe so I joined. They liked my fighting skill, but at that time they didn't know I was the Chosen One. All this about my discovery of my own tribe and the whole thing with my parents was part of an ancient prophecy about a chosen one that would come from my tribe. Since my parents were dulled by Georgian ways, they could never understand the ways of Hawote which was also part of the prophecy. So, my life was kept secret, and it was said a great one would come from the lost Falcons which is basically what happened. Well, I worked my way up to captain, which was the highest rank, and from there I learned of the Crackedskulls, and I was able to command and free all of the enslaved tribes. They call me the 'Liberator' and many other things like that. Recently I was promoted to admiral until a phony chieftain, who is a Crackedskull—I found out only a few days ago—disbanded me under false charges. Well, I also got mad at him and punched him in the nose, so that didn't help. Now everyone is trying to get me back in, and Raven has been plotting this whole big scheme and it is connected—somehow, but I don't know what his next move is—yet."

"Good grief! You sound like a hero! You know, I like you already—you would be a good Attack Packer. No wonder Raven wants you out and why Bloodhawk is in love with you—you're pretty; I wouldn't be surprised if they'd try to kidnap you."

"Aw, shucks, you little smoothie, you!" Neiko chuckled.

"You said something about a dope head earlier. Who was he?"

"Oh, him. Some Crackedskull that came into my house dressed up like Ramses. He did a great job at scaring me. I would give him an Oscar for flawless acting, but I knew it was one of Raven's tricks."

"Somebody dressed up like Chrome Gas? For real? What kind of stuff did he say?"

"Well, I won't kill you, I am Ramses, I work for no one—um, I will return, and I have a surprise for you when I do. Stuff like that."

Quickstrike shuddered. "That sounded like him. He says stuff like that. Was he five-inches tall or whatever?"

"Heck no! He was taller than me! He was taller than Michael Jordan! He was six feet eight easy! Now I definitely know he was lying, but I wonder how he got his eyes to glow like that, and his armor was super shiny! I never saw armor shine like that! It looked like he ran through a drive in car wash!"

"Hmm, six feet eight is the exact height of Ramses, good observation. I have no idea who Micheal Jordan is. Ramses has been acting somewhat odd lately. He used to have green scum on his armor, but now he shines it every weekend and sometimes every day. He looks like a god, a mean scary one too. Did anyone else see him? He was here when I was outside."

"No. I was here alone, and I just got home from my cousin's. The neighbors were outside, but they didn't even notice him come to the door. Crackedskulls wait till dark or when no one's around or they go undercover. I would think somebody could spot him a mile away! I was the only one who saw him, and I almost had a heart attack! He left before my mom came. It was like he *knew* she was coming. He went down the hall and disappeared. My mom missed him by a few seconds, and she didn't see him either. He killed a three-inch cockroach near my head with his dagger, and I thought I was a goner—see—here's the hole right here. He didn't want to kill me, and he called me sweetie, eww!" she said as she pointed to the hole on the top of her nightstand.

Quickstrike examined the hole then looked at Neiko with terror in his scorpion eyes. "I'd recognize this hole anywhere! It's the dagger of Ramses alright! It *was* Ramses! What did you say to him? He actually *called* you that, Iforgotyourname?"

"Yeah, yuck! Well, I called him: a loser, Crackedskull, junky, and I told him I was sick and tired of Raven's stupid fiasco. My name's Admiral Neiko Kidd—just call me Neiko. Man, I hate to see that surprise he has in store for me!"

"Me too. It's not death because you would be dead by now. He doesn't go around calling every girl he meets names like that!"

"Yeah, well, do you know who Ramses really is?"

"The first-born son of Osiris and that other stuff, right?"

"No, you don't know the truth?"

"No."

"He's the Dark Pharaoh," Neiko replied cautiously, and there was a clap of thunder outside.

They both jumped.

- CHAPTER 20 -

THE RAIN AND WIND got up as a thunderstorm moved in. Neiko caught her breath, and Quickstrike asked, "He's the Dark Pharaoh? I mean, how do you know? What else do you know about him?"

"Well, I know that because that's what I imagined him to be. All I know is that he's immortal, and he's more powerful than an ordinary Pharaoh. I made this up only a few weeks ago, and I hadn't said anything to my cousin about it yet."

"Does he know that you know?"

"I'm not sure—I hope not, but I could be wrong. He may not be the Dark Pharaoh."

"Well, nobody knows that the Dark Pharaoh really exists, and most say he is just a legend. Some don't believe at all. Some say that in ancient times they saw him. They only documented his appearance as a shadowy form with red, glowing eyes. He was mostly spotted at night; no one knows his identity. There were many people who wanted to find out what he looked like and who he was, but they found nothing. If he saw anybody, he would kill them, and the deaths were mysterious. So after that, anyone who went on this 'wild goose chase' was laughed at. The person who knows the most about him is Genghis Khan. He doesn't know the identity either, but he has the most understanding. I've always wanted to ask him, but I was always told not to mention it."

"Hmm, red, glowing eyes kind of gives it away, doesn't it? I mean, that's the kind of eyes Ramses has, right?"

"You know what else? No one has ever seen the face of Ramses. Not Lydia, Osiris, Menes, or anybody. What's more is that he eats alone, and if he sits with them, he just sits there."

"You know, that really makes it obvious. I mean, Osiris would know what his own son looked like, if he was really his son. I mean, people aren't born with armor on. He really must be on a roll if he won't even show Lydia, and he loves her; not eating at family meals and only eating by himself just really puts the icing on the cake."

Quickstrike rubbed his head with his claw. "Hmm, this all makes sense now; the clues are everywhere. The reason why no one has thought anything about it is because no one thinks about the Dark Pharaoh at all. And you know what else? Lydia asked him what he knew about the Dark Pharaoh, and he got so mad he slapped her face, and told her to shut up."

"That really proves it! He's really touchy about that subject to get that mad, especially at Lydia of all people. Why was she with him? Was she having dinner at Skull Fort or something?"

"Well, she was probably forced to have dinner with him, so she tried to find something to talk about. None of us has ever been to Skull Fort, including Lydia, because we were always able to find her in time, and we don't know where the fort is," Quickstrike replied.

"Well, you've been there tons of times according to me, but I was wrong about that."

"Yeah, I believe you're right, and I'm wondering why he came here in normal size and why I'm small. I guess it has to do with his power."

"Yeah, I guess so," Neiko said and sighed.

"When you were playing with us, did you have Qari, Tiawuk, and all?"

"Yeah, sure did, and you're in Saudi right now. My dresser is the Pinnacle, and you can probably go from there. Khali was this little fort, tree house, and these two barns, the floor was Pitfall Plain, and we're on the Great Plateau right now," Neiko replied as she pointed to everything and constructed it the way it was in her imaginary Saudi. "Qari is my yard and where you were this afternoon, and Tiawuk is at my grandparent's house, Occorom is in my cousin's house, and Iduas is my cousin's yard including the woods."

"Wow! Where's the Tatowee Road, Tiawuk Trail, and the Highlands? I was in your Qari, and I saw this tower of blocks, and under this tree was a temple of rocks with these weird sticklike house things."

"Oh, I don't have those in Qari, and the tower of blocks is Skull Fort, and that other place is the abandoned village," Neiko replied.

"Norak was never abandoned, and you are missing a lot in your Qari; it seems that your version and the real thing are different."

"Do y'all still live in Saudi?" Neiko asked.

"Nope, we moved out into Qari a long time ago; we didn't live there long, did we always live in Saudi in your version?"

"Yeah."

"It really is different. Tell me all you know about us, and let's get everything straight, shall we?" Quickstrike said.

"Well, most of y'all are from a island named Etowah that is part of Saudi, and one day this black demon-like thing came and destroyed it, killing your families, and the rest of what was left were dispersed everywhere. The same thing happened to Darkclaw,

Glacier, and Rip Rat, but they lived in Eht Dnalsi that is also an island but is a part of Iduas. The Pharaohs destroyed Sandstorm's people, and Lydia was with him after her long history with Monster Gas. Y'all all started to come together and found each other like Cheetor trying to find his adopted mom Lydia." Neiko went on to tell him about some of the battles they had, and everything she had told Dr. Macintosh.

"Well, all of the background stuff is right, but most of the battles with Ramses you mentioned didn't happen. What do you know about the ordinary Pharaohs?"

"They're all descendants of Rumi, who was the First Pharaoh, and once was one big family, but they were killed off and all that remained were Menes, Re, Tut, and Osiris, and the phony son, Ramses. I wonder how Osiris actually believed he was his son, and he swore up and down he witnessed his birth—but the truth was, the whole thing was made up by Ramses, but I didn't ever think too much about that."

"Well, all of that stuff on the Pharaohs is correct. Hmm, as for the question, I'm now wondering that myself. I also wonder why he is pretending to be something he's not; unless, he has this big sinister plot."

"Well, I'm wondering why he says he's the first born and not the youngest or whatever," Neiko mused.

"Hmm, good one, but I know the answer to that one. The first born of the ruling Pharaoh becomes the supreme of the entire Pharaoh family after the father's death, regardless of age, unless he is unfit. In which case the second born will challenge his authority. However, if the father has more than two, and they want the crown, then they fight each other in a fight to death, and the winner will overthrow the ruling brother by exiling him and taking his place. Xerxes, the son of Rumi, set up all of these rules, but I don't think there was ever a situation like this because of these harsh punishments. That's all I know of their codes on that stuff. I don't know what they do if the ruler has no son, or he becomes unfit or sick, but doesn't die. Osiris is not dead, and he is capable of fighting, and I don't consider him unfit. Why is Ramses the ruler?"

"I wished I knew, but I think after he brainwashed him and whatever else he did, he started taking control by handling things smoothly. So then Osiris gave him more and more power till finally he just handed everything over and decided to become a follower. Ramses probably made this speech about his so-called father and this honor and junk to put them in line so they wouldn't object, and the whole time he was lying his helmet off. That's what I think happened. Oh, how old is each Pharaoh, and how old does Ramses say he is?"

"Osiris is four million, Menes is two million, Tut is one and a half million, and Re is one million, and Ramses says he's three million."

"Hmm, directly between Osiris and Menes and just old enough to create an alibi, and so Menes and the rest have no doubt about it. Was he there before they were all born, and were there any more Pharaohs then? What happened to the rest?"

"Yeah, he was there when Menes was born, and he witnessed the rest of their births. Omar, Sandstorm's father, was born fifty years after Ramses' so-called birth year. They didn't hear much out of them especially after the fall of Geezah, the Pharaoh City. Ramses was the one that led the war that wiped out their long-time enemies, the Saracens, and I believe that was his crowning moment. But the cost of Pharaoh and Skull Bearer casualties was extremely high. For the first time in Pharaoh history there was mutiny brewing, but then there was a plague that wiped them all out except for the 'Final Five'—or should we say four. The plague was so awful the word spread through every land by the morning of Osiris, and a total of two million Pharaohs died from some unknown plague. The total casualties from the war and plague were eight million Pharaoh dead. The war cost about four million Skull Bearers, but the total annihilation of fourteen million Saracens. The only survivor of the Saracens is, of course, Sandstorm."

Neiko whistled. "Whoa! That's a lot of deaths, did they name that the Season of Blood? Hmm, the timing of that plague was too perfect, and I think Ramses sent that plague on them to do away with them nicely, and he even didn't have to get his hands dirty. He probably faked his mourning and put on airs to keep it like he didn't do it and cover it up. Are you sure all two million were involved in the plot to overthrow Ramses?"

"Hmm, I believe you're right! Well, I can't answer that because I don't know if all of them were guilty; if so, then they were killed. But if not, I suppose he just did it that way to insure no more attempts, or he didn't find out who was responsible, but it would probably take that many to get rid of him."

Neiko shook her head. "I wonder how he found out. Well, we've pretty much covered everything by sleuthing our way through his scheming to cover up his true identity, and a lot of it is so obvious when you think about it. When did Geezah fall? Did the Pharaohs keep records on births, deaths, and stuff like that?"

"Well, Geezah fell during the reign of Thutmose XVIII the Mighty, the father of Anubis the Terrible. They were attacked by the Marauders, a group of giant stick people who wanted to end the iron reign of Pharaoh rule. They killed many, including Thutmose, and laid Geezah to ruins. The survivors fled and took Anubis with them, and they hid from the rioting Qarians. A wizard cast a spell on all of Qari to make them forget where Geezah was so that it would never rise again, and it has stayed that way. The Pharaohs had scribes that kept extensive records, but they were kept at Geezah. They would be out of date and the last recorded birth would be Anubis; Thutmose's death would not be recorded

"How did the Pharaohs get back on their feet and start their road to recovery?"

"Well, Anubis is the one responsible for that. When he grew up, he took his father's place, and his mother told him everything that happened, so he wanted to avenge the defeat and his father's death.

When he took power, the Pharaohs were a profitless rabble, but he made them into what they were by whipping them into shape by using terrible threats if anyone opposed him. He felt that death was a release, so he used torture that was so bad they pleaded for death, but it was not granted. After being tortured, they would be put with the others in hard training. They became greater than ever before, and he built Skull Fort as the new place they would thrive. Cheetor killed him in his search for Lydia, so then his son Saber the Strong took over, and he was Osiris' father. Skull Fort was the place they thrived till Ramses came to power, and we know he could care less about Geezah and anything of the Pharaohs' that doesn't apply to him." Cheetor was the fierce giant cheetah in the Attack Pack whom Lydia raised from a cub.

"Wow! Anubis was terrible! Why did Cheetor kill him, and was Thutmose capable of holding off the Marauders?"

"Cheetor killed him because he thought he was the one that took Lydia; Anubis wanted her to be his. Ajax said no, so he threatened him saying he'd kill him and take her himself. That's what he found when he came home; he thought he did it so he killed him, but found out that he wasn't the one, so he went on his search. Well, Thutmose was capable of destroying them, but he made a costly mistake. The Marauders had the perfect plan of a fake surrender. It was a surprise move, and they were more than a match for the Pharaoh forces, so they struck with a lightning speed attack, and there you have it."

"What a history lesson! Where did you learn all of the stuff that didn't apply to Attack Pack members? Is that all you know, and oh yeah, why didn't Lydia—along with you guys—know that Ramses was around before Osiris?"

"We had many talks with Genghis Khan, and we soaked up all the history, legends and knowledge that he had to share. Sandstorm also wondered about how his great enemies fell to almost nothing, and you helped me figure it all out. Every mishap after the death of

Anubis was all of Ramses's doings. Lydia doesn't believe that is the same Ramses, and vice versa, and we go on her word because she knew him before anyone else did."

"How in the world can she think that? I mean, he's kinda hard to forget, unless that is what the scum on his armor was about. But when he got rid of it, she should've recognized him. Unless, he did something to her mind and just fooled around saying it's a different one when he knows good and well it's her. He knows she's eight-million-years old and not two hundred! I believe that's why y'all don't know about it, and Cheetor believes the guy he wants to claw is dead! Man, he is a good liar!"

"Well, that makes good sense. Well, I don't think Ramses will be so happy to know what we found out by putting our heads together. I'm not so sure we should say anything about what we have discovered."

"You're right, but at least tell the Attack Pack—that is—if we can find a way to get you back to Qari," Neiko said rubbing her chin.

"Amanda, what are you doing?" her mom called.

"Just playing with my toys," Neiko answered.

"Well, go to bed! It's one in the morning! And who are you talking to? You sound like you are carrying on a long conversation with someone!" she said.

"I was talking to myself! Good night!" Neiko called back. "Well, let's go to bed, shall we? All that thinking made me tired," Neiko said as she stretched and yawned. Neiko put on her pajamas and crawled into bed. Quickstrike crawled over Neiko's head on her pillow, rested his head on his claws, and covered himself with his tail. Neiko turned off the lamp, and they both went to sleep.

- CHAPTER 21 -

A TERRIBLE RACKET AWAKENED NEIKO. T-bird was squawking and fluttering, and the cover on her cage was moving. She also noticed Quickstrike was missing. Neiko got up and uncovered the cage, and Quickstrike was stalking T-bird and ready to kill. "Hey, don't kill my bird!"

"I need something to eat, and it looks really tasty," Quickstrike complained.

"No, we're not going to eat the bird—I'll get you something." Neiko said putting her fists on her hips.

"Is it your pet cockatiel? What's its name?"

"Yeah, it's a cockatiel, and it's my pet; her name's T-bird."

Quickstrike looked at her startled. "You mean like the great T-bird, the wise cockatiel? But why doesn't she talk like we do?"

Neiko scratched her head. "What?! Well, she doesn't talk because she's a bird, duh! Does this wise bird talk? And where does she live?"

"She lives in Saudi with Tweety the Brilliant in Pitfall Plain. They don't live in cages or in the same place. Both of them are giants, and they are extremely wise."

Neiko bit her lip. "Is this Tweety the Brilliant a yellow and white parakeet by any chance? Is there a blue parakeet that lives in Occorom, and a blue and purple fighting fish named Ramses?"

"Why, yes! The blue parakeet is Babe the Magnificent, and Ramses the Betta is a jolly old fish and friendly. How'd you know?"

"Well, Tweety was the name of my parakeet that died about six months ago, and my cousin has a parakeet named Babe and a betta named Ramses.

This is really cool that our pets are just like your pals."

"Yeah, and about that stuff we talked about last night—I have more things I wish to discuss."

"Me too. Especially the part about Lydia forgetting and some of his habits around the fort."

"Yeah, a lot of the things surrounding Lydia don't add up, and he had plenty of chances to mess with her mind. I wonder if Dark Pharaoh magic has any type of mind control. I know that her 'forgetting' is too perfect especially since they saw each other while she lived with her foster father. Pharaohs have the ability to impose a trance so that someone will do their bidding if they refuse, but no type of memory erase, wild spells, or spell to change the memory."

"Oh, I think I get it. I think he may have erased her memory of those years he held her and all that so he wouldn't be exposed. Ajax believed him because Lydia backed up his story because she had no account of who he was, but there's one piece missing. He had to pull it off before he went before Ajax because she would have spotted him."

"Oh, I see. He had to do it like when she was asleep; later he came and made a request for her hand. Of course, he had no idea that was the one he was to avoid, and Lydia simply said it was not the man, so they fell in love and the betrothing part, and here comes

Sandstorm showing that Ramses is evil and a Pharaoh. He probably did the same thing to Osiris by changing his memory and erasing the real memories of what happened. The Osiris incident must've happened before he found Lydia and destroyed the Saracens, but Sandstorm got a very good look at him. So he exposed him as being the son of Osiris who is the murderer of his people and family. And, of course, he carried her off the day before Sandstorm and Lydia's wedding and on the honeymoon."

"Well, when Phoenix returned, how did she remember him, unless Ramses thought he was dead and didn't bother to erase that."

"Probably so, and I think he did something to Phoenix to make him think he was someone else and not the same Ramses. So the rest of us think that the other guy is still looking, and Cheetor thinks he'll never find the guy that ruined his life."

"I wonder how Ramses met Osiris, and how he might have brainwashed his wife," Neiko mused.

Quickstrike shrugged. "That we'll never know, but he probably pulled that off on his wife when Osiris brought him home. And, of course Menes and the rest have no idea or suspicion because he was there when each were born."

"I wonder what would happen if Menes ever found out the truth. I bet Osiris would be devastated."

"Yeah, and if Menes found out, oh boy. Menes has a very violent temper, and he would try to kill Ramses, but he would have no idea who he was dealing with. He would probably say that Ramses is an infidel that learned a few magic tricks and say that he is a peasant who wants to be a Pharaoh. He wouldn't believe Ramses is the *Dark Pharaoh* and say it's a cheap joke to save his chrome hide. Tut used to be the one that picked fights with Ramses, and Menes was the loyal brother, but now Menes is right with Tut, and Re is just tagging along. Osiris is totally clueless about their quarrels, and Menes would really be mad to know that Ramses stole his birthright to be the First Pharaoh."

"Did Osiris always wear a mask, and what happened to his wife?"

"No, he was terribly scarred in a battle against Omar, and his wife died when Re was a year old, of leukemia. Osiris' face was slashed ten times with the scimitar of Omar in his younger days even before he reached his hundreds. Osiris was mean in his heyday, and he just wanted to murder Omar. That battle was an attempt to slay him. But instead of killing Osiris, he simply cut his face to remind him of his defeat, so that no woman could possibly love him That was worse than death."

Neiko grimaced. "How awful, but he deserved it. Why did he want to kill him, and was Omar married yet?"

"He just wanted to kill him for the fun of it and he hated him, and no, Omar was not married. Osiris made the mask he wears this day, and he didn't let what happened stop him; it just made him meaner. When Omar married Persephone, he wanted to kill them both, but when Osiris did find a wife, he became not so evil."

"Wow, how did they meet and how could she love him because Pharaohs have a problem with getting women to love them?"

"They met when she heard of him and she sought him out. She found a picture of him somewhere— I forgot where, and it was one without his scars. Osiris was very handsome before he received his scars. When they met, Osiris was wearing the mask, and he showed her his scarred face. She took pity on him and became his wife. She helped him put the hatred away and deal with the pain, and he didn't hurt anyone else till she died. The hate returned with the help of Ramses, of course."

"That was a really good wife, and what was her name?" Neiko asked.

"Leah, and Osiris was a wreck when she died; he still mourns her."

Neiko whistled. "Oh yeah, you said Anubis is the grandfather of Osiris. How was Saber born if he was after Lydia?"

"Oh, I forgot to mention that. Well, he had a wife named Libra that gave birth to Saber, and she died of cancer when Saber was two. Anubis wanted a new wife and someone to take care of Saber. He stumbled on Lydia, but of course Cheetor did away with him, and you know that story."

"How did Saber survive without his father?" "I suppose someone adopted him, raised him, and put him on the throne, and I think it was his uncle, Amenmehet IV."

"Well, that's that, but back to old Chromy. You know, I wonder if he ever takes a bath, and if he does, does he take it in his armor?" Neiko asked as she rested her cheek on her hand.

Quickstrike giggled. "Well, he used to not take but one once a month, like Menes, Tut, and Re. Now, he takes one twice a day, while Osiris takes only one a day. Those three need to stay clean if they want a wife. Osiris gets on to them about it constantly saying they stink to high heaven, and they will attract vultures. When Ramses used to be scummy and smelly, I think that it was a disguise. He felt he had to be like his 'brothers' for his plan to work. His 'strange' behavior is actually his old habits, and I don't think he liked being dirty and smelly even though he said it is the life of a Pharaoh. Osiris scolded all four of them saying that they are a disgrace, and Pharaoh is not a dirty, smelly ogre that brings in the scavengers, and they do realize they smell like carrion and that it smells like a dead brachiosaurus is in the fort. Ramses probably has his own private bath so that he won't be seen by anyone because he takes off his armor both times, and I believe no one knows where it is, so then no one will spy on him or play pranks. Like if Tut wanted to steal his helmet and hide it, then his endeavors to hide his face would be shot."

Neiko shrugged. "Well, that's a wrap. We know everything about Ramses except what he looks like, how old he is, and where he came from. Now I understand more about Qari, the Pharaohs, and all that other stuff. It all fits together."

"Well, not all of it may be so, but that is our best explanation for some of his actions; they are probably fairly close. Some of them are extremely obvious as you pointed out, but as for some of the ones we we're unsure of, we have a good insight on."

"Well, I'm ready for breakfast, I'm starved! I'll bring some to you because I don't want my mom to see you because she'll freak out."

"Alright, but why would your mom go nuts if she saw me?"

"Well, she thinks you are just a lifeless toy, and the two animals that she hates most are snakes and scorpions, and you're both. She'd freak out."

"Yeah, please hurry and bring something good."

"Okey dokey. Be back in a few minutes." Neiko got up and walked to the kitchen.

- CHAPTER 22 -

NEIKO SHOVED THE REMAINING bit of honey bun into her mouth and carried another into her room, but on her way she ran into her mom. "What are you doing with that?" she asked.

"I'm so hungry I thought I might have seconds, and I've got a drawing to finish," Neiko replied.

"Alright," she said. Neiko walked into her room and closed the door. "Well, I got you a honey bun, and I hope you like it," Neiko said as she unwrapped it and laid it down on top of the wrapper. Quickstrike scurried over and looked at it doubtfully.

"I want bugs or something," complained Quickstrike.

"I'm sorry, but that's all I have. I can't really find bugs here because there are no woods. Will you at least try it?"

Quickstrike grabbed a claw full and shoved it into his mouth. "Mmm, not bad. Your food is kind of strange, but it tastes good. Just wait till you try ours."

"What do you mean? I'm not going to Qari. What type of food are you talking about anyway?"

"Oh, I didn't mean you were coming; I was just saying maybe I'll make a dish or something. Well, like barbecued velociraptor, marinated beetles, wild cherry muffins, and Lydia's famous slug casserole, fried snails, and my favorite, parched rollie pollies. We have much more selection, but we would be here all day if I have to name them all."

Neiko grimaced. "Yuck! The only thing that sounds good is wild cherry muffins. Do you ever eat deer?"

"Oh yeah, we do a lot. Is that something you like?"

"Yeah, barbecued deer is my favorite, and I like it hot and spicy." Neiko said as she dreamed of a steaming bowl of the stuff.

"You eat hot stuff? I'm not particularly fond of hot and spicy food, but you can try some of our food, and you wouldn't die if you eat it. Maybe you can try something like snake, frog legs, alligator, or crawfish."

"Mmm, I've always wanted to try snake and that other stuff, but do you eat fish?"

"Oh yes, we eat every kind—catfish, bream, bass, and even pirhana."

"What does pirhana taste like?"

"I'll surprise you, you'll know when you try some, believe me. It's good. I like it with a side dish of worm pasta with katydid dices."

"Eww! What's for dessert?"

"Cricket cobbler, chocolate covered fire ants, or any type of fruit cobbler or pie."

"Sick! I'll just stick with just plain chocolate. Can you put almonds or nuts in chocolate?"

"Yes, I prefer plain chocolate too because fire ants give me gas," Quickstrike said groaning.

"Oh, did they give you a stomachache?" Neiko said laughing.

"Yes, you bet! I also wondered why Buzzclaw and Torca kicked me out of the tent."

Neiko laughed so hard her side started hurting. "That bad, huh?"

"Yes, hee, hee, they said I was making too much noise because they were trying to sleep, and need I say more? Glacier, Darkclaw, and Rip Rat said I could stay with them because I can't possibly bother them, and I believe you know why."

"Yeah, well—" Neiko started saying, but her mom called.

"Amanda, I'm going to the bank and to the post office; I'll be back in about forty-five minutes!"

"Alright, mom!" Neiko called back. "You want to play video games?"

"What? What are those?"

"Oh, uh, they're games you play on the TV, do you want to watch?"

"Yeah, can I get on your shoulder?"

"Sure, I'll pick you up, and you can hop on." Neiko laid her hand on the bed, Quickstrike crawled onto her hand, and Neiko carefully placed him on her shoulder. "Hang on, sitting down may be rough." Neiko sat on the floor, but Quickstrike held on with no trouble. "Very good! You had no problem hanging on?"

"Nope, I have eight legs and two claws to hang on with. Give me a real challenge," said Quickstrike. "And all I needed was my legs."

"Which one do you want to see?" Neiko asked as she laid them out.

"Hmm, I don't know. They all look interesting. How 'bout that one with the guy that looks like Ramses on it?"

"Oh, you mean Killer Instinct? Fulgore does look like Ramses, kind of. You know, I never thought about it till you mentioned it, but I don't think he acts anything like him."

"Yeah, he probably doesn't, and Ramses has lied so much that he wouldn't know what the truth was if it came and bit him in the nose," said Quickstrike in a scathing manner.

Neiko laughed and put the game in and grabbed the controller.

"Is that so?" asked an angry, cold voice.

Neiko was so startled she threw the controller in the air, and Quickstrike landed on the bed because he was so startled that he jumped. Neiko looked, and Ramses stood leaning on the inside of her door with his feet crossed and his arms folded over his chest; he was glaring at Quickstrike.

Neiko stood up and gathered her composure. "Well, speak o' the devil," she said moodily.

Quickstrike hissed at him. "I heard about you coming and harassing my friend; what do you want here, Pharaoh?" he asked angrily.

"That's none of your business, bug brain," he snapped coldly.

"You know, you lied to her when you asked what this place is when you knew exactly where you were, liar and cheat!" Quickstrike yelled fiercely.

"Watch your mouth and hold your tongue, or I'll remove it for you. I did not lie," Ramses retorted.

Neiko folded her arms and stared at him sternly. "Yeah, where did you hear the word 'Hawote' then, hmm?"

"That voice that I heard summon me told me to come to Hawote, and it was the voice of Raven. So this is the place you call home? Then I cast a spell to come to this 'Hawote', and I find it exists. I have noticed you know who I am."

"Yeah, what's your point? Well, it's seems you found out everything you wanted to know, so I guess you will be returning to Qari then. Besides, there's nothing here you could possibly want except to pick a fight with Raven and Bloodhawk, but they'll cream your butt. Well, this is it then, huh?" Neiko said, shrugging.

"Yes, I will return to Qari, but I won't leave empty handed; I wish to take a souvenir with me," Ramses said mischievously.

"Well, if you're looking for the Eye of Mohica, I don't know where it is. You can find it yourself," Neiko snapped sarcastically.

"I am not interested in that worthless talisman. Maybe I should've said I won't leave alone," he replied in a soft tone.

"Oh, you want to take Raven and Bloodhawk with you? Go ahead be my guest; we've been waiting a long time to be rid of those two. You're welcome to it," Neiko replied ushering toward the northwest.

"I have no use for those two overgrown idiots! Oh, they are no match for me, and *I'll* cream them."

"You sound just like Arnold Schwarzeneggar," Neiko muttered. "Well, there's nothing else I can think of, so what *do* you want?" Neiko asked aggravated, but Quickstrike stared at Ramses nervously.

Ramses said nothing, and his eyes shimmered with a terrible red light, and they had a sinister look in them. Then he took a step toward Neiko.

Cold fear gripped her stomach, and her mind started racing. "Oh no! I'm not going anywhere with you! I'm staying right here in Hawote where I belong! You won't get me without a fight! If you want me, come and get me, but you have to take me down first!"

Ramses laughed evilly. "You want to fight against me? Why don't you just come quietly—for old time's sake. What are you trying to prove? If you insist on this stupid last stand, so be it. I haven't had one this brave for some time, and I'll enjoy this even though this will not take long. Enjoy your freedom and the last look at your land because it will be the last time you see it! Where is your weapon, dear?"

Neiko jumped on the bed and grabbed her stick from the corner; it had a club-like end on it, and she held it on the slender end. "Right here, Monster Gas! I'm not trying to prove anything! Neiko Kidd surrenders to no one, and when I get done, you're gonna wish you never wanted to take Admiral Kidd!" Neiko said as she spun her stick.

Ramses laughed even harder. "Oh, you'll eat those words once I have you. You'll wish you hadn't resisted me. When we return, Hawote will be destroyed! You are going to fight me with a *stick*? It doesn't matter to me what weapon you use because I will win. I don't need a weapon. I am going to take you down with my bare hands. So prepare to be captured!"

Neiko bared her teeth and hissed. "Ooooh, come and give me your best shot, Chrome Scum!" she said as she beckoned him with her hand and then replaced it on the grip of her stick.

Ramses angrily stuck with lightning speed as he tried to grab her ankle. Neiko jumped and just barely dodged his sweeping hand and landed at the head of the bed. Seeing an opportunity to attack, Neiko swung the stick over her head and sent the head of it crashing down on the end of his middle finger with every ounce of her strength, and the pain rushed through his glove into all of his hand.

"Owww! I'll get you for this, Neiko!" he growled as he rubbed his injured finger to ease the pain. It lingered, causing him to get angrier.

"Ha! Ha!" Neiko said jeeringly. "How do you like fighting Indians now, hmm? I guess it's not like it's cracked up to be, huh?" she punned, laughing. "Oh, by the way, you need to get your eyes checked, Ramsneeze. It doesn't profit much in trying to catch air!"

Quivering with rage, Ramses shouted, "Oh, you'll see, I'll get the last laugh; you won't think your loss and your captivity are a bit funny! Consider that miss a gift, and I will not grant you any more!"

Seeing an opportunity, Quickstrike shouted, "Attack Pack!" as he ran and jumped on his face blocking his view. Ramses growled fiercely, and he tried to get him off.

"I forgot my manners. I forgot to welcome you to Hawote, and this is how we greet uninvited, evil guests—Quickstrike, watch out!" Heeding the warning, Quickstrike jumped off, and landed on the bed beside Neiko. "Eat stick!" she yelled and hit Ramses right in the face with the stick, but the end snapped off because of the force of the blow and the hardness of his helmet; the hit didn't faze him. Neiko looked at it surprised because she had used it against titanium Crackedskull armor, and it didn't break. Seeing his opportunity, Ramses hit Neiko in the back of the legs with his arm in a sweep, sending her falling on her back onto the bed, and the fall caused her head to spin. Ramses stood over her, but Neiko still had her stick and she attempted to hit him in the top of the head. Knowing her move, he stopped her in midswing by seizing her wrists, and with his free hand, ripped it from her grasp and threw it on the floor. Quickstrike scurried over to help his fallen friend. He jumped onto Ramses' face again, but this time he grabbed Quickstrike and threw him against the wall. Quickstrike groaned and lay still.

"Quickstrike!" Neiko yelled as she tried to crawl to him, but Ramses grabbed her ankle and yanked her to him. He turned her over and seized her by her wrists; Neiko tried to free herself by struggling, but Neiko had no idea of his strength, and he laughed at her puny attempts to free herself. "Quickstrike, say something, help! Somebody help me!" Neiko saw some of her neighbors in the yard. "Help!" she screamed at the top of her lungs, but they didn't hear her.

"Be quiet. No one can hear you, and there is no one to rescue you. Let's go."

"No! Please! I won't call you names again; please let me go!" Neiko begged.

"No, it's not about name-calling! I decided this long ago, the day I saw you. Don't fight me, or I'll tie you up. I suggest you relax."

"Let go of me, Chrome Breath, or I'll—"

"Shut up! You'll what? You are at my mercy. I am not releasing you, so don't ask again." Neiko started to sob, and then she saw her mom's red car pull up. Ramses showed a great deal of annoyance, and he let go of Neiko. "Well, you get your wish this time because I let you win, and since I don't want to be seen by anyone here. Next time you won't be so lucky, and your mommy won't be around to save you, so be warned. I'll be back, and you'll be mine!" He laughed wickedly and all of him disappeared but his eyes. "I've been watching you, and I'll keep watching!" he said then his eyes disappeared, but she could still hear his terrible laugh. Neiko sighed with the utmost relief as her mom came in. Neiko rushed in and hugged her. "Mom, I love you," she said squeezing her eyes shut to keep the tears from coming.

"I love you too, honey," she replied. Neiko then ran to her room to check on Quickstrike.

- CHAPTER 23 -

NEIKO RAN INTO HER BEDROOM with her heart thumping. She dove over her bed and looked in the small aisle on the opposite side of her bed. Quickstrike was still lying there unconscious. Neiko gingerly picked him up and set him on the bed. She carefully placed his limp tail beside him. "Quickstrike, can you hear me? Oh, please don't be dead, Quickstrike," she said as she gently poked him.

Quickstrike groaned. "Ohh, Mom, it's Saturday, and I'm not ready to get up yet," he said doggedly, but his senses returned. "Am I dead? Neiko, what are you doing in heaven? Did he kill you too?" he asked as he rubbed his head.

"Of course not. You're alive, silly," she said, giggling.

"Ohh, I'm hurting so bad that I want to be dead. I can't believe I lived through that! He threw me really hard, and he was pretty mad. Wait a minute, how come he didn't take you?"

"Boy, that was a close call because my mom drove up when he was about to leave with me. I'm glad he didn't go ahead and carry me off anyway. He said he'll be back," Neiko said, rubbing the sweat off her forehead with the back of her hand.

"Yeah, but did he say when?"

"No, he just said he would be coming back, and my mom won't be around to save me the next time. He said he'll be watching."

"Hmm, well, that in itself is a threat, and he will live up to it because he doesn't bluff. He won't leave till he has you, and is that all he said?" asked Quickstrike.

"No, he said something about he has been watching me."

"Yikes! Did you have any idea about that?"

"No, but there was three occasions when I had these terrible chills, and I felt that someone was watching me. Could that have been him?" asked Neiko.

"Yeah, maybe."

"Oh, I just realized something. He didn't say anything about us knowing about him being the 'you-know-what' or anything else we talked about, so I guess he doesn't know that we know."

"Phew! That's a relief, but we need to not talk about it because he could find out about us knowing; he won't be so generous in letting me live or letting you stay free long," said Quickstrike with a sigh of relief.

"You're right, and if we have to say anything about it, then we'll say DP or you-know-what, and he could be listening right now. Oh yeah, when those strange feelings came, they got worse when I said 'Ramses' or anything about him," she said urgently.

"Well, that explains it then; he was watching you at those times that you knew of, and there might have been times that he was there, but you didn't sense him," Quickstrike said affirmatively.

"We need to be ready for him when he makes his next attack because I need to win to stay here."

"Well, if you defeat him, he'll come back again and again. He doesn't give up till he gets what he's after," he warned, waving his claw.

"Well, I'll feel better if I have a plan of defense, and I need a battle plan. Does he have any weaknesses you know of like chinks in his armor or whatever?" Neiko asked.

"Well, he doesn't have any chinks in his armor or any known weaknesses," Quickstrike replied shrugging.

"Darn! Well, what about his eyes? That's the only part of him without armor on." Neiko picked up her broken stick. "What is his armor made of anyway? I mean, Crackedskull armor is the hardest there is, and I've hit plenty of them in armor, and it didn't break. This was my favorite stick! I mean, look at it!" Neiko groaned. "I'll lose a lot of good sticks fighting him!"

Quickstrike laughed. "Oh, it's okay, Neiko. Wait! His eyes are his weakness! I've spit venom in his eyes many times to blind him, but now it doesn't even faze him! My venom is supposed to paralyze and cause permanent blindness, but of course you know he ain't at all blind! I know it's because he's the Da—I mean the you-know-what."

"Hmm, that gives me an idea. If your venom won't work, then I know what will, and he will be blind for a while. He will be dancing because this will sting so bad! What happens when he gets really mad? I've noticed pain makes him angry," Neiko said as she rubbed her hands together smiling.

"Well, tell me. When he gets extremely angry, he loses all sense of thought and the only thing he focuses on is trying to kill—or in your case—capture the person responsible for the pain."

"That's kind of a weakness, but it's a dangerous one. However, I have just the thing for that, that is, if I can get past him to make an escape."

"Tell me! Please? I need to know," said Quickstrike, jumping with anticipation.

"Well, okay. I'll make this solution of all types of hot stuff like pepper powders, hot sauce, and pepper juice. This will sting on impact, and as he gets madder, it gets hotter!"

"Oooh, I like the sound of that! What's the other part you were speaking of?"

"Oh, that's if I can get out of my room without him catching me because the fighting space is small. Okay, if I can get down the hall, then I can throw this can of marbles on the floor, so he'll trip for a while. He will get madder, and he will still be blind, and, that will buy us time. I'll run in the woods across the big road even though that's Crackedskull country. I'll stay there till it's almost time for my mom to come back, so I'll need to take a bow and arrow, a tomahawk, a walking stick, my backpack, and canteen."

"Hmm, good plan. When Ramses comes in the woods, how will you get past him? I mean, how will you dodge him that whole time and how will you know if he won't just wait for you to come out and set a trap for you?"

"Good point. We won't have to worry about running into him in the woods because they're pretty big; I went into them a few years ago. Like you pointed out, coming out is a problem. I got it! I'll walk toward the northwest and then come back south past my house in the woods. I will exit then, and walk to my house from the back, see if he's waiting, or if my mom's home. If I see neither, then I will wait in a concealed spot and wait for my mom to come home. I will just tell her I hid in the woods because some lunatic tried to break in the house but lead on that it wasn't Ramses, and that he wasn't here trying to kidnap me. That's it so far."

"Well, one more thing—actually two. You need something for self defense against Ramses. The weapon you will use cannot be breakable when it hits his armor, but I don't know what it's made of. The weapon should be metal at least. Also,when do you suspect he may try to attack? Like, is your mom going to be gone for a long period of time?"

"Hmm, I know! My aluminum baseball bat! Oh yeah, that oughta give him a headache to think about or ring up his helmet! Well, I'm not sure about when or if my mom will be gone for a really long time." But then the thought hit her. "Oh crap! I almost forgot! My mom, dad, and sister are leaving for that business trip Friday. They will be gone for a whole day, and come back at about ten or eleven that night! He'll probably attack sometime that day! Oh man, he definitely won't pass up that opportunity! We'll have to go on with the plan even though we haven't worked all the kinks out. I have exactly five days to plan and get everything I need. Well, at least I suspect him, and we'll be ready!"

"What will you use to throw that solution in his eyes? I mean, you would have to throw it at a distance and be accurate, and if you try to blind him at point-blank range, then you're as good as captured. Oh yeah, one more thing, once he's blinded, he will try to locate you with his hearing, and he is very good at that. He can hear extremely well. There was once I blinded him trying to protect Lydia, but he chased her like he wasn't blind. Phoenix swooped down and saved her, but then Ramses ran into a tree and he fired arrows at him by listening to the beat of his wings. He barely missed."

Neiko eyes widened. "Gosh! I hope I can do something about that! I'm glad you warned me! The marbles will help in the escape, I hope, but what about in my room? I know just the thing that'll do well in throwing the stuff. Water guns! I'll find a pistol, a Super Soaker 200, and a tiny one for you, but I have to go and buy them along with some of the ingredients for the Pharaoh Spray. I have plenty of allowance money, so I can buy some of this stuff. Mom said we're going to the grocery store and to Wal-Mart tomorrow, so I'll go in the kitchen and see what we have."

Quickstrike giggled. "Pharaoh Spray?"

"Yeah, like the catchy name?" Neiko put on a commercial act. "Have you had a Pharaoh in your house, and you can't get rid of him? Then try Pharaoh Spray. It gets rid of those pesky Pharaohs for good, and all you do is spray it in the eyes, and he'll run away forever, and it's only $1.50 a gallon. Call and order your Pharaoh Spray today because it's the only one in its class, and our secret recipe works like no other."

Quickstrike laughed. "Oh, that was hilarious! I bet you would have to keep reapplying for a D-Pharaoh! Go and see what we have to get, and I'll think of some more ideas for the room."

Neiko returned about ten minutes later. "Well, we have black pepper, red cayenne powder pepper, chili powder, pickled jalopeño juice, red sauce, and a few banana peppers, cayennes, and jalapeños. All I need now is Tabasco Sauce and pickled pepperoncini pepper juice."

"Yeowch! I'd hate to be Ramses about now. Oh, I thought of the bed being a barricade, and I also thought about clearing an aisle just big enough for yourself, then you have an escape route. Once he's blinded, I'll make noise to distract him, and you can grab me on the way out."

"Good one. I also thought that I'd leave my backpack and other stuff in the living room in the coat closet, and I'll hide the marbles behind the pillow on the couch on the big day. I'll put my compass, binoculars, my logbooks, matches, a lighter, a flashlight, a pen, a pencil, food, this letter too and this printout stuff on Francesco, and my machete in my backpack. I'll have to take this walking stick, and I'll have to visit the armory and take a tomahawk and a bow with a quiver of arrows; oh yeah, and this dagger I ripped off a Crackedskull. Then I'll fill my canteen full of water, that'll do it."

"Why are you taking your logbooks and the papers on Whatshisname? When are you gonna pack your backpack?"

Neiko grabbed her backpack and slung it on the bed. "I'm taking my logbooks and these papers because I don't want any Crackedskull to get their dirty hands on them. These papers are important because they are dirt on that phony Indian chieftain that's a Crackedskull, and if Raven finds them and this letter, then I'm screwed for good because Francesco will stay Grand High Mohican, and me just an Indian—powerless to do anything. Raven will find out what I know then he'll definitely take me out by kidnapping," Neiko replied as she packed her backpack. "Well, all I need now is a lighter, matches, and food for the backpack, and I can get that when I go get gas for my car at the store. I can visit the armory later tonight because they stay open all the time, and I'll make something up like I'm going for a walk. I'll hide them in the laundry room behind all those boxes of junk. While I'm out there, I'll get the bat. That's that, except for the canteen, but I'll get that Friday. Did I miss anything?"

"Nope, that's it except for the Pharaoh Spray and the guns, but that's tomorrow's project. When you leave, can I come with you?"

"Yeah, sure, I guess I'll make the Pharaoh Spray on Thursday, but I'm leaving for the store now. You'll have to go in my purse because of people; I'll switch to this big purse so you'll have room." Neiko put her wallet and Quickstrike into the purse and walked into the living room. "Mom, I'm going to the store to get gas."

"Okay, honey, be careful, and here's ten dollars," she said. Neiko thanked her and walked to her car.

- CHAPTER 24 -

NEIKO ARRIVED AT THE store in ten minutes. She pumped in five dollars in gas and went in to get the supplies. Neiko got several bags of chips, beef jerky, three Paydays, five Slim Jims, salted peanuts, sunflower seeds, and two packs of Reese's pieces. Neiko found the matches and a lighter at the register. Neiko paid for everything, and walked to her car, but two boys cornered her.

"Hey, baby!"

"Look, pal, you and skanky friend need to get lost, okay?" Neiko snapped coldly.

"Where are you going?" asked the other.

"None of your durn business! Go away, loser!" Neiko snapped and tried to open her car door, but the boy slammed the door and spun her around, and then Neiko felt her silent visitor come; this time he was angry. She could feel it, and fear went into her eyes. "Uh, I wouldn't do that if I were you," she said as he looked as if he was going to kiss her. Neiko unzipped her purse, but his friend took it away. He opened it and Quickstrike hissed at him, his tail poked out ready to bite. He dropped it and screamed like a girl.

Quickstrike crawled out facing them. "Alright, punk, show's over," Quickstrike said menacingly.

"A talking scorpion with a cobra tail! Run!" the boy shouted as he grabbed his friend, and Neiko felt the invisible watcher leave and pursue them.

"Thanks, Quickstrike, I owe you one," Neiko said graciously.

"No problem. Let's get home. I would hate to be those two if Ramses found out."

"Uh, get into the car, I got something to say," Neiko said as she picked him up and put him on the seat. Neiko shut the door and started driving. "I have bad news, Ramses *did* see it."

"How do you know?" asked Quickstrike puzzled.

"I felt him—I don't know how, and he was real mad; I could feel his anger. When they ran off, he went after them because I felt him leave, but he was invisible," Neiko replied with her eyes wide open.

"Oh, gosh! They are in for it! They're as good as dead. I wonder why he got so angry about it?"

Neiko shrugged. "Beats me! Maybe because he doesn't want his souvenir to have cooties."

Neiko got home and slipped the food into her room and put it into her backpack. Neiko replaced it into her closet. "Well, now for weapon pick up."

Neiko arrived at the armory at seven thirty. Neiko kept Quickstrike in her large purse, and she walked inside. "Hey, Bear Claw, how's it going?"

Bear Claw looked up. "Evening, Admiral! So nice to see you; I've missed you. Everything's fine here, but how are you?" Bear Claw was the armory keeper for the Tribes' warriors and a member of the Cheikomaguan Brave tribe. He was a sensible man, but a bit of a neat freak.

"Oh, just fine. I was wondering if I could borrow a tomahawk and a bow with a full quiver of arrows. I'll gladly pay you four quartz for the trouble since the GHM is so stuck up on keeping me shut out," Neiko replied.

"Oh, I don't care about him; I'll loan them to you free of charge. You can keep these quartz. I have plenty of money. So, are you off to war?"

"Well, kind of. You see, my parents are going off, and I need some defense just in case of any Crackedskull trouble."

"Oh, I see. Do you want me to contact Xartna and send some sentries?" "Nah, I'll just stay in the house. I'll be fine," Neiko said reassuringly.

"Well, alright. I'll get these for you, and you'll be off." Bear Claw came out with the tomahawk, bow, and arrows. "Alright, just do the paperwork, and take off. Come back to visit, okay?"

Neiko signed the paper. "Yeah, sure. You take care, and I hope to be an Admiral again soon," Neiko said as she did the secret handshake and left.

Quickstrike poked his head out after Neiko unzipped the purse after she left the armory. "That was easy enough. Is that guy your friend?"

"Yeah, sentries did sound good, but I wouldn't want any Indian fighting against an enemy they can't beat. Ramses would probably kill them if they got in his way, and that's what they would do."

"Well, it seems you have a good rep with your friends because they help you against that retard's say so."

"Yeah, and once I get out of this mess with Ramses, then I'll get that beanpole for every rotten thing he has done to me and for all the tricks against the Tribes. That is, if I get out of this without getting into bigger trouble because death, destruction, and trouble follow Ramses wherever he goes."

"That's an understatement," Quickstrike said as he went down into the purse. Neiko put the weapons in a concealed area, and she got the baseball bat. Neiko fixed the passage under her bed and got everything else ready but the final touch. Neiko fell asleep that night.

- CHAPTER 25 -

NEIKO WOKE UP THE NEXT morning and got ready to go do the final touches. Quickstrike came along in the purse, and the first place they came to was Wal-Mart. As soon as they got finished with the needed stuff, Neiko and Quickstrike headed to the toy department. Neiko went to the aisle with the water guns, and then she unzipped the purse. Quickstrike poked his head out and looked at all the guns.

"Wow!" said Quickstrike.

"Hmm. Look here. There's a pistol and a tiny gun just for you, and it's only $3. Super Soaker 200 is $15. Do you like this small gun?"

"Yeah, it's perfect. Well, that's that. Now all we need is those two things for the Pharaoh Spray to make it."

Neiko zipped the purse then her mom came up. "Do you need all of those? Are you about to have a war? How much is all that?" she asked.

"Yeah, it's only $18 for the whole shebang, and it's fun in the pool, you know," she said casually.

"Alright, honey."

They arrived at the grocery store a few minutes later. Neiko ran and got the pepperoncini peppers and the Tabasco sauce, while her mom shopped. Neiko put them in the buggy. Her mom asked, "What are you doing with those? We have hot sauce at home."

"I've been wanting some of these peppers, and I want some real hot sauce, I'll pay for these, mom. Please?"

"Alright, but I'll pay for these," she said.

They returned home, and Neiko was sent to get the mail. Neiko got the mail out of the mailbox, and she found the local paper. She unfolded it to read the cover story. Neiko's hands went cold, and her stomach went numb when she read it. The pictures on the front were the two boys at the gas station.

DOUBLE MURDER CASE

Toby Jackson and Bobby Vaughn's bodies were found in the ditch on Rabbit Farm Road and the causes of death were different. Bobby died from a dagger wound to the heart. Police say it was a fourteen-inch blade, razor sharp and curved from the autopsy report. Toby was evidently tortured by cuts with the dagger and horrible burns all over his body, but the cause of death was the neck crushed by strangling. The bones were crushed to tiny pieces, and both boys had a frozen look of terror on their faces. Police say the murderer had to be abnormally strong in order to crush Toby's neck, and there were no traces of any evidence to convict the killer.

Neiko's mouth flew open as she read the article. "Toby, that's the one that looked as he was gonna kiss me; he was tortured and then killed. That's an awful way to die," Neiko said shaking her head. "Man, I didn't want them to die. I just wanted them to get lost, and I know who the killer is, but I can't turn him in because more people will die." Neiko ran in, gave her mom the mail, and ran down the hall with the paper to show Quickstrike.

"What's with you?" he asked seeing the look on Neiko's face.

"Read about the dirty work of Ramses," she said tossing the paper on the bed.

Quickstrike read the article, and when he finished, he replied, "Those are the guys from the station, and that one that was tortured was the one doing most of the stuff; he died slowly and painfully."

"They deserved a spanking at most, but not to die like an execution from the Comanche, and this is all my fault. Maybe if I gave myself up, then they would be alive today," Neiko said hopelessly.

"Now, don't go blaming yourself!" Quickstrike scolded. "Being held by Ramses with no hope at all is much worse than the way this boy died, and people will have died trying to free you. Ramses kills without a care, and people and beasts die all the time because of him, so don't even think about giving up."

"Has Lydia always had hope?" Neiko asked wiping away a tear.

"Yeah, she always had hope, even when one hundred thousand years came around she didn't give in to his demands, and she had never given up hope. See, if you surrender, then you won't have any hope. Lydia always had fame to back her up and searches sprang up, and she knew it. but I'm the only one that knows about you, besides Ramses. If you give in, I'll be stuck here with no hope, and nobody will save you because Ramses will make sure of it. No one will ever know you exist, and he'll be the only one you'll ever see. How can anyone save you if they don't know Neiko Kidd exists but Ramses, hmm?"

Neiko shuddered. "What does he want with me anyway? I mean, he's really going through a lot of trouble to make that scenario you just pointed out, and it'll be that way if I get caught."

Quickstrike shrugged. "I wish I could answer that. You'll find out when he takes you, I suppose. You're right, that's exactly how he wants it to be, and we must make sure that he never gets you."

"Well, when my parents go to bed, let's make the Pharaoh Spray. Tomorrow is the eve of the great battle, and my destiny is on the line here. If I win this, then it'll be hard for him to make another flawless attempt, and you know what will happen if I lose," Neiko said with dread.

"Yeah," Quickstrike said in the same way.

It was about twelve o'clock when Neiko could hear her parents snoring. Neiko tiptoed into the kitchen and found the bowl she laid out. She flipped on the light and found all of the ingredients to make the concoction. First she put in the Tabasco sauce, Texas Pete hot sauce, and all of the pickled pepper juices. Then she added the chili powder, black pepper, and red cayenne powder pepper to the mixture and stirred it well. The solution was thick, so she put vinegar in a large pan, dumped in the mixture, and stirred it. Neiko bent over and sniffed, and the pepper smell was so strong it took her breath. "Whoa Mama! Ramses will be hurtin' for sure! Get a whiff o' that, Quickie!"

Quickstrike obeyed and coughed. "Oh my, this will definitely do the trick."

"Well, now let's put it in the guns because it's hot and ready to go, and it'll get hotter as it sits."

"I'm glad I ain't Ramses!" Quickstrike said playfully.

Neiko giggled as she put on her rubber gloves. "I'll do the small guns first, then I'll get the humdinger," Neiko undid the plug on Quickstrike's gun and dipped it in the Pharaoh Spray then she did her pistol. Neiko looked in the cabinet and found the funnel. She poured the rest of it in the bottle of the Super Soaker, and she closed the hole. She put the dishes in the sink, washed them, and sneaked back into her room. "Now I'll hide these so that no one will Pharaoh Spray themselves and be in for pain, especially my nosey sister," said Neiko playfully. Neiko hid them under the bed, and they went to sleep that night.

- Chapter 26 -

Thursday passed quickly, and the dreaded day came. Neiko's parents backed down the driveway and waved as they left Neiko behind. As soon as they were out of sight, Neiko sprang into action. She put the water in the canteen, got the weapons, and put them in the coat closet with her backpack. She found the marbles and hid them behind the pillow on the couch. She then sprinted to her room and fixed the barricade; she laid the Super Soaker on the bed and laid Quickstrike's gun on the top of the entertainment center. Neiko put on her buckskin tank top and shorts, her socks, and her black Nikes, and she put the pistol in the belt of her shorts. She put on her bead headband with a falcon in the center, and she painted her face for war in red and blue stripes on her cheeks and chin; the battle was ready. Neiko waited for several hours behind the barricade, but there was no sign of Ramses. "Man, is he coming or not?" Neiko asked irritated.

Quickstrike drummed his legs on the entertainment center nervously. "Hmm, he's coming alright, but he wishes to attack when he gets ready, and probably when we least expect it."

"Let's play some music," Neiko said. After she had listened to all of her tapes, she played video games, but every creak or noise made her jump. Neiko threw her controller down in disgust. "I can't play games!"

Neiko looked at her clock, it was five. "He ain't coming, it's five—"

"I'm here!" Ramses said as he walked into the door to her room. "Have you been waiting for me?" he asked sweetly.

Neiko did a backflip into her barricade and grabbed the Super Soaker.

"Yeah, and I have a present for you, and it's called Pharaoh Spray! Have some!" Neiko said as she fired at him, but she sprayed him in the neck, in a drenching blast. "Oh, darn I missed."

Ramses wiped some off and smelled of it then looked at Neiko angrily. "So, you wish to blind me? Is this your game? Ha! I presume you wish to continue this idiotic combat. Well, let's get started!" he said then he did a side slap and sent the gun flying out of her hands landing at the head of the bed. Neiko dove for it and was able to retrieve it, and she spun dodging his sweeping hands. Neiko got a good aim at his eyes and before she could fire, he snatched it out of her grasp and threw it behind him. Neiko jumped on the floor and she headed for the door, but he tripped her with his foot. Neiko tried to crawl out, but he grabbed her ankle, yanked her to him, and held her upside down by her ankle. "Now, do you yield?"

Neiko dangled with her hands over her head, her other leg bent, and swinging dazedly. "Yeah, you win. I bet Qari is beautiful this time of year, and I bet Skull Fort is a wonderful place to visit," Neiko said quickly with a twinge of fear.

"That's better. Now let's be off." Neiko's pistol slipped on the floor, and she tried to reach it, but Ramses kicked it out of reach. "Uh, uh."

"Hey, Chrome Daddy! Put her down!" Quickstrike yelled from the floor.

Ramses dropped Neiko and turned to Quickstrike. "You! I will crush you like the bug you are for insulting me!" he said as he went after him trying to stomp him with his armored foot. Seeing his narrow escapes, Neiko grabbed the bat and hit him on top of the head. Ramses cried out as his helmet began to ring. He grabbed it to stop it from ringing then he turned and faced her. "Argh! You won't get away with this!" Neiko swung it several times, but he blocked it with his arms and with the backs of his hands because of the hand guards, and it clanged on every hit.

"Dang! C'mon, eat chrome!" Neiko growled as she tried another hit. Ramses fended off the attack with his arm, and then he backhanded it, and it fell behind the entertainment center. Seeing Neiko disarmed, his sightless red eyes glowed with triumph, but Neiko was not giving up. She ran and jumped on him trying to claw at his eyes and trying to clobber him with her hands, but he threw her on the bed and pinned her by her arms, yet Neiko still fought by trying to kick him and fighting to get up.

He laughed cruelly. "I've got you now! It seems the fight hasn't gone out of you yet!"

"Yo! Chrome Sneeze! Look over here, I stole your mom's platinum panties!" Quickstrike yelled from the top of the entertainment center with his gun aimed. Furious, Ramses looked as he jerked Neiko up to her feet. Quickstrike hit the trigger, and he scored a direct hit in both of his eyes. Ramses screamed in pain, and he released Neiko immediately because the pain was so intense. Neiko moved quickly, but he had her cornered. Neiko ran behind the barricade and started to go under the bed. In his fury he had forgotten where the bed was, and he tripped on it. Neiko popped out the other side, ran, and grabbed Quickstrike. Hearing her footsteps, he charged after her. Neiko barely got past him and into the hall, and then he ran into the wall with a crunch of sheetrock breaking. Neiko sprinted down the hall and threw the marbles all down the hall. Neiko ran to the closet to get the weapons and backpack, and she heard him trip on the marbles and hit his head on the wall making a huge hole. Growling with rage, Ramses tried to get up, but then he tripped on his cape and on a few marbles and fell on his back. Neiko saw it and started laughing as she peeked around the corner of the hallway.

"You just wait till I get my hands on you, Indian! You will not get away so easily!" Ramses snarled indignantly.

"Watch me if you can!" Neiko shouted back as she headed for the door.

Hearing his quarry escaping, he growled in a seething tantrum, but then an idea popped into his head. He smiled in spite of himself, and he began to chant the spell, then he clapped his hands. Once he finished, he touched his eyes to get rid of the sting of the Pharaoh Spray, and walked after them. Neiko ran out the door, but once she ran out, there was a light, and then a strange land spread before her. Neiko saw enormous trees with strange leaves, and a dusty road reached as far as she could see. Neiko spun around, and she saw her front door hanging in space closing. Neiko ran to it trying to go back in. "Please don't close, please!" Neiko prayed, but the door closed and disappeared. Neiko then heard a thunder of hooves coming. She spun around and saw an army rushing to her. She dove into the ditch, and they rode past her; when they were gone, she came out and looked for Quickstrike. She called his name, but he was nowhere in sight.

Suddenly, she heard a clap of thunder, and Ramses came out of the sky and landed catlike on the ground one hundred yards away! Neiko ran into the woods, and she searched for a place to hide. Moments passed slowly as she ran, taking cover behind trees and bushes as she tried to find a better hiding place. Finally, there was a tree that had a split in it big enough for her to fit, and it was fairly concealed. The land was getting dark, and she went into the tree and sat down, pulled her knees to her chest, and wrapped her arms around them. She heard him running in the woods looking for her, and then he came into sight. Neiko closed her eyes and pressed her lips on her knees. *Please don't find me*, she prayed over and over in her mind.

Ramses stopped and looked around, but Neiko was nowhere in sight. "Well! I know you are here somewhere! You may have escaped this time, but you can't hide forever, and I will find you wherever you go! Welcome to Qari, my dear! Ha, ha, ha!" He left the woods laughing wickedly, and Neiko huddled up tighter in the tree, shuddered, and closed her eyes.

"Neiko!" Quickstrike's voice called. "Where are you?" Thinking Ramses was trying to trap her, she stayed silent, closed her eyes, and started praying.

- CHAPTER 27 -

"NEIKO, WHERE ARE YOU?" Quickstrike called. Neiko got up and she looked outside the tree, but she didn't see anyone.

"Quickstrike!" she called back as she stepped out of her hiding place. Suddenly, the bushes started to move in front of her, and then a cobra shot out of them. Neiko screamed and grabbed her tomahawk out of her backpack.

Quickstrike came into view, and he was three feet from the end of his claw to his rear, and his tail was four feet long. "There you are, I've been calling your name like crazy, and I was afraid it was too late."

"I'm sorry, Ramses was here a minute ago scoping the place for me, and he just left. Then, I heard you, but I thought it was him trying to trick me. I also barely got clear of that army, and I thought I was a road pizza," Neiko said, relieved.

"Phew! That was too close. That was a Skull Bearer patrol,

and I bet ol' Chrome Butt is on his way to alert them about you, so I guess we should start moving."

"Wait. I need to find out where we are and plan on which way we should go. There is a road just outside these woods, and do you know where the Attack Pack is?"

"I don't know where the guys are, but I think we are in Woodchuck Woods, and I think this is Tatowee Road. If you head north, you will head toward Saudi, but south will take us further into Qari."

They walked to the road; Neiko got out her compass and lay it in her hand. "Hmm, north is directly in front of us, and that's the way that patrol was heading, so if we do an about face we'll head south. I'm sure we'll dodge the patrol, but I'm keeping my fingers crossed we don't meet Monster Gas. Are there any Skull Bearer camps or any place we can shack up for the night? It's getting late, and I'm tired, but I can't sleep in the woods because we'll be discovered."

"Well, Camp Steal is ten miles away from Bronto's Tavern, and that's the only place there is for miles. Bronto is quite brash, tough, and he is a hard bargainer. However, I can say he totally despises Pharaohs."

"A tavern? Oh well, that's the only hope I have right now. I'm glad he won't tell the Pharaohs about me. Does he have rooms to stay in? But the trouble is I don't have money. Will he accept quartz?"

"Hmm, that is a problem, and I'm not sure if he'll take it even though quartz is extremely rare, almost like diamonds. Like I said, Bronto can be hard. I must warn you; Skull Bearers go there all the time to get drunk especially when there is no Pharaoh around," Quickstrike said as he scratched his head.

Neiko scratched her head. "Quartz is rare, huh? It's really common in Hawote. Anyway, what's a few wasted Skull Bearers? They'll be pushovers, and my main concern is Bronto. What kind of guy is he? I mean, is a human or beast man?"

"He is a Brahma bull man, and he was once a general in an army years ago."

"Oooh, bad combo. Brahmas are known to be mean, and an army officer? I would hate to be a private under him—yikes," Neiko said, cringing. "Boy, I have my work cut out, but I would rather deal with him than Ramses any day."

"I agree, but those Skull Bearers could go and tell their friends about you, rumor will spread, and the Pharaohs will be alerted. It'll eventually get to Ramses."

"Good point. Well, let's move on."

Neiko and Quickstrike walked down the dusty road for several hours. The sun started rising and she could see the tavern; it was about two miles away. Neiko shielded her eyes as she walked to get a glimpse. "Man, I could use a rest about now. I'm so exhausted, and it's getting hot."

"Yeah, we're almost there, just a few more miles."

They walked and finally reached the porch and lounged in some of the large wooden chairs. They watched as people would come in all sorts of attire. Most were civilians, but suddenly two Skull Bearers came their way. They were dressed in black armor with a silver skull on the breastplate, and their helmets had outstretched batwings on the sides and a spike on the top. Both had a sword on their waist, a dagger, and they were carrying a mace apiece. Neiko and Quickstrike went inside when they saw them. The two Skull Bearers came in and ordered a bottle of whiskey for the two of them and started drinking it.

"Phew! That was close," Neiko breathed.

"Yeah, let's go speak with Bronto and see if he can help us out. Neiko, will you do the talking?"

"Yeah, sure" Neiko walked up to the barmaid. "Excuse me, can I speak to Bronto please?"

"One moment," she said.

"I'll go and take care of the stuff," Quickstrike volunteered.

Bronto walked up to Neiko and stared at her. "Yes?" he asked gruffly.

Neiko swallowed. "Um, I was wondering if you are willing to let me and my buddy have a room tonight."

"Yeah, but do you have any money?" he asked. Bronto was huge. He had two massive horns coming out of his head, enormous muscles, and he stood seven feet—every detail of a huge brown Brahma bull complete with a gold nose ring.

"I have four quartz," she said then laid them on the counter.

"Quartz? What do you think I am—a rock collector? I have no use for these! Where did you come from to think I would accept worthless rocks!" he thundered. "Go on your way now."

"If you must know, I'm from Hawote, and there, quartz are our money!"

"Where? Well, I will not accept them, so be off," he snapped and walked away.

Neiko cocked an eyebrow. "Quickstrike wasn't kidding when he said he was brash. Man," Neiko turned around and started to walk off, but she ran into something. Neiko looked up and the Skull Bearers stood right in front of her smiling.

"Aww, what's the matter? Can't get a room? Just come with us to Camp Steal, and we'll give you one for free," he said slyly.

"No thanks. I'll pass, besides I'm a survivor, and I can make it alright. Now if you'll excuse me," Neiko said as she tried to walk past them, but they blocked her path.

"You're not going anywhere, Pretty," said the other. "You're a new barmaid, and a strange looking one at that. We always take one with us and have a little fun," he said in his drunken stupor.

Neiko gagged at the heavy smell of whiskey and the grotesque invitation. "Hey, you need to lay off because you have no idea who you're dealing with. If I were you, I'd take a hike," Neiko said folding her arms.

They both laughed. "Feisty you are, and what will you do, huh?" he slurred.

"This," she said as she pulled her dagger out of her pants and stabbed him in the neck. The Skull Bearer gave a look of shock as he fell to the floor, dead. His friend looked at her with rage.

"You little—" he snapped and started swearing at her. He began charging with his sword drawn. Thinking fast, Neiko swiped the sword from the dead Skull Bearer, and she fended off the attack and stood ready. They got into a duel and neither made any progress. The Skull Bearer kicked her in the leg and she fell on the floor. He kicked the sword from her hand and sheathed his own. "Alright, when I get finished with you, I'll let the officers have their turn, and I hope you stay because I'll make you pay for this by making you my slave!" he growled, and he seized her. Suddenly, the Skull Bearer was lifted off the ground and Neiko heard a mighty crack, and he flew against the wall lifeless.

Bronto stood over her. "You okay, warrior?"

"Yeah, thanks. I owe you one. Well, I guess I should be going."

"Wait just a minute. I would like to repay you for showing those vermin what for and showing them that some people have some backbone around here. I'm sorry about before, and I'll gladly let you stay the night free of charge. Those two and their friends have been preying on our women, as you could see, and I knew one day they would stumble on the wrong one."

Neiko stood up. "Well, I really appreciate it, but why do you serve them if they cause you these kinds of problems?"

Bronto shrugged. "Well, no choice actually. The camp is only ten miles away. So what do you do?"

"Yeah. Well, I'll get my dagger, their daggers, and these swords are cool, so I'll swipe one." Neiko retrieved the weapons. "You can carry out the trash."

"Gladly," Bronto said as he lifted them and threw them outside. "I'll let their friends pick them up, and I'll warn them not to mess with our women. Well, do you need anything else?"

"Yeah, do you know where the Attack Pack is?"

Bronto scratched is chin. "Hmm, nope, I don't," he said as he shook his huge head.

Suddenly, the door flew open, and a company of Skull Bearers came in. One began to play his trumpet, and Menes, Tut, and Re walked in, and everyone began to murmur; Neiko hid under a counter on her hands and knees behind Bronto. Quickstrike scurried into the hiding place beside her. Upon seeing them, Bronto narrowed his eyes. "Take your worthless lot out of here, Pharaoh Scum!" he said as he shook his fists at Menes.

"Shut up, or I'll make steaks out of you!" Menes snapped. "I've come to announce that there an escaped outlaw among us who is inquired of by our brother Ramses. This person is a newcomer to Qari, and may be dangerous and must be delivered into our hands upon sight."

Everyone began to look at each other and murmur. Menes was a triceratops with orange skin with a blue stomach and beak. He had three horns, and his top two were covered in a red Pharaoh cloth. He wore armor over his chest and it had a red triangle over the right plate, and the armor covered his back. He wore green pants, no shoes, and he wore a purple and silver glove on his left hand, which had spikes on it. His right hand had a purple armband with a silver plate on the back of his hand; he was carrying his battle-axe.

Bronto stormed. "You come into my tavern asking me to do you favors? I bet this newcomer is only dangerous to Pharaohs, and they probably had a stomach full of your despicable brother! I suggest you get lost, horn head, and take your filth with you! I would never send a newcomer into the hands of scum like you or that metal-headed scrap pile you call your brother!"

Tut was fuming. "Oh, there are a few things you should consider, hamburger meat, before you go protect this outlaw. Read them, Re!" Tut was a mole that wore black pants and no shoes. His pants were torn at the knees like crude Capri's. He wore a camouflage tank top along with his Pharaoh war helmet. He wore red, fingerless gloves, and he carried his long, curved sword. His fur was grayish brown, and his fingernails and toenails were long and black.

Re unfolded the scroll. "Articles concerning the outlaw Admiral Neiko Kidd from Hawote: Neiko escaped seizure from Ramses in Hawote and is hiding somewhere in Qari. If you deliver Neiko to us, then Ramses will personally reward you with the Amir diamond and anything else you desire. However, if you are caught hiding the outlaw, then the conspirator and his family will be killed, and Neiko will be taken. If we find Neiko in your custody and you resist us and hinder us from taking Neiko, then you will be arrested along with Neiko; Ramses will personally execute the conspirator and family by a slow, painful death." When Re finished, he rolled the scroll. Re was a wolf with brown fur and long curved fingernails and toenails. He wore spiked plates on the tops of his thighs and wrists. He wore a breastplate that was brass-colored with a red triangle similar to that of Menes. He wore his Pharaoh war helmet and carried his mace. He had long, curved, sharp teeth that were yellowed.

"So you see, impudent dog, you're better off handing over the outlaw, and if you are hiding Neiko Kidd, give him to us," Menes trumpeted. Menes did not know Neiko was a girl.

"I've never heard of this Admiral Kidd and, there have been no newcomers here today, so I wouldn't be hiding him, so be off. Tell Ramses he can stuff his threats down his throat and wash it down with strychnine, and I hope this Admiral Kidd gets the better of him. Get out of my sight, worthless trash!"

"Well, before we leave, we must ask and see if any of you rodents be Neiko, and if you are, surrender!" Tut said folding his arms.

Bronto laughed. "I don't think he would be that stupid. I think you better leave before I have a Pharaoh killing!"

"Just testing the bravery of this Desert Storm Falcon, and I don't believe Neiko is as brave as we thought. As for you, we will deal with you later, farewell," Menes said then they all turned and left.

"Phew! That was close. Thanks again, Bronto," Neiko said shaking.

Bronto looked at her puzzled. "Wait. Did you say you were from Hawote?"

Neiko fiddled with her hair. "Yeah."

"What's your name, warrior?"

"Admiral Neiko Kidd. Put her there," Neiko said as she stretched her hand in a friendly manner.

"Oh my. You're the newcomer. Well, welcome to Qari. Are you traveling alone?"

"No, Quickstrike is with me, and that's partly why I need to find the Attack Pack. I can't hold out against the Pharaohs without their help. I need to find my way back home. I'm an outlaw, and I've only been here for twelve hours. I hope I didn't endanger you."

"No, no. Don't worry about it. They can threaten me all they wish, but I will not let them have their way; I despise them all because most Qarians do, and I've fought against them years ago."

"Yeah, Quickstrike told me."

"Oh—well—is Ramses responsible for you being here, and what does he want with you? That is no cheap reward he is offering because the Amir diamond is the largest diamond in the Five Lands."

Neiko whistled. "Well, he is the reason why I'm here, but I have no idea why he wants me, and that is some reward he's offering. I had no idea he wanted me so badly."

"Come on, go lie down. You look like you've been through a lot. Here, I'll carry you." Bronto lifted her up with his huge hands, took her to the bedroom, and gently laid her down on the bed. He left the candle on and he quietly closed the door. Neiko could hear his hooves clomping down the hall, but she was so overcome with exhaustion she fell asleep instantly.

- CHAPTER 28 -

"Prepare to move in!" Raven shouted at his warriors to move in the attack against Neiko. The Crackedskull warriors moved in, and Raven and Bloodhawk waited patiently for their chance to apprehend Neiko. Several minutes passed then they came out of the house, but there was no sign of Neiko.

"Well, where is she?" Bloodhawk snapped.

"She was not there, my Prince," he replied.

"What?!" he boomed.

"Bloodhawk, silence," Raven said with a scowl. "Is there any trace of her?"

"Well, there was no sign of her, but there was evidence of a battle, and I think someone else beat us to the job and kidnapped her."

"Kidnapped her! I'm gonna kill the person responsible for this!" Bloodhawk growled then clawed a tree.

"Tell me everything you saw," Raven commanded.

"Well, um, there were water guns filled with this pepper concoction lying on the floor. Her bed was set up like a barricade, and she had an aluminum baseball bat lying behind her entertainment center, and I found this," said the warrior as he handed the broken stick to Raven.

"I recognize this stick. How can this be? This stick has never broken, so whoever did this has extremely hard armor. Is this all?" Raven asked.

"There were marbles down the hall, and a few were crushed. There were holes in the wall where something hit it. There were wet spots in the floor. It is that solution, and it has only been there for about one to two hours. There is a possibility she may have escaped him, and I have to say this was way too clean to be the work of an Outsider; they do not wear armor. The only evidence of his presence is the battle and the holes in the wall," replied another.

"Hmm, it seems she knew this person was coming, and we just missed it by a few hours at most. Did you touch anything besides this stick?" Raven asked.

"No," they all said in unison.

"Good. When her parents return, they will notify the police, and we will learn more about this. I will get some of my winged warriors to circle the woods, and you take some more ground warriors and patrol the ground. Do not return until every inch of my territory has been searched. If there is no trace, I'll contact Francesco and tell him to report any activity on the matter in the Tribes. If she did escape, we'll find her. Is that understood? Oh yes, return this stick back where you found it. I'm glad you're wearing gloves, but check for any hairs. I want no traces of our presence, and once you've finished, begin the patrol," Raven said.

They saluted smartly. "Right away, Majesty."

A few hours passed, Bloodhawk was pacing the floors. "When are they coming back?"

"Patience. I know you're worried—so am I," Raven said. "Here they come now."

Karo and Condor came in and bowed, but Neiko was not there. "Ground troops found nothing, not even a broken branch," Karo, the Crackedskull general, replied. .

"We didn't find anything, either," Condor said. Condor was the second in command of the winged warriors beneath Deatheagle.

"Argh!" Raven snarled, and Bloodhawk shook his head. "Well, nice work. We must contact Francesco immediately!"

Francesco ran in about an hour later. "I came as soon as I could. Is something wrong?"

"You bet there is!" Bloodhawk snapped.

"Well, do you have Neiko?" he asked.

"No, that's the problem," Raven replied.

"What?! She escaped *again?*" Francesco asked, worried.

"No! Worse. Someone else took her," Bloodhawk said, putting his hands on his hips.

Francesco's mouth fell open. "How? Who? I can't—oh no. Was it an Outsider?"

"We don't know. If it is an Outsider, there will be evidence. But my trackers tell me that the person left no known evidence except he was wearing armor because of crushed marbles and holes in the wall. Oh yes, you know that stick Neiko fights with? Well, it finally broke, so this guy was not wearing our traditional titanium armor."

Francesco put his hand on his forehead and shook his head. "This is unbelievable. Outsiders don't wear armor, and not even steel armor could break that stick. Well, what shall we do?"

"First of all, we'll wait on the police report, and you will tell us everything you hear in the Tribes. Once we get all the information, we'll find out who's responsible, and Bloodhawk and I will tear him apart," Raven sneered and Bloodhawk smiled cruelly.

"Well, I'll get right on it. When I find out all there is to know, then I'll report," Francesco replied and left.

- CHAPTER 29 -

NEIKO'S PARENTS CAME HOME later that night and notified the police once they discovered their daughter was missing. Several of Neiko's friends were also there in their disguises to offer support and get any information on the occurrence. The police had just finished searching the house for evidence when the detective approached her parents.

"Well, we found no fingerprints other than your daughter's, and I have no idea why this pepper concoction was made. The holes in your wall had to be made by someone or something metal that weighed at least 500 to 600 pounds. We'll notify you if we find the trail. Good day, Mrs. Hawk," replied the detective before he got into his car and left.

"Oh, I can't believe someone kidnapped Neiko, and there was hardly any evidence!" Pike said shaking his head.

"You're telling me! From what I could tell, this had to be one tough cookie to be able to take her when she was ready and leave no trace. That's even too good for a Crackedskull," Nighthawk shrugged.

"Yeah, if it was a Crackedskull or an Outsider, then there would've been blood or something. Well, let's go tell Xartna and see what else we can find out," Pike suggested.

"Well, we should ask every Indian and see when they saw her last," Xartna offered. The three of them called every Indian.

"The person who saw her latest was Bear Claw when she picked up weapons? That's a little odd, and they didn't find either in the house. I mean, this doesn't make sense," Pike mused.

"If she was in trouble, why didn't she tell somebody? She knew this guy was coming for her, and she tried to handle it herself. But why?" Nighthawk thought.

"Hmm, there is more to this mystery than meets the eye. Maybe this person was a danger to anyone that got in his way," Xartna shrugged.

"Maybe she was protecting us."

"Yeah right! We coulda helped her! We can handle a Crackedskull or an Outsider! We ain't kindergarten warriors!" Pike snapped.

"This guy is not either a Crackedskull or an Outsider judging from evidence," Xartna said.

"Well, who is he then, huh? I can't just stand here and let this jerk get away with this. He could be doing God knows what to her, and she could be dead!" Pike stammered.

"Pike, don't say things like that! We need to keep a positive mind. Well, I'll schedule a meeting tonight and tell everyone about the bad news and all the info, and please, Pike, keep your hopes up," Xartna said shaking his finger at him.

"Everyone, please be seated," Xartna said to every Indian who attended the emergency meeting that had been called earlier that day. "I scheduled this meeting on such short notice because I have dreadful news. Neiko is missing." Great hubbub broke out, and people looked at each other horrified. "That is why the three of us called to see when she had been seen last."

"Who is responsible?" White Fang asked his brother Pike.

"We don't know, but we do know it was not a Crackedskull or a Georgian," Pike replied.

"It has to be Iraqi or Iranian terrorists! Then we're all dead meat!" cried Hawk, a Mohican.

"Everyone, stop jumping to conclusions!" Monganata scolded. "Besides, terrorists do not wear armor. This person's armor was so hard it broke Neiko's famed fighting stick," he said holding it up and the end that broke off.

"How can this be? Who on earth has armor that hard?" asked Hawk.

"There's more. She evidently used her aluminum baseball bat as a weapon, and she made some type of extremely strong pepper solution as a blinding agent, so this guy had to be totally covered in this armor. There were no fingerprints, hairs, or blood even though she did hit him several times because the bat was dented. The police also noted holes in the wall, and the detective said that a metal object weighing up to 600 pounds could crush marbles and put those kind of holes in the wall," Nighthawk replied.

"Marbles?" Hawk asked.

"Yeah, they were lying in the hall, and it looks as if she put them there to trip him after she blinded him, and it looks as she had a foolproof escape plan, so he must of got her on the way out," Pike shrugged.

"No way! That stuff she made would make that guy cry mommy for hours! There ain't no way he could go after her if she blinded him, so she had to miss. Or, that guy chased her out, and the Crackedskulls nabbed her. That guy's armor weighed that much? I can't even bench press that!" Hawk said.

"No that is the gross weight of the man and armor. The armor itself may weigh up to 250 pounds. So the man could weigh up to 350 pounds," Monganata mused.

"Whoa! That guy had to be huge! He had to be in his upper sixes to weigh that much and that's a lot of muscle. Boy, I couldn't imagine that much weight on my body, so that had to slow him down, and I don't think he could easily catch someone as nimble as Neiko," Eagle, Hawk's brother, said.

"This is what makes it really strange. The man chased her as if he was wearing *clothes*, so the armor didn't even faze him. It had to be carefully made in the joints to prevent any hindrances to his movement, and nobody is that strong or makes armor like that," Nighthawk replied.

"Gosh, when people wore that much armor on themselves, they couldn't even get on a horse, and if they fell then they couldn't get up. How can you tell she barely escaped to make it outside?" Eagle asked.

"Well, I don't think she would have holes in her wall, and I don't think she would have to go to the armory and get a tomahawk, bow, and arrows, and have a plan that elaborate—just call it a hunch. Oh, yeah, the tomahawk and the bow and arrows were nowhere in the house. It does look as she escaped, but knowing Neiko, she would've came back at least by morning so we know he got her or the Crackedskulls did. It seems we are going in circles. Let's all go home, and pray that Neiko will safely come home," Monchiska said sadly.

During the prayer Francesco slipped out to go report to Raven.

- CHAPTER 30 -

I'm here!" Francesco said as he ran into Raven's fortress.

"Well, did they find anything new?" asked Raven.

"Not really. The police found zilch, and the only thing different was that they deciphered that the man was wearing armor, and the gross weight was up to 600 pounds. This guy could probably play pro football. It also seems that this guy was quite an adversary, but it sort of seems she did escape."

"How so?"

"The pepper stuff was used to blind him, she used the bat, and the marbles were used to trip him after blinding. You know what else? She went to the armory and picked up a tomahawk, bow, and arrows, and they were not in the house anywhere," Francesco replied.

"What else did they say about this man?" asked Bloodhawk.

"Well, the armor may weigh up to 250 pounds, and he may weigh up to 350 or more. The armor did not hinder him at all, and it seemed to be carefully made. This was a hunch of Monchiska, and we all know his gut is no liar. He said this was like clothes to this guy, and it seems he is abnormally strong and possibly covered head to toe in armor."

"My, my, it seems we are going nowhere fast, and there is no one I know of that could possibly be that large, strong, or possess armor. It seems both the Indians and we are going in circles. I have to say that Neiko Kidd is presumed dead unless she is found or returns home," Raven said sadly.

Bloodhawk's eyes widened. "Father, no!"

"I'm sorry, but there is nothing more we can do. You may have to move on."

"I can't, and I won't. I will not rest till I find her or her body! If she is dead, I'll avenge her by tearing this man to shreds! He may be a large man, but he is not a giant, and that armor will not save him from my wrath! I will never love another," Bloodhawk stormed.

"As you wish, and do you feel that the land of Hawote is partly responsible? If she was with us, then she would be alive today. Do you agree? They partly blame us and suspect we possibly took her, but we will show them."

"Yeah, are you saying that we can release our wrath on the entire land of Hawote?" Bloodhawk asked wiping away his tears.

"Yes, let's make them all pay, and we won't stop with the Seven Tribes, but every Indian!"

"Yes, let's do it!"

Neiko woke up and heard a clap of thunder. She looked out the window, and she saw it raining heavily. "That's just great. Well, a little rain never hurt anybody, and it'll slow down Ramses at least." She got up and walked into the main room.

"Did you sleep well?" asked Bronto.

"Like a rock," she replied. "Well, thanks. I think I'll head out."

"Are you crazy? The monsoons are moving in, and it will rain for days! Besides, there are floods, tornadoes, and dangerous lightning. Only a fool would travel in this. I doubt the Dark Pharaoh would travel in this," Bronto said, and Neiko looked at him with a cocked eyebrow. "Oh, I didn't mean it literally, it's just a figure of speech. He doesn't even exist and just an old tale to make kids scared of the dark."

"Uh-huh, that's one heck of a tale to scare kids with. Are you trying to make your kids scared stiff?"

"Well, we usually say that thunder is him calling for his bride; lightning is him hunting for his next victim. If a child was disobedient or didn't eat their dinner, parents would say 'Eat up or the Dark Pharaoh will come,' 'You better obey or I'll tell the Dark Pharaoh on you,' 'Clean your room or he will tear your face off.' They would say to walk in a dark room with a candle because he may be in the closet or under the bed with his dagger drawn, and they will tell their kids not to wonder off, or he will carry you off and make you his slave. Some of the boys would scare the girls by hiding in the bushes and saying they're the Dark Pharaoh, and they are going to take you off and make you his queen. They usually used scary voices, jump out of the bushes, and scare the daylights out of them; I've done that in my younger days," Bronto said.

"Shame on you! My gosh! I think that would make grownups scared of the dark. Well, I'm glad he ain't real," Neiko fibbed. "I need to go see Quickstrike."

"Well, nice of you to join us," Quickstrike teased.

"Oh, well, I slept really well despite the nightmares I was having, and I bet you could guess who was chasing me and all that stuff," Neiko said. "Bronto was telling me of some of the things they say about the DP, and I don't think that's a good way to scare your kids. I thought the boogie man was bad, but they make the DP really bad, and I wonder what Ramses was like in those days when he lived up to his title and deity."

"He was probably really bad—worse than he is now. I'm kinda glad he is pretending to be an ordinary Pharaoh. I'm also glad those bygone days are long gone."

"For now," Neiko said. "Well, we need to plan our next move; I hope Bronto has a map. This rain will also give Ramses plenty of time to plan his next move, too." Neiko came back a few minutes later with a map. "Well, there's not much civilization on this road, and I have no idea where to begin."

"The best place to end is at Norak because it's the safest place in all of Qari. The Pharaohs have been trying to invade it for years, but no luck. You will be safe from Ramses for sure; that is, if he doesn't get you first."

"There's always a catch. You suppose we could send someone to find the Attack Pack for us?"

"Yeah, I'm sure we could."

Neiko scratched her head. "Norak is a heck of a long way. Which way do you think is best?"

"We only travel on the Low Road till we get to the Short Road which leads directly to Norak."

"The High Road leads to the mountains. Why can't we go that way?

Ramses may expect us to take the Low Road."

"You have a point, but that would take a lot longer, and the mountains are said to be haunted. There are old winding roads that are perilous, and there is a possibility we may get lost. As you can see, there are no roads drawn on this map, and it's pretty old."

"Aww, c'mon, why not a little adventure? You know, we may have to go that way if Ramses is waiting for us on the Low Road, well, at least we have plan B. I'm ready for a challenge; it's exciting to think I could explore some unknown terrain, and a little mountain climbing is all I need for a balanced diet of adventure. Besides, I doubt if

Ramses is crazy enough to follow me in the mountains because that armor would slow him down, and I can climb really well," Neiko said as she flexed her arms.

"You're right, that's a good back up plan. You seem to love adventure, and you know how to explore just about anything. I hope I can keep up with you on all of those steep hills."

"Yeah, I'll try to keep a slow pace, and I'm a little out of shape."

"You seem in good shape to me."

"Not like I used to be. Back then you could eat my dust on that road.

Well, let's get some grub, I'm starved." Neiko ordered roasted quail, and Quickstrike got parched beetles and they began eating.

"Well, did you find anything?" asked Ramses as Menes, Re, and Tut walked in.

"Nope, not a trace of him anywhere. Are you sure you lost him at Woodchuck Woods?" Tut replied.

"You morons! Neiko Kidd is a *female* warrior! No wonder you didn't find her. She was probably right under your noses, and you didn't even notice! Never mind. This time I will send copies of her picture to the soldiers in this camp. One thing is certain, she did not go far," he said, holding up a picture of her.

"Where did you get that? Can I see it?" Menes asked.

Ramses handed the picture to him, but didn't respond to his prior inquiry. The others stood behind Menes to get a look. Menes whistled, and he looked at the others slyly, and they had the same look.

"That's enough. Give it back. I'll keep the original if you don't mind. I'll give you copies," Ramses snapped coldly. "You will pass these out, and tell General Scythe to send patrols down the road. Oh yes, one more thing. I want a blockade put three miles inward on the Low Road from Tatowee Road, and step on it! I don't have all night, and I wish to mobilize right after the rain stops because I'm sure Neiko will as well. Hurry up!" he shouted as he threw a pile of the copies he made of Neiko's picture at them.

Menes picked them up as Ramses turned around, and when he did, Menes shot him an icy stare and mouthed his commands in a mocking manner. The three of them stamped out and followed their instructions. After they finished, they walked into Menes' tent.

"Menes do this—Re do that—I'm getting tired of him telling us what to do!" Menes growled. "Why can't he get off his lazy butt and do his own stuff? He is really getting on my nerves!"

"You said it!" Tut agreed. "He is really pushy this evening—more than usual."

"Yeah, he wouldn't even let us get a good look at that picture, and it was the original. He acted like it was the only real picture of her in the world, and we would mess it up," Re moaned.

"It *is* the only real picture of her, dodo!" Menes snapped. "You're right, I don't think he could stand us looking at her, and I really want to know why he is so anxious to get this girl. He didn't even want us to have a copy. Well, we have a copy!" Menes smiled slyly as he put the copy on the table, and the three of them sat down and studied her warrior picture. She was wearing war paint and her falcon headband, and she was holding a tomahawk and a bow and arrow. It was a picture of her entire body, and she was wearing a red tank top, black shorts, and her black Nikes. A dainty smile creased her face.

"Hubba, hubba," said Tut. "You know, she's pretty."

"I saw her first, nitwit!" Menes snapped.

"You mean Ramses saw her first," Re jabbed.

"Shut up! Don't remind me, moron. So what do you think? Do you think we make a cute couple?" Menes asked.

Tut giggled. "Yeah, but don't hog her. Can the three of us share?"

"Yeah, Menes, you ol' woman stealer," Re teased.

Menes waved his hand. "Oh stop," he said smiling. "Why not? Surely all Ramses wants is a slave, but I want a wife! I don't think he'll have a problem, do you think, Re?" he asked putting his feet on the table.

"Uh, guys, you gotta come see this," Tut said.

"What? Can't you see I'm daydreaming, Tut?" Menes growled.

Re ran to the door of the tent. From their tent they could see into Ramses' cottage. "What the heck is he doing?"

"Who?" Menes asked curtly as he stood up.

"Ramses, dufus," Re said. "Come over, see this, and bring the telescope."

Menes did just that. "Well, he's sitting there looking at something, but I can't tell what."

"Let me see," Tut said taking it. He saw Ramses looking at the object, but then he saw him run his fingers down it like he was stroking it. "He's probably looking at a picture of Lydia, no biggie."

"Hey, he doesn't have a picture of Lydia, fool," Menes hissed. "Give that to me!" He grabbed it and adjusted the sight. Menes gritted his teeth and snarled as he folded the telescope. "He was looking at this!" he snapped in clenched teeth as he held up the picture of Neiko. Re and Tut looked at each other puzzled. Menes ran back and unfolded the telescope. He watched him slip the picture in his belt and look out the window in a distant gaze with his eyes shining in an unusual glare. Menes was so angry he couldn't stand it. He placed the telescope on the table and slammed his fist on the table.

Re folded his arms. "I think he may have a slight problem."

"Shut up! Shut up!" Menes growled. "We let her escape, and he blames it on us, and he's had that the whole time! He always says it's our fault! Oooh, I'm gonna get him!"

"How bad is it? What is he going to do if he catches her?" Re asked.

"I don't know, but I intend to find out," Menes snapped. "I'll make her my wife despite what he has planned. He may like her a little bit, maybe, but I'll fix that."

"A little bit? Is that what you call it? I've never seen his eyes shine like that!" Re squealed.

"Stop jumping to conclusions, Re. It'll wear off. I'll bet you on that. He may be acting weird, but I think he was thinking about Lydia, and he didn't realize that was a picture of Neiko. He imagined it was her, that's what I think," Menes shrugged.

"You're right, but I want to keep an eye on him just in case," Re said casually.

"Don't worry. It's not like he's in love with her or nothing, and I'll get her, no problem," Menes said as he folded the picture and put it in his pocket. "You two better not tell him, alright?"

"No problem," they both said.

- CHAPTER 31 -

A FEW DAYS PASSED AND the monsoon continued to let the rains fall. As Menes, Re, and Tut walked in to have a word with Ramses, they saw him looking at the picture. Menes quivered with rage. "Oh, come on in," Ramses said, barely noticing them, and he put the picture in his belt.

Menes eyed him contemptuously. "We gave out all the copies, and the general said he will launch the patrols and prepare the blockade when the rain stops," he said curtly, trying to control his growing wrath.

"Very good—well—nice work," he said, half-paying attention.

"Will we attack Tenev when the rain stops? I mean, the patrols will let us know if they see anything," Tut said, trying to get his attention.

"Yes, of course. I haven't forgotten. We will attack as soon as the rain stops," he replied not looking at him.

Menes was seething. "Are you paying any attention, Bro, or have you been at the tavern getting snockered like most of the Skull Bearers? Or have you even noticed? It seems you left your brain in your other helmet."

Ramses looked up and his eyes flashed. "I don't think I like your tone. You better watch your mouth. I *have* noticed, and why not let them have a little fun? It's not often they can celebrate our progress."

Menes looked at him like he was crazy. "Are you ill? You usually hit the roof when you hear stuff like this, and it sounds like you have been smoking stinkweed or joining them at the tavern. It's a zoo out there!"

"Do I have to explain myself every time? They will be ready. Tonight is their last night, and I will deal with them tomorrow, and I don't believe the rain will be letting up anytime in the next few days."

Menes laughed. "Okay, *God*, if you say so, and since when have you been playing The Almighty anyway?"

Ramses stood up. "Back down and shut up. It was only an educated guess. Don't call me God. I am not as knowledgeable as he is, and you know it. If you don't have anything else to report, then leave. I don't even want to argue with you; I have my mind on other matters," he said and turned around.

"Oh yeah, like Neiko Kidd," Menes said, slipping up. "I've been wondering what you are going to do with her when you catch her."

Ramses spun around and narrowed his eyes to flaming slits. "What did you say?" he asked angrily as he drew his dagger.

"Just asking. You don't have to get in a tizzy. I'm just curious," he said, putting his hands up in an innocent way.

Tut and Re winced as they saw the horrible glow in Ramses' eyes.

"What I have planned for her is none of your business!" he snapped coldly. "Why are you so interested in my plans and her all of a sudden? You better not be getting any ideas in that pea-sized brain of yours! Remember what curiosity did to the cat," he said as rubbed the blade in a harsh, subtle warning.

"Uh, Menes, maybe we should go and let him cool off," Re said nervously as he put his hand on his shoulder, but Menes wrenched free.

Menes was fuming, and he shook his finger at Ramses. "I'm not finished yet! What are you hiding, Ramses? What's the matter? Afraid I'll tell the whole army about your little schoolboy crush? Oh, I wonder what Neiko would think about that, and I'm just *dying* to let the entire Five Lands hear about it!" he yelled at him.

"I am not *hiding* anything! There is no crush! If you spread lies about me then you *will be* dying, even if you are my brother! So I would take Re's advice and go while the going's good," he said, trying to control his urge to throw the dagger.

"Oh, yeah, coulda fooled me! All you seem to do is gawk at her picture, sit on your lazy butt, and think about her so much you don't even know what day it is!" Menes growled harshly while Tut's and Re's mouths fell open in shock as he slipped again.

Ramses' eyes glowed brighter and to a darker red in his growing wrath. "How do you know that I gaze at her picture?" he asked, seething and in clenched teeth even though it could not be seen. "Well, if you must know, she will be my personal slave, and I'm seeing what she might wear, satisfied?"

"Yeah, well I came to that conclusion when we walked in. You were staring at her like that was the real thing, and you treated us like we were made of glass!" Menes yelled, shaking his fist at him.

Ramses simmered down a little, sat down, and propped his feet on the desk. "I still don't like you prying into my business or letting your little imagination run away with you. And it seems to me you've been doing some daydreaming of your own; let me warn you. I saw her and claimed her first, so she's mine, do you understand?" Menes didn't answer. Ramses cupped his hand over the right side of his helmet. "Speak louder, I can't hear you." Menes' only response was when he slammed his fist on the desk and kicked the table and knocked it over. Maps, papers and food spilled on the floor. "Oh, clean that up on your way out."

"Why don't you get up off your lazy duff and clean it up? Unless you can't pull the weight of your armored tail," Menes snarled indignantly.

"Alright fine. I am not lazy; just wait, I'll fix you. I hope you haven't forgotten that I am the First Pharaoh, and it seems you don't remember I make the decisions around here. I give the orders, and I definitely hope, for your sake, the order I gave you about Neiko Kidd belonging to me is crystal-clear."

"You're just using that ancient protocol as a crutch because you are a wimp!" Menes shot back.

Suddenly his dagger hissed by him and dug itself in the wall, and as it passed, its edge cut Menes' arm. Menes grabbed his arm and looked at him angrily. As he bellowed at the sting, blood trickled down his arm, and splattered on the floor. Re whimpered and quickly cleaned up the mess, and Tut licked his dry lips.

"You better be glad Re is kind enough to pull your weight, and the next time you insult me or pry into my business, I will not be so forgiving. I will not injure you but kill you. If you *ever* try anything or lay a finger on Neiko, I will cut off your fingers one by one, then your hands, then your head—understood?"

"Yeah," Menes snapped, turned around, and stamped out; the others followed him. "Liar. He *is* hiding something—and slave my foot! I wouldn't be surprised if he was picturing her in a jeweled gown. Well, now I know what he's up to, yet I still don't know how bad it is, but it will not involve marriage at least."

"Oh, it looks really bad to me. He was actually going to kill you in there, and he is in one of those dangerous moods. I couldn't believe you kept pushing him. Not only are you on to him; he is on to you," Re whimpered.

"He *is* lying! I mean, you asked him a simple question, and he flew off the handle. Every time you mentioned her name or something we saw him do; he got paranoid. You really saved your hide by not telling him we were spying on him the other night," Tut whined.

"You have a point there, Tut. Did you notice he made plenty of threats concerning her and the bad ones at that. I always thought he talked to us all the time about what he planned with Lydia, and why is he being so secretive about Neiko? He really got dangerously angry the more we talked about her, but it delighted him to talk about Lydia, hmm," Menes mused as he rubbed his chin.

"Have you noticed he hasn't said a word about Lydia in days, and he's been in this dangerous mood ever since he got back from that place, whatever it's called?" Tut asked.

"Hawote," Re corrected.

"Whatever," Tut snapped.

"Yeah, I noticed that too, and I don't like it. It'll probably get worse once he gets her. I noticed he thinks about her more than Lydia, and he seems to be putting all his energy into trapping Neiko. If she's so dangerous, then why did he bring her here in the first place? What all does he have in store for her?" Menes asked.

"Good question and we won't know till she is brought to him," Re replied. "I wonder what would happen if he had a picture of Lydia. I wonder if he'll forget about Neiko?"

Menes finished wrapping his injured arm then snapped his fingers. "That's it! Re, you're a genius! If I can get someone to paint a picture of Lydia for him maybe he'll change his mind. Then I could get that original of Neiko. The portrait would have to be better than life, but who can paint that good? Definitely not a Skull Bearer and I can barely draw stick figures; he wouldn't look at my effort."

Re smiled sheepishly. "I can. I can paint well."

"Huh? I didn't know you could paint. Can you create a masterpiece quickly because I need that photograph ASAP?" Menes asked.

"Why, yes I can. But who will give it to him, and how would you get the photo that he keeps it with him all the time?" Re asked.

"You will take it to him, and when he starts staring at your work, then ask him for it. He will give it to you because it will not compare," Menes said smiling slyly. "Go start it now."

"Why do I have to—" Re whined.

"Because you are the good one, and he likes you better."

"Okay," he said as he grabbed some paper and started to paint. A few hours passed, and Re was still painting. Ramses addressed the Skull Bearers, and Menes listened closely.

". . . After we destroy Tenev, then all companies will patrol the Tatowee Road and assist in the blockade at the Low Road. When Neiko is spotted and captured, then you will bring her straight to me and me alone. Report any sightings to me as well. When we strike Tenev, leave nothing standing and no one alive. After we destroy Tenev and I have Neiko, then you can party as much as you wish till I need you again."

Menes quivered with rage as he heard the Skull Bearers cheer for him and his flawless plans. "This can't be happening to me. Now he won't even let us bring her in. They love him! Argh!" he snapped pulling at his Pharaoh's head cloth. "He's giving them what they want, and they give him what he wants, and it's not fair! Hurry up, Re!"

"No wonder he is the First Pharaoh," Tut grumbled. "

"Shut up, Tut!" Menes hissed.

"I'm finished," Re said as he held up his masterpiece, and they whistled. She was better than life, and her peach skin shone, her blonde hair glistened in the painted sunlight. Her white and gold suit was painted perfectly.

"Well, Re, you know what to do."

Re walked up to Ramses' cabin and knocked on the door nervously.

"Come in," came his harsh voice.

Re walked in and tried to swallow the knot in his throat. "Evening, Ramses," he said smiling shyly.

"What a surprise! What brings you here?"

"Uh, I have a present for you. I painted it."

He folded his hands on the desk still holding Neiko's picture and looked at him surprised. "Oh?"

Re presented it to him, and he noticed the picture in his hands. "It only took three hours," he said trying to break the silence.

Ramses barely glanced at it, and he laid it down on top of his maps. "It's very good. I didn't know you could paint—how nice. Maybe I'll get you to paint pictures for me since you do so well and in such short time, thank you," he said kindly, then he turned his chair around facing away from Re and started staring at Neiko's picture once more.

Re peeked over his shoulder. *Menes is not going to like this*, he thought.

"What? What do you mean he just *glanced* at it? It was a knockout!" Menes said high pitched in anger.

"He said maybe I could paint for him, so he did like it. I tried my best," Re said flatly.

"Yeah, paint pictures alright, but of Neiko Kidd or himself! This will be harder than I thought," Menes mused.

"No it isn't. I'll just paint one of Neiko and then you can have the photograph," Re suggested.

"No! It isn't about the photograph! I want him to forget about her completely!" Menes yelled shrilly.

"You don't have a prayer on that, Menes! You would have better luck trying to steal the photograph," Tut said flatly.

"Steal the photograph—good idea. I may just do that," Menes said as he rubbed his hands together, smiling wickedly.

"Are you out of your mind? That was just of figure of speech. Besides, how will you steal it? He keeps it with him in his belt or in his hand. Ohh, he'll be mad. Besides, what if you get the person? He seems more interested in that photo than Neiko herself," Tut shrugged.

"Oh, that's where you're wrong. That photo keeps her fresh in his mind, and I wonder why he wants the original so bad. Why couldn't he settle for a copy? Actually, I'd rather he not have one at all."

"Menes, you're raving mad. I think he'll know you did it," Re warned. "Oh yeah? What if I hide it really well? He'll expect it to be on me not in some secret place," Menes smiled even wider. "He can't kill me without proof, and he can't risk killing me on suspicion; the truth would come out if he tried to cover it up because he was searching for it right? He has too much at stake." He saw Ramses walk outside of his cabin and head for the chieftain's tent on the other side of the camp. Seeing his opportunity, Menes ran out.

"Crazy fool's gonna do it," Tut said shaking his head. Ten minutes passed and he came back smiling big. "Did you get it?"

"Yep, here it is," he said holding it up, and their mouths dropped open. "It was easy, and he'll never look here," Menes said pointing to his breastplate, but he took a minute to look at it. "You know, I like it better than this copy," he said as he put the corner of the copy on the candle flame, and he let it burn to ashes.

"Menes, look, there's something written on the back," Re said. "You may think that was easy, but you got lucky because he coulda took it with him, and the hard part is hiding it from him."

Menes flipped it over. "To Neiko, with all my love and friendship, Monchiska. Neiko, it is a pleasure for us to be friends and serve in the Tribes together. Keep this as a gift from me and my family."

He finished and looked puzzled. "So, this person is a friend, and I guess he took this picture of her. Ramses took it from her house, and I bet he never saw this because he was too busy staring at *her*. No wonder it's so important—" Suddenly, they heard Ramses cry out in rage as he found it was missing. Heeding the warning, he slipped it into his breastplate, and smirked. They could hear him throwing things in the floor in his frantic search. He came out and slammed the door so hard it broke, and Skull Bearers came out to see what was wrong. "No crush, huh?" Menes asked sarcastically.

"Who has it? Confess now, and I'll let you off, but you have ten seconds! No one will sleep until it is found! Whoever did this will know this prank was not funny because this camp will hear his screams until dawn!" Ramses shouted as his eyes flashed continuously, and they continued to darken and blaze with every passing moment as he grew angrier.

"What was lost, master?" asked one.

"The original photo of the outlaw! I want it, and I want it now!" he ranted. The Skull Bearers were frightened at the horrible fury of Ramses and it continued to grow; they scattered trying to find it. Ramses continued to get hotter and yelled at them continuously.

Re and Tut looked at his eyes and shuddered. "Menes, you had your fun, now fess up and give it back," Re whined in fright, and Tut nodded.

"No, I plan to keep it and Neiko, so stop whining." Re and Tut knew that this was going too far, and they headed to tell Ramses. "Where do you—oh, no. Please don't!"

Tut put out his hand. "Give it, and I'll say I did it. Why I should stick my neck out for you is beyond me—"

"I knew it!" Ramses growled behind them seething, and all three of them spun around. "Menes, give it to me, or I'll burn out your eyes!" Menes saw the intense anger in his eyes, so he pulled out the photo from his breastplate and handed it to him. "You two remain here, but I want to see you outside," he said to Menes as he grabbed him by the throat. Ramses choked Menes with his steely grip, and slammed him on the ground. "I warned you," he snapped as he kicked and punched him several times battering him. When he finished, he stormed back to the cabin. Menes stood up; he had cuts on this left eye, cuts and bruises on his stomach, and his right eye was black and swelling. The Skull Bearers went back to their tents horrified, yet relieved.

Menes stormed into the tent. "Thanks a lot, you two!"

"We just saved your life. If you kept it, and if he found out later, then you would be dead meat," Tut snapped, putting his hands on his hips, "Forget about making him forget about her; just focus on the girl. Like, if we nab her and say she likes you, and we know she hates Ramses, so doesn't that sound more interesting? Either that or when she is brought to the fort, then try to make her like you—"

"Yes, that'll work, and I'll plan and not pester Ramses. Working on her is less painful," Menes moaned as he rubbed his black eye. "I look a mess, but I'll be ready upon her arrival." They sniggered and planned that night.

- CHAPTER 32 -

THE RAINS STOPPED AND NEIKO prepared to leave. Bronto strapped a haversack full of food on Quickstrike's back. "Thank you so much for all you've done. Wish me luck," Neiko said shaking Bronto's huge hand.

"You made a good choice in going to Norak. Let me warn you. Not everybody is like me. Some would turn you in in a heartbeat, so don't trust everyone you meet. Ramses has a lot of allies, and I bet he has traps set everywhere, so be careful. I wish you well; come back to see me if you make it. Farewell, warrior," Bronto said as he waved.

Neiko waved back and started walking down the road.

"I bet we have enough food to make it to Norak—that is if you don't eat it all. I had no idea scorpions ate so much. I know snakes don't. Are you sure you're not part pig, too? Is that too heavy?"

"Nope, it's fine. I promise I won't eat it all, and I have no pig in me. I'm just part scorpion and part cobra," he said laughing. "How did you like the beetles?"

"That was the best thing I ever tasted! I think I have snack ideas for the next party I have in Hawote, and I wonder what their faces will look like when I tell—" Neiko stopped in mid sentence as she saw a column of smoke rising above the trees and a trail leading to its source. The sign said: *Welcome to Tenev*. There was a stag beetle carved in the sign. Neiko examined it. "This is fairly new. I gotta see what's going on," she said, going down the pathway to Tenev.

"No, Neiko! It's too dangerous! This is the Pharaoh symbol, and there could be Pharaohs in there! Wait!" Quickstrike yelled.

"Shh!" she said as she put her finger over her lips. "I gotta see what's going on, and I don't want them to hear us. I'll use the road and go in the woods. When I get fairly close, I'll watch with these," she said as she pulled out her binoculars.

They ran down the road and into the woods. Neiko found a hole in the ground with a rock concealing it. It was on a hill, and she could see the wreckage. Buildings burned and there were screams of pain. Women and children were crying and screaming in terror as Skull Bearers chased them with weapons drawn. Neiko pulled out the binoculars and watched in horror as people were being rounded up and killed. She watched as a Skull Bearer on a horse hit a woman in the head with a mace killing her, and she landed in a lifeless heap. Horsemen with axes, maces, and swords rode around killing others. Archers fired arrows felling victims, and others shot flaming arrows, hitting people and catching houses on fire. Catapults threw fireballs, stones, spiked balls; spear launchers fired huge arrows and spears at the soldiers of Tenev. "My gosh! They have all types of hardware, and the defenders don't stand a chance!" Neiko exclaimed. "I don't think they'll spare anyone!"

Thirty minutes passed and the city was laid to waste—the survivors were lined up. Archers fired and killed them as they stood in a firing squad execution. The king's castle was nothing but rubble; the treasure was brought out in wagons, and the four Pharaohs started to walk to the wagons. Skull Bearers brought a man, woman, and two boys to them and threw them at their feet. Neiko adjusted the focus to get a clearer view. "Oh no. It's the king and his family," she said. "I can see their crowns." They stripped them of their royal clothes till they were naked and threw the jewels and clothing on the wagons. The king was forced to watch the execution of his family. The wife was hung, and his two sons were beaten to death with cat-o'-nine-tails. The king collapsed at the feet of Ramses pleading for his life to be spared; Ramses drew his sword, raised it, and beheaded the king. They gave the signal, and they began to march away. Neiko heard the beat of drums, rhythm of the feet of their march, and the rumble of their weapons of war.

"What all did you see?" asked Quickstrike.

Neiko put her back against the rock and slid down as she sat down. "I have never seen so much bloodshed in my entire life! The Crackedskulls were never that cruel. The king pleaded for his life, but Ramses showed no mercy and killed him just like that," she said then snapped her fingers.

"I know. The Attack Pack can't even recall horror like this."

Neiko closed her eyes. "I miss home," she said, then opened them.

"Let's go see if anyone was lucky enough to make it." They walked down the hill and into the ruins of Tenev. Charred houses and bodies were everywhere. Some looked as if they were killed as they tried to escape their burning houses. The trees were laden with dead, and people were also crucified. Heads were put on posts. Neiko covered her mouth as she looked at the carnage. "I feel like I'm gonna puke," she said. "I have never in my life seen so much merciless killing. And for what? Treasure?"

"No. The people of Tenev have been a thorn in their side for years, and they've planned this for about as long. The treasure is just spoils—not even the cattle were left alive, so no one made it," her companion said sadly. "C'mon, let's go before we're seen. I bet they'll celebrate the night, so we may get ahead."

Neiko bowed her head and walked to the road sadly. The two of them walked for miles in silence as they prayed for the people of Tenev.

Neiko wiped away a tear in anger. "I'm gonna get you, Ramses!" she hissed in clenched teeth. "I'm gonna nail you to the wall, you just wait—"

"There she is! Get her!" cried a voice behind them. Neiko spun around and saw three Skull Bearers on horses racing to them, and two whipped out their nets ready to catch her. Neiko had time to yank her bow off her shoulder, notch an arrow, and fire. The leader flipped off the back of his horse and landed in the road with the arrow stuck in his stomach. He crawled, moaned, and then died. Neiko jumped in the ditch to dodge the net and drew her sword. The Skull Bearer turned around for another attack while his friend waited. He rode toward her, and she cut the net in half. He turned and rode again, but this time she stabbed him in the side, and he fell off, dead. She pulled her sword out, but then a net covered her, and she screamed.

"Help!" she cried, as he got off to secure his prisoner. Quickstrike ran like lightning even though he had the heavy sack on his back. He ran and faced the Skull Bearer, and the Skull Bearer drew his sword. When Quickstrike's tail fired venom in his eyes blinding him, he screamed in pain and in fright. Then Quickstrike struck him in his unprotected face. The Skull Bearer shuddered and lay still. Neiko struggled to get out of the net, but she got entangled.

"I'm coming," he said. He tore the net with his sharp claws and got it off of her, and she stood up.

"Thanks. That's like the fifth time you've saved my hide," she said sheathing her sword and picking up the bow and putting it on her shoulder. "Let's get them out of the road." After they dragged the bodies and laid them in the ditch, the two continued their journey.

Night began to fall, but they kept walking, and they watched for anyone that may attack. They traveled at a fast pace, covering about twenty miles.

"Nice night for a walk, eh?" asked a voice. They froze, and Neiko drew her sword.

"Who wants to know?" Neiko challenged trying to locate where the voice was coming from.

"Doing no harm, warrior, just asking a simple question. Why are you so paranoid?" he asked.

"Genghis Khan, is that you?" asked Quickstrike.

"Yes," he said and appeared. He was a bullfrog man wearing a purple smock and a gold pendant around his neck. His back had smooth green skin and his underside was white. "Howdy ho, Quickstrike, what brings you here on this side of Qari?"

"It's a long story. This is Admiral Neiko Kidd of Hawote and of the Desert Storm Falcon tribe," he said introducing her to him.

"Uh, sorry about my rudeness—just heeding Bronto's and my own advice," Neiko said sheathing her sword. "Nice to meet you," she said stretching her hand, and they shook hands.

"Apology accepted. Why are you here? I don't recall a land by that name," he said. "Bronto, huh?"

"Well, like he said, it's a long story," she said casually.

"Well, in that case, maybe we need to go to my camp, and let's hear it." Genghis Khan said inviting them to follow him.

- CHAPTER 33 -

GENGHIS KHAN FED THEM a dinner of fish. They told him of all their adventures, how they met, and how they arrived. "I should've known. Well, I didn't think he had enough power to reach Hawote. He has attempted before and failed. I think the Boundary has been broken."

"What?" they asked in unison.

"The Boundary of Reality and Imagination. It has separated our worlds since the beginning of time—I always wondered for what, from what, or why. You thought we were made up and vice versa. Not even the Dark Pharaoh is powerful enough to break it. The only way it could break is if a powerful person from Hawote summoned a powerful person from the Five Lands to come through. Yet, the person from the Five Lands would have to be as powerful as Sisper-Bijou, and no one can match him, so how could Ramses enter?"

"You lost me," Neiko said, shrugging. "Who is Sisper-Bijou?"

Genghis Khan chuckled. "No knowledge of magic, eh? Sisper-Bijou is an ancient tongue and it simply means 'Dark Pharaoh'—so that makes it self-explanatory. It is just his title, and no one knows the first name, so Sisper-Bijou is like a last name."

Neiko drummed her fingers on the table as she thought, and it dawned on her. "Of course! Raven somehow summoned Ramses in that plot I told you about, and he is the most powerful man in Hawote—the only one with extensive magical knowledge! I bet he has the Eye of Mohica—no wonder. So when Raven called him, and that's exactly what Ramses said, and it opened it for him! Now I get it! Now he can come and go as he pleases, but how can I get back? This is totally not what Raven and Bloodhawk had planned."

"Wait. Hold on. Ramses does not have that kind of magic! What do you think was the scheme of these enemies of yours?"

"Oh, yes he does! Now I know *exactly* what they were up to! They used him to destroy my reputation, and *then* one day they'd kidnap me. It was probably the same day Ramses brought me to Qari! They were close to carrying it out. If Ramses hadn't gotten me, then they would have! I think Ramses butchered their plans; they had no idea he was real and that he was after me. I bet they have no idea what happened to me. I wonder if family, friend, and foe all think I'm dead," she said weakly. "There is something you need to know about Ramses—but first, tell us everything you know about the Dark Pharaoh that Quickstrike doesn't even know."

"Alright, he is immortal; he was never born. He is the most powerful being just below The Almighty himself. He is extremely evil, even worse the devil—even though the devil doesn't reside here. He is capable of killing immortals because of his power just as easily as he can kill a mortal. Only immortals can kill each other in case you were wondering. It is said that he left his dark kingdom in search of a bride, and he had been gone for countless years. There were sightings of him in the Five Lands, and they stopped after the death of Xerxes, thirty billion years ago. There have been no more sightings reported since then until there was a case about thirty years ago where a man saw a dark, shadowy form kill his brother in the woods. The moon shone on it, but it was still black and didn't emit light. He supposed it was the Dark Pharaoh, and he was sent to the loony bin because the trauma made him insane. People didn't believe him because no one really ever believed the Dark Pharaoh was real. Now he lives as a hermit in Bird Wood near Norak. I followed the case for years, yet I've never found any more information on Sisper-Bijou, or better yet, his identity. Sometimes I feel that he could still be living among us—hiding—and no one would ever know. He probably laughs at people's unbelief in him. If he revealed himself—oh, how the Five Lands would panic!"

"That's it!" Neiko exclaimed. "Now I know why Ramses is hiding his identity! He would get more panic by revealing himself now than if he did it years ago! Ajax would've never let him see Lydia if he knew the truth! She came too close several times!"

Genghis Khan's eyes widened. "Are you saying Ramses is—" he couldn't finish because he swallowed hard.

"Exactly," Neiko said, reading his thoughts. "I knew before he came to Hawote, and don't ask *how* because I don't really know. We figured out his schemes to hide himself in society. The Pharaohs were perfect because they had magic and hearts like his, and he is a Pharaoh himself. Do you know what would happen if a girl married Sisper-Bijou and the nature of his magic?" Neiko also told him everything she and Quickstrike discussed about the deaths of the Pharaohs and everything he did to hide his identity.

"It all fits, as you point out. He's able to fly, disappear, change form, throw anything, cause things to fly and place them where he desires without touching them, cause natural disasters, cause disease, multiply himself, and create any monster he desires. He also can control the mind by changing memories, erasing true ones and filling the head with what he wishes, and much more. Yet, I don't know what would happen to a girl or Lydia in respects to marriage. Probably take her to his kingdom and never be seen again."

"He's immortal, so if his wife dies, then he'll seek another and so on?" asked Quickstrike.

Genghis Khan shrugged. "This is all I know. Is Ramses aware that you know that he is Sisper-Bijou?"

"Nope, not to my knowledge. If he knew, I think he would probably kill me or capture me and lock me up in a hole somewhere and say I'm dead to cover up his operation. I probably wouldn't be here now," Neiko replied.

"You must be sure he never finds out for that same reason. You must tell no one about what you know for the danger Ramses finding out. Why does he seek you?"

"I have no idea. I need to tell the Attack Pack, and definitely Lydia because she's in big trouble."

"Yes. You are not at all safe yourself. If The Almighty sees fit, and you find more proof or more of his secrets. You must not tell those or where you found them because he will destroy the records and seek you out. There has to be more information."

"Have you tried Geezah?" Neiko asked.

"No, no one has ever found it ever since it fell. I want to explore the mountains, but I'm way too old for that type of adventuring. Besides, I could never hike in the mountains. What if I got lost? Those roads are perilous," he said, stroking his white beard. "I'm three billion years old!"

"Is it possible that Geezah is in the mountains? It seems logical because it has never been found, and it was a long time before it fell. I think I'll try to look for it someday. Besides, I don't think Ramses would attempt to explore them, either. He doesn't know I'm a good climber, explorer, and adventurer. All he knows is I'm a warrior, a pain, and he wants me in his custody ASAP. Three billion years old? That makes Methuselah look young—that makes me feel way young!"

"Oh, I do know a little of your land, and your time goes by slower than ours. Multiply your age by one million, and you have your age in our time. Christ died in your world two billion years ago. We know this from ancient legends passed down through the generations. However, many believe Earth not to exist since the times of old."

Neiko thought and figured her age. "I'm eighteen million years old. Okay, that means I'm older than Lydia by ten million years, and Ramses's so-called age by fifteen million. How old is he *really*?"

"No one knows, but he is older than sixty billion because that was the first sighting. I definitely have no idea what he looks like underneath his armor, so don't ask."

"Do you know anything else about my world?"

"Why yes, most of everything I know comes from visions or old legends like I mentioned earlier. I know that our universe was created before yours, and you are in a totally different universe, and yours is ten times larger than ours. Our planet has no name unlike yours, and our constellations are different than yours. We have four moons, but this one always shines, and the other three are new. We have one sun just like you, but it rises and sets in the opposite direction of yours. The Almighty exists in both our universes simultaneously because he is omnipresent, and he is the only being able to do so. Our calendar consists of twenty months and each moon sets in a quarter of the year. The new year begins when all four are full, and we are in the last quarter of our year, which is only five months till the new year. We do not have changing seasons like you do, and the monsoons come in the beginning of the fourth quarter of the year which was last week. Our week is seven days like yours, and our months consist of twenty-eight days apiece. Do you understand everything I'm saying?"

"Yeah, I took astronomy. I learned some stuff about my own universe. So I gather we are separated by space and time of trillions or quadrillions of years, and this Boundary thingy blocked a shortcut of seconds! I think The Almighty created this to keep our universe safe because we don't have magic to protect us from Ramses. But Raven had to screw up this order, and Ramses said he may even destroy Hawote because I resisted him! Oh gosh! I definitely know he won't stop until my whole world is under his heel, but couldn't he reach us by going through space?"

"Hmm, he probably didn't because it would take too long, and you know Ramses hasn't got any patience especially for that length of time. Besides, The Almighty would probably stop him; our magic is no match with his. We barely can hold out, so how do you think you could fare against him? So he threatened you; he *will* destroy Hawote once he captures you because he doesn't kid around. Your world doesn't stand a chance against him even as a mortal Pharaoh. Did you say something about magic earlier?"

"Yeah, Raven is the one who can do it, and his son, Bloodhawk, is learning. We have a stone called the Eye of Mohica, but no one knows where it came from. We call it that because it was found in the Mohican Territory in the year 1902. It stayed there till 1930 when it was stolen, probably by Raven's father, Claw. No one has found it, and I think that's why Raven is so powerful. It is useless against Ramses; I think I could use it against anyone else. Do you suppose it could have come from here? It's the same size as a grapefruit, and it glows a green light."

"Hmm, that sounds like the Eye of Cygnus or also known as the Heart of Rumi. This talisman belonged to the Pharaohs of old, and it was lost after the death of Rumi, the owner. It just vanished into thin air, and that may be it. I have a picture of it. Could you identify it if you saw it?"

"Yeah, I've helped trying to find it! You mean to say that Raven possesses Pharaoh magic? Where did it come from?"

"Rumi made it. He found an ordinary rock and put in it every type of Pharaoh magic, including Pharaoh black magic; their magic is not related to demons, but are just forces and that includes both types: light and dark. "Black Magic" just means it is a stronger type of

Pharaoh magic and the dark arts by their dark gods. No magic in this universe is demonic," he replied going through the papers. "Here it is," he said handing the picture to her.

Neiko's mouth fell open. "Oh, my gosh! It is! So this is where it came from! So basically Raven is using Pharaoh magic. I wonder what else he's done with it! How in the crap did it get on my world?"

"That you will discover on your own, and those are mysteries in your own universe. Oh, yes—Rumi also learned the Pharaoh black magic, and he wrote them down in twelve volumes according to their strength—one is the least and twelve the most powerful and complicated. Ramses has been searching for them and the Eye of Cygnus."

"Like he needs it! Why does he need more magic, and is it anywhere close to his own?"

"Well, Dark Pharaoh magic can be extremely destructive, dangerous, extremely strong, and very complicated. There is an old tale that Ramses came from the distance of the Great Beyond in search of these in the distant past before they were made, which also could mean he can fortell the future to some capacity. I believe Raven used a volume twelve spell to summon Ramses, and of course, Ramses used Dark Pharaoh magic to reach Hawote. I have noticed that the Eye of Osiris has a multiplying effect on Pharaoh magic, and I'm sure it can multiply his Dark Pharaoh magic at least one hundred times, and the Eye of Cygnus about eighty times in addition to whatever spells and power they contain. He may even achieve some some level of omnipotence with all that in his possession. So you see why he could want them."

Neiko's eyes widened. "Whoa! I can't even *comprehend* any level of omnipotence whatsoever. I'm glad he didn't get the Eye of Cygnus; he said it was worthless; I wonder what happened when Quickstrike left. Did Osiris create the Eye of Osiris?" she asked, judging it by the name.

"Well, that is one secret you need to keep, and just call it the Eye of Mohica. He said it was worthless because he knows your world has no magic, and if any, it is weaker than peasant magic which he isn't looking for. When he heard you call it by the Eye of Mohica and not Cygnus, he figured it was not what he was looking for. No one ever believed it would be in your universe. As for the Eye of Osiris, no he didn't create it. No one knows where it came from. Osiris found it and named it after himself, but no one has ever claimed it, and he doesn't know where it came from. You have learned much young one, and you have helped me solve some great problems. You have much to think about, and the fate of both our worlds depends on you. Not only that, you are running from the very one who can destroy them both. As for what happened after Ramses and Quickstrike left, I don't know, but the Attack Pack would know."

Genghis Khan shook his head at her question. He had no idea.

"Ouch! Sigma asked me to take on more responsibility. If I knew this was coming, I would've said no. Now since I know this, I don't even know where to begin. Life was easier when I was captain. Since I became admiral, my life has turned upside down. I was comfortable fighting Crackedskulls, but a Dark Pharaoh is way too much. I can never beat him; I know knowledge is power, but this could get me in more trouble. I've become a magnet for secrets because I found out a bunch in my own world—now this," Neiko said in despair.

"T'will be alright. I know this is a lot to sort through, but don't give up. The Almighty has set this challenge before you, and you may be the beacon of hope we have been searching for to rid us of Sisper-Bijou."

"Hey, wait a minute! Are you saying I have to fight him in a duel? I know nothing of magic; I can't even make rabbits come out of a hat! He'll cream my potatoes! I just barely escaped him in Hawote, and that's because Quickstrike saved my bacon! I ain't cut out for fighting something I can't kill," Neiko squeaked. "Raven and Bloodhawk may have Pharaoh magic and be giants, but at least I know I can kill 'em!"

"Oh, no, no. I didn't mean that. I just meant you can find out everything one day, and he wouldn't stay around."

"You hope," Neiko said, folding her arms. "I wonder if I'll just make things worse by digging up his secrets. I ain't got time to look for 'em either because Ramses is on my tail, and he could find my trail any minute. He probably has traps set everywhere; I hope he doesn't read my mind and have one set for me in Norak."

"So, that's where you're heading—the safest place in Qari. Knowing him, he will cover the entire land with traps because you have escaped his so-called brothers and those Skull Bearers. Be proud you made it this far."

"But it's still so far away," Neiko moaned. "Those are the first of many traps; if he finds my trail, then he'll be in hot pursuit, and even try to head me off. I just want to go home—I miss my family and friends, and I have unfinished business to take care of; I left a mess. Speaking of home, how am I gonna get back? Where is the Attack Pack, or do you know?"

"Well, the Attack Pack was last sighted in Norak. The only way I know you could get home is if Ramses sends you there, but there could be another. Only The Almighty knows."

Neiko slammed her head on the table in disgust. "Wo!" she yelled in Greyhawk rubbing her head. "Like that'll happen. I'm stuck here for good! In that case the next time I see Hawote is when I'm in chains beside Ramses as his POW, and it'll look like Tenev. I'll see my friends and foes alike dead, and maybe even my family! I won't let that happen! I'll stay here and die before I let him massacre and destroy my world!"

"You know of Tenev?"

"Yeah, I watched from the woods as I saw people die, and I watched Ramses kill the king in cold blood! I can't stand the thought of that happening to Hawote and people I don't even know in the Outside World outside of Hawote! I went to see if somebody made it, and I saw stuff not even Bloodhawk would do in anger. I never saw anything that horrible in all my days as a warrior," Neiko said, shaking with anger.

"Yes, well, it's time to rest yourself. You must leave early tomorrow, and you've had a busy day," Genghis Khan said as he prepared her bed. Neiko went to sleep, but Quickstrike stayed up. "Poor little warrior. She has suffered so much in such a short time, tell me all about her." Quickstrike told him everything about her, her life, the Indians, Crackedskulls, Hawote, and Georgia. "How interesting. A totally unknown civilization, and she is very important there. I bet she has had enough of Ramses Sisper-Bijou and his reign of terror."

"Yep," he said stretching. He crawled beside her and fell asleep while Genghis Khan watched them.

- Chapter 34 -

LATE THAT NIGHT, TWO Skull Bearer officers walked into Ramses's cabin, took off their bullhorn helmets, and bowed. "Ah, what do you have for me? Any luck?" he asked folding his hands on the the desk.

"Uh, there are five dead Skull Bearers, Majesty. Two at Bronto's Tavern, and three were found in the ditch on Tatowee Road about five miles south of Tenev. The ones at Bronto's Tavern have been dead for a week, but the ones on the road were only dead for only a few hours when we found them," said the lieutenant as he toyed with his beetle antennae on his helmet.

Ramses rolled his eyes. "You bring me bad news? What were the causes of death?"

"The ones at the tavern died of a dagger wound to the neck, and the other was killed by Bronto as he defended a girl, so I guess the girl killed the other. They were stripped of their daggers and one sword," replied the captain.

Ramses looked up in surprise. "Go on."

"Well, one of ones on the road died of an arrow in the stomach; another died of a sword wound to the side; the third was blinded by venom, and had a purple snake bite on his face. One of their nets was torn like they caught something. There was a sword drawn, and it was the one that was bitten," replied the captain.

"Aha! That's them! Nice work. It seems to me that one of them trapped Neiko, and Quickstrike saved her again!" He slammed his fist on the desk. "Drat! That stupid scorpion is more trouble than he is worth! Well, at least I found their trail. I want them both brought to me. Neiko Kidd is an extremely talented warrior, and she will fight you with everything she's got—tooth and nail if need be, and she is like a wild beast. To ensure their capture, get a company of fifty or more and attack them in teams. I will take the pleasure in killing Quickstrike, and Neiko will watch," he said with cruel pleasure. "Make sure they are unharmed."

"What will you do with Neiko? Kill her?" asked the lieutenant.

"No, what I've planned to do ever since I saw her the first time," he said as his eyes flashed in evil delight. "Dismissed!" he said, waving his hand. The two bowed and left. They put on their helmets and gathered seventy Skull Bearers and horses, and rode out that night.

Neiko and Quickstrike woke up the next morning refreshed. Waving and thanking Genghis Khan, they walked down the road toward Samoan territory. "How are you feeling about all we talked about last night? Still pessimistic?" asked Quickstrike.

"No. I feel better knowing who I'm dealing with, and nothing will take me by surprise—" suddenly a branch snapped and Skull Bearers on horses ran out from the side. "Run!" Neiko screamed as she saw more coming from behind. They ran about ten feet as more came in front and from the other side, closing them in.

"Oh great, we're trapped! We can kill three, but not thirty!" Quickstrike whimpered.

"Try seventy!" Neiko corrected.

"How can you count that fast?"

"Believe me—lucky guess. I've been in situations like this, but this time the Seven Tribes aren't here to save me!"

The lieutenant rode up. "That's them! Capture them!" he commanded. They closed in the circle as Neiko drew her sword and tomahawk; Quickstrike got his tail ready to spray, and they got close to each other. Twenty jumped off their horses, drew their weapons, and walked toward them while the other fifty kept them surrounded, not letting them escape.

Neiko let loose a shrill war call as she brandished her weapons. Neiko struck at the nearest Skull Bearer with her tomahawk, but he fended off the attack with his shield. One grabbed her from behind and pulled her arms behind her back, while two more disarmed her . She struggled, but the other two came and helped hold her, while a fourth came with a rope and gag. First he tied her hands behind her back, then tied her arms down and gagged her. She fell to the ground, and they rushed to help trap Quickstrike.

They surrounded him, and he hissed at them and tried to spray several, but they ducked behind their shields. He lunged at others trying to injure them with his powerful claws as he struck with his tail; he fought like an angry scorpion. Several came from behind hitting him with the butts of their spears and pikes. He hissed angrily, and he tried to shake them off by slapping with his tail; he tripped one, and they closed in and started to beat him. They knocked him senseless, yet they kept pounding him.

"No! Don't kill him! The master wants him alive too. Tie him down in the wagon and put a net over him," commanded the captain. He got off his horse and walked over to Neiko strutting. "Not so tough are we?" he sniggered. Neiko narrowed her eyes at him and wriggled trying to loosen the ropes. "The master's been expecting you, and he'll be so glad to see you. I know he has something special planned just for you," he said proudly. Neiko's eyes widened, she shook her head, and gave horrified mumbles. "Oh, don't worry, he won't kill you—just your friend. He'll be the last person you'll ever see," he laughed cruelly. "You deserve it after what you did to our friends, and I'll take pleasure in your screams of helplessness as you watch us kill your friend. I can't wait to see what the master has in store for you, but I can tell it scares you, doesn't it?" Neiko struggled more frantically and she screamed under the gag, as they all laughed. "Grab the girl, put her on a horse, and let's go. He awaits our arrival, and you know he doesn't like to wait long," he said. "I want her to be nice and awake upon her arrival. Save your strength, Admiral. I want you to be presentable."

Two seized her, and she struggled, kicked, and screamed as they dragged her to a horse; two more lifted her and put her on the horse. One of them on a horse took the reins, and his buddy got on behind him. Neiko looked back to see Quickstrike, but he was still unconscious. They turned to head back to Camp Steal when a flurry of arrows came out of the bushes felling several. People ran out with spears, and they started killing the Skull Bearers till all seventy-two were dead. They started talking in a language that was familiar; it was Greyhawk!

The leader pointed to Neiko and Quickstrike. "Eitnu dna eerf meht." Neiko gave a sigh of relief as they helped her off the horse, cut the ropes, and pulled off the gag.

"Sknaht," she said. They turned and looked at her puzzled.

The leader looked at her amazed. "How can you speak Samoan? No one in Qari can speak it, unless you are the outlaw," he said in Greyhawk.

"You're right, I'm not from Qari. I am Neiko Kidd of Hawote. My tribe, the Desert Storm Falcons, speak this same language, but we call it Greyhawk. I mean you no harm, and I thank you kindly for freeing me," she answered. "How is my friend?"

"He's badly injured, but nothing a night in our city can't help. You are welcome to stay with us. My name is Radge, and I am the leader," he said bowing in courtesy. "A female warrior. I am honored."

The Samoans took them into their village and treated them well. Neiko got a bath, and was fed. "Here are your weapons. One of my trackers found this on the leader," said Radge as he handed her a piece of folded paper.

"What is that, and what did he say?" asked Quickstrike. "This salve of theirs works wonders. If it wasn't for them, we would be in the hands of Ramses right now."

"Yeah, I know. They were going to kill you, and Ramses is going to do God knows what to me. I don't like the way it sounds because he said it was something 'special just for me'," she said then shivered. "The sky's the limit, but I know he isn't going to kill me, but I kind of wish he was. Radge said he got this off the leader, and he just gave me my weapons." Neiko unfolded the paper, it was a copy of her warrior picture, and she gasped. "It's a copy of my warrior picture that Monchiska gave me as a gift. Somebody has my—ohh!" Neiko quivered with rage as it dawned on her. "I'm gonna kill that sleazy Dark Pharaoh! That was given to me by one of my best friends, and I have a secret crush on him too, but he doesn't know. I suppose Chrome Scum is the one with the original, and I'm gonna get it back! In fact, I'm in love with Monchiska. So, this is how they know what I look like." Neiko told everything to Radge about what had happened, and about her life, but she mentioned nothing about Ramses being the Dark Pharaoh.

"Oh how dreadful," Radge said. "We will mount you up horses, more rations, and a pad for Quickstrike in the morning. We also have beds for you, so go on to bed. You need an early start to get ahead of Ramses."

"What about y'all? You could be in danger by helping me. Ramses will massacre you for taking me from him and for those Skull Bearers," Neiko asked, worried.

"No need to worry. We have a hiding place, and he couldn't care less about the Skull Bearers, but he would definitely kill us for you. He can't burn us out because we are underground about fifty feet in a secret passage, besides, we normally stay out of his way. We helped you because we heard his name, your fright, and desperation to escape, so we knew he had something awful planned for you, and it was not death," he said as he showed them to their room. "Good night and I'll see you before dawn," he said and left.

Neiko translated everything Radge had said. "It kinda reminds me of being in my tribe," she said sadly.

"It's okay, Neiko. Why don't you tell Monchiska how you feel about him. I'm sure he would like to know."

"Well, it's not that easy. You see, he is seeing this Georgian named Rebecca Cunningham; she is extremely wealthy, and she adores him. All he feels for me is friendship, although I'd like to bash that girl in the head because she sometimes treats him like crap and takes advantage of his good nature. She drools all over him, and Indians hate that!"

"Oh well, you have good reason to dislike her, but stuff like that never stopped Ramses," he said, laughing.

"Ooh, bad example. I wouldn't ever go that far because I respect his wishes and that's true love, you know. She has never met Sigma and Puma, and she thinks his name is Antonio Alvarez and not Monchiska! She even said she doesn't want to meet them, and they are his parents, mind you; she has no idea she is dating an Indian! Sigma and Monchiska have the darkest skin in the Seven Tribes, and she is as white as a cloud! She thinks he's Hispanic Georgian! Ha! She'd freak out if she knew Antonio was actually a Scraah named Monchiska, and Amanda is a Falcon named Neiko, and we're Indians; she said she hates Indians with a passion! Wouldn't that be funny? It's a rule if an Indian marries an Outsider, they must meet the Seven Tribes, and they must approve. Believe me, the Seven Tribes wonder if she has him in a trance, and they hate her as much as I do."

"You know, that's a splendid idea. It would be hilarious to see her face when she found out there were that many Indians!" They laughed, Neiko blew out the candle, and they fell asleep.

- Chapter 35 -

WHEN MORNING CAME, NEIKO and Quickstrike were both refreshed. "I feel wonderful, and I don't hurt anywhere!" Quickstrike said. "If I get hurt next time, I'll come here, but I wish I could understand what they're saying and vice versa."

"Yeah, I'm glad they speak a language I know all too well," Neiko replied as she lifted and put her backpack on her shoulder. "Does anyone else speak a different language? It seems everyone else speaks English or how we're talkin' right now—English is what the Outsiders call it."

"No, the Samoans are the only ones that speak a different language, and no one knows why, but it is believed they speak the language of the ancients. They can't learn how to speak like anyone else because they isolate themselves, and they can't understand the dominant language. They want to keep their customs. No one knows where they came from, not even the Samoans. Some say they live like what Qari was like before Rumi, but it's a guess. No one has anything to do with them because they feel like they are backward, old fashioned, and not aggressive fighters like everyone else. Of course, language is a problem."

"They seem fine to me, and I gathered that when Radge told me they usually don't help or fight against Ramses, but they did a very good job. He also said they saved me because they know that name all too well; they saw how frantic I was, and they don't like acts of cruelty. He was glad they rescued us when I told him about our adventures, but I didn't say anything about our secrets about Ramses."

"Good. They would definitely be scared if they knew the truth, more than anybody."

"Yeah. I'm still worried about them getting exterminated because Ramses would have a fit to know he lost me because of them. He won't take it lightly, but Radge says they have a secret stakeout. I just hope he doesn't find the door."

"Good morning. Everything's ready, and you must hurry," Radge replied. "I'm sorry to rush you, but I feel better if you leave before sunrise."

"Alright, thanks for all your help. I want you to go underground and stay there. Take down your teepees and set up down there, and I don't want anything to happen to you guys. I think of you as a brother tribe, and I care," Neiko said as she hugged him and shook his hand.

"I feel honored, and you're the first to care for us. We will follow your instructions and go take our teepees to our underground city, but we do not have to set up because we have buildings of stone. Don't worry about us, the caverns are a maze, and only we know the way, farewell," said Radge, touched, and he left to start the evacuation.

"Okay, it's a go," she said jumping on the horse, and Quickstrike jumped on the pad on the rear. "They'll be safe because they'll be underground in their hidden city, so let's move out!" Neiko signaled the horse to a steady walk. "You okay back there?"

"Yeah, now I know why they call them the Vanishing People. They are there for a little while, then they go underground, and it looks like no one was ever there. We'll keep that secret between us. Neiko! Skull Bearers behind us! Kick it!"

"Okay, hang on! This'll be bumpy because I'll try to ditch em in the woods!" Neiko shouted and kicked the horse. The horse dashed forward and headed for the woods; Neiko found a clearing, and she ran off the road into that clearing. There was a thicket of trees she went into. She jumped off the horse and looked through the trees. She could see the road clearly, but no one could see her.

"Did we lose 'em?" asked Quickstrike, but Neiko pressed her finger against her lips. The Skull Bearers came into the woods and stopped on the road.

"Do you see anything?" asked one.

"No, but they couldn't have gone far! Let's go back and report to Ramses immediately! We must tell him we spotted them and about the seventy-two casualties!" cried a sergeant. They turned around and headed back to Camp Steal.

Neiko breathed with relief. "Well, we're safe for now. Where are we anyway? I haven't been able to check our progress, so let's find out." Neiko pulled the backpack off the horse, and she retrieved the map. "Okay. Let's see. Here's Tenev, and we just left the Samoan Territory, and we just entered the woods called Fleetwood Forest. So—The Split is a few miles after we get out of this forest, and the Low Road is on the right. The High Road goes straight into the mountains and comes out on the Low Road, so plan B is in check. Maybe we'll be lucky and just go down the Low Road, up the Short Road, and right on to Norak Pass, and then right to Norak."

"That sounds easy enough, so now what?"

"We'll travel as much as we can till nightfall, and then we'll make camp. We'll get up before sunrise and get ready to rock."

"Good plan. That's sounds fine to me."

They mounted and traveled deep into the forest till nightfall. They pulled off the side of the road and made camp. They ate their

supper and kept the fire going. Neiko looked up at the stars as she lay on her back while Quickstrike kept a watch. "Wow, this is so cool! I like looking at a different set of stars, and there are even purple and green ones in this place. We never had those colors," Neiko said.

"I never thought about it really, do you want to play connect the stars?"

"Yeah!" she said. They played for thirty minutes and created endless shapes. "Well, let's go to sleep. Quickstrike, have you seen my tomahawk?" Neiko asked, saw it, and picked it up. "Never mind, I found—" Neiko stopped as she saw vulture men surrounding them. They were holding tridents. Their bodies were covered in black feathers with a white ring of feathers around the base of their necks. The skin on their bald heads and necks was red or black; their beaks were white, sharp, and curved. They had arms and legs like a man, but vulture feet and wings on their backs.

"We have trespassers!" one growled.

"Let's take them to King Carrion and let him decide what to do with them," said another.

Neiko stood up with her tomahawk ready. "Oh yeah? You ain't takin' nobody to your dead head king! Give me your best shot, road kill eater!"

"Put the weapon down, or your friend gets it!" shouted one named Scavenger as he let her see that Quickstrike was surrounded and they had their tridents ready to stab him. Seeing no escape, Neiko threw it down in disgust and put her hands up. "That's better. You two, take care of her and fly on."

Neiko watched as they killed her horse, and they picked up all of their things. They put Quickstrike in a bag after they knocked him senseless. They seized her and tied her hands behind her back and blindfolded her. They picked her up and she could feel her feet come off the ground; they turned to the southwest as they headed to their kingdom.

- CHAPTER 36 -

The sergeant and a tracker came in to report. Ramses looked up. "Yes?" he asked coldly.

"We saw Neiko and Quickstrike, but we lost them in Fleetwood Forest. We sadly report there are seventy-two dead Skull Bearers; they were found seven miles north of the Samoan Territory," replied the sergeant.

"Is that all?" he asked in fury.

"No. It was evident they had them, but someone came and bailed them out. There were no dead of the enemy."

Ramses was so angry he overturned the table; food and papers scattered everywhere. The two shrank back in fear. "Seventy-seven casualties in two weeks! Impossible! How could they escape seventy-two men?"

"Maybe some ragtag group helped them and then left," suggested the sergeant.

"How can you be sure it wasn't the Samoans?" Ramses asked, seething.

"Well, they help no one, and they are too frightened of you to even think about fighting you."

"You're right. Well at least I know they are walking right into my blockade trap. Never mind about the patrols, I will go to the blockade and wait for a week. If there are no signs, I will return to Skull Fort. I will send word to my allies, and I will send out bounty hunters! She will not escape me this time!" he said as he got on his black Clydesdale, Goliath, and rode across Prosper Valley to the site of the blockade.

Neiko and Quickstrike were brought into the castle, and they were unblindfolded. The vultures prodded them with their tridents, and they finally entered the throne room. "We found these two trespassers camped near the road, Majesty, and we brought them to you to seek your discretion," replied Scavenger.

King Carrion looked at them. "Hmm. What do you have to say for yourselves, wanderers?" King Carrion was a condor who looked just like his followers. He wore a large gold crown and carried a scepter with a golden skull that had ruby eyes.

"Oops," Neiko said sarcastically.

"You have no respect, do you?" he asked angrily. "We have one from the Attack Pack, but who are you?" he asked, looking at Neiko.

"What's it to ya?" she snapped.

"Answer the question," said Scavenger, shoving her.

"Neiko Kidd from Hawote, and we're travelling to Norak. We weren't planning to stay till morning. We're just passing through, so can you just give me back my weapons and our food and let us go? We'll gladly leave right now."

"Majesty, there were Skull Bearers that came in the north end earlier, and we found them hours later, so it seems they were searching for them," replied a buzzard named Cleaver.

"Really? How interesting. Is it possible that they are outlaws or hunted?" asked the king. "Put them in the dungeon till morning. So, Neiko, you aren't leaving. Take them away."

They brought them in the dungeon and they chained them with balls and chains and locked them up. "Well, this sucks," Neiko grumbled. "Are these twerps friends of Ramses?"

"Hmm, I'm not sure, but I have a feeling we'll find out," replied Quickstrike.

"Great, I hate long waits," Neiko grumbled.

When morning came, the guards brought them before the king. "Well, I haven't decided what to do with the two of you. I may do away with you, Attack Pack slime, but as for you, stranger, I may just make you my personal slave," replied King Carrion.

"Majesty, there is a letter for you," said a vulture named Grinder as he ran in and handed it to him.

"Thank you," he said. He unrolled it and read it. "Aah. It has been sometime since I have heard from Ramses, and it seems the girl is an outlaw; he wants her delivered to him as soon as possible. We may do as we wish with her companion. Well, I will execute the scorpion in the morning, and I will hold the outlaw until he arrives. Grinder, you will go find Ramses and tell him we have caught the outlaw on her way to Norak, and that she is awaiting his arrival."

Grinder bowed. "Right away." He bowed again and left.

"Great. That's just wonderful. Well, that answers my question," Neiko grumbled moodily.

"Well, well. You seem to be important, and I will need to take care of you till he comes. You will have dinner with me tonight, and you will be cleaned. Guards, take them away."

The guards chained them back as they were before. "Great. Now what? I'll be dead by dawn, and they will keep you till Ramses comes to pick you up," grumbled Quickstrike.

"I have to have dinner with birdbrain tonight, and it seems he keeps my weapons near his throne along with our food for some strange reason, but he might ditch it later. I'm trying to think of a way to bust out, and it's gotta be tonight."

"A jailbreak? How will you get past those guards? We have a very big problem. What about the chains and the door? If we do get away, they'll tell Ramses we got away, and now he knows where we're headed. Also we don't know how to get back to the road, and it's possible they may try to stop us from escaping."

"One thing at a time. When I have dinner with the king, I'll find something to pick the locks. We'll slip out and get our stuff and make a run for it. I'll use my compass to find the way back. Ramses won't know we're going to Norak till they tell him, and we may already get there. They're coming."

The guards came in. "Alright, let's go, girl," said one as he used the key to unlock her chains, and they took her upstairs to bathe. Women washed her clothes and bathed her. Then she was taken to the dinner table, and seated. King Carrion sat down at the head of the table, and the food was brought. There was fruit, vegetables, and raw horse brought in, and Neiko grimaced at the sight of the raw horse. She pushed it away and started to eat the fruits and vegetables.

"Are you a vegetarian?" he asked.

"No, I don't eat raw meat or anything that is rotten or part rotten, and is this my horse? What is this, a gimmick to rub in my face my defeat?" she asked curtly.

Carrion chuckled. "Really? Yes, this was your horse. I do not make one's defeat so unbearable, and horse is my favorite." As they talked Neiko measured up their plan, but she found nothing to pick the locks.

Darn! Well, I have to find a way to get the keys, she thought. After dinner the king went to bed, and one jailer took her back to the dungeon. Locking the door behind him, he headed to the place to chain her. Neiko got Quickstrike's attention to strike the guard before he chained her. His tail was chained down, but he was able to aim it to blind him by spraying venom like a spitting cobra.

"Hey, baldy, you're so ugly, roadkill looks better!" Quickstrike yelled. The jailer looked at him angrily, and Quickstrike sprayed him in the eyes with his venom with great accuracy. He let go of Neiko, and she hit him in the back of the head, knocking him senseless. She ran and unlocked Quickstrike; she chained the guard up and put a band on his beak. She unlocked the door, and they slipped up the stairs. They noiselessly put on all of their equipment, slipped in the main entrance, and saw sentries outside in the light. They slipped past them in the shadows and ran into the woods. Neiko got out her compass, aimed the sight at the castle, and saw that the castle was west. "We need to head east to find the road, and we need to get out of the forest tonight. Vultures, condors, and buzzards are day birds, and they have no night vision, so we're safe as long as it's dark," Neiko whispered. They stole out into the shadows of the woods aided with the little light of the moon. They walked for several hours before finally coming to the road. They walked for about another hour, and they could see the end of the forest. The sun started to rise; they kept walking and exited the woods.

- CHAPTER 37 -

"FINALLY, WE'RE OUTA THE FOREST," Quickstrike cried with relief.

"Yeah, but I love the woods, yet I don't like 'em crawling with friends of Monster Gas. I hope it's a while before Grinder finds him. The Split is just ahead!" Neiko said as she started to run. They approached the Low Road. They started to go down, but something caught Neiko's eye. There were many people in a group about two miles away behind a huge line that seemed to go on forever in the distance. "Thank Yahweh we're in the plains so I can see for a long distance. Do you have traffic jams on the Low Road a lot?" Neiko asked worried.

"No, why? Neiko, what's wrong?" asked Quickstrike, but Neiko didn't answer. She spotted a climbable tree, and she got out her binoculars. She strapped them onto her neck and started to climb. Near the top she found a good branch and checked her footing. Holding on to the tree with one hand, she pulled the binoculars up to her eyes. She saw people being checked as they passed by Skull Bearers under the watchful eye of Menes, Re, and Tut. A woman under a hood walked, but they stopped her and pulled it off revealing a lynx woman.

"There's the goof troop, but where's—" she thought, but something shiny caught her eye under a tent. She adjusted the focus, and she saw Ramses reclining under the tent and fanning himself. She gulped and climbed down the tree. "We gotta take the High Road," she said as she took off her headband, wiped off the sweat with the tail of her shirt, and replaced the headband.

"Why? What did you see?"

"Oh, about five hundred Skull Bearers, three Pharaohs, and one Dark Pharaoh, and they're checking everyone and asking them if they saw me as they showed them a picture. They have wanted posters everywhere, and I bet they'll put them all over the land. If I didn't notice nor had that bad feeling, we woulda just walked right into a trap, and we wouldn't stand a chance."

"Yeah, Ramses was right there, and you would see him in seconds. Alright, let's do it."

"Yeah, let's move out now. We'll be safe once we get to the mountains, and we'll take a break."

"Good idea," Quickstrike said as they turned around and headed back to go to the High Road. They walked on the High Road for several hours in the plains, and the mountains towered over them. The road was in extreme disrepair as grasses grew in it, but the road was still there.

"I can tell no one has been this far down the High Road in a very long time. I need to take a break now," she said pulling her shirt to release the heat coming from her body; she set down her weapons and spotted a sign. She ran to it. Although the letters were faded and barely legible, Neiko read it carefully and was able to make it out: *Kilowee Mountains entrance two miles.* "Yes! The entrance to the mountains is only two miles, and we can go ahead and take a breather because we're close enough to the mountains," she said then plopped down beside him.

"Phew! I didn't think you would ever stop! Let's get a bite to eat and drink."

"Sure thing," she said as she got out a piece of Slim Jim and the canteen. She cut the wrappers with her dagger and handed Quickstrike his. She opened her canteen, gulped the water, and let him have a gulp. After they finished their snack, they started their journey. Neiko saw another sign, but she couldn't read it, so they moved on. The ground started to slope upward and gradually got steeper. "Well, we're in the mountains. We probably entered them a while back near that sign we couldn't read."

"How can you tell?" he asked.

"Easy. The ground's sloping, and I can tell we went further than two miles. Believe me, I've been exploring in the mountains before. I go on hiking trails or explore near my aunt's mountain cabin. This isn't any different than that except no one lives here or comes here."

"I'm glad you know how to do all of this stuff. If it wasn't for you and your fighting and wood skills, we would've never made it this far."

"Well, don't give me all the credit. You saved my hide plenty of times, and you helped construct the Norak plan. Your knowledge of Qari and your people skills also paid off."

"You're right. We used teamwork, and we make a good team." They talked more and more as they traveled further and further into the mountains.

"It's really getting steep. We must be getting in the tall ones now. Wait. Here's a lookout point." They went and looked down. "Wow! This is great! I wished I had a camera!" Neiko said as she could see a river snaking through the plains, the roads, and the forests. "Ha! Ha! Do you see that black dot?"

"Yeah, what is that?"

Neiko giggled. "That's the blockade! I can see them, and Ramses doesn't even know I'm up here watching him, and what a laugh because he will never think I came up here! We can say we outwitted the Dark Pharaoh and not lie!"

"I never thought of that."

"What a view! The mountains are sloping down now, so there must be a valley up ahead; then we get to the really big ones," Neiko said as they walked back to the road and saw the road sloping down. The slopes were so steep that Neiko had to dig her walking stick into the ground and walk sideways to avoid falling. Rocks would cause her legs to go downhill; she would almost do a split. They finally got to low ground after an hour of coping with the shifting steepness of the road. "Let's take a break," she said, and then she caught the sweet smell and heard the trickle of a nearby creek. Neiko got her canteen and all the ones the Samoans gave them and started off.

"Where are you going?" he asked.

"I'm gonna get some water because there's a creek down this way. I'll be right back."

"Okay, how do you know there's a creek down there?"

"I can smell it and hear it," she said then disappeared while Quickstrike scratched his head. She came back with eight canteens full of creek water. Her hair was wet from dipping her head in it and cooling herself. "The water is good! Let's move on. We should reach the large mountains by nightfall, and we'll call it a day. If we see any berries or a river, we'll stop to get food. We'll use what we got for emergencies, and we'll need to stock up soon. Let's boogie."

They walked in the valley for an hour and they came to a fork in the road. Neiko saw several crude signs that pointed to both forks but they were illegible. The post had a carving that said: *Welcome the Great Fork.*

"Great, now what? Well, which way do we go—left or right?" asked Quickstrike as he threw his claws up in confusion.

"You got me, but wait. Left is going toward the tall mountains and that's where we are heading, and I have no idea where right goes. Left it is."

"Lead on, Admiral," he said, and they started down the left fork. They walked and saw many little side roads, but they stayed on the main road. The road never got intensely steep, but it started to wind, and it became very narrow. It was carved in the granite of the mountain's side. The air began to get thinner and night fell. They found a berry patch. They picked, ate many, packed some in reserve and camped out. They arose early and traveled for weeks in that same fashion. Then the road got to a high level and the air was frigid. White-gray clouds came up, and a snowflake dropped on Quickstrike's head.

"Oh no! It's gonna snow. We gotta keep moving or we'll freeze to death. We gotta find a cave or something or move until it stops then build a fire," she said rubbing her arms a little.

"I'm f-f-freezing! You're barely cold," Quickstrike said shaking. Then they heard a rumble of thunder, and a flash of lightning cut the sky.

"Holy cow! We gotta find shelter like now! It's gonna be a bloody blizzard!" Neiko said, horrified.

"How do you know?"

"I was in one once, and it thundered and all while it was snowing! The wind is just getting started, and the snowflakes are getting larger," she said frantically, and they picked up their pace. Within minutes the howling wind was blowing so hard it was hard to walk. The snowflakes pounded them, so they had trouble walking and seeing. Neiko's skin was numb from the cold, and she was getting so tired her limbs were killing her, but she wouldn't stop, and Quickstrike followed. The thunder rolled continuously and the lightning flashed. Suddenly a bolt struck a tree, and Neiko heard the pop and the crackle of the tree right behind them. The tree groaned, and Neiko saw it falling. She sprinted, even in her exhaustion, with lightning speed. Quickstrike started to run too, but the tree landed on his tail.

"Neiko, help! I'm stuck! Oww! This hurts, and I think it's broke! I can barely feel it. I can tell this tree killed it!" Quickstrike yelled in pain and fright. Neiko pulled him frantically, but he wouldn't budge. "I'm gonna die! I think my butt's stuck too!"

"No, we're gonna get you outa here!" she said then she sensed another presence. She turned around and saw a figure in the falling snow. Neiko reached out her hand weakly. "Help us!" she said in a strained moan, and then she collapsed face first in the snow because of cold and exhaustion.

- **CHAPTER 38** -

"IT HAS BEEN THREE WEEKS! What do you mean there has been no trace?" Ramses yelled at three trackers.

"We've searched everywhere, and the Damonites, Cannibals, and Pirates haven't seen her either," one said, shaking.

"Is it possible she went home or even died?" asked another.

"No, she is not dead, and she can never return home," Ramses snapped, putting his hands on his hips. "Go fetch me the ten best bounty hunters in Qari and tell Quicksilver I wish to see him."

They bowed and left. He sat down on his throne and drummed his fingers on the arm. His thoughts were scattered when a voice said, "There you are! I've been looking everywhere for you! Have you been here at the fortress the whole time?"

"Aah, Carrion, nice to see you. Why have you been looking for me? I have been at Camp Steal for a week and the Low Road for a week. I came back here two weeks ago. Did you get my letter?"

"Yes. I sent Grinder for you because I got your letter, and I had the outlaw with her friend, but they escaped. I planned to execute the scorpion and let you come get the outlaw," Carrion replied.

Ramses stood up. "How did they escape? Do you know where they were headed?"

"She obviously was the brains. They permanently blinded one of my guards, Neiko's keeper, and slipped past my sentries. They got the key somehow. I can't believe she outwitted me! I'm sorry I let you down."

"I pay it no mind. Now I'm beginning to realize how smart she is, and it seems I will have to keep a close watch. Do you know where they were going?"

"Yes. She said they were going to Norak. If you were waiting on the Low Road, then she should've been there in two days at most. Do you suppose they took another route? What is she capable of? Could she already be there?"

"Well, she can go in any way she pleases because she is capable of traveling in any terrain, but she would have been spotted by one of my allies, so she hasn't traveled through the plains. She couldn't go around me because I had the blockade in the plains and close enough to the Tatowee Road to prevent any such movements. If she was there, then Vipra would have told me because she is an undercover spy to keep an eye on that annoying Attack Pack."

"Do you think she would be daring enough to attempt to go through the mountains? There are old roads that would take her to the Low Road, and maybe even right behind where you were set up."

Ramses rubbed his chin. "Hmm, well, it's possible. It would take several weeks or months to travel through them, and no one has been through them in thousands of years. In that case I will go ahead and send out the bounty hunters. They will find her when she comes out of them."

"Have you considered Quicksilver? He won't fail you if you want the job done right."

"Yes, I have. I told those addle-brained trackers to fetch him for me. I know he will find and catch her. His skills are unmatched, and he has things to trap a T-rex. He is very loyal to me, and I think I will promote him in time. Instead of being a mercenary, I will make him a Shadow Warrior; you know that has been his dream."

Carrion cocked his head. "You think that highly of him?"

"Why not? He has taken care of little tasks for me, and he does very well, second to me."

Carrion nodded. "Well, I must go, I hope you succeed."

"Don't worry. If everything else goes wrong, I'll do it myself," Ramses said rubbing his hands together smirking.

Neiko awoke, warm and wrapped in a fur blanket. Her limbs ached, and she was very groggy, yet she checked her surroundings. She saw she was in a house, and a candle flickered.

"So you're awake," said a kind voice in a High Alpine dialect that sounds much like Irish.

Neiko looked around to find the speaker. "Where am I?" she asked weakly.

A golden eagle lady came to her with a bowl of steaming soup, and Neiko shrank back in a little fear. "Oh, don't be frightened. I mean you no harm. Welcome to our village, Eagle Nest. How do you feel?"

"I feel terrible. I'm groggy, and my arms and legs hurt. How did I get here, and how long have I been out?"

"You have been asleep for four days. You must have seen a lot of action. My husband and his hunting party found you in the blizzard with your friend. Your friend is in the guestroom with a broken tail, and he hasn't yet awakened. Here, have some of this."

Neiko took the soup. "Thanks. My name's Neiko, what's yours?"

"My name's Talon, it's nice to meet you." Talon was made just like the vultures, but she was a golden eagle. She had on a green dress and a red shawl on her head.

"Who was it that I saw in the blizzard? How did y'all know I wasn't bad or whatever?"

"Oh, that was my husband, Warbeak. They have been tracking you ever since you came in the mountains. We assumed by your behavior that no one would come here unless they were in some type of serious trouble, and Ramses is a very good excuse. Oh, don't worry, he won't find you here."

Neiko sat up. "How'd you know I was running from him?"

"You talked in your sleep," Talon chuckled. "I've been taking good care of you and watching over you. Just rest yourself. Oh yes, I heard you say that Ramses is the Dark Pharaoh, and no one has ever known that."

Neiko groaned. "No one was supposed to find out about that. I wished I knew exactly why I know, but I really don't know how something I dreamed up could be so real."

"Don't worry, your secret won't leave this village. Warbeak says King MacPhearsome wants to see you when you get good and strong. He is a good eagle, and he wants to help just like everyone else."

"When do you suppose I should get moving? I know I'm safe here for a little while. I know I'm safe from everyone but Ramses. He has no patience, and I would bet fifty quartz he would do a covert Dark Pharaoh assault and kill everyone here and carry me off. Besides, I need to find the Attack Pack to get Quickstrike home and find my way back to Hawote."

"Oh, probably not for another month or two," Talon said gently. "A month! Am I really that sick?" Neiko shrieked.

"Please calm down. No, the snow hasn't let up, and it will take that long for it to melt; you need to be able to tell which way you should go, right?"

Neiko lay back down. "You're right. I'm sorry I yelled. I just want to go home, and I wish this nightmare was over. I would like to stay if I didn't have a Dark Pharaoh on my trail."

"Yes, I know. You need to eat your soup and rest. You need to be strong when you start your journey."

Neiko took a sip, and the soup felt good to her hungry stomach and her aching body. "Deer soup. This is good! I feel better already, and I'll have seconds because I'm starved."

Talon smiled. "I'm glad you like it. I have plenty, so don't hesitate to ask."

"So one's awake," said a male golden eagle.

"Hello, honey, meet Neiko," Talon said to Warbeak.

"Nice to meet you, well, I'm glad to see you're feeling well," said Warbeak as he took off his overcoat and leaned his spear against the wall.

"Alright, go check on the other one. Neiko needs to rest, so you can chitchat with her later," Talon said thoughtfully.

"Sure thing," he said as he hugged his wife, and patted Neiko's head gently. Neiko finished three bowls of soup and fell asleep.

- CHAPTER 39 -

A FEW DAYS PASSED AND Neiko was feeling refreshed; she got up and got dressed. "It's nice to feel like me again," she said to Talon.

Talon smiled. "I'm glad to know you're feeling better. Are you ready to meet with the king today?"

"I guess so. Why is he so anxious to meet with me?"

Talon shrugged. "I wished I knew. Who knows, he may even have the answers to all of your struggles, and he wants to help you find your way home."

"How's Quickstrike?"

"He's fine. His tail hurts, and he is quite tired, but by the time you leave he'll be as good as new. Oh, he won't be coming with you tonight."

"Oh well, at least he'll be fit when I'll need him; he has got me out of jams several times," Neiko said as she put on her headband.

"Well, I'm glad y'all use good teamwork. What is that symbol on your forehead on your headband?"

"Oh, it's a falcon, and it's one of the symbols of my tribe," Neiko replied pointing to the white beaded bird that stretched its wings over her forehead.

Talon gasped. "Could it be? No, no. MacPhearsome knows about it more than I do, and I don't need to fill your head about wild, crazy stories."

"What? Aw, c'mon, tell me. It seems lately that the imaginary is real and terrible."

"You can ask the king; he's a big expert on many of these old tales, and you can pump him for all of them because they may help you in your struggle against Ramses."

The door opened and Warbeak came in. "Well, it's time. Let's go, Neiko, and you can come too, dear."

The three came to the small castle of the king, and the friendly guards greeted them, led them into the throne room. MacPhearsome walked in and sat down. He was a large bald eagle man in purple and gold robes with a small crown on his head. "Well, now, I'm glad to see you feel well. Have a seat, we have much to discuss, lass," he said in a heavy High Alpine dialect.

"That we do, Great King, and I wish to ask about all of the tales you know," Neiko said bowing her head.

MacPhearsome smiled. "You don't have to use that title with me, but first things first. I promise we will get to the tales later, and I guess Talon told you I know a lot about them, I reckon."

"Yeah, and she said they may help me," Neiko said politely.

MacPhearsome held up his hand. "That they might. I know you are running from Ramses and you were taken from your homeland,

Hawote, and how I know you wish to return because you fear the worst from your enemies there. You came a long way to avoid your pursuer, and I am aware he has set many traps for you."

"Do you know how I may get home?" Neiko asked.

"I'm not sure, but you may ask our brethren, the Hawks, who live near Cougan's Bluff. They have a secret, and it may be a way, but don't bank on it."

"Do you know how I can get out of the mountains?"

"You should have taken the right fork, but the Almighty has sent you here for a reason and in our care. We know of the terrible secret you carry about Ramses, and no one else must know, especially him. Do you know why he's chasing you all over the tarnation?"

"Nope. I know I can't go back. What's at the end of this road, and is there anyone else that can help me?"

MacPhearsome rubbed his beak. "Yes there is. Our other brethren, the Falcons, are there on the road as you exit the mountains. They can help you, and you can go there for lodging and food. I will send word to King Greytail that you are coming, and there will be no doubt you will make it. I will tell him you aren't just another one of those pesky treasure hunters, yet I have no idea what's up there. We don't go that far because of unknown perils like the giant grizzly, wolves, and alike."

"Treasure hunters? How could they find anything here? I'd rather tangle with the local wildlife than Ramses because at least I have a better chance against them."

"Oh yes. They come here bugging us in their search for that stupid Pharaoh's treasure, and they think it may be here, but no one knows where it is. So they think it's here, and some speculate it's in Geezah, but no one knows where Geezah is. I know what you're thinking. It is not the secret of Cougan's Bluff."

"How can you be sure?"

"I know about Pharaohs, and they are not cave dwellers, and the Hawks wouldn't lie to their kin about something like that."

"Oh, I see. Can we get to the stories now please?" Neiko asked in an innocent child's way.

"Why certainly. Which ones would you like to hear?"

"Tell me anything that has to do with Geezah, the Pharaohs, and the Dark Pharaoh, and anything that Genghis Khan doesn't even know."

"Alright, I will start off with Geezah. It is said that the city was built on the ruins of the ancient city of Shadazar. Shadazar was the ancient capital of Qari, but it fell hard during the rule of King Silas. Silas was the keeper of many mysterious caverns that contained lore of the Dark Pharaoh written in an unknown tongue, and he hid the secrets during the rise of the Pharaohs. Rumi was a scholar on the Dark Pharaoh. It is said that he collected much information on him on his travels because he would ask the locals about any tales, and he wrote them down in a journal.Unfortunately, they are probably in Geezah."

"How did he go around and no one know who he was?"

"I suspect he was in disguise; no one knows the extent of his knowledge, and no one will ever know if he found the caverns. All of the Pharaohs are buried in tombs at Geezah except Thutmose, his followers, and his lot. Some say that the tomb of Thutmose and Anubis are somewhere inside of Skull Fort, and Anubis placed his father there after he built it, and he told Saber he would join his father in the day of his death. Saber did carry that out, but there is a graveyard with the rest of them, including Saber. The old ways and rituals died with Anubis. The Pharaohs of old are much different than they are today. They did not wear torn clothes, but only their armor and war helmets. Ramses is very much like the ancient ones, except he wears his armor all the time, and we know why; they could never possess any that well made, and we know why. The Pharaohs are said to have had a huge amount of treasure—the one I told you about earlier—which is probably in Geezah and well hidden. Did any of that help?"

"Yes it did. It seems Geezah is really important, and it contains many of the answers of the old days and all of that other info. I'd bet a Pharaoh's uncle that's where the books of black magic are. It seems like a good idea to try to find it, but I can't lollygag, and I have to get home."

"Do you realize that you are no longer safe from him wherever you go? He'll always hunt you. I am not saying this to scare you, but he has gone to great lengths to get you here and capture you. Hawote is in danger as well, but you are the one who will always be threatened by him," he said then looked at her forehead. "What is that symbol on your headband?"

"It's a falcon, and Talon had a fit about it earlier. It is a standard of my tribe, the Desert Storm Falcons, and she looked as if it was real important."

"Yes, it is quite important. 'One day there will come one from Earth with a falcon on their brow to find a liberator and uncover the secrets of the Dreaded One' is an old phrase my father always told me when I was going to sleep, but it seems to be true."

Neiko's eyes widened. "Earth is the name of my planet which is in the other universe, and I had no idea the falcon was so important, and we call ourselves the Desert Storm Falcons which we have always been called since we migrated from the west to where we are now. Also the desert is where we used to live before my forefathers traveled east. The falcon is one of my many personal symbols. It's really weird that y'all knew about me already."

"Not you personally. The Almighty has chosen you to be the Chosen One to expose the Dark Pharaoh; you have done that now, but your work isn't finished. You must find out about all of his secrets, and you must find the one to battle him and bring down his reign of terror. I believe you are going to have to watch your back because Ramses is a great peril, and the danger will increase if he ever gets wind of who you are."

Neiko giggled and clapped her hands together. "I knew it—I knew it! I warned him not to mess with me, and now it's *really* gonna bite him. I can't wait till I blow him out of the water, but he is a time bomb waiting to happen if people start suspecting him because of me, but I can't let that stop me. I have two universes to save along with my country, my family, and friends. It seems I just got warmed up because I've already started sucking up tons of info on him. Quickstrike and I sat down and figured out all of his schemes against the Pharaohs themselves."

"You are doing well, but you must be cautious, and I wouldn't get too comfortable just yet. You still need to find more. I would hate to see you face him in his old ways; you think he's bad now, but just wait."

"Well, you're more right than you realize, and that's when the ground falls from under your feet when you get too confident, but I do need to warn Lydia and the Attack Pack who he is because they face him all the time."

"Yes, but don't tell them everything just yet, and don't get any crazy ideas like trying to blackmail Ramses."

Neiko laughed. "Well, darn. That would've crossed my mind, but that would be a mistake. Well, that's that then, huh? I plan to go the rest of the way down the unexplored part of the road, and visit the Falcons on the way out. I'll go to Norak, wait for the Attack Pack, and visit the Hawks."

"Very good. I'll write letters to Greytail and Wartalon, and they will help. Be sure to tell them you are the one we've been waiting for. Wear your falcon proudly, and you will remain with Talon and Warbeak till I say it is safe for you to go"I thank you for all you've done, and I have two more questions. What will happen if Ramses finds out who I am, and where do I look to find someone that strong to battle him?"

MacPhearsome shrugged. "That you'll have to find out on your own; the Attack Pack is a wise choice for help. Go now and rest. You have much to think about and you must be ready. I will counsel with you on your departure, and I will give you the letters as well, good night."

"You too," she said as she shook his hand. Talon and Warbeak took her home that night.

- CHAPTER 40 -

THE SKULL BEARERS USHERED THE bounty hunters into the throne room. "These are the bounty hunters you requested for, Master," replied one of them.

"Splendid. Now—have you told them about their mission and the reward?" asked Ramses.

"No, we left that for you," replied a Skull Bearer.

"Alright. As you know, I seek the renegade Neiko Kidd, and she has eluded me thus far, so I am asking you to bring her to me alive. No annihilation."

"As you wish," replied Armos, an armadillo.

"What about her companion, the Attack Pack scorpion?" asked Raker, a velociraptor.

"You may do as you wish, but I'd like him dead. You can use him for sport. I don't care how you do it, but bring me his head in a box wrapped in his tail, and I will reward you well with anything you desire as long you do my bidding to the letter. Understood?"

They bowed, turned, and left. As soon as they dispersed, Quicksilver came in. He had on steel armor that was silver. His breastplate had a skull carved on it and his shoulders had spikes on them. His arms and legs were bare except for wrist guards, and plates on his thighs and shins, and they had spikes on them too. His helmet had a part that covered his face to his nose and was shaped kind of like a skull. The top was covered in spikes and two horns coming out. His hands were protected by spiked handguards. "Have you summoned me?" he asked.

"Guards, leave us," Ramses said waving his hand, and everyone scurried out, leaving them alone to converse. "Did you take care of that little task for me?"

"Yes, Dark Lord, Silas the Ninja is dead just as you commanded," Quicksilver replied in his creepy, even toned voice.

"Now I have a new task for you. I want you to bring the outlaw to me alive. Do you know which I speak of?"

"Yeah, I know. Neiko is the one you seek, and what is your bidding for Quickstrike?"

"Kill him. Do it any way you like, but remember, I want Neiko alive. Understand?"

"Loud and clear; is it possible she could be dangerous to you and your secrets, the ones only I know?"

"Maybe not, but if she does know, then that is just another reason why I want her brought in quickly. I know you will not fail. Only return if you succeed, and if someone stops you, report to me, then I will get her myself and you will aid me if I desire. That will be all."

Quicksilver bowed. "I understand all, Dark Master. I shall return." He turned and left.

Several months had passed in the mountains, and the two were ready to start their journey. "Good luck to you both. I hope you will come back one day," MacPhearsome said as he shook her hand and gave her the letters.

"You know, I have a lot of visiting to do after I get out of this mess. Y'all aren't the only ones who want a visit," Neiko said, teasing.

"Good luck to you both," Talon said as she hugged Neiko. The two left the village waving back to the entire village as they watched them leave.

"You know, I kinda hate leaving them," Quickstrike said. "They were so kind."

"Yeah I know, but we've got a lot of work to do," she said as they walked on the road.

"Man, I can't believe you're so important. I wonder if Ramses saw this coming."

"I wouldn't think so, but I really am getting antsy about what he has waiting for me."

"Please don't! That gives me the chills just thinking about it," Quickstrike said, cringing. Suddenly there was a rustle in the bushes. "What was that?" asked Quickstrike, worried.

Neiko quickened her pace. "I don't know, but it sure was big—let's get a move on." They walked a short distance, and there was a chasm up ahead. The only way across was a rickety, old rope bridge that had planks of wood for footing. Neiko tested the wood carefully, and she waved her hand at her frightened companion. "Come on."

"Are you crazy? This thing's as old as the dickens, and I could fall through! Besides I hate heights!" Quickstrike wailed.

"Don't worry, I tested it. Indian secret—don't look down and shift your weight. Some of the middle ones may be weaker."

"Oh, that's comforting," he grumbled.

"Okay, now just stay to the sides, hold on to the rope rungs, and always keep a hold on something," Neiko said as she started to cross.

"Uh-uh, I am not that brave," he shouted as she made it all the way across.

"C'mon, scaredy bug!"

Quickstrike looked down at the dizzying drop, the sharp, jagged rocks and cliffs, and thousands of feet down was a raging river. He shivered, and cold sweat broke out of his hard scorpion skin and his scales. Suddenly a deep growl came from behind him, and he spun around. The largest grizzly that anyone had ever seen towered over him as it stood on its hind legs. It growled, and Quickstrike was so scared he froze, and the bear dropped to all fours and came toward him. "Oh no!" he groaned in terror.

"Across the bridge! It's your only chance!" Neiko shouted to him. Without thinking, Quickstrike ran like lightning across, and the bear was on his heels. They reached the middle and the bridge swayed greatly due to their combined weight. Quickstrike safety got past the center, but once the bear stepped on the old wood, the planks gave way to its enormous weight. The bear fell through the bridge and plummeted down into the chasm while Quickstrike made safely across.

"That was too close," he said as he breathed hard. "I knew you could do it," Neiko said, smiling.

"Let's keep going, shall we?" said Quickstrike trying to stop his body from shaking. They walked for hours, and the ground sloped upward more, and then in about an hour it started going downward. In the setting sun Neiko could see the shape of a nearby city. "Could that be the Falcon city?" asked Neiko with hope in her voice. Neiko pulled out her binoculars, but all she could see was the overcast shadow. No one was stirring. "Hmm, that's weird. No one's moving; it looks as if it has had its better days, and it's sitting on a plateau on the highest peak. MacPhearsome said the Falcons lived on the lower peaks, so let's go check it out."

"Uh, Neiko, do you think we took a wrong turn?" asked Quickstrike worried.

"No, there were no turns," Neiko shrugged.

"Just checking," Quickstrike said, gulping.

"Let's go see what this place is, and we'll spend the night," Neiko said as she started to walk.

"Great," Quickstrike said uneasily as he got himself ready for any unknown perils.

"What's with you?" asked Neiko, annoyed.

"I dunno. I have a weird feeling about this place. It's so quiet it's creepy."

"Aww, see, look there's a sign." She studied it, but the carved words were worn off; there was a stag beetle carved on it, and twenty feet away were tall obelisks and an old battered gate that was once a fancy entrance. "A beetle? Weird name, so I guess this is Beetleville," Neiko shrugged.

"Uh, no. The stag beetle is the Pharaoh symbol. This place might have been destroyed by them."

The two friends walked past the obelisks and the gate and saw the rubble within. More obelisks lay broken on the ground, and elaborately decorated buildings were smashed, and the once colorful paint was faded. Statues stood without heads and for some only the feet remained. Sphinxes of all kinds were worn by time and pieces were broken off. A pyramid in the distance still stood, but there were holes in the sides. Some buildings still stood, and others were partly standing.

Neiko walked over to a headless statue and found an inscription. "Fidel IV," Neiko read aloud. She walked to another. "Thutmose I." Neiko walked to one with just feet. "Seti X," she read the name.

Quickstrike saw three without their torso and up. "Imenhotep II, Sesotris XII, and Ra II. These are weird names for falcons."

Neiko rubbed her chin and she saw two whole statues of two birdmen. One was a falcon and the other was a hawk. They wore a head cloth, a long kilt, and robes. The head cloth was fixed with a band with a stag beetle in the center. Neiko bent down and cleared the dust from the pedestal from the falcon. She blew into it and a cloud of dust went into the air. Neiko gazed into the letters. "Rumi," Neiko said as she gazed at the proud stance of the man, as he held his his shield at his side and his sword high.

Quickstrike read the name of the hawk. "Xerxes," he said puzzled.

"You can tell these are Pharaohs. They dress like the ones from my world, but they have a tad more style. So this is what the great Rumi looks like," she said then it hit her. "Do you know where we are? We've just stumbled on Geezah!"

"Wow! This place is kinda cool. I suppose you wanna look around, but can we sleep first? We have plenty of time to explore tomorrow; besides, this place gives me the creeps at night."

Neiko built a fire, and they slept under the stars that night.

– CHAPTER 41 –

THE NEXT MORNING NEIKO woke up refreshed and ready to explore. "I'm gonna explore every crack and crevice; I don't want to miss anything because there is said to be a lot of cool stuff in here."

"Where do you want to start?"

"We'll start in these other buildings first, and then I want to explore that pyramid. I wonder what they used it for."

They searched all of the wreckage of the smaller buildings, but found nothing. "Hmm, I think all of these were homes, but I wonder what the First Pharaoh stayed in."

"How can you tell?"

"Well, there are a lot of broken pots, beds, and all that stuff, and that one place had a fireplace."

"Good point. Now I guess you want to explore the pyramid."

"Right." They walked to the monument itself. Several obelisks surrounded it and there was a great door in between two sphinxes. The door was faded by age; they tried to pull it, but it wouldn't budge. "I guess it's rusted, but what's this?" she asked as she spotted a camouflaged beetle on the door after searching it after several minutes. She just barely touched it, and it went in with a clank. The door rumbled as locks from the inside loosed and it swung open with a groan. "Wow! That's really awesome, now let's go inside."

The holes in the side of the pyramid allowed some of the light to enter, and she could see pictographs on the walls. Some were smeared with dirt. In the floor before them was a mosaic of colorful stones that formed a stag beetle, and there were pillars that had pictures on them as well. They could see a hall in front of them, but it was dark. Neiko got out her flashlight and turned it on when they entered the darkness of the hall. She whipped her flashlight around seeing carvings on the stone walls, and a mouse scurried in front of them. They entered a large room. She fanned the light around and found many shelves carved on the walls and something shiny caught her eye. Neiko walked up closer and there lay the remains of a dead Pharaoh.

The Pharaoh lay there dressed in his clothes with his jewels; his shield and mace lay over him. His name was written in gold letters on the slab that separated him from the one below him. *Thutmose I*, it read. The room was filled with remains of millions of the dead. "I wonder which of these are the older ones," asked Neiko.

"Thutmose I is one of the older ones, I think Ra I came after Xerxes." Neiko walked to the left from where Thutmose lay. At the very top in the furthest to the left lay Ra. "They buried them in order, but the burial columns start with Ra, but where are Rumi and Xerxes, who came before him? The pyramid is the burial ground for Pharaohs, and all of 'em for that matter. The ones in my world would build something this big just for one, but they quit very soon because it took twenty years to build one."

"Boy, that was one bad drag. Let's go outside, look, and see if there's something we missed." They exited the pyramid and looked around. Neiko looked behind the pyramid and noticed a building they didn't notice before.

"Wow, look at that!" Neiko said as they found a building that was untouched by the assaulting Marauders. The building had steps going up to an open door and two griffins stood at the base of the steps. They approached the building and took in the overpowering grandeur of it. Even though it was waxed old by time, it was still majestic. They sprinted up the stairs and entered the door. Inside were tattered tapestries and an old faded chair that was a throne. Marble floors and pillars were covered with color. They walked and explored all of the halls and found the bedrooms, baths, ballrooms, and dining halls.

"I think this is the palace of the First Pharaoh. Boy, life here was pretty fabulous. Well now what? We searched everything, but we haven't found anything that you said may be here."

Neiko sighed as they entered the throne room, but then a door they hadn't noticed before caught their eye. They ran and opened it. A desk was set before them, and a skeleton was slumped over it with a quill still stuck in his hand. A book lay open just in front of him along with a stack of another three. They looked around and saw that it was a library. Neiko walked over and looked at the book. She blew off the dust and saw a list of names written in the English-like language of Qari: *Anubis I, Saber I, Osiris I, Menes I, Tutankhamen II, Re I.* They looked at it then at each other. "This is the Pharaoh birth log, and did you notice that everyone's name is in here except Ramses I? We just found more proof that Ramses is not an ordinary Pharaoh. I think they have all of them in categories like a split off in the family tree. I wonder what kind of other names they have. She flipped through the pages and read the names: *Siberius I, Bengal I, Cobras III* . . .

"Let's look at those other three books," Quickstrike suggested. Neiko opened the first one. She flipped through the pages, and she found pictures of each Pharaoh and their accomplishments, and it was in the same order as the previous book. "Who is Tutankhamen II? You mentioned his name after Menes I."

Neiko flipped to the next to the last page and found a picture of him and showed it to Quickstrike; it was a picture of Tut. "Tutankhamen II is also known as Tut."

"I wonder who Tutankhamen I is."

Neiko flipped and found him toward the middle. "He is just like Tut, but he's cleaner, and he was a First Pharaoh," she said as she skimmed the page of his life and accomplishments, and looked at his picture. She looked in the other two books. One was the list of all the First Pharaohs from Rumi to Osiris, and the last was the names of every Pharaoh that ever lived in alphabetical order. "Haven't you noticed something? There is no mentioning of Ramses anywhere even though this guy lived to record the birth of Re."

"What about the one with all the names listed?"

Neiko turned to the R's. "Nope, and check this out. There has never been a Pharaoh named Ramses, and they haven't named a single one in any form or fashion. There were twelve by a similar name on Earth. They spelled their name differently than old Chromy, but we don't have Pharaohs anymore; they didn't rule in Hawote. I can't believe this, not even a smidgen close, and isn't that ironic?"

"I know! It seems that 'Ramses' is a little too upper class or something, but they had no idea it was the name of the *Dark* Pharaoh, and what does the name mean anyway?"

"I have no clue, but we are getting somewhere. We thought these would be incomplete, but there's still more to find, and I have a feeling the answers are in this library."

"We'll let's see what we can find. What are we looking for anyway?"

"Rumi's journal on Ramses and the volumes of Pharaoh black magic or anything else along that line." They looked at each of the books and skimmed through them, but there was nothing on what they were searching for.

"We looked though every book but found nothing; we haven't checked the desk," said Quickstrike.

Neiko looked all over it, in the drawers, and every compartment, but nothing. "Well, that's just great, I ain't leaving till I find that journal and those books," she said as she leaned against a flat wall. Neiko didn't notice a hidden button, and she leaned on it by accident. The button went in, and the wall gave way; she toppled into a secret tunnel. She slid in a sightless abyss with her backpack on, and she screamed as the ride got faster.

— CHAPTER 42 —

NEIKO PLUMMETED INTO UNKNOWN DARKNESS and slid in an abyssal joyride. Suddenly the ride stopped, and she toppled on a floor, rolled, and collided with a wall. She then heard Quickstrike hit the floor just a few feet away. "Neiko, are you here?" he asked.

"Yeah, what a rush," she replied.

"Where are we anyway?"

"I dunno."

"Turn on the light, will ya? I can't see a thing."

"Sure thing, just as soon as I can find my flashlight," she said as she groped in her backpack. Neiko found it and turned it on. The wall behind her was a low platform and she used it to hoist herself; her fingers brushed something hard and dry. "Man, what stinks?" she said as she turned around and was face to face with a skeleton; she jumped.

"What or who is that?"

"It's Rumi, and Xerxes is right beside him," she said as she read the names engraved in the stone and filled with golds and jewels, "We found their tomb!"

The two just lay there in their garb and they had their swords and shields placed on them just like the others. Neiko whipped her flashlight in the tomb and she found a passageway. She found a torch on the wall. She got it down, dug out the matches, lit it, and put the flashlight and matches back into her backpack. With her newfound and better light, she explored the walls of the tomb. She found pictures that showed the life of the two, but in the midst of the pictures was a picture of a shadowy form. She walked over to it to get a better look and Quickstrike followed her. "What on earth is that?" he asked.

She examined it closely, and saw the familiar shape; the red eyes came out of the figure's terrible stance. "It's the Dark Pharaoh. So this is what people saw, and you can tell it's Ramses. See, you can tell. Paint black on his armor and what do you see?"

Quickstrike looked at it as he rubbed his head. "I believe you're right, and I wonder if he used to wear black instead of chrome."

Neiko rubbed her chin. "No, it doesn't look like it. Genghis Khan said that he has the ability to change his form, and he said that guy saw a form that was dark even though light shined on it; metal emits light, so he doesn't have a different suit. Let's go on shall we?" The two turned, left the tomb, and walked down the hall. The hall walls were barren with a musty smell of a cave after years and years of closure. There was a room to their right, and there was a glitter. They looked into the room and there lay the treasure of the Pharaohs. Gold, silver, jewels, crowns, and countless rings, earrings, and necklaces littered the floor. The two friends gazed at it, then they turned and left to explore the rest of the hall. They then walked into another room, but this time it was a dead end. There was a great stone desk with a shelf just overhead that was carved into the stone. A large chair was pushed underneath, and a small candle lay on the desk. Neiko picked up the candle and lit it with the torch, placed the candle on the desk, and handed the torch to Quickstrike. One solitaire book lay in the desk covered with dust and cobwebs. She scraped off the webs and opened the book. It was written in the ancient language that was just like Greyhawk. Neiko was able to read it, but she had to read it aloud to Quickstrike.

"This is a record of my findings on the roads I have traveled to find out all of the mysteries of Sisper-Bijou... —Rumi." Neiko read aloud. "This is it! Let's see what he found out." She flipped through the pages and skimmed looking for anything they didn't know.

"Found anything new?"

"Oh yeah! Let's see, The Dark Pharaoh engages war against the mortal beings but not against God. Spiritual warfare is only for Satan, and we all know Satan wants to do in Yahweh. Ramses is smart in not trying to overthrow Great Spirit because he knows he can't, and it's not possible to invade heaven while God's around, and that's always."

"So we know that he wants to rule all mortal beings, but until when?" Neiko read on. "Till the coming of Christ and only Yahweh knows when that is, and it also records there was a Bible written by Great Spirit himself for this universe. No one has ever found it; the Bible is taught by mouth, and Great Spirit has guided other men to write copies, but the original is lost. Ramses wishes to dominate both universes, but Yahweh has stopped him."

"Does it say anything about his strengths and weaknesses?"

Neiko flipped the page. "He is not as powerful as Yahweh, and that means he is not all knowing, all powerful, or everywhere at once like Great Spirit is. He *does* have the ability to see into the future, go anywhere he desires, and all the other stuff we know already. His power at full strength is one thousand times weaker than God, but that is way too much power for a mortal to handle, and we can't imagine Great Spirit at full strength. I bet The Great Spirit is not even trying at that measurement in this book. It also says that the Dark Pharaoh also possessed a large purple sphere called the Dark Pharaoh's Eye or the heart of Sisper-Bijou. It has a picture of it, and it is the Eye of Osiris; now we know he lost it and why he is so anxious to get it back."

"So, you're saying that we are trying to take something that is his? Have you found anything about what will happen to someone who marries him?"

Neiko flipped. "Here it is," she said and started reading and her mouth fell open. "Oh gosh."

"Is it bad?"

"Oh yeah—listen. Anyone wed to Sisper-Bijou will encounter the worst bondage ever known. When the vows are said and sealed with the kiss, her fate is sealed with it. She becomes immortal, and she will possess powers similar to his, but she cannot use her powers against him and is subject to him. He will isolate her from everyone, and she will remain with him in his kingdom till the end of time. Yikes, my idea would have been to marry him and give him a taste of his own medicine, but it wouldn't even faze him. Oh, it also says that they will be linked in heart, mind, and soul. She will not be able to hide. Parts of their spirits will go into each other, and he can find her wherever she goes. Also, she is bound to him in death. If someone finds a way to kill him, then she will die with him."

"Man, Lydia's in bad trouble."

"Not really, there is someone in worse shape, if he ever finds someone who fits this criteria."

"What are you talking about?"

"There are two love stages. Level one is the least severe and Lydia's life is an example. Level two has never been reached, and it is dangerous. Level two is known when Ramses shows extremely irritable behavior to anyone else, and if the girl's name is mentioned or if any of his behaviors concerning her is spoken of, he gets paranoid, and he may even kill someone. He is also extremely secretive about it; he may even dream about her so much, he may be in La La Land so much he may forget he's even alive. If there is someone he loved in the level one and finds a level two, then the level one may even face death because he will turn on her and the love he felt will turn to hate. There will be only one person that will ever encounter level two, which is true love, but this will destroy the beloved's life because he will stop at nothing till she is his completely."

"Whoa! That is really bad, and has he ever found a love like that?"

"Hmm," she said as she turned the page. "In fact, he has. Oh no, it's somebody from Earth! Let's see, it says he loved her from the day he saw her when he was only three days old—however long ago that was. He looked into the window of the future, but she could not be reached, so he had to find another, but no one knows her name. She's probably dead by now, if not, I hope it's not anyone I know. If she was ever reached, then Lydia would be in big trouble and may even end up dead. If this person got married, then her husband's dead meat, but we still don't know how old he is, and we could figure how long he's dreamed about her."

"We still don't know where he came from, and how did he acquire that much power, and where do we look to find someone to face him?"

"Beats me, and that's all, but that helps a whole lot! Wait, what's this?" she said as she found something protruding out of the back. She pulled it out, and it was a map. Many strange landforms were on it and a mean looking idol. The names were written in some strange language. Neiko examined it carefully. "I know this! Me and Monchiska wrote in these symbols all the time in coded messages to hide important info from Crackedskulls, and these are Ancient Greek letters. I have a decoder in the front of one of my logbooks that I brought that has all of our secret coded Intel in it. This right here in big letters looks like the name of the place," she said as she pulled out the book and turned to the front. Each letter had its capital, lowercase, and English equivalent. The title was Ερα∝τηγιν. "I'll decode and see what I get—it may not work, and it may not say anything at all." She jotted each letter down on a blank sheet and it read Eramthgin. "Wait, 'eramthgin' is Greyhawk that simply means 'nightmare'. I wonder what this place is. I'll decode a few more and see what kind of place this is." She looked to the idol and it read ςυλ–Καρ Ιδολ, and it decoded to Vul-Kar Idol. Other names were: Μουνταινσ οφ Μαλιχε, Λακε οφ Λαχιωιουσνεσσ, ανδ ςολχανο οφ ςενγεανχε. These were decoded as: Mountains of Malice, Lake of Lasciviousness, and Volcano of Vengeance.

"What names! That place is a nightmare! The name is the only thing that's not in English. Who writes in that crazy stuff, and is that place real? What does it have to do with Ramses because it's in that journal, and where did he find something like that?"

"All he says about it is that he found it in Eht Dnalsi in a historian's shop, and he bought it. It seems no one has been able to read the names. I think he assumed it has something to do with him, but no one is sure. It looks like a place he would hide out at. There is said to be some secret caves in the ruins of Shadazar, so let's see if there is a secret lever or something in here."

"What are those books up there?" asked Quickstrike as he looked at the shelf.

"It's the Twelve Volumes of Pharaoh Black Magic! I gotta take a look, then let's snoop around, and see if we can find those caves. I think they will have more of the answers we're looking for," Neiko said as she took down Volume Six; the books were also written in the ancient language that she read aloud. "Time travel," she said and turned the page. "Fireball. Wow! I gotta see volume twelve. "Transfer spell, and specialty crystal—I wonder what that means? Let's look and see if there's a secret passage in here. Once I find everything, I'm gonna record them in this blank logbook.

"Why won't you take everything with you?"

"I don't want Ramses to destroy the evidence or find these books—remember we heard that he was looking for these. I'll only take this map just to be safe, and I want to do some more research on it."

"You must make sure he never finds out where you found everything because he will finish what the Marauders started and maybe loot the treasure. Who knows, he may even find what's left of Shadazar; that is, if we find it."

"I agree, and I won't record where I found it just in case he ever finds this book. Let's go ahead and look around, and let's be careful. I don't want to fall into the dark again."

The two looked around the room carefully for quite a while but found nothing. While Neiko was thinking as she walked around. She stubbed her toe on something. "Wo! What in the—" she bent down and looked at a box that was partly buried. "Help me dig this up."

"What is it?"

"Some box," she said as they started to dig it up in the soft, dusty dirt.

After she dug it up, she used her tomahawk to break the lock. She opened it and found a sticklike object and an armlet. The stick-like object was open at both ends and it had gold engravings on it. It was made of black onyx, and had a large ruby on the side. The armlet had three jewels on top, a diamond, a ruby, and an emerald.

"What's this?" asked Quickstrike handing her a piece of paper and a belt. The belt was thin with a buckle depicting an eagle with red eyes carrying a skull with long, curved fangs. The eagle was gold, and the skull was jade with ruby eyes. The belt was black leather with gold designs, and it had a hilt for the strange object. Neiko slipped it on with a perfect fit, then took the paper from Quickstrike.

"This says this stick is a lightning sword, a magical armlet, and the belt is magic too. It also says what they do, but Rumi hasn't been able to activate the lightning sword. These are Dark Pharaoh weapons, and I bet Platinum Puss is missing these."

"What do they do?"

"The sword has blades made of lightning coming out of these holes, and it also throws lightning bolts. The armlet has magic stones. The diamond throws ice; the ruby fire and the emerald controls water and air; no one knows what the belt does, but it carries the lightning sword. I wonder how this sword works," Neiko said as she tried different techniques but no avail. Then she accidentally moved the ruby upward, and the blades shot out of both sides. She tested it by spinning it, and she found it was an easy one to fight with. Suddenly, she pressed the ruby, a bolt shot out, hit the box, and turn it into splinters. She hit the wall with the blade, and it cut a chunk out with the greatest of ease. Neiko moved the ruby back, and the blades went back in.

"Wow! I bet that will come in handy, and you can fight with DP weapons. Neiko, you're amazing!"

"Not really—it seemed natural and just came to me—I don't know how. I like it so much that I think I'll keep it. Finders keepers; losers weepers. I wonder what other weapons he has," she said as she put it in the hilt, strapped on the belt, and put on the armlet.

"Well, we found Dark Pharaoh weapons but no secret passage."

"Hmm," she said then she looked under the shelf where the volumes were. "I think I found something," she said as she pressed the button, and the desk moved then there was a secret passage. Neiko grabbed the torch and walked into the passage, and she was blinded by a reflection of light.

- CHAPTER 43 -

AFTER HER EYES ADJUSTED to the glare, the two friends could see there was a cavern that was full of perfect crystals. They were in all shapes, sizes, and colors and they came out of the walls, floor, and ceiling. The beauty was spellbinding. "Wow! If I found this in Hawote, then I'd be rich! This is a rock collector's dream come true!"

"Yeah, but didn't you say that there were writings about Ramses somewhere in here? I wonder where the ruins of Shadazar are," Quickstrike rambled.

"Somewhere in here, I guess. I think we're close. Let's keep walking and look at the walls. If there are any branch-offs, then we'll split up. If you find anything, then come looking."

"Actually, I'd rather stick together, so we won't get separated."

"Good idea, well, I like that idea better too," she said as they journeyed deep into the caverns. They walked and looked at the walls, but all they found were arrangements and shapes created by crystal; they gleamed and sparkled when the light hit them like multicolored diamonds. Luckily for them, there were no branch-offs, and the caverns appeared as if they were carved into the crystal. New formations were growing in the hewn walls. Neiko found several broken pieces on the cavern floor; she picked them up and slipped them into her pocket.

"Look, there's an exit up ahead," said Quickstrike as he saw a break in the glamour and a darkened cave. As they entered the door, darkness overtook them and there were ruins just ahead. "We found what's left of ancient Shadazar!"

"Yeah, and we have an underground lake to cross. I wonder what's on the other side."

"I dunno, but I've noticed the further we go in, the further we go back in time, so that could mean the writings are probably after the lake. How do we get across?"

"There's a boat right there." They climbed into the boat, and Neiko got the oars and began to paddle while Quickstrike carried the torch. They could see broken columns and the remains of a bridge that possibly was a shortcut long ago towering over them. She kept paddling, and then they saw a waterfall just ahead. Neiko paddled around it and parked the boat on the bank of the hidden cavern. When they entered the hallway, there were pictures and writings. "Neiko, look! We found it!"

"Hmm," she said as she looked at the letters which were surprisingly in the alphabet of her tribe. "Well, it's written in English, but it is written in the alphabet of my tribe. This will be easy for me to translate."

"That's good. So, what does it say?"

Neiko looked at the battling figures and the dark, shadowy form of the Dark Pharaoh fighting and slaying them. She ran her finger under the letters as she read. "This is talking about something called the Good Pharaohs. It says that Great Spirit created powerful beings called Pharaohs to protect the universe from evil. They possessed magic that Great Spirit gave them, but he made them to be his children—kind of like us. They protect this universe while he created angels to protect mine. There were few evil spirits floating in this one, so Great Spirit told them to find and destroy them. There was one he created to be the best and most powerful, but something happened to him. Sometime after Satan fell, he somehow was turned on his brethren and slayed many. He developed the desire to dominate the mortals, so then he called himself the Dark Pharaoh. Yahweh sent the remaining Good Pharaohs after him to stop him and banish him to limbo, but he destroyed his pursuers. Great Spirit hasn't given up, and he's all under control, so I'm part of this plan. I wonder if he is trying to turn him back."

"His evil hasn't even begun yet. I think turning him back is a lost cause."

"Yeah," Neiko sighed and read on further. "Ooh, check this out, he looks at the Pharaohs as sons and Pharaohesses as daughters. So he looks at Ramses as being a wayward son, and sending him to limbo is like he's sending Ramses to his room and grounding him even if he was turned against his will or something..."

"Yeah, that makes sense. That means that they have been around before The Almighty created mortals."

"It also says that he made them before the universes had form, and Great Spirit only knows how long ago that was."

"Phew! What about that one?"

"It's about the 'Chosen One'. Okay, it says that the chosen one will be from Earth, and he will wear a falcon on his brow. He will dwell in two lands at the same time, and will be a part of a hidden civilization. He will be great in both places and be a child of God. He will be unusual, and he will know about this universe in play; what seems to be imagined will be real. He will also possess a toy that looks like Sisper-Bijou as mortals have seen, and the great understanding of our world and the Dreaded One will be implanted in his mind by Great Spirit himself. Toys of good and evil people he will also have, and no others will know whence the ideas cometh. That's me to a T. The prophet that wrote this uses 'he' because he didn't know if it would be a boy or girl, and that's how they put it in the Bible in distinguishing anyone. I wondered where those ideas came from, and I also wondered why I would sit down and go on adventures with you guys and with my cousin a lot, and every now and then, not much, go with y'all alone. So now I know why I know."

"Wow! Now, what's other one say?"

Neiko looked at it and read. "Oh, man! This is really important too! This says why a beloved is so important to Ramses. Everybody immortal or mortal except Satan wants to have someone. It's for personal gain, and it has some merit too. Great Spirit told him he would punish him for his wickedness by sending him to limbo, not hell, for all eternity. There he will live in solitude in a place of nothing. If he can ever find one to love, and she loves him in return, and she gives him true love's kiss on the day of marriage, then he can return to heaven at the end of time with her. However, he may not use any type of trance or memory erase to do so, but anything else is acceptable. This must the the plan to turn him back to the good side, but the clock is ticking. If time's up, then he's up the creek. He'll be dreaming about the woman he couldn't have on Earth for all eternity in a place of nothing."

"Sounds dangerous—why doesn't The Almighty just throw him in hell?"

"I suppose out of sheer mercy, and maybe it couldn't hold him since Pharaohs are stronger than angels. Yahweh doesn't really want to condemn anyone except Satan and his angels. I have a feeling limbo is more powerful place than hell is. I don't really know, but that's all. We've found everything we need to know, so the combatant we need to look for is a Good Pharaoh, if there is one."

"What about a Pharaohess?"

"I don't know either a Pharaoh or Pharaohess will do."

"So in that case that girl from Earth is his only hope, but can he make it with anyone else?"

"Nope, so basically he's finished, unless he finds her, and if she still lives. The two who know are Great Spirit and Ramses, but neither will tell who she is, so I have to find out on my own. C'mon, let's make tracks." The two walked on further, and they entered into more crystal caverns, where the crystals were larger and more exquisite. They then entered a room that had a circle of huge white quartz stalagmites; in the center was a quartz podium, and on it laid a book with a gold cover. Neiko ran to it and the title was written with gemstones: *The Holy Bible*. Neiko opened it and inside it read: "Here are my words so that ye may know me and live likewise. Feast and live on my words of truth.—God."

"You just found the Bible that The Almighty wrote himself!"

Neiko turned to Genesis 1:1, "In the beginning The Almighty created the heavens and the earth. It matches exactly except for what you guys call Great Spirit! In this universe Yahweh wrote the Bible by his own pen, but in ours he spoke to men who wrote down his words. I hope that everything is in check here, and if not, I'll take this and give it to someone who can teach."

"Well I guess we'll find out, so let's take it with us because people have been searching for it."

"Okay," she said as she closed it and placed it in her backpack. "It's a dead end, so there must be a way out." The pair searched the room carefully for hours and testing every rock and checking every formation for hidden switches or doors.

"How about this lever?" asked Quickstrike as he pointed to an amethyst lever that was cleverly hidden on a wall of purple stones. The lever had a perfect crystal handle with a straight crystal shaft. They had passed the lever several times during the search.

"Bingo, nice work. I was beginning to think we were going to be stuck here or have to go back," she said with relief as she pulled it down. The wall lifted up in a secret door and sunlight shone in. The two shielded their eyes and walked outside. As they left, the door closed and disappeared behind them since it was a cleverly hidden entrance that was made to look like the landscape. They walked down the steep slope for thirty minutes, and they could see a town just below them; it was about two miles away downhill. Relieved to have found civilization, they traveled at mind-boggling speed the rest of the way and entered the village.

The Falcon gatekeeper saw them approaching. "Can I help you?" he asked, puzzled, in his Low Mountain dialect that sounded much like Scottish.

"Yeah, we're the ones from Eagle Nest, and here's a letter from MacPhearsome," Neiko said as she took off her backpack and fished out the letter to King Greytail.

The keeper read it carefully, and when he finished, he smiled. "Sorry about my rudeness, but the security is tight nowadays because of those gold hungry fiends. What took you so long? Well, come with me and I'll let you speak with Greytail, welcome to Falcon Ridge. My name's Yuri and I'm pleased to meet you," he said politely.

"Name's Neiko and this is Quickstrike," she said as she shook hands with Yuri.

"Aah, one from the Attack Pack and you're the outlaw, and this says you're the Chosen One. Welcome, I bet you'd like to have some rest after you speak with Greytail. The longer I babble, the longer you have to wait."

Neiko giggled. "Okay, lead on." Yuri opened the gate and led them inside.

- CHAPTER 44 -

NEIKO AND QUICKSTRIKE WALKED behind Yuri, and they could see the small castle in front of them. Falcons stopped what they were doing to greet the newcomers. The two friends were overwhelmed by the hospitality as they walked on. "They aren't afraid of us," Quickstrike said.

"They know you're coming because a few Eagles came and told us you were coming. The only ones I'd let in are you two; they told us the good news of you, Neiko," Yuri replied.

They entered the palace, and Greytail sat on his throne waiting. "Nice you could make it. What took you?" he said in a heavy Low Mountain accent.

"Took a slight detour in Geezah, and I found everything, including the Bible The Almighty wrote personally," she said as she took it out of her backpack and gave it to Greytail.

Oohs and Aahs filled the room. "You are amazing. You have found out all in such a short time. Well, no one else must know what you have found or where you found it. I hear you will want to warn Lydia and the Attack Pack, but the information you give them must be limited. I will send word to the Eagles of your progress. You have done so well, and now all you need to do is find your way home. Once you get there, you mustn't tell anyone of your importance or about your adventures here, unless Ramses proposes a threat to the well-being of your world along with yourself."

"Gotcha. Has he still got that reward on my capture?"

"Oh, that. He would never give that up. It's all one large trap. If a civilian is that dumb—and many are—to turn you in and ask for that idiotic diamond, he would slay them without thinking."

"From what I gather, I seem to be extremely important to him, but I don't think he knew anything about me being the one to expose him. I also know he loved someone from my world, but I wonder who she was—is. Do you think the Chosen One and the mysterious woman could be the same person?"

Greytail pondered. "Well, I'm not very sure, but it is possible that the Chosen One could suffer that peril as well, but that would be a lethal combination. If this were so, and then you would suffer in his hands after you bring him down, so be careful. What are your plans from here?"

"I plan to go to Norak and wait for the Attack Pack; they will take me to the Hawks."

"Good plan. Well, you must get some rest, and we will send you in the morning. I wish you well."

"Before I leave, I have two questions. Who will I stay with?"

"Oh, well, I—"

Before he could finish, Yuri volunteered. "They can stay with me!"

Greytail chuckled. "Alright, that answers one but ask away."

"Where do I find a Good Pharaoh?"

Greytail cocked his head. "I have no idea. I didn't even know there was such a thing. I'm sorry. I wish I could help you there, but that is all I can do for the moment. Have a good night," he said as he saluted them, and Yuri took them to his house that night. They bathed, ate, and talked with him, his wife, and their ten children; they slept well that night.

Early the next morning, they left the Falcons on their long trek to Norak. She left them as they waved good-bye and took note of their invitation for her return soon. "Well, we're almost to the Low Road again, and it should be smooth sailing from there," Neiko said, relieved.

"You hope," said Quickstrike, reminding her.

They walked for a couple hours down the smooth, sloping road, and they came to another plank and rope bridge, but this one was in better shape. "Yuri said that this bridge is the halfway point. Can you cross it?"

"Yeah, this will be a cinch after the last experience," said Quickstrike, and they both laughed as they crossed the bridge. They quickened their pace, and the remaining time was only an hour. They approached a sign that clearly stated: *Low Road ½ Mile*. The two ran until they were safely on the Low Road once more. The pair walked and cut up for several miles, but then they saw a man twenty feet in front of them, and his armor glistened in the sun. The pair looked at him. It was not Ramses, but he began to charge. Neiko got her walking stick ready and Quickstrike pulled his tail into attack position. The man took out an object, pull the pin, and he threw it at Quickstrike. It rocketed to him on target, and it exploded in the air right over him. He was covered in spider webs and he was unable to move; Neiko looked at him horrified.

"Yuck! I hate spider webs!" he said as he tried to free himself; he could clearly see their attacker. "Neiko, run! It's Quicksilver—save yourself!" said Quickstrike as she turned and ran in a zigzag pattern to dodge the web bombs he threw at her, just barely missing. Seeing that the bombs were ineffective, Quicksilver lifted his left arm and aimed it as a hidden rocket, fanned its wings, and he fired it right on target. It exploded just behind her, and rope bound her from her shoulders to her ankles within seconds; she fell hard on the ground unable to move. She struggled, but these were no ordinary ropes. They glowed with blue-green light, and they were stronger than any that she had ever encountered. Her strength started to dwindle. Quicksilver smiled at his handiwork and at his helpless, vanquished captives.

"The great outlaw is now prisoner to Quicksilver," he said, smirking as he swaggered to her.

"You won't get away with this, creep!" Neiko yelled at him angrily, shuddering at his sinister looking armor.

"Oh? And who's gonna stop me? There's no one to save you this time, and my Master is waiting. You will make me a Shadow Warrior."

"Hey—whatever. What's a Shadow Warrior anyway? Can I reason just a tad? Can I offer a bribe?"

"No. I will accept no bribe. You will never know what a Shadow Warrior is, and Quicksilver does not reason. I only follow my Master's command. Come," he said as he picked her up and flung her over his horse. He drug Quickstrike and put him in a cage on a wagon still wrapped in webs.

He led them away and made a camp by the roadside. He built a fire, and he left Quickstrike in a cage. He cut part of the rope that snagged her and tied her up tightly with it but leaving her legs and feet free. Neiko struggled to free her hands and arms, but she started to weaken. "There's no use in struggling. The more you wriggle the more strength you lose. I designed them."

"Good, so you should be proud of yourself, scum wad," Neiko snapped at her captor with contempt.

Quicksilver chuckled. "You have spunk. Oh, just one more thing. When we leave before dawn, I will leave Quickstrike behind for the birds and jackals to feast on."

"Oh, you just wait till I get loose because I'm gonna smash your face in, jerk!" Neiko growled as she fought, but her energy drained.

"I think not. If you do get loose, you can't get past me, and you can't defeat me, so don't tempt me to kill him now," he threatened. She said nothing and slumped down in her bonds. "I don't want to hear any talking from either of you or any attempts to escape, or I will slay Quickstrike."

The next morning, Quicksilver prepared for his journey back to Skull Fort. He tied Quickstrike down to the ground with rope and stakes, and he left him there in the hot sun. Neiko sat on his horse tied up as he walked in front leading it. Neiko looked back at her friend with sadness until she could see him no more. She rode with her head down, and terrible thoughts of what lie ahead swam in her head. They walked for several miles in that same fashion. Suddenly, there stood someone in the road just ahead, and Quicksilver pulled out his crossbow just in case of any trouble. Neiko looked up in hopes of freedom, and she yelled as loud as her vocal cords would allow, "Help! Please help me! I'm in trouble—help!"

The man bounded up, and Quicksilver fired his arrow at him; he jumped in the bushes, but the arrow caught him in the leg. He disappeared.

"Nice try. Try another stunt like that again, and I'll tape your mouth shut," he snapped at her angrily because of his close call. The bushes began to shake all around them, and hundreds of jaguar men jumped onto the road. Before Quicksilver could reach any of his weapons, ten pounced on him. Growling, clawing, and battering came from the eleven, but Quicksilver ignited a smoke bomb and disappeared into the smoke without a trace. Several more appeared along with the injured one with an arrow in his leg. He limped, and two of his friends carried him.

"Neiko, are you okay?" asked a familiar voice, and Quickstrike appeared out of the ranks of warriors.

"Yeah, how'd you get loose, Quickie?"

"The same way you're about to," he said as they took her off the horse and cut the ropes off.

"Alright men, let's take them to Tsarmina's castle," said the leader.

Quickstrike look at them with terror.

"What's wrong?" asked Neiko.

"Uh, Tsarmina doesn't like people near her kingdom; the only type she prefers is woodlanders, and only special ones at that, and she can be mean.

But the thing is we are not even near her kingdom."

"Tsarmina wants to have a word with you two," said the leader as he led them down the Low Road, but they turned left on Jungle Pass and entered the Malibu Rainforest.

- CHAPTER 45 -

THEY WALKED BEHIND THEIR guides on the trail into the colorful foliage of the forest, and then suddenly thousands of huts in the trees appeared as they entered the village. The largest and nicest hut was Tsarmina's, they led them inside; Tsarmina was sitting on her throne looking at them with her golden eyes. She wore purple and gold royal robes, and she had a golden crown on her head with a large opal in the center. "Welcome to my jungle kingdom, newcomers."

"We weren't anywhere near your kingdom. Are we in trouble?" asked Quickstrike.

"Silence," she said waving her paw. "You are not in trouble with me, I am curious to know why you were attacked by Quicksilver. My warriors have been watching you for a while since you entered the Low Road from the mountains. They had been watching Quicksilver as well; they knew he was up to no good. I gave the order for you to be rescued once he sprung on his target since I knew Quicksilver was lying in wait for someone on the Low Road. I wasn't sure who it was at the time or what their fate was."

"Boy, you've been sheltered; I thought everyone knew that," Quickstrike snapped.

"What's with you? Oh no. Is she gonna turn me in even though her warriors kicked Chrome Butt Jr.'s behind? She won't get that reward."

Tsarmina chuckled. "Heavens no. I wouldn't do such a thing. So you are being pursued by Ramses? Poor dear. I can tell you are a woodlander."

"We are heading to Norak, and we have taken a slight detour." She told her about all of her adventures except Geezah, all the things she found there, and what Genghis Khan had told her.

"So, you have quite a story. Well I have news for you. Those hawks are hiding nothing, and MacPhearsome is a senile old bird. Besides, the only way home is by the Eye of Osiris, and it is in the possession of Ramses at present, so basically it's hopeless. Well, you cannot go the way you came because Quicksilver could be waiting there, and so you must go through Velociraptor Ravine."

"Oh, no! We gotta go through there alone? You're crazy!" Quickstrike squealed. "We will be snacks for raptors!"

"Oh, don't be silly. I will send Jaguas with you; he is skilled in trekking through. Velosos could help you, but no one can find him."

"Who's that?" asked Neiko.

"Velosos? The raptor hunter. He lives there, and he has lived there since he was two, but I would think of him as dangerous because he hunts like them. Jaguas will leave with you at dawn tomorrow, and he will escort you to Norak." Jaguas stepped out. He was stout-looking and had on all types of adventure equipment. "I bid you good night," she said waving her paw.

Neiko and Quickstrike stayed the night with a good jaguar family. "You know, she's the one that's senile," Neiko said curtly.

"MacPhearsome was perfectly fine, but I gotta find out what the secret of Cougan's Bluff is."

"I believe Ramses got his Eye back, and if that's the only way back, then your chances of returning are slim to none; you can tell she trusts no one or no one's as good as her, but at least she's helping, and she rescued us from that creepola." They talked more then went to sleep that night.

The following morning, Jaguas was ready to leave for Velociraptor Ravine. They walked on Raptor Pass and they could see the ravine clearly. They ventured in cautiously as they came into raptor territory, and Neiko could feel that they were being hunted. They neared the middle of the ravine. Suddenly they could hear the purring of raptors, and the bushes began to empty their contents of raptors. The three were totally surrounded by fifty or more hungry raptors. They let loose a shrill cry of glee and poised themselves to spring and kill the three trespassers. One was about to run and pounce on Neiko, and then a blur came from nowhere as a human man pounced on the raptor and slayed it with a simple dagger. He let loose a shrill call of a raptor, and they recognized him; they turned and fled. The man was wiry yet stout, and his hair was extremely long. His only clothes were a loincloth, and he was covered with necklaces and bracelets of raptor claws and teeth. "Strangers you are. Why have you come?" he asked in his quirky, jumbled speech. Velosos had difficulties speaking with normal folk because of his raptor upbringing.

Neiko listened and scratched her head in trying to figure out what he was saying. After she was able to piece together the question, she said, "Travelling to Norak, sir. I'm Neiko of Hawote, this is Quickstrike, and this is Jaguas, our guide from the kingdom of

Tsarmina," said Neiko stretching forth her hand, but he cocked his head like a confused raptor.

"Nice to meet you it is. Velosos I am, and kind people are you. The outlaw you are, and running from Ramses you are. Glad to help I am. Neiko, home is far away, yes? Help you I will. Hate Ramses I do, and want you he does. Know you are here because he seeks you, yes?"

"That's right. I go to Norak—"

Before she could finish, he said, "Seek the Attack Pack you do. Return Quickstrike, and need them against Ramses. Wise choice it is, and want to return home you do. First come eat lunch with me you will, and lead you to Norak I will," he said smiling at Neiko. He took her hand and led her while the others followed.

At his camp they ate roasted raptor till they were stuffed. Velosos talked with Neiko about her adventures. "Enough about me, why do you live here alone?"

Velosos cocked his head and a tear came into his eye. "Black creature slay my parents it did. Come for me it did, but run I did, and here I did hide. Raised by good raptors I was, and now dead they are, killed by bad pack that live here. That why I know raptor way. Good raptors like Raptor of Attack Pack, only two there were, and came from Etowah they did, kin of Raptor, yes?"

"Man, I'm sorry. I would think that those are kin of Raptor, so can we leave now? I'm ready to get to safety," she said putting her hand on his shoulder. He looked at her happily, and he took off one of his necklaces of teeth; it had one of the side claws in the center. He put it on her neck gently.

"Gift to you. Remember me. Visit you will? When you go to Norak come back to home I will. Can't live in city. Not accept raptor man. Leave now we will," he said as he combed his long hair, armed himself with a homemade spear and his trusty dagger. He led them safely down the other side of the ravine and walked them on Norak pass.

"There it is! At last!" Neiko said as she could see Norak on the hill half a mile away, and the four started to run for it.

- CHAPTER 46 -

WHEN THEY REACHED THE gate, they were let in
immediately, but Velosos would not come in. He looked
in the city with terror.

"Must return home I must."

"Wait! Can you at least come and have dinner because I want
to repay you for your kindness. Maybe the Attack Pack may even
make you a member. Besides, I have something to say about that dark
creature."

"Alright. Stay I will, and thankful I am," he said and shuddered
at the mentioning of the thing. "Fear the black shadow I do. You
know what is?"

"Yeah, it's the Dark Pharaoh."

"Terrified of Dark Pharaoh I am. Saw it before on Ravine I
have. It only thing I fear, mortal it is not, and strong it is."

" Also I know who it is, and it's Ramses."

Velosos's eyes were filled with terror. "Hate Ramses I do, but fear him too, now Velosos tremble. Two nightmares in one. The ones I fear most I do. In trouble you are and protect you I will, fight for good I will. Be brave I will, and take you away he will not, and come with you I will. Home no safe no more, and nothing there is not," he said, walking in with them.

Neiko walked up to a man. "Excuse me, is the Attack Pack around?"

A kangaroo turned around. "Nope, they left several days ago, but they be comin' back. The only two here are Lydia and Air Hammer," he replied in a heavy Desert Bushman accent that sounded much like Australian.

"Well, can I talk with them?" asked Neiko.

"Sure thing, mate, name's Boomerang Joe Dundee, ma'am," he said as he tipped his hat to her. He wore a snakeskin vest, jeans, but no shoes. His hat was black and decorated with crocodile teeth. He carried a large knife on his hip with a snakeskin hilt.

"Neiko Kidd, put her there."

"Blow me down, it's the jolly old outlaw! You made it to the safest place in Qari, and you managed to get past old bucket head."

"Well, thanks, but I ain't outa the woods yet."

"Well, no worries, come and follow me," he said then he led them into a small house and knocked on the door.

"I'm comin'," said a male voice, the door opened and there stood Air Hammer. He had a hawk's plumage on his body and he walked like one. His head was that of a hammerhead shark; he had a tail of a shark and a dorsal fin of a shark on his back; his sharkskin was a blue color; the rest of his body was that of a hawk. His legs had on red bands from his knee to his ankles. "Quickie! Oh, I'm glad to see you! You've been on the news lately along with your friend here. So you're Neiko. Well I'm glad to meet you," he said as he shook her hand with his claw.

"I'm glad I found you guys. I need your help big time," she said then told him all about their adventures in Hawote and Qari, but leaving out everything they found out about Ramses.

Air Hammer whistled. "That's too many close ones for me, but at least you suckered him; I can tell he's just got started. Besides, we gotta get you home, just like you got Quickie here. I know one thing, Ramses won't stop, and he's just started in trying to screw up your life."

"I know, and I don't like the sound of it at all."

"Well, come on in, and who are these two gentlemen?"

"Oh, this is Velosos and Jaguas."

"The great Velosos? Oh, I always wanted to meet you, and I reckon Jaguas is from Tsarmina's place."

"That's right, but I will leave in the morning. Tsarmina commands," said Jaguas.

"Stay I will, and join Attack Pack," said Velosos.

"Alright, cool! Well, come in and eat and take off a load. I'll tell Lydia y'all are here," he said then went upstairs.

"Good, she's awake—we're in luck, but we gotta wait till they go to sleep," said Neiko.

Lydia came down, and they told her everything they told Air Hammer. "Oh, you poor dear, I know exactly what you're going through," she said sweetly.

"Oh, there's some stuff I gotta tell you later, and it's gonna scare you," said Neiko as she fingered her long black hair.

"Oh really? What?"

"Me and Quickie have to tell you in private—alone."

Velosos and Jaguas went outside to talk; Air Hammer went upstairs while Lydia, Quickstrike, and Neiko stayed at the table. Quickstrike took a deep breath and said, "Ramses is the Dark Pharaoh."

Neiko looked at her. "It's imperative you never tie the knot or the consequences will be horrible," Neiko said, but before she could say more, Great Spirit told her not to say anything else. "I know much more, and I could nail him to the wall, but that's all you need to know."

"Oh my," she said shaking. "Where did you find all this?"

"I can't say; it's classified. But I knew who Ramses was even before he came to Hawote," she said then bells started ringing, and people started screaming.

Air Hammer raced down the stairs. "It's a Pharaoh attack! They're gonna try to invade! Quicksilver may not have had time to tell Chrome Stack you got away, but he could find out now!"

Everyone raced to the ramparts. Neiko brought her binoculars. She looked, and she saw hundreds of Skull Bearers with Menes, Tut, and Re leading the attack. "Well, I got good news. Ramses didn't show up, but the three dumb Pharaohs are here."

"How many Skull Bearers are there?" asked Jaguas.

"All of 'em I think. There's probably about eight hundred. We need to mobilize defenses now, and tell about sixty archers to come to the front wall. Get all types of defenses and protect the gate, hurry up! They're about to storm," said Neiko urgently.

"You know your stuff," said Jaguas.

"Yeah, I fought in plenty of wars back home, and some old Indian tricks may be what the doctor ordered."

"Get the archers I will," Velosos said as he disappeared like lightning. Within minutes he came with eighty.

"Alright, form four lines of twenty. The first line will fire when I say, and follow my lead. We have to hold them off till we can get backup."

The Skull Bearers began to run to the gate with a battering ram on the command of Menes. Neiko waited till they were on the steep hill in which the city sat upon. "Front row, ready—aim—fire!" she yelled then they fired, and they felled many including the ones carrying the massive battering ram. All of its bearers were struck down; the ram rolled down the hill injuring and tripping anyone in its path, and the ranks scattered. "First row, down and reload. Second row—up—ready—aim—fire!" she said. They fired on the confused Skull Bearers. Many fell dead and several were injured. Wasting no time, she called the third row, then the fourth, and kept the cycle going. The tactic kept them pushed back till the ground force came out and smashed into the weakened force.

Seeing the battle was going sore against him, Menes quivered with rage. He could see a figure leading the archers. "I have never in my life seen a move like this in all my days!"

"Me neither," Re said, scratching his head.

"I'll have a look at the brains of this defense," he said as he pulled his telescope to his eye. "Well, well. Won't Ramses be happy to know that his little prized sweetheart just stopped us from taking Norak, and she outwitted him! He can't blame this one on me!"

Tut sniggered. "Well, I guess we oughta tell him. So should we call off the attack?"

"Yes. I have a feeling he will not be happy about this." "

He will be when we tell him where Neiko is," Tut said.

Menes groaned. "Maybe some, but she is in Norak, stupid. He can't get to her, so basically he's thwarted either way. The Attack Pack will be back soon. I don't want them to whip up on us anymore and add to our humiliation."

Re tapped Menes. "No need to call them off. Look."

The Skull Bearers were retreating as the ground warriors were chasing them, and Neiko's archers kept a steady rain of arrows until they were out of range. As they turned and left, Menes could see everyone raising their weapons in the air and shouting at their swift victory.

Menes looked at Neiko's shadow from afar. "It's not over yet. You just wait. If I don't get you, then Ramses will," he said he and his two brothers they rode away. The three of them giggled.

That night the city of Norak celebrated their victory with dancing, feasting, and games. All of the leaders were congratulated for their fine efforts including Neiko. The High Elder personally approached her. "You have risked yourself further for our sake, and you helped us cut a week's battle into only a few hours with that tactic. Very good."

"No problem. It's one of my most effective moves in Hawote."

Boomerang Joe slapped her on the back in friendship. "Well enough talk, mate, let's dance in a chieftain's dance." They danced, and everyone celebrated the entire night.

- CHAPTER 47 -

QUICKSILVER RAN INTO THE throne room, and Ramses knew something went wrong. "What happened?" he asked.

Quicksilver trembled. "I had her, but I was attacked by soldiers of the jungle kingdom, and there were hundreds. There was no way I could keep her because they had me surrounded, and I barely escaped to tell you. Oh, please, be merciful and not slay me because I know how you hate failure."

"I wasn't even thinking of that—this time. Things have been going her way, but that will soon change. I can't use normal methods, so I will have to use some of my more elusive ones. I have a few more tricks up my sleeve because I will have a few surprises waiting for her when she arrives in Norak. I will need you to find her location and watch her for me. Do not try to take her because that senile old cat probably has guards all around her, and they have identified your target. I will contact Vipra, and she will have a few surprises from me waiting there."

Quicksilver bowed. "Thanks for your mercy."

"I will reward for your efforts once she is in my possession. At least you found her because she seems to know how to hide. You found her rather quickly unlike those other imbeciles."

"She had just exited the mountains when I apprehended them."

"Excellent."

"Yo! Bro! I'm back!" Menes said as Tut and Re followed close behind.

Ramses look at him and rolled his eyes. "Well, how'd it go?"

"We got spanked. We lost in only a few hours, and we had five hundred casualties. Your surprise attack was mowed down by archers."

Ramses stood up. "What? Are you lying to me?"

"Heck no! I never saw a tactic like it! They had rows a coordinated attack, and they hit us every time we tried to climb the hill."

"Well, who led the defenses?"

"Boomerang Joe led the ground assault, and your little sweet Indian led the archers."

"Stop badgering me about that! So she made it to Norak. If you say anything else like that to me again about Neiko, I will beat you with a cat-o'-nine-tails!"

"Touchy, touchy. Well, tah tah, Lover Pharaoh," Menes said to anger him and made kissing noises, and Ramses clinched his fists, and his eyes blazed as he boiled. Menes laughed and left the room.

"One of these days!" Ramses snarled as he was seething. "I will be glad for the day I renounce being that idiot's brother! I grow tired of him pestering me and living this stupid mortal life! I will reign here, and that ruffian will regret the day he ever angered me! Well, now to important matters. Go to Norak and tell Vipra I want her to call me. You will keep an eye on Neiko. Alert me as soon as the Attack Pack arrives. Get there tonight."

"Yes. I understand."

"Help me get her, and I will make you a Shadow Warrior—not just any, but my personal warrior."

"Thank you," he said as he bowed. He left the throne room and flew into the night.

The following morning the rest of the Attack Pack arrived. They each in turn gave their greetings to her and introduced themselves Then she told them about her adventures.

"Well now, you are quite amazing, and you brought Quickstrike back to us; we've been wondering what happened to him. Now we need to get you home," said Phoenix the Pack leader. Phoenix was part eagle and part wolf. He had the face of a wolf, and he walked on all fours. He had large wings, and his front legs were larger than his hind legs, and they possessed claws of an eagle. He had copper bands on his legs and toes. He had gray fur with a large black spot on his back, and he had an eagle's tail. His wings were gray with black tips and copper-colored trim.

"I'm glad to get to meet you," said Sonar in his Transylvanian type dialect. He was a giant vampire bat. He had a red face, and the rest of him was dark gray. He had the large front wing hands, and two small ones in his rear. His wife Rosenar looked just like him.

Ramulus was a large ram with red, brown, and gray fur and a green stone on his forehead. He had two huge sharp edged horns that curved to the back. His wife Aries, twin brother Sichus, and sister-in-law Daisy were like him.

Noctorro had the body of a bat and the head of a Brahma bull. He had brown and black fur. His hands were different than Sonar's because he had five fingers instead of two.

Buzzclaw and Sky Shadow were brothers, and both were part lizard. Buzzclaw was mostly praying mantis, but his back feet were a lizard's and he stood upright. Sky Shadow was mostly lizard and part dragonfly.

Cheetor and Cheetara, another look-alike couple, were cheetahs.

Scarem was a large stag beetle with razor-sharp pinchers. His shell was blue and green and shiny. He had a green and brown face with his huge, red eyes and long, orange antennae. He has six orange legs.

Raptor was a velociraptor with white skin, a blue snout, and a purple spot on the top of his head. He had a long tail fixed with razor-sharp bone protrusions at the end of it. He had the side claws and he had extra long toe claws on his feet; he had the front hand like feet of a raptor. His haunches were purple with red spots, and his mouth contained razor-sharp teeth with two front curved fangs on his top jaw.

Torca was part whale and part elephant. He had the legs and body of an elephant complete with tusks and trunk. He had the back and the teeth of a whale.

Injector was part lionfish and part hornet. He had the body of a hornet, complete with a large black and yellow stinger. His head was that of the venomous lionfish.

Waspinator was a huge wasp. He had a red body and green wings.

Bantor was part tiger and part baboon. He had a body of a tiger and the head of a baboon.

Diana and Sandstorm were the only other "people" besides Lydia. Diana had blue eyes, red hair, and fair skin like her sister, Lydia. Sandstorm, the second in command of the Pack, was a camel man in the attire of a Saracen prince. He wore a red fez with a gold tassel. He wore a white shirt with a purple sash draped over his left shoulder that draped across his chest. He had gold plates on his shoulders that flared outward. He had a curved Saracen knife in his chest, and he wore green pants. He wore no shoes, and on the left leg of his pants was decorated with a purple cobra that was sewn on.

Darkclaw and Glacier were twins. They were unusual batlike creatures with four legs and unusual toes. Darkclaw was black with red and silver eyes and white teeth. Glacier was white with orange teeth filled with venom and orange and green eyes. Rip Rat was similar to his brothers, but he was a giant rat with two curved fangs in the front of his mouth that were filled with poison. Each of these creatures and people made up the Attack Pack.

Everyone came into the house and ate dinner. Neiko tried several of their favorite dishes. "How do you like snake?" asked Rosenar in her Transylvanian type dialect.

"It's great, I didn't know that cobra was so tasty." Neiko replied.

"Good. Next time let me cook ya something," Raptor said smiling. For the next hour and a half, Glacier and Raptor told jokes and made fun of Ramses. Lydia got up and left.

"What's with her? I thought she liked our jokes, and she always had a few of her own," said Rip Rat concerned.

"She's been acting a little strange lately," Air Hammer said. "It's probably nothing."

"Well, there are some important matters to discuss," Phoenix said as everyone gathered around the table. "Alright, Neiko, do you have any ideas on how you may return to your homeland? I also gladly accept Velosos into the Attack Pack," he said, and Velosos thanked him kindly.

"Well, I first plan to visit the Hawks and see if the secret of Cougan's Bluff can help me, and if not, the only hope I have is with the Eye of Osiris."

"Aye, there's no problem in visiting the Hawks, but if we have to use the Eye, we have a huge problem because the Pharaohs got it when Ramses and Quickstrike disappeared, and we had to bail out Lydia from a company of Skull Bearers," said Sandstorm.

"Well, that's it for the time being," said Phoenix. "We can resume our party time."

"I'm gonna check on Lydia," Neiko said. "I'll come with you," said Raptor.

Neiko and Raptor walked through the streets of Norak trying to find her. They finally found her under a tree talking with someone.

In seeing them, the man got up and left, and Neiko had great suspicion. "Well, there you are, we combed the whole place for you. Why didn't you introduce me to your friend? Is he scared of raptors?" asked Raptor.

"Uh, no, he just remembered he had errands to run, that's all," she said nonchalantly, but Neiko eyed her suspiciously. "What's wrong with you, is it wrong for me to have friends outside of the Attack Pack?" she asked coldly. Neiko didn't answer, but just cocked a questioning eyebrow.

"Lydia, she didn't mean anything by it. I mean, she's been through a lot, and she's tired, that's all."

"Just checking, and it seems she's giving me the look like I'm making a boo boo," she said as she marched in front of them in a snobby fashion.

"Neiko, what's wrong?"

"Nothing. I had a bad feeling that's all," she said casually. "Don't worry, it's probably me."

A few minutes later they arrived at the house. Neiko kept her eyes fastened on Lydia, and a bad feeling rose from her insides from time to time. "I gotta see if she's up to something, but I can't let her know I have the woolies," she thought. Every time Lydia glanced her way, she hid her gaze and acted like nothing was wrong. Neiko went outside, but Lydia was right behind her.

"What is your problem?" she asked coldly. "And don't tell me any more stories."

"Well, it's that guy you were talking to. The fact is he gives me the shakes, and I don't like him," she fibbed in trying to hide her suspicions of her.

"Well, he's just a friend, and do you feel like I'm cheating on Phoenix? Well, I'm not."

"You know, that's what they all say, but hey, who knows? That guy could be Ramses in disguise."

"Oh, don't be silly. I think I would know if it was Ramses or not," she said.

"Obviously you don't know him like I do," Neiko said testing the waters.

"You are to tell me you know him better than I do, and you have known him personally for maybe thirty minutes altogether while I have known him all my life? Do you really believe all of that nonsense is true? There is no such thing! If it were true, he wouldn't go out on a limb like that to see me, and he wouldn't want to expose himself, would he? I can't believe I'm even wasting my time with you on this subject. If it makes you feel any better, I won't see him anymore. Satisfied?" she snapped, turned on her heel, walked into the house, and slammed the door.

Neiko giggled at her. "She is up to something all right, and I thought she would be a little more careful since I told her the truth. I'll keep an eye on her," she thought as she followed her into the house.

- Chapter 48 -

Several days passed and the Attack Pack went into Bird Wood and set up camp. Everyone pitched in helping set up the tents and the beds. They gathered wood and dinner for the entire group and set up room arrangements; Neiko was assigned with Lydia. Neiko distanced herself from her, and stayed closer to the rest until bedtime that night. Lydia stayed in the tent that night, but she stayed up late like she was trying to wait till Neiko went to bed. Neiko did so, but she feigned sleep. She watched her through tiny slits. Lydia walked toward her and rubbed her face, but she faked groaning and rolling over, and said, "Mom, is my favorite cartoon on yet?"

Thinking she was asleep, Lydia walked to a secluded corner and pulled a crystal out of her shoe, rubbed it, and Neiko pulled the covers over her head, rolled back over, and opened a hole so she could see. Lydia cautiously hid it, and she looked at Neiko for a few minutes and studied her, but Neiko didn't move, so she pulled out the crystal once more. She rubbed it and asked, "Master are you there? It is I, Vipra."

The crystal shone a dim, green light, and Neiko watched in horror as a familiar figure appeared inside of it. "It's about time. What took so long? Have you met with Quicksilver?"

"I have met with him, and he has told me all. I had a problem trying to call you because of that stupid Attack Pack, and Neiko has been watching me like a hawk ever since I saw Quicksilver. She does not know it was him; she doubts me, but at least she thinks I'm cheating on Phoenix."

"Where is she now?"

"She's here with me asleep. I made certain of it."

"No more talk tonight. Meet with me at the Great Oak tomorrow night at midnight and make certain no one knows where you are going, farewell," he said then disappeared, and Vipra put the crystal back into her shoe. Neiko pulled the covers over her head, and fear crept into her soul. She thought heavily about what had been said, and she fell asleep despite all the things in her mind.

The next morning Neiko got up early to avoid Vipra before she got up. She ran outside and found Raptor. "Where's the Great Oak?" she asked.

"It's down that little trail right there on the right. You can't miss it. Why?"

"I—uh, just want to go there to relax that's all," she said casually then she walked down the trail and found the great tree. Neiko found a bush about five feet away from the meeting place, and it offered suitable camouflage; she would not be seen in the night. The trip was about ten minutes. "Okay, hiding place and timed the trip. I gotta find the time to get into my spot before Vipra comes and meet with Chrome Gas. I gotta find some excuse to leave, and I can't be spotted because I'll be caught if I do, so I really got to be careful."

That day she found a way to make it, and she waited till that night. She pretended to go to bed early, which was about nine. She laid in bed till about ten thirty. She put pillows under the covers to make it like she was still there, and she hid under the bed. Vipra came to the door and peeked, and she left thinking it was she. She slipped out the back of the tent, and carefully went into her hiding place at the Great Oak. She waited the remaining time until Vipra appeared. Suddenly out of nowhere appeared Ramses. "I am here and no one followed."

"You can take off that disguise," he said. Then she changed into her true hideous form. She had black skin and yellow eyes with two pointed fangs coming from her top lip, and she wore a black cloak. "I have a job for you, and there can be no mistakes. Take this phial of sleeping potion and give it all to her, and she must take every last drop. I know exactly how to do it. You will give Neiko her favorite dish, which is deer barbecue, and put this in it. Make it a dinner with just you and her, alone. She will gradually grow tired, and you will put her in bed. Summon me, and I will take her away, and you will handle the Attack Pack. I want this done tomorrow night. If I don't hear from you then, I will come anyway."

"I understand," she said as she took the phial from him. "Before you leave, I have something to tell you. Neiko knows who you are and of your secrets."

"How? Who told her?"

"Nobody. She said she has always known, and that is not all she knows. She said she knows much more to 'nail you to the wall' is how she put it. She was hoping to warn Lydia; she is dangerous. Should I kill her to avoid your secrets from being revealed?"

"No. Do as you're told. I will handle this little problem myself, and is there anyone else who knows?"

"Quickstrike, my lord."

"Neiko will tell no one once I have her, and you will slay Quickstrike. I have a feeling she may know just about everything, but there is one thing she will never know until it's too late. So, she is the Chosen One as well, but that will not change what I have planned, and it will not save her from—never mind. The fact remains if she stops me from reigning, she will never see the last of me. Go now, I will be waiting for your call," he said as he disappeared into the foliage without making a sound, and Vipra turned and ran back to the camp. Neiko took the long way back and made it to bed, but she couldn't sleep that night.

- CHAPTER 49 -

NEIKO GOT UP THE next morning ready for action. On her way out of the tent, Raptor stopped her.

"Why did you sneak out late last night? Don't tell me you went exploring because I won't buy it."

Neiko drug Raptor to a secluded area and told him everything about what she found out last night and all she knew.

"Oh boy, you're in trouble now! So now what?"

"I'll turn the tables on that Vipra somehow; well at least I know the secret ingredient in Vipra's recipe of deer barbecue. At least I knew this was coming, or I would be gone by tomorrow, and after that she'll try to kill Quickie. Tell him about the news, but don't tell anyone else yet."

Raptor mused. "I wonder where the real Lydia is."

"Probably at Skull Fort, and we got to find a way to get her out, but it's probably another trap. I would bank that it would mean the end of the Attack Pack and my hopes of ever returning home. I still don't know what he's got planned for me; he didn't spill his guts to Vipra either, but we gotta risk it to save her from the worst fate of all."

"You're right," he said.

"Neiko, I want to talk to you, please come here," came Vipra's voice.

"I'll play along. Hide out in the back just in case."

"Right," Raptor said with a nod as he headed to a good hiding place.

Neiko ran up and tried to hide her anxiety. "What's up?"

"I have a surprise for you. I made your favorite—deer barbecue. I will gladly eat some with you, and I wish to say I'm sorry for being so mean to you," she said sweetly, and Neiko followed her inside.

Neiko smiled and thought, *The joke's on you! If I didn't know about that meeting, then I would be buying this.* "How'd you know I like deer barbecue?" Neiko asked.

"Oh, Quickstrike told me," Vipra lied.

Yeah right! You mean Ramses told you, she thought in her mind.

"So when do we eat?" she said.

"It's ready now and it's waiting for us. I love deer. I cooked this meal especially for us."

Neiko looked on the table and saw two identical plates of the stuff. The smell filled her nostrils, and her stomach growled. "Boy I'm starved!" she said and caught Vipra's insidious smirk.

Vipra seated Neiko, and Neiko studied the situation and tried to concoct a plan to eat deer and thwart her kidnapping scheme. She saw wooden forks beside the plates, and a floor made of dirt. When Vipra wasn't looking, Neiko licked her fork all over and set it on the table. Vipra handed Neiko her glass of mango juice. Neiko purposely reached for the juice, and then she slid her elbow and knocked off the fork onto the dirt floor. "Oops," said Neiko as she picked it up and it was covered in grit. Vipra thought it was an accident, and she covered her mouth in fake dismay. She got up to get her another. While she was finding her another fork, Neiko switched the plates quickly and unnoticed; Neiko gave Vipra the drugged meat. Vipra sat down and Neiko said the blessing. Neiko began to devour the meat, and Vipra watched with wicked glee; she unknowingly took a fork full of the doped venison. Neiko and Vipra both finished their plates, and Vipra began to feel the effects of the potion. She looked at Neiko with hatred as she found she had been caught in her own trap. Neiko looked at her with a smile and said, "Thanks for the deer, Vipra."

Vipra's drowsiness increased and she started to sway. "You won't get away with this! You can't escape from the Master forever! He will get you! You wait and see."

"Yeah, yeah, that's an old one. You may have told him who I am, but I will succeed in kicking his chrome butt all the way back to the Stone Age."

"You can do no such thing, Neiko. That is not what you are chosen for, surrender, you don't stand a chance," she said just barely able to hold up her head.

"No chance," Neiko said then Vipra collapsed, and her face landed in her plate.

Raptor ran in. "What happened? What'd ya do?"

"Oh, nothing really, just gave her a taste of her own medicine."

"Well, let's put her to bed, and you better stay with me and Quickie tonight because even if she doesn't summon him, he will come and see what happened. If you are asleep in here and he finds you alone, he will carry you off, and all this will be for nothing."

"You're right, let's do it," she said as they put her into bed. They headed to their tent, and they told Quickstrike about all that had happened.

"Oh my, he's not gonna stop there. I think he's gonna use a covert Dark Pharaoh attack next, and you're really gonna have to watch it, Neiko."

"Yeah, I know, that's what I was thinking, and it's getting more and more dangerous. I gotta find a Good Pharaoh and quick before something really awful happens," said Neiko.

"Guys, look," said Raptor as they saw a shadow approach Vipra's tent, and it disappeared into the shadows of the woods.

"There he goes, and now the fun really begins," Neiko said nervously, and the three of them went to sleep that night.

- Chapter 50 -

THE NEXT MORNING THE three got up early, and they stayed away from Vipra the entire afternoon. She remained with the rest of the Attack Pack while Raptor, Neiko, and Quickstrike watched from afar and tried to find ways to get rid of her. "I can't think of anything because she'll sic the Dark Pharaoh on us," Raptor said as he kicked a rock.

"The only thing I can think of is wait till everyone else catches her in a lie," Neiko suggested.

"That'll be hard to do because she does such a good job at lying. Besides, it may take a long time," Quickstrike replied.

"Just think what Cheetor will do if he ever finds out," Raptor purred.

"If I find out what?" asked Cheetor from behind, and they spun around in surprise.

"I was just thinking about if you found out someone found a surprise for you, that's all," said Raptor casually.

"Oh. Neiko, can you go pick some berries for me? Cheetara needs you two to help with dinner. Will you be back around sundown?" asked Cheetor.

Neiko nodded. "Sure thing. I'll take my tomahawk, my armlet, my little stick, and belt, just in case. If I ain't back, and if you find my tomahawk, you know something's wrong," she said as she put on her lightning sword, belt, armlet, and picked up her tomahawk.

"Roger. Be careful, here's a croaker sack," he said handing it to her, and she headed off into the woods.

As Neiko walked, she found many berry bushes, and picked and picked while she sang.

Suddenly, a branch broke, and she jumped, froze, and looked around. A deer galloped by and disappeared as Neiko laughed with relief. She traveled deeper into the woods in the cool of the evening, but it was almost time to go back, so she picked up the sack and started to head back. An eerie, chilling feeling penetrated the woods. The bugs and birds no longer sang, adding to the creepiness. Neiko's heart started thumping, and she quickened her pace. A few branches snapped behind her; she spun around, and there stood a large black Clydesdale horse with a silver plate on its head. It had fiery red eyes, and its rider was a black shadow with the familiar red, flaming eyes of the Dark Pharaoh himself. Neiko's courage left her, and panic surged through her as her mouth fell open; her eyes widened in fear. She dropped the bag and her tomahawk and started to run. The black rider charged, and she could hear the hooves of the horse as he pursued her. She only made it a few feet when he leaned over and caught her in her middle, lifted her up, and sat her in front of him. She screamed and fought, but he was too strong. He wrapped his powerful arms around her.

"I have you, and there is nothing anyone can do to take you from me this time," said the familiar voice of Ramses with wicked delight. He held her closely to him with one arm and turned his mighty horse with the other, and he disappeared with his helpless prisoner. Neiko cried and yelled as he carried her away.

It was thirty minutes after sundown, and Cheetor was getting
worried. "It can't take three hours to pick berries, and the patch is

only a few yards away, I gotta go check on her," he said. He returned in ten minutes. "Guys, I didn't see anything. We gotta get the Attack Pack and search the woods.

Cheetara, go tell Phoenix right away."

"Will do," she said then ran like lightning. The search sprang out in only a few minutes. They went into the woods and called her name, but there was no answer. They traveled deeper and deeper into the woods, and Cheetor found the bag and her tomahawk lying in the ground.

"Well, this is the last place where she was, I gotta see which way she went from here, and see if a bear or something might have attacked her."

Cheetara searched the perimeter, but she found nothing. "Cheetor, I don't like this. Her trail leads to this spot and it just vanishes. It's like nothing came at all except her. This is really strange. There is no other scent but hers—wait—I smell something," she said pointing to their left.

Cheetor stalked to that area and disappeared into the trees. They heard a shrill scream of fright. A man ran with Cheetor right on his heels, and he was only greeted by angry snarls from the Attack Pack.

"Where is she?" asked Waspinator, the wasp, shaking his leg at him. The man's eyes were wide as saucers, and he was shaking uncontrollably. He was so terrified he didn't answer.

"C'mon tell us, and we'll spare you," Scarem, the beetle, said as he brandished his deadly pinchers, but the man just covered his face and shook with fright.

"Guys, I don't think he did it, I mean, look at him. It looks like he saw a ghost," said Torca, the elephant-whale.

"Well, let's see if he knows anything," said Bantor, the tiger-baboon.

"I'll handle it," said Diana, Lydia's sister. "I'm sorry about before, sir, what's your name?"

"J-jinx," he managed to gurgle.

"Okay, Jinx, we're looking for our friend, and she is lost, have you seen her?"

Jinx nodded.

"What happened?"

"It took her. He rode on his dark steed and grabbed her. He vanished without a trace just as he came," he said then swallowed.

"Who?" she asked.

"The demon of the shadows—it's the same creature that killed my brother years ago."

"You mean the Dark Pharaoh," said Quickstrike, and Jinx nodded.

"Oh no," Cheetara said sadly and in shock as she covered her mouth with her paw.

"Could she be dead?" asked Buzzclaw, the mantis-lizard.

Jinx shook his head. "The Dark Pharaoh kills men where they stand, and he usually takes no prisoners, so your friend is lost. He may have chosen her to be his queen."

"We can't give up. There must be hope. We can't let her go through all of this for nothing. We will find her no matter what it takes," said Phoenix bravely.

"Where do we start? No one knows who the Dark Pharaoh is and he is long gone by now. It wouldn't take him long to disappear with her, and he'll hide her well," said Noctorro, the bullheaded bat, rubbing his left horn.

"There *is* hope. I know where Neiko is," said Quickstrike.

"And we know who's got her," added Raptor, and everybody looked at him with surprise.

"Let's go back to camp. Will you be alright, Jinx?" asked Sandstorm.

"Yes, I'm fine. I'll go home. I've been through this before. I'm just really scared of him," he said, being fully recovered and he left. The Attack Pack left and returned back to camp.

- CHAPTER 51 -

T HAT NIGHT EVERYBODY MET to see what the two had to say. "You said you knew who the Dark Pharaoh is, so tell us," said Sichus impatiently.

Raptor took a deep breath and said, "It's Ramses."

Everyone gasped, and Quickstrike told them everything that he knew.

"So basically he probably took her to Skull Fort, and he has no idea that all of us know, and we must keep it that way. We will treat him like we know no different, but he is aware that I know, and he's got the person who found everything. I can tell he's almost ready to reveal himself. Now we're kinda ready for what lies ahead, and we know what he's capable of."

"Your right, we must do exactly that. We have to mobilize tonight because I don't know what he's got in store for her, and I will waste no time to let him get away with this." Lydia got up and was about to leave, when Phoenix asked, "Where are you going?"

"To bed. I'm tired," Vipra lied. When she walked to the door Velosos and Raptor stopped her.

"Lying you are," Velosos snarled. "Tell Dark Pharaoh our plan you were, Vipra."

Seeing they had discovered her, she looked around in fear. Angry beasts surrounded her, and she turned into her real self. Cheetor sprang onto her and sank in his claws and teeth while many others followed, and Vipra lived no more. "We have another problem. We have to find Lydia and now Ramses may know what Neiko knows, and maybe we stopped her from telling him."

"No, he knew before he kidnapped her, but he doesn't know the extent of her knowledge," Quickstrike said in dread.

"We can't waste time trying to find a Good Pharaoh now, we must handle this ourselves, and we'll save that for more dire emergencies," said Sonar.

"We have to find the fortress, and we must plan carefully because he will expect us to attack when he discovers Vipra is dead—we have no time to lose! Let's fly!" said Phoenix, and everyone flew into the night, the ones unable to fly riding on the ones that could.

Ramses and Neiko rode into the Giant Forest, and the giant trees towered over them. The forest was somewhat dark because the trees were so thick the sun could barely penetrate. They crossed over the Schism Canyon on a wooden bridge that was guarded by Skull Bearers. They let him pass, and then they entered into the Dark Forest. This forest was pitch-black, and suddenly Skull Fort towered before them. The huge stone fortress was enormous, and its towers reached up into the tall trees' limbs. Crow cages contained the bones of dead men, and the skeletons of the tortured added to the morbid appearance of the place. He rode across the drawbridge, and when he passed the gate, the drawbridge closed, and they lowered the gate. He kicked the horse to a run as he approached the stronghold. "Open the doors," he commanded.

"Yes," they said then opened the doors. He stopped Goliath in the foyer, and waited till some of them came to steady the horse.

"Hold her till I get off," said Ramses to two Skull Bearers, and they did as he bid. As soon as he slipped off, he said to them as he grasped her arm, "Take him to the stable," noticing the armlet and lightning sword complete with belt. "So, you found my lightning sword and armlet? I'll take those if you don't mind," he said as he took them off, and Neiko gritted her teeth knowing she was trapped. Goliath pawed the floor, and they backed away. He walked up, nuzzled his master, and looked at Neiko intently as he licked her face and sniffed her hair. Neiko looked at him puzzled. "He likes you," Ramses said. "Goliath, go with them now, and I will come later." Goliath grunted. "I will bring her along," he said as he stroked his nose. The two Skull Bearers came and the gigantic horse left with them. "Let's go," he said then led her into the hall.

As they entered the throne room, Osiris saw them. "Well, so you finally caught her, and I didn't expect you back so soon." Osiris wore one large purple suit with black stripes with shin and wrist guards. His breastplate came up over his shoulders, and his entire armor was covered in razor-sharp blades. His helmet was black with silver designs. Two large stag beetle pinchers extended from both sides of his head, and the only parts of his body that showed were his hands and his eyes.

"Well, it was easier than I thought it would be," he said gruffly. "I'm proud, son. Welcome, Neiko," he said kindly.

"Thanks," she said bluntly.

"Be sure to introduce her to your brothers, especially since she will be living among us."

"Alright," he snapped moodily.

"Don't be temperamental. I'm still your father even though you are the First Pharaoh," said Osiris sharply as he left the room, and the three waltzed in.

"Hey, look who's here!" said Tut.

"Oh, look it's Tutankhamen II," Neiko said jeeringly.

"Don't call me that! I hate that name! I only go by Tut, besides, I can't even spell that mouth full of a name."

"You know, people should be able to spell their own names, and by the way, Tut is harder to spell than Re," she said mockingly as Tut gritted his teeth.

"Enough," Ramses growled harshly.

"I'm Re, and this is Menes," said Re, smiling.

"Yeah, nice of you to join us," said Menes slyly.

"Yeah, how'd you like my defense move, Menes?" she said, and before she could hurl any more insults, Ramses tightened his grip on her arm and gave her a warning look.

"Oh, I wouldn't be so smug about that because we got you, and you have no archers to mow us down," Menes said proudly as a shrewd light came into his eyes.

"What do you mean *we*? It's time for me to show her to her room, excuse us," snapped Ramses as he led her down another hallway. He led her down the long hall and stopped in front of a door. He pulled out the key, unlocked it, and opened the door. The room was fancily decorated with a bed, a table, a closet, and a desk. The wood on the furniture was beautiful, brown, and elaborately carved. The bed had red velvet covers with gold tassels and matching pillows. In all its grandeur it lacked windows.

Great, no windows? Neiko thought in desperation.

He let go of her arm and shoved her inside the room. "Stay put. I'll be back later," he said as he closed the door. She could hear the clank as he locked it, then she could hear his footfalls down the stone hall.

"Great, now what? How am I gonna get out of this one? No windows, locked doors, plenty of guards, gate and drawbridge, and moat to go with it. So I'm stuck here. My only chance is if Ramses leaves and goes somewhere. I may have to wait till the Attack Pack comes, but they don't know where this place is," she grumbled as she plopped on the bed. "Well, at least the bed's comfy. Nice prison," she said in dismay then she heard voices outside.

"The master wants you two to stand guard, and you will keep this extra key. She will not come out, unless he says so," said a commanding officer.

"Aye," they said in unison.

"Great, now I have guards," she fussed fiercely. "I guess he really wants me to stay." She covered herself with the blanket and went to sleep.

- Chapter 52 -

THE NEXT MORNING SHE woke up and checked her surroundings a little more. She walked to the mirror and fixed her headband and her hair. She found a small lamp close to the bed on a small table. She checked for any objects on the floor to pick the lock, but there were none. Escape was almost hopeless. The door started to unlock, and Ramses came in. "Good morning. Sleep well? Dad has breakfast. Come."

"Correction, he's not your dad," she corrected.

"That is something he'll never know. Now let's *go*," he said pulling her out in the hall. They walked into the dining hall where a long table was set up with food everywhere.

"Oh, yum. Food," she said as she sat down close to Osiris, and Ramses sat down right beside her. After she prayed to herself, she began to eat. Menes watched her as he ate. Ramses touched no food, but he watched her continuously. She kept glancing at them as she ate. Menes smiled slyly, but Ramses caught him and shot him daggers in warning. *Ooh, I wonder*, she thought. Osiris didn't even see the looks the two gave each other. Menes glared back at him wrathfully. *I wonder if I could stir up something here, and why is Ramses looking at me weird?* She thought as she also tried to think of a plan.

"Do you like your room?" asked Re.

"Yeah, beats staying in a dungeon," she said then drank her water.

"Really? It was my idea," said Menes.

"It was not! It was mine," snapped Tut.

"Mine nitwit!" Menes retorted back.

"It was neither of yours. It was my idea," Ramses thundered.

"Stay out of it, loony Pharaoh!" Menes said shaking his fist at him.

"What did you call me?" Ramses asked as he began to boil.

"You heard me unless you have too much chrome in your ears."

"Shut up, wet behind the ears!"

Neiko giggled at the intense fighting at the table between the three. "Don't take that, Menes! Let him have it!"

"Make me, Chrome Bucket!" Menes retorted.

Ramses looked at Neiko then at Menes wrathfully. "I will, you smelly guttersnipe!"

"You won't neither, chrome behind the ears!" Tut said in defense of Menes.

"You go, Tut!" Neiko said, trying to stoke the fire. Ramses became angrier, and Neiko knew something wasn't right; it wasn't the insults that did it.

"What's the matter? Jealous because she's taking up for me because she likes me better?" Menes said, taunting.

"I have no idea what you mean, you two stupid morons!" Ramses snapped indignantly.

"That is *enough*!" Osiris scolded. "Can we have one meal without the four of you fighting? I'm so weary of your endless bickering. Now, I want peace and quiet from here on out."

They nodded at each other but they kept glaring at each other. Neiko looked at each of them, and the great annoyance in each of their eyes, but death was written in the eyes of Ramses, especially when he looked at Menes. His eyes softened when his flaming eyes fell on her, and for the first time she looked into them in attempts to read them, but she could not decipher much for what she felt; she turned away and shuddered.

"Hmm, I wonder," she thought.

"When do you plan to go visit the Damonites, Ramses?" asked Osiris.

"I will do it tomorrow," he said, and Menes perked up. This time he didn't notice, but Neiko did.

"Well, the sooner the better," he said, shrugging.

"I must take Neiko back to her room, excuse me," he said as stood up and taking hold of her.

On the way back to her room, she began to ask Ramses several questions. "What are you up to anyway? Why am I so important to you? Obviously it isn't because I am the Chosen One."

Ramses turned and look at her surprised. "You'll find out soon enough. I promise you."

"Why can't you be straightforward for once? Why are you being so secretive about it—" she began but stopping abruptly by putting her foot in her mouth and thinking she may have said too much.

He stopped right in front of her door and turned around. "Persistent you are on the matter. Like I said, all in good time," he said as he put his hand on her cheek and looked her in the eyes. His eyes burned into hers, then he proceeded to unlock the door, and she went inside.

"Okay, that was weird. So much weird stuff happened today, and I kinda get a drift from him that unnerves me. I think he likes me, and that's not good. What makes it worse is that he's hiding it. Menes kept badgering him about it and he looked as if he wanted to kill him—yikes. I also get the distinct impression that Menes is contesting Ramses over me, and Ramses doesn't like it. I just gotta find a way to get Ramses mad enough to slip up and tell me, but how? So when I stuck up for Menes—I got it! I'll pretend I like Menes, and that oughta make him really mad. Oh, I also forgot that Lydia isn't here; I wonder where she is. Obviously that adds to the hint that Ramses has got his sights on me at the moment, but why? I'll find out in this little scheme of mine," she mused as she paced the floors in her prison, and she then heard Menes and his two brothers outside of her room.

"You better hope Ramses doesn't find out, or your dead meat. Do you remember what he said the last time?" said Tut.

"Yeah, he just loves making empty threats at me because I get to him," Menes retorted.

"They didn't sound empty to me. They used to be empty, that is until Neiko showed up," Re replied.

Neiko ran up and put her ear to the door and listened in closely.

"You also remember what *I* said? I was gonna let him do all the hard part, and I was gonna steal her from him. I wished he would admit he's smitten with her instead of denying it all the time, but it is so obvious. Well, in that case I'll just make him look like a fool when she and I are happily married. I bet he'll wish he never tried to play dumb with me!" Menes trumpeted.

"I hope you know what you're doing," Re said cautiously.

"Oh, Re, you sound like my mother and a worry wart! I have it all under control."

"That's what you said when you stole that picture, and he took you outside and cleaned your clock," Tut reminded.

"But this is different. I think you should give it up. I have a bad feeling about Ramses like he isn't the brother we've always known him to be, and his love for Neiko is a lot stronger than anything we've ever seen," Re said, whimpering.

"Love? Is that what you call that little excuse for a crush? Ha! That stupid chrome spud doesn't even know the meaning of the word. Besides, when I bag Neiko, he'll go on with Lydia or either he'll go on alone and let Lydia rot in Fort Kill. He'll be moping around like a kicked puppy with his tail between his legs."

"But you know what Dad will say," Tut said.

"Yeah, he always lets Ramses get away with everything! He gives him everything he wants and who he wants. He gets all the ones with class, and it's not fair! That lying, no-good cheater! Now it's my turn!"

"Menes, there are plenty of women with class in the world. Who knows? Maybe you can get Lydia on the rebound."

"No! I've made my choice, and it's Neiko, no exceptions! There is nothing Ramses can do or say to stop me!"

"Shh! Menes, not so loud! Neiko could be asleep now, and you don't want to wake Ramses do you? He will be doubly angry to know we were on this hall near her room, and remember he said he would boil us alive if he ever—"

"Oh hush, Re! You seem to let every little thing he says scare you, but we need to scoot because he gets cranky if he doesn't get his Pharaoh sleep, c'mon, let's go."

Neiko got up and thought about everything she had heard. "Oh boy, Ramses's case of lovesickness is worse than I thought, and it almost looks like stage two, but I'll go on with my scheme. Now I know where Lydia is, and he's just left her there, how mean! Menes is so love struck that when I play him for a fool, he won't even know it! I bet I can get plenty of info from him too. Re is the weakest link in the chain, and I'd like to tell him that his suspicions are right on target. Well to bed," she said as she jumped into bed and went to sleep.

- CHAPTER 53 -

THE NEXT MORNING THE door was unlocked, and Menes came in, but this time he was clean and well kempt. "Mornin'—wanna have breakfast with me and my brothers?" he asked sweetly.

"Sure do since Ramses isn't here to bother us," she said as she flicked her hair in his face in a flirting manner. They walked to the table, and sat together. *This is so easy!* She thought as she ate.

"What do you think about me?" he asked.

"You are a really nice Pharaoh, and you're kinda cute, unlike that mean ol' ugly chrome-plated jerk," Neiko said watching him intently, and Tut and Re gave each other high five.

"I'll let you stay out all afternoon instead of leaving you cooped up in that room all by your lonesome," he said as he moved closer to her and put his arm around her.

"So, uh, Menes, what would you do if you found out that Ramses was not your brother?"

Menes looked at her puzzled. "I would take great pleasure in cutting off his head with my axe and throwing it into the moat to feed the piranhas."

Neiko looked at him puzzled. "You got piranhas?"

"Yeah, dear, want to see 'em eat?" he said as he took a huge ham and led her to the moat by the hand. He walked her to the rampart and handed her the ham. "Go ahead, feed them," he said, and she threw the ham into the moat. As soon as it hit the water, the water boiled with the onslaught of raging, hungry piranhas, and all was gone including the bones.

"Whoa! Do you ever feed 'em?"

"Once a week, and if anyone falls in the moat then they will be piranha food," he said. "Let's go inside and chat with my brothers."

They stayed in that afternoon and talked. Neiko found out all kinds of things that happened in their family life, and how Ramses acted around the fortress; all of her suspicions were right. Menes slid closer to her, put his arm around her, and looked at her with a large grin. He tilted her chin up and puckered for a kiss, and Neiko's mind started racing.

"Why you—" said a cold, hard voice, and all four looked and saw Ramses in the doorway with his eyes burning like fire and narrowed to slits. He was breathing so hard his shoulders heaved up and down in rhythm of his breaths which were fast in his fury. Menes gulped as Ramses stormed up and grabbed him by the throat. Losing all sense of reason, he revealed his true strength as he lifted him off the ground with one arm and pinned him against the wall. Menes choked and wheezed as he fought to breathe. He tried to pry the fingers off of his neck, and he kicked trying to stay alive while Tut and Re looked at him with terrified looks. Neiko stood there in shock, but seeing the door open, she sprinted to make a hasty escape. Seeing her running out of the corner of his eye, Ramses threw Menes against the wall like a ragdoll, spun around, thrust his hand forward, and said an unknown word. The doors slammed shut in front of her, and she frantically tried to open them, but they wouldn't budge. He walked up and seized her, and his grip was like steel.

"So, this little game is to get back at me? Well, let me tell you something. The only Pharaoh you will be marrying is me, understand? If you must know, I came to Hawote and brought you here to make you my wife! I hope the three of you hear that, especially you, Menes. Let this be a warning, and if you *ever* try this again, then I will finish what I began, is that clear?" he said as he stormed up to them drawing his dagger as he dragged Neiko behind him. He thrust the point into Menes' chin as it started to prick it. A small trickle of blood oozed as the point stung his chin.

Menes grunted in between his gasps to get air back into his lungs. For the first time Menes feared Ramses as he looked at the hard, merciless glare and the others flattened themselves against the wall. Menes sat up, and his brothers aided him and helped him stand up. The three left the room and were gone leaving them alone. Ramses pinned her against the wall, and he tilted her head up into his piercing eyes with the handle of his dagger.

"There is something else I will let you know and remember it well. I saw you in the windows of time, and I loved you before the universes had form. You seem to know what I speak of, don't you?" he said seeing Neiko's terrified eyes, and she nodded, shaking.

"I-I only imagined you only half of what you really are, and you only loving Lydia like this—not me!" she managed to rasp out of her frightened body.

"Things change, my sweet. I know you know a lot about me, yet there is still so much you don't know among which are my age and my appearance, but that is not important now. I know *everything* about you."

"What do you look like under there?" she asked as she touched his helmet.

"I will show you one day. You will be the only one that I will allow to look at my face and live to tell about it. It matters not where you found the information on me, and if you try get smart and try to tell anyone, they'll die—just like Quickstrike has died now."

"How much do you know about me?" she asked.

"You love to explore, adventure is your middle name, Kidd is not really a last name for you, defending the Indians of Hawote against the Crackedskulls, and Bloodhawk wants you to be his. You became Admiral this year, the only one in history, and you became a Desert Storm Falcon in 1985, became Captain in 1988, the youngest officer in your tribe's history—the only time a child was able to lead the victory. You love deer barbecue, hunting, and you love Monchiska of the Scraah, son of Sigma and Puma, who are the leaders of that tribe. I was also perfectly aware of where I was when we met the first time—I only pretended I didn't know since I was unaware that you knew my true identity, and I had planned to hide it from you until we were married in hopes for my success of eternal matrimony. Did you honestly think that the Heart of Rumi arrived on your world in your area of Hawote by some kind of freakish happenstance? *I* sent it there! I also know that it is in Raven's possession, and its location hasn't escaped my notice—I only *pretended* I didn't know. Foolish girl. My focus is on *you*, and I will retrive it in due time when *we* return to rule as husband and wife for eternity. Everything has been intricately planned milennia in advance, and nothing will stop me now. Need I say more?" he said as he slipped the handle from her chin, down her neck, and down her chest.

She shuddered with a million thoughts racing her head. *The mystery of the Eye of Mohica—or Cygnus is finally solved.*

"You will spend the rest of this afternoon with me, alone, my diamond," he said as he led her down the hallway to the ballroom.

Later that afternoon the three brothers had a meeting on the day's events. "You see, Menes, I told you a hundred times there's somethin'

that ain't right about Ramses. Would you listen? NOOoo!" Re retaliated.

"You're right, Re. He has never lifted me off the ground in his life, and he almost killed me! Where did all of that strength come from all of a sudden? If he woulda squeezed any harder, he woulda crushed my neck. He was never that strong even in anger."

Tut swallowed hard. "So what do you think we should do now, Menes? You remember that question she asked you earlier?"

Menes rubbed his chin. "Oh, you mean like him not being my brother or something? Why?"

"I've been noticing that he never eats with us, and he isolates himself like he's too good for us or somethin'," Re suggested.

"Well, two can play at this game. Maybe she knows something we don't, and she was testing the waters. I wonder what, and I still won't give up on getting her," Menes smiled wickedly.

"Are you crazy? After he tried to kill you this afternoon? He said he'll do it the next time!" Re squealed in a high pitch.

"Oh, Re, I'll be much more careful this time. I know one thing; he will too, and I probably won't be able to be within ten feet of her. I could just look at her cross-eyed, and he'll have a hissy fit. I just—just want to kill him!" Menes said snarling, and then he had an epiphany. "Kill him, that's it! If he's not here to give me problems—"

Tut and Re smiled devilishly. "That's the best idea you've come up with. I'm getting sick and tired of taking crap off of him," Tut said.

"I agree, let's do it! I hate him so much because he bullies me all the time because he knows I'm scared of him," Re said with evil glee.

"You can't be scared of a dead Pharaoh then can you, Re? His chrome breeches have got a little too big, and we will cut him out of the picture."

"How we'll we do it though, Menes? I mean, Dad will really be mad to know we killed him on purpose," Re said.

"We have to make it look like an accident, and I will need the two of you to help me."

"Gladly," Tut said, sneering.

"Just think, you'll not only have Neiko, but you'll also be First Pharaoh, and neither of us oppose," Re said, smirking.

Menes rubbed his hands together. "I love the sound of that. I'll teach Ramses a lesson he'll never live to tell about."

"The sooner the better," Re sniggered.

"Let's go find him," said Tut, and the three of them went to find him.

They looked everywhere he usually was, but they couldn't find him.

"Well, where is he? Well, time to plan more. Let's get a snack," Menes said as they approached the dining hall. There were two guards at the doors. "Hey, what's the big idea? Do we have a food shortage?"

"The First Pharaoh is having a private dinner with the outlaw and wishes not to be disturbed," replied one of the guards.

Menes shook indignantly then pushed the guard out of the way, and tried to open the door, but it was locked. He then banged his fist on the door. "Open this door right now, Ramses! This ain't fair! There are other hungry Pharaohs in this fortress, you know! Hey, are you listening or are you having problems with your brain? Or do you have one?"

Ramses did not answer.

"What do you think you are doing, you three?" Osiris scolded.

"He's in there hogging all the food! Can he go someplace else to have dinner?"

"Menes, I have news for you. Ramses has informed me today that he is courting Neiko and later will be marrying her. You would want privacy on your date too, would you not? He will join us for dinner tonight along with his chosen, so you can hold a little longer. You aren't wasting away, so leave him alone," Osiris said then walked away.

"Well, we gotta do it and fast," Re said. "Your chances aren't looking good, and—"

"I know, Re! I am getting ready each minute to do him in. Wait and see, he'll be dead soon, and the next wedding news will be mine and Neiko's! The only music will be for Ramses' funeral and my wedding, along with my coronation!"

"Come on, let's plan a little more, and let's scram before Ramses finds out what we're up to and does all three of us in. I don't want Dad giving us another one of those Pharaoh brotherly love lectures," Re said walking away.

"I agree," Tut said as Menes followed suit in following Re.

- CHAPTER 54 -

THAT NIGHT ALL FIVE Pharaohs and Neiko had the family dinner. Osiris sat at the head, and Neiko sat in the first seat to his right with Tut across from her. Ramses sat beside Neiko with Menes in front of him, and Re sat on the other side of Menes. The three eyed Ramses in a sly look, and he watched them carefully. Neiko interrupted the staring contest by asking, "Osiris, do you believe in the Dark Pharaoh?"

Ramses looked at her coolly as he listened intensively.

Osiris looked at her puzzled. "Well, yes and no. I believed in him as a boy, and I passed the tales on to my sons, but I don't concern myself so on the matter like Rumi did."

"What about you, Menes?"

Menes rubbed his chin. "Well, yeah I do! I'm scared of him! One Halloween I tried to dress like him, and I scared the daylights out of Tut and Re; they believe in him too."

Funny they have that holiday here. "Did you scare Ramses?" she asked.

"No. I guess because I looked so silly, but the real thing would scare the chrome off his armor," Menes said.

Ramses shot him icy daggers as he grabbed and held Neiko's hand trying to control his rage. Neiko tried to pull away, but he tightened his grip.

"Must we talk about these childish stories? I have never believed in this ridiculous legend!" he said in attempts to hide his anger.

"Aww, c'mon. If it's so childish, why not talk about it? I think it's fun!" Neiko said, turning the knife.

"So be it," he said as he gave her a warning in his eyes and squeezed her hand reminding her he was there.

"Ramses, you need to learn to live a little instead of being as hard as your armor all the time," Menes said as he flicked an onion onto his breastplate.

Ramses looked at it coldly, picked it off, and look at him with his frigid eyes.

"I know all about the Dark Pharaoh. I plan to hunt him like Rumi did, and I'll find him," Menes said with a mouth full of corn.

Ramses stared at him as he narrowed his eyes with venom, and gripped her hand even tighter.

"Oh, really, and how will you do that?" she said trying to wrench her hand free from Ramses's grasp. "Will you let go? I need my hand to eat with you know!" she snapped as she slapped his gloved hand several times, but she hit his hard hand guard by accident with her middle finger. "Oww!" she said as she waved her hand side to side then popped her aching finger in her mouth.

"Aww, did you hurt yourself?" asked Ramses sweetly as he took her other hand in his affectionate grasp, and he placed it over his mouth plate as if he was kissing it. The pain mysteriously vanished, but he refused to release either of her hands, and Neiko gave an annoyed look.

"How am I supposed to eat now?" she asked ruffled.

"The food can wait," he said passionately.

Menes was hot. "You know what, Neiko? I'll hunt him down like the mouse he is! I can spot him a mile away, I could!" he said as he tried to put all of his wrath on the unknown, and Ramses gave him a poisonous stare.

Neiko looked at him like he was joking as she tried to free herself still. "You could, huh? You know what? You wouldn't know who the Dark Pharaoh was even if he sat down right in front of you!" she said trying to stand up, but her loving captor forced her to remain seated. "Okay, I'm really—" she said bristling at him but he refused to release her.

"There's no point in resisting me. Get used to it because when we're married—"

"I'll never marry you! Never! You hear me? Reven!" she shouted at him as she fumed.

"It's useless to resist!"

"I'll resist you as long as I live, Chrome Dome! Pharaoh Scuzz Bucket! The butt end of everyone's jokes and the Pharaoh of Scum! If you wanna marry something, marry the bumper of my car because it's just like you, Chrome Turd!" she boiled.

Ramses laughed at her as he pulled her into his arms and embraced her, but she bucked and struggled. "I think not. I will crush that will of yours like I did that roach in your room, and there's nothing anyone can do to stop me."

"Stop it! Let go of me! The Attack Pack will fix you! If you go to Hawote, then the Indians and Crackedskulls will. I'd rather marry Bloodhawk than you any day, you monster!"

"Are you still counting on them to save you? I have news for you. I will destroy the Attack Pack and Hawote. Hawote will end up like Etowah unless you marry me."

"Oooh, you're despicable! You won't get away with this! Ohh, get your hands off me!"

"I already have, my sweet," he said sniggering as he held her tighter. "No one or nothing can stop me."

Menes was seething. *I'll be the one to stop you*, dead *in your tracks*, he thought smirking.

Osiris was feeling sorry for Neiko. "Ramses, that's enough. Don't torture her so. It is hard for her to adjust as it is; be gentle."

"I've already tried that, but it will not work. I refuse to take no for an answer, so she brought it on herself."

"Just send her to her room, and leave her in peace till tomorrow," Osiris said sympathetically.

"You are so soft, Dad. No wonder you gave up long ago."

"I'll take her to her room," Menes offered, and Ramses narrowed his eyes viciously.

"Menes, that is kind of you, but I will have escorts to take her to her room."

"But—"

"Menes, you better mind your father or the Dark Pharaoh will come and tear your face off," Neiko said in a subtle warning, and Ramses looked at her in wicked agreement.

"Alright, Dad, but first I want to show her something," Ramses said as he got up, and leading her by the hand. He walked quickly, and she stumbled behind him.

"So be it," Osiris called after him. "You bring her back to me, and I'll have her sent to her room."

"As you wish," he answered.

He stopped in front of a wall, he pushed in a brick, and a secret door opened. A staircase wound into an unknown basement. They walked down it and came into a small room, and there was the Dark Pharaoh's Eye. "Look there," he said pointing to two golden sarcophaguses. They were the tombs of Anubis and Thutmose. Anubis was a jackal man with black skin and icy blue eyes, while Thutmose was a saber toothed tiger man with long curved top fangs, and both were in Pharaoh robes. The sarcophaguses had been made in their likenesses as if they were alive. Neiko looked at them with amazement. "Now, come here to the Eye. Ask it what you wish to see and rub it three times."

"Show me the Seven Tribes," she said then rubbed it. She saw the entire Seven Tribes along with most of Hawote in mourning. She could hear them weeping, Xartna was giving a speech, and each of her friends were crying along with Monchiska.

"Oh, ye great land of Hawote, we lift up in memory of Admiral Neiko Kidd, who has given her life in service so that we may be free today. She was the greatest friend that anyone could have. Let Great Spirit have mercy on the soul that took her life in cold blood, and may even God's wrath, ours, and the wrath of our enemies, the Crackedskulls, be heavy on his conscience. A cold-blooded murderer of the Outsiders shed innocent blood. May Neiko's memory go with us everywhere and when we go to battle . . ." Xartna preached as tears streamed down his eyes and in seeing this, Neiko began to cry.

"Show me Raven and Bloodhawk," she said and rubbed it again. It showed the mighty Bloodhawk doubled over in sorrow wailing like a baby. He was professing his undying love and making curses to the man who supposedly murdered her. His eleven-foot, massive body shook in grief, and he buried his face in his hands. Raven was in just as bad shape, and he put his hand on his broken son's back as he wept sore as well, and all of the visible Crackedskulls were lamenting as well, except Francesco who was faking his mourning. Seeing this, she cried harder. "Show me my parents," she said and rubbed it. Her parents were in just as bad of shape as everyone else, and Neiko sobbed. "Everyone thinks I'm dead," her voice was a whisper. She looked at him with pain in her eyes. "How can you be so cruel?"

"That is why I am the Dark Pharaoh, dearest. Besides, mourning your feigned death is less severe than if they knew the truth. They are the ones who believe you were murdered; I had nothing to do with their judgment. In their eyes I am make believe, and they will never know the truth. It is in their best interest if they don't know and meddle."

"You didn't have anything to do with it my foot! You may not have made it look like I died, but you are the one who stole me from my land, toilet face!" she hissed with hate as she shook her fists at him angrily.

"Temper, temper. Name-calling will get you nowhere. Besides, once my mind is made up, there is no changing it, so I'd give this up if I were you. If you do, then I will be more lenient."

"Yeah, right. I know what will happen to me if I get hitched with you! I'll become a Dark Pharaohess and your eternal prisoner, and you'll go ahead and destroy Hawote anyway! I know your type, Chrome Commode. Nice try, but no cigar, Chrome Snitcher," she scowled.

"You're absolutely right, but your knowledge won't save you. I'll win you, you'll see. I will change back to good later, and you know that as well."

"Gimme a break. I don't want to spend another minute with you, so you can take your marriage proposal and shove it down your throat!"

"This is far from over. Like I said, I have just begun, and I will never give up."

"What are you gonna do, put me in a trance or erase my memory or some crap like that?"

"No. I want you to love me with no tricks. If I do that, then I cannot have you forever like I want or like I was promised, and you know that."

"You know that won't happen, so give it up already. You'll have an easier time trying to get Bloodhawk to fit in a kid's funhouse!" Neiko stormed.

"You underestimate me. Quelling your spunk is much easier than you make it out to be. It seems you want to do this the hard way, so be it. It seems Neiko Kidd is the one to do things the hard way."

"Good. I don't want to see your ugly face for another minute even though it's not your real face," she snapped and started up the stairs, and he followed her.

Everything's going according to plan. She thinks she's won, if she keeps this up, little will she realize I'll be wearing her down. Her friends will pay for her impudence, and no one insults me without paying a price, he thought as he followed her.

Osiris personally escorted her to her room. "I never thought I'd be glad to see a prison in my life, and I don't know how much more I can take of this. I was rejecting him with everything I had, but he pushed harder and harder. If I stay here much longer, then I'll get myself in trouble or someone will get hurt. It seems Hawote is next on his hit list, but one thing is certain: I can't give in, or I'll be in bigger trouble. Everything will be fine when Judgement Day comes, but until then—" she shuddered. "I gotta find a way to escape and soon. I have to get back to Hawote, tell everybody I'm alive, and get things back to normal, sort of. My life will never be normal now thanks to Ramses," she said as she devised an escape plan.

- CHAPTER 55 -

LATER THAT NIGHT SHE thought of the plan. "Now, all I gotta do is get this door open," she whispered to herself as she approached the door. She knocked on it to see if there was a guard. "Hello, is anyone out there?"

"What do you want?" he answered gruffly.

Her mind started going, and she found a brass pitcher. She grabbed it and answered, "I've gotta use the restroom," she said.

"I am not supposed to let you out because the First Pharaoh commands," he answered.

"Do you want me to make a mess and tell Ramses why?" she asked.

Then he started to unlock the door. "Alright, you get your wish," he said as he came in, but he didn't notice that she was hiding the pitcher behind her back. When he approached her, she struck like lightning, and hit him in his chin knocking him senseless. She dragged him in her room and took off the keys. She shut the door and locked it and tiptoed down the hall.

Yes! She thought as she sneaked into another hall. Two sentries walked past her, so she flattened herself against the wall and froze. When they turned down another hall, she sneaked into the throne room, which was lit by torches. Two guards walked in, and she hid behind the throne. They walked into the next room, and she slipped into the foyer and listened for any guards. She crept for the exit, but there were two guards by the door. She backed up and slipped into another room. This one had a window, and she ran to it and opened it. It squeaked as she opened it, and all of her muscles tensed at the sound as she froze. No one came around, so she climbed out of it and stole across the courtyard. She used the shadows to get a closer look to see if the drawbridge and gate were open, but they were closed, and the gatehouse was far away with sentry towers along the way and very little cover. She took a deep breath, and measured up her first dash. She sprang and sprinted noiselessly to a nearby bush. A long run across four towers lay ahead. Before she could go, a sneeze started to come into her nose. It burned and she took a deep breath, and it went away. As soon as she was about to make her run, it came and she sneezed so hard she hit the bush and it rustled.

A bell started to ring. "Prisoner is escaping!" one shouted as others were alerted. Skull Bearers came and ran into the yard. Wasting no time, she ran as fast as she could to the gatehouse. She made it, and she found the levers to the gate and drawbridge. She quickly pulled them. Before the gate barely opened she crawled under it, and the drawbridge slammed on the ground because she allowed too much slack. She quickly ran across it, but at the end were horsemen, the outside sentries, and the ones on the ramparts had their bows drawn. More came from behind, and she was surrounded. Her escape plan was thwarted, and she was intercepted. Two came and took hold of her, and a general swaggered to her.

"You just wait till the First Pharaoh hears about this, you little savage. Trying to escape from Skull Fort are you? Well, I have news for you, no one escapes and lives, and I wouldn't be surprised if he triples the security around here. This little escapade of yours will not go unpunished, even if you are his chosen one. Come and bring her, I believe First Pharaoh Ramses wants an explanation," he said then turned on his heel while her two captors brought her back into the throne room.

Ramses was waiting in the throne room with his hands on his hips looking at them. "What is this? Someone owes me an explanation! Explain this!" he fumed.

"The prisoner was trying to escape, Majesty, and we intercepted her at the drawbridge," replied the general.

His gaze fell on her, and she gulped. "You still haven't learned, have you? You will never leave this place—ever! Have I made myself perfectly clear? General, I want this place guarded well. Quadruple the guard around here, and step on it!" he shouted. The general bowed and left. Then the guard of her room came in with a swollen chin. "I thought I told you not let her out of her room, did I not?"

"She said she had to use the bathroom, and I thought you would be displeased—"

"You idiot! She was playing with you, you simple-minded fool! I'll fix this. There will be no guards by her door because I'll have the keys. Give them to me!" he said as he thrust his hand forward, and the frightened guard did as he was told. "Alright—memo—maim you after I take care of Neiko. The next mistake made by anyone will be death as punishment, and you better make that clear to the rest of the Imperial Guard! Get out of my sight, you worthless ignoramus!" he said as he cuffed the terrified Skull Bearer, and the guard ran away. "As for you, my flower, I'll ensure you'll never pull a stunt like this again! Bring me a chain, one that goes on arms and legs and are linked together, and give me the key."

A few minutes passed, and they brought him what he had asked for. They put the fetters on her wrists and ankles; they locked them with the key and handed it to him. Neiko had trouble moving because the chains were heavy, and she looked at them sadly as she held her arms in front of her. "I wouldn't have to put these on you if you wouldn't try to escape. This is your punishment. You will wear them at all times except when you are in my presence, alone. Now, let's go back to your room. You two, go back to your posts," he said as he grasped her arm and pulled her behind him. She stumbled because of the added weight, which made it difficult to walk. When they got to her room, he opened the door and shoved her inside. Neiko tripped on the chain, and toppled onto the floor. "I bid you good night. See you in the morning," he said then shut the door.

Neiko felt hopelessness well up inside of her, and she could not sleep. She stared at the door as she sat on the bed fingering her bonds as some of her spirit was broken. "I hope the Attack Pack can find me," she moaned as she bit her lip.

"The only place I can think of where it might be, is in one of the forests past the San Antari Grasslands," Phoenix said to his followers.

"Well, let's do it!" Bantor shouted. "She's counting on us!"

"Yeah, we're the only hope she has!" cried Sky Shadow, the lizard-dragonfly. Then all of the Attack Pack took flight as they started their trek to the Giant and Dark Forests. They flew days across the San Antari Grasslands before they spotted the Giant Forest.

"Air Hammer and I will circle over the woods at high altitude and see if we can find it from the air, and if not, we must approach it from the inside," Phoenix replied. "Remain here till we return," he said, and the pair shot up into the sky like arrows.

The two flew overhead, but they saw nothing but the green tops of the trees, and the divide of the Schism Canyon. "Well, Phoenix, I can't see anything but trees, and you and I have the best vision," Air Hammer replied.

"I know. The trees are so tall and thick that no one could see it from the air. If I figure correctly, Anubis probably built it in the Dark Forest because it could easily hide something that large. Let's go back and tell them," Phoenix said as he dove back down with Air Hammer closely behind him. They told them their strategy, and the entire Attack Pack wondered into the Giant Forest. They traveled at random as they tried to find a road. They found one and started to follow it. They trekked along it, and in the distance Phoenix spotted a bridge crawling with Skull Bearers.

"We don't need a bridge, but if they see us, then they'll tell them we're here, so let's kick their behinds because we can't go around; we can't lose the road," mused Ramulus, one of the rams.

"Yeah, let's do it!" said Sandstorm, and the Attack Pack let out all types of calls and charged at the bridge. Surprise and fear took the Skull Bearers as they saw an onslaught of maddened, attacking beasts. A small group was blocking the bridge.

Air Hammer dashed forward. "Hammer Head!" he called as he rammed into them with his hard hammered head felling several, some into the canyon. Scarem and Raptor followed him slicing and killing many. A large force began to come across the bridge.

"I'll handle this!" Cheetor yelled as he leaped in front. He fired his rocket and hit the bridge. The bridge exploded, and collapsed taking most of the force with it, while others were flying in the air from the explosion, but they all plummeted into the canyon. Seeing this, the rest tried to make a retreat, but the Attack Pack closed them in and did away with them.

"Onward!" Sandstorm pointed down the road with his scimitar, and they ran into the Dark Forest following the road to find the fortress and rescue their imprisoned friend.

- CHAPTER 56 -

THE NEXT MORNING NEIKO came in to eat breakfast with everyone. She walked in front of Ramses in her shackles with a gloomy look on her face, and they looked at her wryly. She sat down in her usual spot and said nothing the entire time. "What's the matter, cat got your tongue?" Menes asked trying to pick conversation, but Neiko wouldn't look at him or answer. She just ate her food and stared at the table.

"Aww, c'mon, I miss your insults this morning; aren't you gonna call me by my whole name?" asked Tut.

She looked at him with pain-filled eyes but said nothing.

"Shut up all of you! She has a punishment to think about, and a truth to accept," Ramses said happily.

"You're awfully chipper this morning, and you haven't been that way in years," Osiris said looking at him.

"Why shouldn't I be? I've got everything I want, and I just stopped her from escaping. I have made it clear she can never escape or outwit me for long, and now it's over."

"Well, you have made me proud, son," Osiris said, but the praise didn't appeal to him.

"Well, I want to spend time alone with my bride-to-be. Excuse us," he said taking her by the hand and left. He took her into a lounge room and shut the door. Neiko looked around half-heartedly. "You can take those off," he said waiving his first finger; her bands unlocked and fell off.

"Why do you need a key if you can do that," she snapped irritably.

"You know why."

"Why don't you stop pretending that you're something you're not, like mimicking Pharaohs," she said kicking her chains contemptuously.

"Mimicking?" he laughed. "All pharaohs are a mimic of *me*. These of Qari and of Egypt are all wannabes of me. They are somewhat different than I am, especially the Egyptian ones. They dress like me, rule like me, and want to be more like me. The ones of Qari conquer and force like I do. The ones of Egypt do as well, but they want to be an immortal god like me, but not till after death. They rule mortals, but they are mortals themselves, and they make rules to make themselves in my likeness with laws alone. I show my divinity with my might and power. Although those from Egypt say they are sons of the sun and do not know The Almighty, they worship gods that do not exist! I am the only true Pharaoh, and I am not the Bright Morning Star, or the Son of the Sun, or any of those ridiculous titles and protocol. I am the Setting Sun, the Black Nemesis, and many others. That spoiled palace brat you mentioned one time before even mocks me by trying to be merciless like me, but he isn't capable of even handling things himself! He has to have armies to back him up, but I don't! I can do everything without them. They are of no use to me."

Neiko cocked an eyebrow. "The only Pharaoh? I think not. What about the Good Pharaohs? Pharaohs are not supposed to be gods under God, but guardians of good. That's what makes you the Dark Pharaoh, then huh?"

"Exactly. I did away with them long ago, even before The Almighty created Earth! I can remember one distinctly, the one I hate most. His name was Sesmar Repsis-Bijou, but he is out of the picture with all of my goody-goody brethren. I have only one sister, but she is only one day younger than I, and I don't know where she is. No more talk about this," he said as he took her hand and sat on the couch.

Suddenly Quicksilver ran in without knocking. "I have terrible news!"

Ramses looked at him with great annoyance. "You better have a good reason for this intrusion! This had better have profound value."

Quicksilver shook his head. "This cannot wait, Dark Lord. I don't know how much time you have till—"

"Out with it!" he snarled.

"Vipra is dead, and the Attack Pack knows that Neiko has been abducted. I don't think she killed Quickstrike like you commanded."

He narrowed his eyes with frustration, and Neiko perked up. "Did you see her body, and do they know I was the one that shanghaied her?"

"I don't know," he sputtered.

"What do you mean you don't know?! What is it that you don't know?"

"I don't know if they think if you are responsible for her disappearance."

"Did you find Vipra's body or not?"

"I-I can't tell; all I found was a wet spot. The only way I think I know is because I found this," he said as he pulled out Vipra's amulet and the empty phial Ramses had given her to drug Neiko.

Upon seeing and hearing this, Ramses grew angry, and he tightened his free hand into a fist so tightly his glove crackled. "They know! I'm sure of it! Well, I'll just have a warm reception waiting for them—" then suddenly he heard the high-pitched screams of a hawk and an eagle along with the shrill war call of a Saracen along with a smash and the crumble of bricks. Screams of agony and surprise came from outside.

Neiko was so happy to hear the Attack Pack's arrival that she started dancing, singing, and taunting the angry Dark Pharaoh. "Ha-ha-ha-AHA-ha! I'm getting outa here, and you are gonna get spanked!"

He jerked her to him, her nose was touching his armored nose plate, and his flaming eyes were even with hers and they drilled into hers. "I think not. I have a few surprises waiting, and they will not steal you from me that easily. Quicksilver, come here," he said, and Quicksilver obeyed fearfully. He placed his hand on his head and closed his eyes and muttered some weird chant. Blue fire went into Quicksilver, and Quicksilver groaned in pain. His eyes rolled back and his body jerked as he started to change.

"You're killing him, you heartless slime!" Neiko snarled as she tried to free herself from his grasp.

"No, I am making him a Shadow Warrior, which is my army of immortal servants who do my bidding. Transformation into immortality can sometimes be excruciating," he said then Quicksilver got up completely changed. His eyes were no longer that of a man, but they matched those of his dark master. Neiko shrank back in terror as he lifted his arms up in triumph of his newfound power. "Guard her while I destroy those meddling beasts!" he said then left. Neiko tried to run after him, but Quicksilver grabbed her, put her chains back on, and shut the door.

Outside was a great deal of action. The flyers were zipping by and bombing the Skull Bearers with their hidden weapons or anything they could get their paws or claws on. Sandstorm flew on his flying carpet, and he threw a huge boulder on a Skull Bearer who was about to fire on Aries.

One archer tried to shoot Scarem, but he hit him on his hard shell, and the arrow ricocheted off. The angry beetle charged and slashed with his pinchers and beheaded him.

"Fire the spear launchers!" yelled Menes as he shook his axe. They fired and hit no one. Cheetor leaped and caught one, threw it and caught the operator in the stomach with the spear. He was killed instantly.

"Fire the catapults!" shouted Tut as he drew his long curved sword, and Re was standing next to him with his mace in hand. The Attack Packers used the giant stones against them. They hurled the stones and caused great damage and hazard as they smashed them into the ramparts and walls. Ramses was running out of the stronghold, and Glacier threw one right at him. He jumped out of the way and barely got away as the rock smashed in the wall where he previously was. He drew his sword and went to lead his battered forces to victory.

"Kill that scoundrel!" shouted Sichus, Ramulus's brother, as he pointed his hoof at Ramses. The Attack Pack concentrated their fire on the leader. Ramses had many narrow escapes, and he made it to the rampart as Menes, Re, and Tut followed him. Cheetor fired a rocket and it exploded into the wall, and the top was gone. The explosion caused Ramses to lose his balance, and he windmilled his arms to keep from falling into the moat, which was filled with hungry piranhas. Seeing their chance, Menes, Re, and Tut, simultaneously sprinted and pushed him off the wall. Ramses screamed as he fell, and he landed headfirst into the water. The water boiled with the surge of the piranha attack. Within seconds the attack ceased, and a few bubbles came to the surface, along with pieces of his cape. Seeing the sword of Ramses lying on the floor, Menes picked it up, held it in the air as he yelled with triumph at his victory.

"I am now First Pharaoh!" he said then threw the sword out and it dug itself into the ground outside the moat where Ramses had fallen. It quivered, and his two brothers patted him on the back.

"All hail Menes, First Pharaoh, and the greatest of all!" they yelled. The entire Attack Pack was taken aback on what had happened.

Sichus and Ramulus walked up to Menes. "Alright, *First Pharaoh*, where is Neiko?" asked Ramulus with a jeer.

Menes shrugged. "I don't now. The ex First Pharaoh is the one who had her last, and it's too late to ask him; even if he were alive, he wouldn't tell you."

The twin brothers smiled at each other knowing Menes was going to be in very big trouble, and they laughed at each other. "Alright, First Pharaoh," Sichus sniggered. "I guess we have to rescue her on our own," he said, and they laughed at him.

"How dare you! You never laugh at Menes and live, you two stupid sheep! You will never take her out because I own her now. If you want to try, then you have to get past me!" he said flexing his muscles and brandishing his axe; they were laughing hard at each other, while Aries dashed and pinned him.

"That was easy. Ramses was never that easy. If this is the future for the Pharaohs, then the Attack Pack could retire early," Aries, Ramulus's wife, punned, and the Attack Pack laughed. "Do you two want to cause anymore problems for us trying to rescue Neiko?" and they shook their heads. "Good. Can you two strong hunks go in and find her while we wait outside?" she said sweetly and fluttering her eyes at Ramulus, her husband.

The two ran into the fortress to look for their missing friend. They opened doors and called her name loudly.

Neiko was sitting on the couch staring at the floor, but then she heard them calling her name. "Sichus! Ramulus! I'm in here, help! Help!" she screamed as she tried to stand up, but Quicksilver restrained her.

"Be quiet," he growled, but Neiko kept screaming.

"Neiko! Where are you? Keep screaming!" Ramulus said as he tried to get a bead on her.

"In here, help me!" her voice came softly from a distance. They were able to pinpoint her general direction, but it was confirmed by Quicksilver's threats.

"Shut up, the Master will be returning soon," he snarled, and they found the room.

"We're here! We'll have this door open in a jiffy, hang in there!" said Ramulus. Two Skull Bearers charged at them just as they were about to ram the door. Sichus rammed into them and threw them ten feet, and they smashed against the wall with a great noise.

The pair pawed the ground ready to buck. Sichus looked at his brother. "Ready on my mark, one, two, three!" he said then they rammed the door. It moved but it didn't open. They bucked it again and again. Quicksilver drew his dagger and waited. Finally on the fourth one, the door flew open. They ran in and saw Neiko on the couch.

"Guys, I'm so glad to see you!" she said.

Sichus grinned. "I know—" he started to say, but Quicksilver came out of nowhere, jumped on his back, and started stabbing him constantly in the side, and Sichus bucked and kicked trying to get him off. Ramulus ran to help him, and he reared up on his hind legs and slapped him in the head with his front hooves. Ramulus hit him in the stomach, and knocked him off of his injured brother. Sichus slung his head to the side and caught Quicksilver with his horn and sent him hurling into the fireplace. Soot and ash fell on him in a great cloud of dust. The three of them laughed as the blackened Shadow Warrior fell over knocked out. Ramulus had his back turned to the door, and Osiris came in behind him with his war club. It was a ball with two spikes in the sides, and on the other sides were three razor- sharp, jagged blades, and at the top was a razor-sharp, pointed blade for stabbing. He raised it to make the kill.

"Ramulus, watch out behind you!" Neiko said trying to dash forward, hindered by her bonds.

Ramulus kicked his back feet and caught him in the chest, and Osiris rocketed and slammed into the hall with his back to the wall, and was knocked senseless.

"Thanks, Neiko, I owe you one. Let's get outa here before Ramses decides to make round two as Dark Pharaoh."

"What about these chains? I can't run in these, and Ramses has the key," she said hobbling to them.

"We don't have time to break them, and Sandstorm will have to pick them off," Sichus said as he looked at his bleeding side.

"Hop on. Sichus and I can fly, and I'll gladly give you a lift, besides, the Attack Pack is waiting," he said as Neiko climbed on, and the twins ran in the way they came. The Attack Pack flew away from the battered Pharaoh fortress.

- CHAPTER 57 -

AFTER THE ATTACK PACK had left, Menes, Tut, and Re looked at the wreckage, and when they finished, they walked outside to the spot where Ramses fell to look at their handiwork. "Great way to begin your reign as First Pharaoh, huh?" asked Tut.

"Ramses is to blame for this. This is what is left of his reign—wreckage. Our great grandfather and forefathers would be very disappointed in him, and I'm glad I got rid of him. And you know what? He lost because of a *girl*. A girl! The mighty Ramses lost to an Indian chick! If he wasn't so busy gawking at her, and letting little ol' moi have her, then he'd be alive today, and this wouldn't have happened. If only the record books could say what a laughingstock Ramses really is!"

"Yeah, he goes around dressed in his chrome armor because he's so scared the sun will make him uglier than he already is!" Tut taunted.

Re scratched his head. "What does he look like anyway? You know, we have never seen him."

"It matters no more because he is piranha meat!" Menes said smiling proudly.

"Are you sure? I mean his armor is so hard," Re whined.

"Oh, Re, if the piranhas didn't eat him, then he drowned because that is 20 feet deep! He can't swim in all that armor, and I bet the little fishes are nibbling on his eyeballs right now!" Menes flaunted as he picked up a piece of Ramses's cape with the butt of his axe and watched it drip with water. He tied it onto his arm. "I'll wear this to remind everyone that Ramses the Sap is dead!"

The three hung out by the moat and poked fun at the memory of Ramses. The sun began to set, but an unusual silence blanketed the Dark Forest; not even a mouse moved, and Re began to get jumpy. "Guys, I wanna go in now. I'm scared," he whimpered.

"Re, stop. You are always negative. Besides, there's nothing out here!" Menes said, stretching his arms.

"Yeah, that's what scares me. I think Ramses knows we did it, and his ghost is haunting us! There isn't even a breeze!" he squealed.

"Re, there are no such things as ghosts. There are mortals, immortals, and spirits, but spirits stay out of mortal business except The Almighty and the good spirits. Dead mortals don't go around haunting people. You imagine too much," Tut said waving his hand at him.

Re gulped and trembled, but something was terribly wrong, and he knew it. While no one was looking at the moat, two red eyes appeared in the water, and it began to stir. Re turned, looked, and saw the two large flaming eyes, and he started to shake in fright. "I-I-I s-s-aw—" he couldn't finish, and he pointed a shaking finger at the moat.

"What?" Menes said and looked in there, but the eyes weren't there.

"It's your imagination, Re, there's nothing there!"

"R-right. O-k-kay. M-m-enes," he stammered.

Tut scratched the back of his neck. "What's with the moat?" he said when the piranhas started to pop out of the water, dead. Tut picked one up. "Dead as a door nail. I guess Ramses was bad for the fish," Tut shrugged. Re grabbed him shaking, and the water started boiling, changing colors, and churning. The three looked at it, and Re was so terrified he couldn't move. Suddenly Ramses rose out of the water and floated in midair. The three turned pale, grabbed each other, and shook. Ramses was dripping with water; weeds hung from him along with his tattered cape.

"G-g-g-ghost!" they screamed and tried to run, but they were too frightened to move. He stretched his hand, and his sword came to him and he caught it by the handle. The three of them backed up as they saw the cold, hard eyes. His armor gleamed in the moonlight, but suddenly the silver turned to black as he approached them. They trembled, and Menes turned from orange to white.

"D-d-d-aha Ph-ph-har," Menes could barely screech.

"That's right. You three tried to kill me! Well, no one can kill Ramses Sisper-Bijou, the Setting Sun! Nobody! Who is the sap now?" said his merciless voice with a hard death chill.

"It w-was only a j-joke, honest!" Menes pleaded.

"Hunt me down like a mouse and catch me, eh? Those were your exact words were they not? No one can capture the Dark Pharaoh! Especially a mortal baffoon like you! Now, if you want to hunt me, the hunt is over; try to catch me and let's see if you can live!" Ramses challenged as he uprooted a huge oak with ease and held it ready to throw.

Menes quaked at the true being that Ramses was. "R-r-ramses, I didn't mean it! Really. I had no idea that you were the Dark Pharaoh," he laughed nervously.

Ramses changed back into his normal state and threw the tree into the woods.

"Does this mean he's not our brother?" Re said with a wheeze.

"Duh!" Tut snapped as he slapped him in the back of head, and Re looked at him coolly as he rubbed his head.

Before Re could say a word, Ramses shouted, "Enough!" then a crack of thunder followed.

"Y-ya know, Neiko was really telling us all along—" Menes stammered.

Ramses narrowed his eyes and red fire came out of them and burned the ground a centimeter from his feet as a warning. "I don't want you to mention that name unless I say; she is sacred to me. If I *even* have the slightest notion you are trying to filch her from me, then I won't hesitate to kill you. You only say her name in my presence when I tell you. Understand?" he hounded, and they nodded. "I will spare your pitiful lives for the time being as long as you do my bidding to the letter. You will not say a word of this to Osiris, or I will kill him and the person who tells. You will do as before, but this time we will get along. I hope this is not hard for your sakes."

The three of them sighed with relief. "Well, what do we do now?" asked Menes.

"Nothing until I say so."

"Do you realize that your little rose petal is getting away?" asked Tut.

"I am perfectly aware of that," he snapped. "I'll see if anyone brings her to me, and if not, then we will make a visit to Hawote," he said deviously. "She has not seen the last of me, and she cannot hide from me even if she knows everything about me."

"What is going on out here?" asked Osiris as he walked out in his pajamas with a candle. "I find it hard to celebrate after today."

Ramses grabbed the three of them in a group hug. "Oh, just having a friendly, brotherly get together. Right brothers?" he said as he gave them a menacing look. They gritted their teeth in fear and nodded with a fake smile.

Osiris looked at them flabbergasted. "Well, good. At least you aren't waking the dead with endless bickering. Come inside, it's late," he said, and they followed him in silence.

That night the Attack Pack exited the Dark Forest. They found a suitable area and made camp. Sandstorm cut the chains off with his scimitar, and they planned their way to Cougan's Bluff. "I'm sorry to interrupt, guys, but Lydia needs our help too," Neiko replied.

"What do you mean?" asked Glacier.

"Where is she?" asked Darkclaw.

"She's at Fort Kill, wherever that is," Neiko shrugged.

"How do you know?" Phoenix said standing up on all fours.

"I overheard Menes say something about 'Ramses leaving her there to rot' or something like that. I think she got captured while Ramses was giving me trouble in Hawote. I think that Vipra character was there impersonating her to spy on y'all. I can't say what kind of shape she's in because I don't know."

"I hope she's all right. From what it sounds like, she may be sentenced to die. They don't call it Fort Kill for nothing, and she may be crow food."

Neiko winced and stood up. "Then let's go right now! My exploring can wait especially if she's dying."

"Wait just a minute, Neiko. Think about who you're dealing with here. We could be too late, and/or he could have another trap waiting for you there. If we get caught, we will die with her, and you'll be back in the waiting arms of Ramses, and maybe later in Dark Pharaoh matrimony," Phoenix reminded. "Is that what you want?"

"I don't care! I can't just sit here and leave her there to die! She's an innocent victim in all this Dark Pharaoh craze, and she knows nothing about it! I don't care if I have to marry Ramses to save her life; I'll do it if I have to. Besides, I think Ramses is finished with her for now. If she lives now, then he won't kill her the next time because he still cares about her, I guess. So let's go!"

Raptor looked at his reflection in a puddle of water, suddenly the ground rumbled, and a ripple disturbed the serene surface. "Uh, guys, I really agree with Neiko for two reasons. One, I don't want Lydia to die like that."

"What's reason two?" asked Rip Rat. Suddenly there was roar and ten tyrannosaurs ran at them with their jaws snapping.

"Tyrannosaurs!" everyone screamed and scattered, grabbing anyone that couldn't fly. Air Hammer swooped and grabbed Neiko with his talons. She hovered over one's head, and he snapped at her trying to get a meal. She did a split dodging the deadly teeth and jaws.

"Whoa!" she screeched at her narrow escape.

Cheetor was flying and carrying Quickstrike. Quickstrike blinded the dinosaur in one eye with his venom. The Attack Pack picked up speed and lost them. They flew into Manotee Marsh to spend the night. Everyone went to sleep by the serene place.

The next morning Diana went to wash her face in the marsh. She then was surrounded by Damonites. They grabbed her and took her to the place where the Attack Pack was surrounded. "Don't move or the girl gets it!" they menaced.

"Who are these geeks?" Neiko asked, annoyed.

"Damonites. Friends of the ever-present chrome snatcher," Raptor replied.

A king came up in his robes and his golden crown, which was filled with diamonds. He was a mole man with skulls on his arms. "The notorious Attack Pack, and I have the chance of killing you all. Each of your hides would be a useful sell."

Neiko couldn't contain herself. "Who are you, slime sucker? Is this slimy mud hole your home or is it the place you come to visit your brother the slime wad?"

"I am King Skull, ruler of the Damonites, and who are you, you brazen little hooligan?" he said then studied her closely. "The outlaw—seize her! I bet my old friend would be delighted to see you," he said pointing at her.

Neiko backed behind Sichus as Damonites started to close in. Suddenly the Attack Pack exploded in a defensive attack scattering the Damonites. The Attack Pack took flight in a hasty retreat. "Some other time, Damonite scum!" Cheetor called back, as Skull shook his fist at them and cursing them.

The Attack Pack wouldn't stop until they reached Fort Kill to save their doomed friend. They flew into the Drybones Desert and headed to the southeast to reach the dismal place. "We're approaching Wynona's Wasteland, so keep your eyes peeled for pirates," Phoenix replied.

"We're up here, so why worry?" asked Neiko.

"Oh, because they have hang gliders, and they would like nothing more than to blow us to kingdom come, that's why," Phoenix said.

"Oh," Neiko said nodding as she rode on Ramulus' back. Then something behind them caught her eye. She turned around and saw that pirates were on their tail. "Bogies at the rear! Prepare for aerial assault!" Neiko yelled.

"What?" asked Raptor turning around. "Pirates!" Then the Attack Pack put on extra speed, but they were heading right for the camp of the pirate who started firing cannons at them. Phoenix moved to the side as one whizzed right by him.

"Attack Pack, make a hasty retreat! We haven't time to lose, and we'll fight these clowns another time! Cheetor and Sky Shadow, fire your rockets and scatter the ground gunners. Cheetara, fire your rocket at the rear!" Phoenix commanded. The three fired their rockets in the indicated areas. The ground crew scattered and several of the cannons were destroyed, and the dead-on hits killed several. Cheetara was able to obliterate some of the rear attackers, but the rest still followed.

"Those creeps are still after us!" Neiko said as she notched an arrow on her bowstring, turned and fired. She killed him, and glider and flyer crashed to the ground.

"I'll stop them, Cheetor, come with me!" Phoenix said as he and Cheetor flew into them. They clawed the wings of the gliders causing them to crash. Several tried to shoot them to keep the pursuit, but they missed and hit their own mates. The pair quickly dwindled their numbers, and the remaining few made a retreat toward the camp. The Attack Pack flew for another hour, and a fortress came into view.

"Fort Kill dead ahead!" Buzzclaw said, pointing his hooked claw as they raced to it.

"To the ground! We can't let them know of our presence!" Sandstorm said and they made a landing. They crept to a concealed area near the fortress to plan the next move.

- CHAPTER 58 -

NEIKO PULLED OUT HER binoculars to get a good look at the place. The grounds were littered with the remains of tortured people and dead soldiers who had fought to overtake the place over the years. Several cages had skeletons in them, but one of them had Lydia inside of it. She was leaning back and motionless. The sun bleached her face; the wind blew, rocking the cage. "Well, guys, I got good news. She's on the outside of the fort, but I gotta get a better look at her to see if she's alright," Neiko said, putting her binoculars into her backpack.

Phoenix looked at her warmly. "I'm glad we found her. Why did Ramses do this?"

"I don't think he did it directly. I believe he wanted her to stay here unharmed, but I bet someone else wanted her dead. I bet it was Vipra. I believe all Ramses intended to do was leave her here in the dungeon until his beck and call to possible slavery. Well, I'll go and see if she's alive," Neiko said as she got a canteen of water and her tomahawk.

"We'll keep watching to be sure nothing happens," Air Hammer said. "Good luck."

Neiko slipped to the fortress in the cover of trees and bushes till she got to Lydia's cage. Lydia didn't move; she was oblivious to her presence. "Lydia, can you hear me? Are you okay?" she whispered.

Lydia half opened her eyes then shrank back weakly when she saw her tomahawk.

"It's okay. I'm here to help. The Attack Pack is here with me."

"Help me," she said with her voice rasping.

Neiko cut off the lock, opened the door of the cage, and helped her out. "Just relax; here's some water," she said, giving her the canteen, and she drank it all in one big gulp. "Can you tell me what happened?"

"First tell me who you are," she said.

"Neiko Kidd of Hawote, and I'll tell you more when we get to safety."

"I can't believe Ramses wanted to feed me to the crows," she said beginning to cry.

"Did you hear him say that?" Neiko said, putting her hand on her shoulder.

"No. Some hideous-looking woman came and said that he wanted me to be crow meat. I've been out here for two days without food or water."

Neiko gripped her tomahawk with her rage welling up. "Vipra! I knew it! I wanted to teach that witch a lesson. She lied, saying that he wanted it done, but actually she's the one—ooh. If Ramses knew, she'd be dead. Well, she got her desserts from the claws of Cheetor. C'mon, let's get outa here," she said as she helped Lydia to her feet and helped her walk.

"There's someone out there, and the prisoner's escaping!" said a sentry from the top of the wall, and they started to fire arrows at them. The pair started to run, but Lydia had to lean on Neiko because she was too weak to go on her own. Arrows dug themselves in the ground near them, and Neiko tried to keep a zigzag pattern. Suddenly a rocket hissed past them and blew up the wall. Phoenix and Cheetor flew up and grabbed the pair and flew away.

That night they camped near Piranha Lake and talked. Neiko told Lydia about all of her adventures and everything about Ramses. "That tale you heard about the girl from Earth, that girl is me," she concluded.

Lydia shook her head in disbelief and tears came into her eyes. "Oh, you poor dear. You have suffered more than I have in my entire lifetime. Now I know why he didn't come for me or hear of my capture because he was in Hawote trying to take you. I was captured in that battle that Quickstrike told you about, that Vipra person was rescued and not me. She wanted me dead because she wanted Phoenix and me out of the way, but if it wasn't for you, I would be dead in about two days."

"I can't see how you stood it for a hundred thousand years. He drove me mad and weakened me in all about a few days. I knew you had to be somewhere, and I'm glad Menes spilled the beans because if he hadn't, we would have never found you," Neiko replied as she gave her the fifth plate of roasted frogs, and Neiko ate her second piranha. "All I gotta do now is see about Cougan's Bluff, meet with King Wartalon, and then get home."

Lydia put her hand on her shoulder. "We're with you all the way. We will accompany you to Hawote and make sure that everything is all right before we return. We will remain with you for a few weeks to ensure Ramses does not try to get you back because he'll come for you and sooner than you realize. I was able to bear it because he was never quite that forceful with me nor did any of those kinds of horrible things—not that it was ever good."

"Thanks. I need all the help I can get. I have no idea what Raven and Bloodhawk have been up to since I've been gone, and I don't know if everything's the same as I left it."

Phoenix sat down with them. "Like she said, we'll remain with you to make sure that everything is *almost* back to normal. Let's rest, we have a long journey tomorrow; we won't stop till we get to the Hawk village."

The next morning the Attack Pack prepared to leave, and over the hill came several legions of Skull Bearers. The Attack Pack flew over the lake even though there was a bridge that crossed the entire lake. The Skull Bearers came after them along the bridge. As they crossed, Cheetor fired his rocket and most of the soldiers were in the middle of the bridge. The rocket hit, and the bridge fell into the lake. The soldiers screamed as they fell in and piranhas ate them. The water boiled with the assailment of the hungry fish and the legions were gone within seconds. "Phew! That was close! Let's go to Hawk village," Scarem shouted.

"You not go anywhere!" said a huge elephant man in witch doctor attire as he waved his spear while several cannibals surrounded them. He had one broken tusk and carried a cannibal shield.

"Hannibal, I should've known," Sandstorm grimaced.

"Attack Pack make good food for banquet for tonight; I dine on Attack Pack stew," Hannibal said rubbing his chubby belly which had a bone in it.

Neiko cringed at the thought of being eaten. "I won't be dinner to some fat, ugly slob like you."

Hannibal looked at her closely. "You not Attack Pack. You look familiar, like I see on paper. Come, tribe, bring Attack Pack to eat."

Everyone was brought to the cannibal camp. A giant pot was being loaded with vegetables and water as a giant fire started to boil the water. Lydia and Neiko were spared; they were made to watch the demise of their friends. Raptor was the first to go on the plank over the large pot. Two cannibals pushed him, but he grabbed on to the plank causing it to tip, and the two fell into the pot. They screamed as they were cooked alive, and Raptor's tail slapped the water as he fell to the ground. "Yeowch! Ooh, my poor tail," he said as he rubbed it with his claws.

"Kill them! Dinner getting away!" Hannibal said pointing at them. Raptor came and sliced through the ropes binding the others. Everyone attacked the cannibal camp and got their weapons and equipment along with Neiko and Lydia and made a hasty retreat as they caused injury and casualty to the cannibals. Hannibal was severely wounded by the slicing claws and pinchers of Scarem and Buzzclaw.

They traveled directly to the northwest, and a village came into view. "There it is! Everyone prepare to land," Phoenix said as he dove, and the others followed.

"Let me do the talking," Neiko said as she fished out the letter to King Wartalon. Neiko hopped off of Cheetor's back and greeted the gatekeeper.

"I need to speak with Wartalon right away."

"I know you. You are Neiko, and the Attack Pack is welcome with you. The king will see you now. We have heard from Greytail and MacPhearsome. My name is Rocangus, welcome to Hawk Pueblo," he said ushering everyone in.

Everyone was admitted into the presence of the king. "I have been expecting you, Neiko of Hawote, and welcome. What has taken you?" asked Wartalon.

"Well, I had a few encounters with Ramses, and the Attack Pack had to rescue me Well, now I'm here, so what is the secret of Cougan's Bluff?" she asked getting excited.

"Behind Flashflood Falls is a cave, and inside it is a portal in which you can go anywhere you desire. I must come with you to insert the key and chant the spell to send you back. Several of my warriors and I will come with you. You will spend the night here and rest yourselves because you have had a long journey. We have planned a feast for the coming of the Chosen One, the Attack Pack, and your return to Hawote, and I hope you accept, Neiko."

"Oh yes, that is so kind of you. I just hope Ramses don't crash the party. I have a question. Do you know where I can find a Good Pharaoh?"

Wartalon cocked his head. "No. The only good Pharaoh I know of is a dead Pharaoh. If you search for something to match Ramses the Setting Sun, I wouldn't know. Well, enough talk. Let's celebrate!"

CHAPTER 59

THE FOLLOWING DAY NEIKO, the Attack Pack, Wartalon, and several Hawks made their way to Cougan's Bluff. They walked along a trail, and they could see the bluff itself along with Flashflood Falls.

When they came to the bluff, they walked behind the waterfall and into the cave. They continued until they came onto a strange formation. It was a stage with a ramp of stairs going to a flat surface surrounded with columns. In the center of the columns, which were on the outer perimeter, was a podium, which may have been a huge stalagmite in the past, with a hole for the key. "Whoever is going to Hawote with Neiko, go and stand on the platform," Wartalon said.

"Who's all going?" asked Bantor.

Lydia stepped forward. "I definitely am."

Phoenix stepped forward with his wife. "I will as well. Not all of us need to go to Hawote, and most will stay behind. I need only three more volunteers." Cheetor, Ramulus, and Sandstorm walked up.

Aries and Cheetara walked up to wish them luck. "Good luck, guys. Neiko, I'll miss you," Cheetara said, rubbing against her.

"I'm not gone for good. I'll be back," Neiko said hugging her strong neck, and she wrapped one huge arm around her and rubbed her back with her paw.

Aries shook her hand with her hoof. The six leaving for Hawote went onto the platform.

"Go back to Norak as soon as we leave and wait for us to return," Phoenix said to the rest.

Wartalon placed the key to the hole into the podium. The key was a ruby that was carved into the shape of the sun. It glowed red light, and the six were surrounded by blue light. "Farewell, and come back to visit," Wartalon said to Neiko. Neiko nodded and waved to everyone who watched. Wartalon raised his hands and started the chant. "Hawote, Hawote, take your own, these six come back to your bosom. Into the yard of Neiko in whence she came," he chanted then clapped his hands. The six were engulfed in blue light.

The six came into the front yard of her house, and it was dark in Hawote. "Home sweet home, I thought I would never see it again," Neiko said looking at the familiar surroundings. "There are some things I gotta do before I tell my parents I'm back. I have to make sure the Seven Tribes are okay."

Sandstorm put his hand on her shoulder. "Lead the way. I have to say this. You must not tell them about us, and mention nothing of Ramses to anyone because I know panic would spread."

"I got ya. I gotta make up one heck of a story, and I wonder what I should say. I guess I'll tell them I was indeed kidnapped by a guy in chrome armor, but lead on it was some wacko Georgian and not Ramses the Dark Pharaoh."

"Good idea. What should we do now?" asked Sandstorm.

"I can't get to my secret phone, but the armory has a radio with channels to all Seven Tribes. I'll radio them and tell them I'm back. I know they always have listeners. C'mon, let's go."

About fifteen minutes passed when they reached the armory. Neiko knocked on the door, but no one came. She knocked again and said, "Bear Claw, are you there? Hello?" but there was no answer. "That's weird. He's usually here. I know where the spare key is," she said as she pulled it from underneath brick in the windowsill. Neiko opened it, and they went inside. The armory was empty and dust was everywhere as if someone hasn't been there in weeks.

"Neiko, are armories always this dirty?" asked Lydia.

"No way. Bear Claw is a neat-freak, and he would have a *fit* if he saw this," she replied as she went to the CB radio.

"What is that thing?" asked Phoenix as he sniffed it.

"This is the radio. Neat, huh?"

"Hawote has such strange but interesting things," Lydia said looking at it.

"Yeah? Could say the same about the Five Lands. You've only been here thirty minutes, and I hope y'all stick around awhile."

"Of course. We promised to stay," Lydia said sweetly.

"Okay, keep your fingers crossed," Neiko said as she grabbed the receiver and pressed the thumb button, and the channel was set on her tribe's. "Desert Storm Falcon Base, this is Falcon 1, do you read me? Repeat, this is Falcon 1, do you copy?"

There was no answer. She switched it to the Scraah. "Eagle Nest this is Road Runner, over."

No answer.

She switched to the Chang and then the rest one by one. Neiko shook her head as the replaced the receiver. "Something's not right. I wonder what those two cooked up. Everyone thinks I'm dead, and I wouldn't be surprised if they blamed it on the entire land of Hawote and did something rash."

Lydia put her hand on her shoulder. "We're with you all the way."

"What do we do now?" asked Cheetor.

"I'm gonna check out Falcon Base and see if I can find a clue. Let's go!"

They arrived at the building in question that was "Falcon Base" in a few minutes. The door was wide open and Neiko jumped off of Phoenix's back and ran inside. The base had been ransacked, and the place was a mess. Tables were overturned, papers littered the floor, and windows were broken. "It looks like a riot just took place," Neiko said.

"What were they looking for?" asked Ramulus.

"My logbooks, I guess," Neiko shrugged. "I gotta see if there is a clue in these papers on what the Crackedskulls were up to or where everyone is. Neiko picked up papers that were strewn everywhere and looked at them trying to find a clue. She stumbled on a map of Hawote with a red mark over the Okefenokee Swamp and it read: "Emergency Landing." "Hmm, I think they may have gone there. I'll go back to the armory and see if I can find the channel to Emergency Landing. I remember Bear Claw saying that he had the only radio able to reach there because Sito made it that way."

"Is that place a hiding place to be safe from attack? Who is Sito?"

"Sito is our inventor. He mysteriously disappeared eight years ago along with his twin brother Tito and their two friends Mactalon and Panthero. Emergency Landing is an underground refuge in that swamp. We have no problems from Outsiders because the swamp is the same in both Hawote and Georgia. It is quite large, and no one lives there really. So in other words, it's perfect from Crackedskull attack."

"Good. Now hop on, and let's see if we can reach them; to the armory," Phoenix said then they went back.

Neiko turned the knob on the radio, and it whistled as she tried to find the unknown channel. Neiko checked the sheet and found the setting and the codename. "Underground Indian, this is Road Runner, do you copy?"

Static crackled. "Road Runner we read you loud and clear," came an excited voice.

Neiko sighed with relief. "Underground Indian, what happened?"

"Crackedskulls attacked, and they were driven mad. They threatened the entire land unless we surrendered, so the entire land is in hiding. Is it safe to return?"

"10-4. Explain more when you come back—Road Runner over and out," she said then replaced the receiver.

"That's a relief that everyone's okay, and the good news is that they are coming. I bet you're glad," said Cheetor.

"Oh yeah. What will you guys do when everyone comes back?" asked Neiko.

"We will stay but not show ourselves to them. We will stay here for two of your weeks," replied Phoenix.

"Okay, that's fine with me. You guys, I'm gonna go outside and get some air, be back in five minutes," Neiko said.

"Stay close," Cheetor warned.

Neiko nodded then went outside. The cool night air felt good to her lungs, and the smell of home lifted her spirits. She walked out and kicked a few rocks. Suddenly two huge hands grabbed her around her chest underneath her arms and lifted her off the ground. The grip was so strong that it took her breath, and she looked back into the face of Bloodhawk. "Put me down, feather brain! Let me go, bird breath! Help!" she yelled as loud as she could as he carried her back to the Crackedskull fortress.

The five came out and saw Bloodhawk's shadow as he flew away. They flew after him.

- CHAPTER 60 -

BLOODHAWK BROUGHT HER INTO the throne room and Raven stood up. "It's nice to see you, Neiko. I—as well as my son—am overjoyed to see you unharmed."

"I have waited a long time for this moment," said Bloodhawk as he sat her down gently and holding her arm with one massive hand.

"I bet. How'd you know I was back?"

Raven smiled. "Simple. A few of my warriors overheard your call on the Sparra-Mohican radio, and they tracked the signal. Of course, Bloodhawk wanted to make your acquaintance."

"That was too easy—much simpler than your Ramses scheme. You know, that was really lame, and you know what? I plan to expose Francesco once and for all."

"I don't think so, Neiko," Francesco came in sizzling. "We got you this time!"

"So you figured it out all by yourself, very good, but it's too bad that an Outsider took you instead, whoever he was."

"I spent six months with that guy, and I still don't know who he is," she fibbed, using her entire time she was missing in Qari, unwittingly using Qarian time.

"Six months? You were only missing for two weeks," Raven said, laughing.

Neiko scratched her head and remembered the passage of time was different. "It was so awful it seemed like longer than it was."

"I would like to find this Outsider and claw him to a paste for the pain he caused you!" Bloodhawk said as he steamed.

Neiko giggled at knowing what they didn't know. "Oh, well. I couldn't identify him because he never took his mask off." *That part was true.*

"Did he wear that armor he wore the whole time he kept you?"

"Yep. I can only say that this guy was six-feet-eight, weighed about 400 pounds without armor and had on about 200 pounds of armor, and he looks like a pharaoh."

Francesco's mouth fell open. "What kind of a nutcase dresses like a pharaoh and is covered head to toe in armor and randomly kidnaps you?"

"Some loony guy. That's all I know. What's really weird is he didn't do a thing to me, and he let me go," she fibbed again. "For the time being," she thought.

"Well, no more talk about this ridiculous prankster; let's concentrate on your future, Bloodhawk," Raven said.

While Neiko was talking to them, the five were watching in the window. "Those are two gigantic men!" said Lydia, shocked.

"They must be her archenemies, Raven and Bloodhawk. We

have to find a way to get to Neiko without them seeing us. We also have to get them to come over here or something," said Phoenix.

"Wait, fellas. I brought a sleeping grenade I ripped off of Quicksilver when he wasn't looking as he was tying me down. Do you still have it Lydz?" asked Quickstrike.

"Yes. Here it is. We must tell Neiko to not breathe it, but how?" said Lydia.

"We have to chance it. Sandstorm, throw it!" hissed Quickstrike urgently.

"I was wondering how come you became part bird," Neiko said.

Raven shrugged. "I do not know. All I know is that our ancestors were cursed by Yahweh for their actions of conquest, why?" he asked.

"Just curious," she said then the window broke as the grenade flew in.

Gas went everywhere and Neiko ran to the window covering her face as her friends were calling to her to help guide her in the noxious cloud. The two gigantic Crackedskulls went after her, but the gas took effect, and they collapsed onto the floor. Sandstorm grabbed Neiko, and they made a hasty retreat to the armory where they spent the night.

- Chapter 61 -

THE FOLLOWING DAY THE Seven Tribes returned to the armory, and Neiko ran out and greeted them. She was surrounded by thousands of Indians, and everyone expressed their relief and welcomed her back. Monchiska fought his way through the crowd, he made his way to her, and hugged her. "I'm so glad you're okay," he said.

Sigma, Puma, Monganata, Pike, Windsong, Xartna, and Nighthawk all walked up and hugged her in turn.

"Gentlemen, I have something I want to give you, and I have to say that the Grand High Mohican is the long-time traitor," said Neiko.

Everyone looked at each other and murmured.

"Do you have proof?" asked Xartna. Neiko handed him the letter from Raven and the printouts from the computer. Xartna looked at them, and his mouth fell open.

"If you need more, go look in his computer under classified info, and the password is Ramesses the Great," she said proudly.

Xartna smiled. "Well done. You have proven yourself beyond measure, and you are admiral once more. Welcome home," he said, and everyone cheered.

"When did you get all of this information?" asked Nighthawk.

"Just before I was kidnapped by that lunatic Outsider."

"Who was he? What did he look like?" asked Pike.

"Well he was a six-feet-eight, 400-pound man wearing about 200 pounds of armor, and he looked like a pharaoh. Weird if you ask me; I never saw what he looked like underneath, so basically he got away Scot free because I couldn't identify him," Neiko replied.

"That's okay. At least you are back safe and that maniacal madman is long gone, and we have seen the last of him," said Puma.

I wish, Neiko thought with dread. "Let's celebrate. Then I'll return home to my parents."

The next day, she returned to her home, and her parents hugged her and had a happy reunion. Once she was able to go outside, she met with her five Attack Pack friends in the edge of the Crackedskull woods.

"I'm glad to see you so happy. This place is so magical to me in the closeness you have with your family and friends," Lydia said as she hugged her.

"Yeah, I wished I could say the same thing about Georgia, but hey, Hawote is the greatest place to be. Qari is really a nice place, but it would be better without Ramses," Neiko said.

"I agree. Now what shall we do about that Good Pharaoh talk? You said we need one to be able to defeat Ramses, and now we need him to protect you from Ramses," Phoenix pondered.

Neiko scratched her head. "I dunno. I talked to Ramses about it, and he mentioned one in particular along with an unknown Good Pharaohess. The Pharaoh's name was Sesmar Repsis-Bijou, but he said he did away with him. He also said he was the strongest of the Good Pharaohs. I suppose he killed him so we have to find another."

"Our best interest is to find out more on this Sesmar character. Maybe we can find another while we look for him. We'll look around when we return to Qari, and we will contact you if we do."

The six chatted the rest of that afternoon.

The two weeks passed, and it was time for the five from Qari to return home. "Well, this is it. I hope to see you soon," Neiko said, hugging each of them.

"Neiko, I want to give you this," Sandstorm said as he placed a crystal in her hand. "This is your Attack Pack crystal that we made for you now that we know the way between our worlds. Use this when you want to come to Qari, call us here, or if you are in danger. Rub it twice and say 'Attack Pack' if you want to come to Qari. Rub it three times if you want us to come here, and rub it four times if you are in trouble."

Neiko gladly took it. "Thanks."

"Oh, Phoenix, I don't want to leave her. I just fear Ramses may attack as soon as we leave," Lydia fretted.

"I know, Lydia, but Qari needs us too. Besides, he would find a way to make us come back. Neiko, I have a few ideas to make sure that he won't be able to get to you. Don't find yourself alone, especially at night. Stay with someone all hours of the day, and if you have to travel in Georgia, then do it in the day, and make sure there are plenty of people. I stress this: do not find yourself alone, not even for a second. All he needs is a second to take you. I wish you luck," Phoenix warned.

Neiko nodded. "Okay, how do you get back since you didn't bring a spare?"

"Rub your crystal once and say 'send them home'," Sandstorm replied.

"Bye guys. Call me if you need me," she said then they nodded. She did what Sandstorm said, and they disappeared. Neiko ran to the house and stayed in most of the day.

- Chapter 62 -

ONE MONTH PASSED AND RAMSES had not attacked. Neiko acquired a job at Chick-fil-A, and she began to lead an almost normal life as she stepped up into Georgian life. Later that night she called Phoenix, one of her best friends in the Desert Storm Falcon tribe. "Hey, girl, how's it going?"

"Neiko, hi, how was your first day at work?" she asked.

"It went fine. Say, I got free tickets to go skating at Sparkles. I was wondering if you wanted to come with me tonight. You can bring your rollerblades because I'll bring mine."

"Sure! I'd love to, where do you want to meet?"

"Meet you right here at my house and just tell 'em your Georgian name like always, you know the drill, and I'll drive," Neiko volunteered.

The pair went to the roller ring and skated for an hour and a half together. The music was blaring, and it was immensely crowded.

Phoenix and Neiko stopped on the carpet to talk. "I'm gonna get some food and drink, what would you like?" asked Phoenix.

"I'll take some Mountain Dew and some nachos. I'm gonna skate till you get the eats. Fine with you?" asked Neiko.

"Fine with me; I'll flag you down right here."

"Okay," she said then pushed off and skated. A few minutes passed, and she was dancing and skating around the ring. She didn't notice the four Pharaohs come into the room.

Menes looked at all of the people, but there was no sign of Neiko.

"How are we supposed to find her in all of *this*?"

"Are you sure she's here, Ramses? I couldn't find myself in all of this!" Tut grumbled.

"Stop complaining. She's here alright. This is not Hawote but Georgia. I thought I explained that clearly enough," Ramses said.

"I still can't tell the difference. Besides, didn't you say that Indians camouflage with Outsiders?" asked Re.

"Yes. The woodlands are Hawote, and places like this are Georgia," Ramses replied, annoyed.

"Do you still got that whatyamacallit?" Menes asked.

"Oh, you mean the gun? Yes," said Ramses as he pulled out a large Desert Eagle pistol from his belt.

"Alright, everybody, let's skate in the opposite direction," said the announcer, and everyone shouted with excitement.

Two teenagers walked up to them and looked at them mockingly especially at Ramses. "Hey nice outfit. I got one just like it made out of copper," he said then his friends laughed. "Who are you supposed to be— King Tut in a can or perhaps Seti I in chrome? Go back to Egypt, I mean, the pharaoh look is out. I'll bet the kiddies would love your dino friend here."

Ramses shook with wrath; he grabbed him by the throat and lifted him off the ground. "You better leave now or die. Get out of my sight, or I'll snap your neck like a twig," he growled then dropped him, and the young men ran away afraid.

Re laughed. "Ramses, I think you could rule this Georgia place easily. I mean, they're scared of you!"

"Re, for the first time in a while you have given me an idea. Neiko's world will be easy to conquer, and it is much bigger than the Five Lands put together."

"You see that over there? I think we can get Neiko's attention with that," Menes said pointing to the announcer's pit.

"Good thinking, and let's fan out. Tut you go to the left, Re to the right and check the video games. I will go search the center," Ramses said pointing toward the general vicinity of where he was going and walked to the ring.

Neiko was skating and dancing when the music stopped. "Neiko Kidd, we know you are here. Surrender to us now or people will get hurt!" Neiko froze when she heard Menes' voice and saw him in the pit. She took off her rollerblades and frantically tried to find Phoenix. She spotted her, and Phoenix's face was frozen in horror at the mentioning of Neiko's Indian name. Seeing Menes only added to her bewilderment. People stopped and looked at the Pharaohs with shock. Neiko ran through people to get to her frightened friend. She ran into Ramses. Neiko look up in fear.

"There you are. Miss me?" he asked, grabbing her and brandishing his gun. "Scream or resist me and someone will die, and if anyone gets in my way, they die."

Neiko laughed at him. "You don't even know how to use that thing."

"Wanna bet?" he said as he pointed at the ceiling and pulled the trigger. An ear-splitting bang echoed in the ring. Neiko jumped. People started to panic and scream seeing the gun and the frightening appearance of Ramses. People fought to escape, and many tried to run in their skates. They tripped and fell on each other. Neiko saw

Phoenix's terrified stare as she gaped at Neiko and her terrifying captor. The other three came in to join him.

Neiko yelled in Greyhawk to her. "Get help! Call 911! Get to the Seven Tribes! It's him and his buddies! Get outa here!"

Phoenix ran, and Ramses got his gun ready just in case she was to cause problems.

Menes laughed at the panicking crowd. "Look at them! They are running like cattle!" he said mockingly. They laughed at them like it was sport, but then the police came in.

"We need more officers! The ringleader has a girl hostage, and he is one *gigantic* son of a gun! He has three accomplices, and they are not small themselves, but the leader is the biggest! The leader is covered in King Tut chrome armor costume!" he said into his radio. The ten police officers came forward.

"Alright, pal, we got you surrounded. Let the girl go, put the gun down, and put your hands up," said another, and the officers pulled out their guns.

Ramses laughed at them. "I will do no such thing."

"Let her go, or we drop you!" he said; then they cocked their guns ready to fire. One looked into his fiery eyes and shuddered. A large muscle-bound man got Ramses in a headlock and forced him to release Neiko. Neiko ran like lightning to the door to make an escape.

"Don't just stand there! Get her!" Ramses commanded. The three went after her, but the cops blocked them. Ramses threw the man off, and he hit the floor. He kicked him in the ribs fracturing several. The man rolled and groaned. Menes was able to fight past the police about when they opened fire on Ramses. The bullets struck his armor, and sparks flew, but they didn't even make a scratch. The cops' mouths fell open in shock. Ramses shot several, wounding them, and he walked after his escaping prize.

Neiko made it to her car, and she saw Menes was on her tail.

"Come back here!" he shouted as she closed her car door and cranked it.

He jumped in front of her car trying to block her, but she floored the accelerator and rammed him. Menes flipped over the hood and landed on the pavement. She zoomed through the parking lot squealing tires. Ramses came out of the building running about 35 mph, she guessed. Neiko saw him out of her rearview mirror.

"C'mon!" she squealed at the oncoming traffic as she pounded her steering wheel. She saw a space, and the rocketed out into the road. She put the pedal to the metal and went down the road at 75 mph in light 10:00 p.m. traffic. She laughed at her narrow escape, but then she saw him in her rearview mirror, and he was catching up fast. He was still running but at about 70 mph she judged after glancing at her speedometer. Neiko's mouth fell open. "Impossible! Cheetahs can't even run that fast!" she squealed. Then she saw the driveway to Wal-Mart, and she swung hard into the turn lane and whipped into the driveway—just out of the way of an oncoming car, and they blew the horn at her. Her tires screamed as she sped out of the turn and careened into the parking lot. She found a nearby parking space, parked the car, and sprinted into Wal-Mart to find a hiding place.

She looked at the clothes racks, but they offered no cover, and she knew the crowd wouldn't help. She racked her brain. Then she ran to the women's restroom at the back of the store. She found a vacant stall, went inside, stood on the toilet, and waited anxiously.

Ramses came into Wal-Mart, but there was no sign of Neiko. He walked through the store and people stared. He growled angrily, knowing she had disappeared. *I'll just wait outside. She can't stay in here forever*, he thought. As he stood outside, a fat cop walked to him.

"What are you doing here, pal?" he asked harshly.

"I'm just waiting for my girlfriend to come out. Why?" he snapped.

The cop looked at him suspiciously. "Leave the premises or take off that costume."

"*You* better leave or you'll be sorry," Ramses menaced with venom.

"How 'bout you spend the night in jail and think it over," he said, grabbing his arm. Ramses reached to his back and pulled out his dagger and stabbed the cop in his stomach. The cop bellowed in pain, and Ramses stabbed him several more times in the chest, killing him. He dragged the cop's still body and laid it out of sight to the side of the building and continued waiting.

Neiko waited for an hour in her hiding spot, and she thought of her Attack Pack crystal. She felt around in her pockets, but it wasn't there. "Oh crap! I left it on my nightstand. Very bright, Neiko!" she grumbled at herself. "At least I know that the Seven Tribes have that tracking device in my earring just in case. I can't stay here. Maybe he gave up and left. I have to watch out though. Or maybe he's still in here; I have to make a run for it, get to my car, and tell everyone that guy is back."

Neiko left her hiding place and cautiously left the bathroom and looked around. Seeing the coast was clear, she went through the aisles, and checked for her pursuer, but he was nowhere in sight. She slipped out the front door, and spotted a fat cop standing on the porch near the Coke machine. She ran to him and tugged on his sleeve. "Officer, there's a guy dressed in chrome with glowing red eyes, and he's trying to kidnap me. He went to Wal-Mart—and he's still in there, I think."

"Did you see which way he went?" he asked.

Neiko was about to say something, but she saw a trail of blood leading to the side of the store. She followed the trail with her eyes, and she ran to see who might have gotten hurt. She saw the dead cop lying face down. Neiko turned him over, but he looked *exactly* like the man she was just talking to. "Wait a minute, wasn't I just—" she started to say and spun around. There stood Ramses who had been disguised as the cop by using his magic. Neiko knew she was trapped in the perfect ambush.

"Nice try. Like I said, you can't run, and you can't hide from me," he said seizing her and tying her hands behind her back. He walked out to the parking lot with her in tow looking for a getaway transport. He spotted a large Harley Davidson motorcycle that was to his liking, and a man was just about to get on it. "I'll take that if you don't mind," he said.

"Hey, man, these are my wheels and I ain't givin' 'em to a freak like you," he said, and he saw him holding Neiko with her hands bound behind her back.

"I will not ask again! Give it to me!" Ramses growled as he pulled out his gun.

The man looked at him like he was crazy. Neiko started to squirm, and she tried to loosen the rope binding her hands.

"Hey, man, you got a serious attitude problem," he said in a stoned punk way.

Ramses said nothing else, but he shot him in between the eyes, and he fell backward dead. Neiko screamed in rage and fright as she witnessed cold-blooded murder firsthand.

"I warned him. I don't like to repeat myself. Get on," he said as he lifted her in front, and he slipped on behind her. He kicked up the kickstand, cranked it, stomped the throttle, and drove away into the night.

- Chapter 63 -

THE NEXT DAY, THE news of Neiko's kidnapping hit the news even in the Atlanta area. Several Seven Tribe chieftains watched the 6:00 a.m. report at Sigma's house.

A woman anchor said, "At about 9:30 p.m., four crazed madmen went into Sparkles skating ring causing mass hysteria. Police were able to free a hostage taken in the situation, and she was able to escape. Police were able to eliminate pursuit for a short while. The result was five wounded cops who suffered gunshot wounds and are in serious condition. A man with eight broken ribs was released today in his heroic efforts. Witnesses say that these four men were dressed in triceratops, wolf man, and mole outfits. The leader was dressed in a pharaoh chrome armor costume."

"Other late breaking news is the murder of thirty-eight-year-old Sergeant Thomas Murphy who was found stabbed to death in the Wal- Mart parking lot in Lawrenceville. He was stabbed once in the stomach and five times in the chest. A Loganville resident was also found shot in the head in that same parking lot. Some Wal-Mart personnel said they saw a man dressed in chrome apparel walking in Wal-Mart," said the man anchor.

"Another one of today's top stories is that an eighteen-year-old Loganville resident named Amanda Hawk is missing. She disappeared late last night and was last seen at Sparkles. If you have any leads on her please call the police. Police say that the kidnapping can be linked to the man responsible for the murders and the rampage at Sparkles. We hope to find more so tune in at the 5:30 p.m. news..." said the woman.

Sigma turned off the TV. "This is not good. It seems that it is the same man that carried her off before, and he is extremely dangerous. They have a good description of the man, and Neiko gave a good one herself. Neiko's life can be in grave danger."

Nighthawk couldn't sit still. "Phoenix is missing too. Could she be—"

Phoenix ran in. "I'm back. Neiko has been taken by some wacko."

"We know. We saw the news report. Tell us what happened."

"These men came in dressed up like monsters, but the guy in chrome was the one I can remember most. The guy dressed up like a triceratops told Neiko to surrender or people will get hurt, and he called her by her Indian name. She tried to get to me, but that chrome guy grabbed her. She told me to get help. People were screaming and running. Police tried to stop him, but he started shooting people. I saw she got away, but he went after her. I found her car at Wal-Mart, but she wasn't there," Phoenix said as tears gushed out of her eyes.

"Did you get a good look at him?" asked Sigma.

"Yes. I can draw you a picture. He *did* look like a pharaoh, and I cannot forget those eyes. They were red and glowed like hot coals. Sigma, he looked like a *demon* pharaoh. Why is he after Neiko? This is the second time he's taken her from us," she said and buried her face in Nighthawk's shoulder and cried.

"What about that tracking device we put in her earring in case she was ever taken by Crackedskulls? Maybe we can find her and our chrome-plated friend," offered Xartna.

Sigma perked up. "Of course! We can find them that way. When we find her, we will make sure he never pulls this cheap trick again. We will destroy him," he said, slamming his fist into his hand. "He may know who we are, but he won't live to tell about it. Obviously he is not seeking ransom for him to abduct her the second time, and we heard nothing about payment the first time. He is not trying to kill her because she would be dead already, so I do not know what he could want from her. One thing is certain; he won't ever get it from her. Phoenix, will you draw me a picture. Thank Yahweh you are an artist and a good sketcher. Will you also color it so we may know what he really looks like?"

Phoenix nodded. "I want to come with y'all to help free Neiko, and I won't take no for an answer."

Xartna nodded. "Alright. The six of us will go to Falcon Base and pick up the tracker, and we will leave tonight. Bring your drawing with you, and we will meet at Falcon Base, everyone understand?"

Everyone nodded.

"Good, see y'all tonight."

Neiko was taken to an abandoned house in Loganville. The house was empty except for a few chairs and a small table. She was bound to a chair and her mouth was taped; her four keepers kept a close watch for trespassers. Menes, Re, and Tut were engaged in a card game while Ramses was sharpening his sword as he watched Neiko. She watched them all and her stomach started growling.

Menes laid down a hand that won the jackpot. "Ha! I win!"

"Aww, you cheated," Tut snapped as he threw his cards down.

"You are such a sore loser, Tutankhamen," Menes jeered.

"My name is Tut," he snarled in clenched teeth. "Call me that again, and I'll punch your lights out!"

"Quiet," Ramses snapped.

"This is a brother's dispute. No place for an eavesdropping Dark Pharaohs who know nothing of having *real* brothers."

"If you want to bicker, take it elsewhere," he said bluntly.

"Ramses, I am starving, when are you gonna get something to eat around here?" Menes asked irritably.

"Yeah. I want to go and explore this place some, and I hope we stay," Re moaned.

"All you do is gripe and complain. Go, I don't care. I plan for us to stay," Ramses snapped, waving his hand.

"I want to ride that thingy," Menes said.

"No."

"Fine, be that way. Be a stingy, stiff-necked old crone," Menes scowled, and Ramses shot him a hostile glare.

A few hours passed and they returned with two large bags full of food. "This place is great! I could get used to this place," Menes said then took a bite out of his Baby Ruth, and Neiko eyed it hungrily; Menes caught it. "Hungry? I brought plenty," he said approaching her with some food. He ripped off her gag, and fed the rest of it to her.

"I'm still hungry, got anymore? I'm thirsty," she said.

"I sure do," he said as he said giving her a Butterfinger and a Pepsi, and Ramses watched him closely with vengeance. "Stop looking at me like that, you ornery Egyptian relic! You are letting your little sweet cheeks starve to death over here. If this is the future you have planned for her, then I pity her. I wouldn't blame her if she ditched you for that Indian, oh, Whatshisname?"

"Monchiska?" she said then belched.

"Don't tempt me, you pompous, overgrown lizard. I was planning to take her out, but you ruined it by giving her junk food!"

"Well, at least I bothered to give her food, you lazy, good for nothing bum!" Menes retorted.

Ramses snarled, and he threw the sharpening stone and hit him in the nose. "I will let this slide, but the next time you won't be so lucky. I alone am responsible for her. Do you get that?"

"Yeah, I'll just watch her starve to a skeleton."

"Shut up! I don't want to hear another word, and if I do, I will cut out your tongue and give it to Re for lunch."

Re grimaced, and Menes punched a hole in the wall and stormed outside.

- Chapter 64 -

THAT NIGHT THE SIX met at Falcon Base and prepared for the rescue. Phoenix showed them the drawing of Ramses. "This is our man, and he is a scary one too," Xartna said.

"Here are the others," she said.

"Hmm, they all look like Pharaohs, but this metal guy really does."

"Monchiska, will you take care of the tracker?" asked Xartna.

"Will do," he said then turned it on. "Guys, I got a bead. She's in Loganville, down on Shiloh Road, and I think it's that old house. She's basically close by."

Everyone sighed with relief. "We must take a truck, just in case of emergency escape because this guy is extremely dangerous. He may try to kill us because we are foiling his plans. Let's go!"

The six rode to the spot, and the signal got stronger. They saw the house, and Menes was standing outside with his brothers, but they continued to drive by. "Hey, there's the other three, but where's Chrome Puss?" asked Pike.

"Probably in there with Neiko keeping an eye on her. Let's drive down and park on the side of the road. We will come back up through the woods," said Nighthawk as he pulled over. They walked through the woods and they could see the house clearly. Menes and his brothers were complaining about Ramses, and they were having a heated discussion about their misfortune of having to stand outside and guard while he had dinner with Neiko. The six of them got out their sticks, tomahawks, and knockout grenades.

"Three of them, six of us. I think we can take these clowns. We will knock them out, tie them up, and drag them to the woods. We must be careful not to alert the leader; we must overtake him with caution because he has her with him. He could either try to run with her or someone could get hurt," said Sigma.

The six of them stalked the three bickering Pharaohs, and they struck like lightning and accomplished their task by deploying knockout bombs. They dragged them to the woods and tied them to a tree. They peeked in the window and saw her sitting at the table tied up talking to him--apparently having just finished eating. They could see Neiko's scorn for her keeper.

"Okay, his back is to us. So do you have any ideas on how to get past this guy? I mean, he's huge, and it doesn't help he's in armor. All of us can't even take down this guy," fussed Nighthawk.

Monchiska had an idea. "I've got it! The five of you will get him to chase you into the woods while I stay behind and wait for him to leave; then I'll rescue Neiko."

"Good idea. How do we get him to come after us?" asked Sigma.

"You have to make him mad, and it probably ain't that hard. Insults would do it."

"Leave that to me," said Pike, pointing to himself. "Neiko doesn't call me the insult king for nothing. But how do we get him to come out?"

"Pike, do the honors," said Xartna.

Pike walked up to the door and banged on it. "Open up, King Tut! Get up and fight or is your butt so heavy you can't stand up?"

The door swung open, and Ramses was fuming. "Menes, I am really—who are you?" he asked curtly.

"Nobody. I'm not that Menes guy. Who are you supposed to be, Ramesses XIII, the Unlucky? You know why pharaohs are endangered? It's because they have such big egos and small brains. You know, I have seen some dumb pharaohs in my life, but you take the taco, pal. If you had brain one in that overstuffed head of yours, you would go back to whence you came, and that's the local sewer."

Ramses' eyes blazed and flashed as his wrath grew hot. "You will die for this, savage!"

"Your mama!" Pike retorted and flicked him off.

"Ooh, come and get us you moldy, Egyptian mummy bandage!" Nighthawk added, waving his arms.

"Yeah, your mother is the fungus that grows in a mummy's navel!" Xartna countered.

"At least my daddy ain't a fat, ugly tyrant!" fired Sigma.

Ramses shook with rage and went after them. They kept the insults flying, and he kept chasing them.

Monchiska came in and Neiko looked up. "I'm here," he said.

"Oh boy, am I glad to see you guys," she said as Monchiska cut off the ropes and helped her stand up. "Let's get outa here before he gets back!" she said, and they ran outside. They let out a call and let them know that it was time to leave. The five of them came with Ramses close behind with his sword drawn. He yelled in madness when he saw that Neiko was free, and the seven Indians were retreating. He followed them relentlessly. They all sprinted to the truck and piled in the cab and the back.

"Nighthawk, punch it!" yelled Monchiska from the back.

He floored it, but Ramses was gaining. He jumped and caught the tailgate with one hand, but Monchiska hit his hand with his tomahawk. Ramses let go, and he toppled and rolled into the road. As he stood up to come after them, a car slammed on brakes, but it couldn't stop; it hit him, sending him into the path of another oncoming car which ran over him, and the Indians made a speedy getaway.

"Ouch. You know that had to hurt, but he will never hurt you again, Neiko. By the way, what did that creep want with you anyway?" asked Pike.

"Oh, well, he wanted to marry me. He was a Georgian Bloodhawk, but more brash."

"Well, he won't be marrying anyone now, and I bet he wished he never met you," said Monchiska, and Neiko laughed nervously knowing he would be back.

- CHAPTER 65 -

THE NEXT DAY, NEIKO returned from work, and she got ready to go to a party the Seven Tribes were going to celebrate that night. Her mom came in with a letter addressed to her, but there was no return address. Neiko ran to her room thinking it may have been from Monchiska, but it wasn't.

Neiko,

You may have gotten away this time, but I wouldn't be celebrating too much if I were you. Your friends will pay for this one day with their lives. I'll be back for you, and you will not know the time, place, or how, but it won't be long. Enjoy this while it lasts because your freedom will be brief. Good-bye for now, my sweet.

Ramses Sisper-Bijou, the Setting Sun
Dark Pharaoh

Neiko swallowed hard and she found the picture that he had stolen from her enclosed with the letter.

"Who was it from?" asked her mom walking in.

"Nobody. Just one of my old friends," she fibbed.

"Can I read it?" she asked.

"Uh—no, it's personal, *very* personal, sorry," she said, slipping the ghastly letter and picture into the envelope.

"Well, okay. Hurry for that party. Your friend Lynn will be here any minute," she said.

The doorbell rang.

Good, Phoenix is here, she thought as she slipped the ghastly letter under her bed. Neiko ran outside, and the pair went to the party.

At the party the Indians were having a blast at Sparkles. "I hope we don't have another rampage like before," punned Phoenix and the group laughed.

Suddenly Francesco walked in, but he was greeted only by scowls by the Indians.

"Well, Neiko, I'm so glad you are all right—" he said kindly.

"Yeah right! You are lying through your teeth. The only reason you want me to be okay is to save your hide from Bloodhawk," she snapped, putting her fists on her hips.

Xartna walked up. "What are you doing at an *Indian* party, Crackedskull? If you must know, you are no longer Grand High Mohican, but Eagle Claw is a real Mohican and an honest man. If I were you, I would be going before we incarcerate you, you worthless, lying, conniving, traitorous Crackedskull trash!"

Francesco shook his finger at Neiko angrily. "I'll get you for this, Neiko, wait and see. I will make your sorrows a hundredfold," he said, sneering, and he swaggered out of the building.

"C'mon everybody, let's have fun!" shouted Neiko, and everyone continued to party.

THE END

NEIKO'S LOG

PEOPLE IN GEORGIA/HAWOTE

INDIANS

<u>Neiko</u> - Captain of the Desert Storm Falcons and the Liberator of Hawote. Also called the Chosen One. She is the primary target of the Crackedskulls, and she is the chosen of Bloodhawk. She is also the Chosen One in the Five Lands, and she finds her duty there in Qari. She is also the long time chosen of Ramses. She is known for her great fighting skill, love of adventure, and for her kind heart.

<u>Xartna</u> - A member of the Desert Storm Falcon Tribe, the spokesman at the meetings, and one of the Falcon chieftains. He is a close friend of Neiko. He is easy going and kind-hearted and does not like to make waves.

<u>Phoenix</u> - Neiko's best friend and she is a member of Neiko's tribe, the Desert Storm Falcons. She is tenderhearted and easy to talk with.

<u>Pike</u> - He is another member of the Scraah Wareagles, and he can cocky and a quick one to make jokes or be sarcastic. He is one of Neiko's close friends and fighting companions.

<u>White Fang</u> - Pike's brother, and he is just the opposite in being soft spoken and reasonable, but he is a good fighter when needed.

<u>Nighthawk</u> - a Desert Storm Falcon tracker and he is one of Neiko's right hand men.

<u>Monganata</u> - Chief of the Chang Battlehawks, and one of the oldest and wisest of all the Seven Tribes, and he is Neiko's mentor. He still is in very good shape and fights with the rest. He is naturally kind and well reserved, but in a fight he is relentless.

<u>Windsong</u> - Wife of Monganata and she is a Battlehawk as well. She is kind-hearted and understanding and she fights with her husband and her friends on the field as well, and she is a dear friend to Neiko.

<u>Sigma</u> - Chief of the Scraah Wareagles and Monchiska's father. He is almost Neiko's second father, and he is fairly easy going till there is a Crackedskull nearby.

<u>Puma</u> - Sigma's wife and Monchiska's mother. She is normally well reserved, quiet and kind. She is close with Neiko as well since her son and Neiko were close friends as kids.

<u>Aquila</u> - Xartna's twin brother and he was always another one of Neiko's most trustworthy people. She promotes him to Captain when she is promoted to Admiral.

<u>Monchiska</u> - Neiko's great friend and he is always at her side in battle as well. Neiko has a secret crush on him and has for a very long time. Son of Sigma and Puma from the Scraah tribe.

<u>Hawk</u> - a Mohican. He is a great fighter and pessimistic about the outside world, but he is good in a battle.

<u>Wolfgang</u> - a Scraah messenger who was sent delivering the news about the next meeting.

<u>Bear Claw</u> - The keeper of the armory. He is from the Cheikomaguan Braves Tribe.

CRACKEDSKULLS

<u>Raven</u> - King of the Crackedskulls and the long time oppressor and scourge of the Indians. He seeks to conquer all of Hawote and give Neiko to his son, Bloodhawk. He is nine feet tall and has white wings, and eyes and feet like an eagle while the rest is man. He is moderate tempered, yet he is intolerant to failure and when things do not go his way.

<u>Bloodhawk</u> - Prince and future king of the Crackedskulls, and he is the threat Neiko faces in her battles and from day to day because he waits to snatch her and take her in marriage. Indians and Crackedskulls know he will be the greatest ruler to come, and he is feared because of his temper and since he is the largest of his entire bloodline by reaching eleven feet. He looks just like his father yet he is larger and has black wings. Bloodhawk is hot tempered and quick to kill another. He can be impetuous and cocky and a great peril to any when he is angry.

<u>Francesco</u> - A Crackedskull in the high rank of Grand High Mohican who has plotted against the Indians for years, but Neiko has suspected him. Francesco has an intolerable hatred for her and wishes for Raven and Bloodhawk to get her out of the way, and he plots along with them. Later he is exposed by Neiko and disbanded. Francesco is very wily and tries to solve things by thought rather than violence since he is such a small, lanky man. He is quick to plot against anyone if he is not respected.

<u>Karo</u> - Crackedskull general of the ground troops, and one of Neiko's worst enemies. He was sent to search the ground after Neiko disappeared.

<u>Deatheagle</u> - the first in command of the winged warriors

<u>Condor</u> - The second in command of the winged warriors, and he was sent to search from the air during the search.

<u>Dingeye</u> - Crackedskull messenger Neiko jumped and retrieved the letter sent to Francesco. He can be deadly when cornered.

<u>GEORGIANS</u>

<u>Jessica</u> - Neiko's cousin that loves to spend time with her and Neiko is teaching her a couple things about her secret life and passing it off as a game. She is inquisitive and interested in Neiko's life.

<u>Dr. Macintosh</u> - The psychiatrist Neiko visits during her misfortune with Raven's plot.

<u>PEOPLE OF THE FIVE LANDS</u>

<u>FRIENDLY QARIANS</u>

<u>Bronto</u> - The large, Brahma bull man who once was a veteran that owns a tavern on the Tatowee Road. He is brash and hot tempered and hard to bargain with, but Neiko wins his trust and support after a showdown with a few Skull Bearers and with Menes and his brothers. He is also Neiko's first civilian contact when she reaches Qari.

<u>King MacPhearsome</u> - The king of Eagle Nest. He is a bald eagle man with a heavy High Alpine accent, and he is eager to help Neiko and Quickstrike when he hears of their perils and misfortunes.

<u>Warbeak</u> - a golden eagle man who rescued Neiko and Quickstrike from the blizzard, and he opens his home to their aid.

<u>Talon</u> - A golden eagle lady and the wife of Warbeak. She is the caretaker of Neiko and Quickstrike.

<u>Wartalon</u> - King of Hawk Pueblo. He has the way to Hawote, and he is a red-tailed hawk man.

<u>Rocangus</u> - The gatekeeper of Hawk Pueblo.

<u>Greytail</u> - The king of Falcon Ridge. He has a Low Mountain accent, and he is the next contact set up by MacPhearsome as they exit the mountains.

<u>Yuri</u> - gatekeeper of Falcon Ridge and he allows Neiko and Quickstrike to stay the night.

<u>Radge</u> - Leader of the Samoans, and he comes to the rescue of Neiko and Quickstrike. They allow them to stay and give them rations to continue their journey.

<u>Queen Tsarmina</u> - Queen of the Malibu Rainforest and of the Jaguar People.

<u>Jaguas</u> - Guide appointed by Tsarmina to help them trek through Velociraptor Ravine.

<u>Velosos</u> - The man raised by raptors. He guides them safely to Norak and later joins the Attack Pack.

<u>Boomerang Joe</u> - Kangaroo man, and like a typical desert bushman complete with a Desert Bushman accent. He is the first contact when

they arrive in Norak and aids in the defense against the attempted raid by Menes and his brothers.

Genghis Khan - The old frog man that gives Neiko her task and most of the information she needs to begin and understanding of how Qari and the First Universe are relative to her universe.

Jinx - The hermit of Bird Wood that witnesses Neiko's kidnapping. He tells the Attack Pack about it.

THE PHARAOHS

Ramses - The Dark Pharaoh also known as "Sisper-Bijou" who is imposing to be the firstborn son of Osiris and the First Pharaoh. He is the reason why Neiko becomes trapped in Qari. Immortal, evil, and has a deadly short temper. His intentions for kidnapping Neiko are to fulfill his infinite desire to make her his wife. His obsession is older than the existence of either universe.

Menes - The true firstborn son of Osiris. A large, orange triceratops man. Short-tempered and impulsive he is quick to act and ask questions later. His intelligence level is often called into question.

Tut - Osiris's second born who is a mole man. He is also known to me rash and impulsive, but not quite as quick-tempered. His biggest pet peeve is when he is called by his full name.

Re - The youngest son of Osiris who is a wolf man. He is often pessimistic, supersitious and skittish. Very learned and skilled in the arts. Often shy and well reserved unless there is a fight. Can be calculating.

<u>Osiris</u> - The father of Menes, Tut, and Re. He hides his scarred face and is the true First Pharaoh, but put out of commission but spared for Ramses's sinister plot that no one has quite figured out yet. Severly diminished from his true mean, ruthless nature supposedly after the death of this wife Leah.

<u>RAMSES'S ALLIES AND MINIONS</u>

<u>Vipra</u> - Witch that is impersonating Lydia and spying on the Attack Pack for her master, Ramses. She tries to do his bidding for Neiko, but she is foiled. When she is found out, she is killed.

<u>Quicksilver</u> - Ramses' right hand servant. He is the only native of Qari that knows of his secrets, and he is sent after Neiko and later is made into a Shadow Warrior.

<u>Hannibal</u> - Leader of the cannibals and an ally to Ramses. He is a large, fat elephant man with a witchdoctor's look.

<u>King Skull</u> - King of the swamp-dwelling Damonites and another ally to Ramses. He is a mole man.

<u>King Carrion</u> - King of the buzzard, condor, and vulture people of Fleetwood Forest, and he is a condor man and an ally to Ramses. When Neiko and Quickstrike were brought to him he was going to kill Quickstrike and deliver Neiko to Ramses.

<u>Grinder</u> - A vulture who is Carrion's messenger.

<u>Scavenger</u> - A vulture who led the arrest of Neiko and Quickstrike.

Cleaver - A buzzard that is one of Carrion's trackers.

Skull Bearers - soldiers and henchmen of the Pharaohs. Rank is determined by the type helmet worn: soldier/tracker-batwing with a spike on top, captain-bullhorn with a spike, lieutenant-beetle antennae with silver plume, corporal-spikes all over head with dragon wings, colonel-goat horns with long hairlike plume, and the generals have twisted horns on the sides of their head, small bullhorns beside the long hairlike plume.

ATTACK PACK

Quickstrike - Neiko's travel companion through the land of Qari. He is an Attack Pack member who is a scorpion with a cobra tail. He and Neiko must team together to get out of trouble and to get to safety so he will not be killed and Neiko captured. He is a mean fighter when provoked, but most of the time he is gentle and often skittish. He attacks with his tail, claws and sprays his venom at his enemies.

Phoenix - Leader of the Attack Pack. He is part wolf and part eagle, and when Neiko reaches Norak and joins the Pack, he aids her in trying to return home and against her struggles against Ramses. He attacks with his teeth and eagle claws on his front feet. He has rockets on his wing tips. Phoenix is soft hearted to all that are good, but those how do evil, beware.

Raptor - The joke telling, Attack Pack velociraptor who likes to help (he does not eat people). He accompanies Neiko while she is in the Attack Pack and gets her out of Vipra's traps. He attacks using his raptor skills and his teeth and claws. He has a laser crystal in the top of his head. He tells jokes about Ramses when possible and can be quite hasty.

<u>Air Hammer</u> - The hammer-headed hawk. He is Neiko and Quickstrike's first contact when they reach Norak. He is well known for his flight speed and keen eyesight, and his signature attack move is the 'hammer-head', and he also uses his razor sharp teeth and talons. He can be cocky and funny at times, but most of the time he is easy going and easy to get along with.

<u>Bantor</u> - An Attack Pack member who is part baboon and part tiger. He is a good tree attacker and has the ability to fly. He attacks with teeth and claws.

<u>Rip Rat</u> - One of the strange creatures of the Attack Pack from Eht Dnalsi. He has a long snout and they are filled with teeth, and his two front fangs are filled with poison, and his bite is his main attack, and he cannot fly.

<u>Darkclaw</u> - A batlike creature similar to Rip Rat, but his has a rounded snout and it is filled with rows of teeth. His attack moves are his savage bite and eye lasers, and he is able to fly.

<u>Glacier</u> - Darkclaw's twin brother that is white instead of black. He has the same attack moves, but he possesses venom in his teeth unlike Darkclaw.

<u>Sky Shadow</u> - He is part lizard and part dragonfly, and he is able to fly. He is terrific at camouflage and he attacks with a rear rocket fixed on his abdomen.

<u>Buzzclaw</u> - He is a mantis with the feet of a lizard. He attacks with his deadly mantis claws and mandibles, and he is able to fly. He is also Sky Shadow's brother.

<u>Scarem</u>- A huge stag beetle. He attacks with his razor sharp pinchers

and has a hard shell for protection, and he can fly. He has a laser crystal on his belly.

Diana - Lydia's sister who is married to Scarem, and she has no attack moves and does not fight. She is a human.

Lydia - Wife of Phoenix and she was long time plagued by Ramses when he could not obtain Neiko. She adopted Cheetor for a time when he was a cub.

Injector - He is part lionfish and part hornet. He can fly and his deadly sting and spines are a threat and he has a rocket on his stinger.

Torca - He is part whale and part elephant. He cannot fly, but he loves to charge and his tusks are deadly and so is his tremendous weight.

Noctorro - A bat with the head of a Brahma bull. He has long claws on his fingers and his horns are deadly. He is able to fly.

Sonar - A vampire bat that have deadly teeth and claws, and he have a laser crystal on his belly. He can fly and he possesses a Transylvanian type accent.

Rosenar - Sonar's wife who is just like him

Sandstorm - A Saracen prince and the only Saracen left, and he is the second in command of the Pack. He fights with his trusty scimitar and his knowledge of Saracen magic. He can only fly if he is riding his flying carpet.

Waspinator - A giant wasp who is able to fly and has a deadly sting. He, too, has a rocket on his stinger.

Cheetor - A huge, fierce cheetah. He has great running speed and ability to fly. He has a rocket strapped to his back and purple shields strapped to his right front and back legs, and on the hind leg he has a laser crystal.

Cheetara - Cheetor's wife who looks and fights just like Cheetor. She his more reserved but fierce in s fight.

Sichus and Daisy - Flying big horned sheep who love life in the Attack Pack. They use their horns in combat and have a laser crystal in their forehead, and they also attack with their hind legs.

Ramulus and Aries - Flying big horned sheep just like Sichus and Daisy. Ramulus is Sichus' twin brother, and he accompanies Neiko to Hawote.

IMPORTANT HISTORICAL PEOPLE OF THE FIVE LANDS

Rumi -The founder of the Pharaoh family and builder of the ancient city of Geezah. He is also the one who wrote the books of black magic, made the Eye of Cygnus and searched for the lore of the Dark Pharaoh.

Xerxes - Son of Rumi who carried on his father's ways.

Thutmose the Mighty - The father of Anubis the Terrible who lost the battle against the Marauders in which Geezah fell.

Anubis the Terrible - The grandfather of Osiris who built Skull Fort and reawakened the Pharaohs. He also pursued Lydia to raise his son Saber, but he met his end at the claws of Cheetor.

Saladin - The founder of the Saracens, who were Sandstorm's family and people.

Omar - Sandstorm's father who had a duel with Osiris and scarred him for life. Omar was later murdered with all of his kin by Ramses and all of the other Pharaohs which Sandstorm was the sole survivor.

Ajax - Father of Lydia who suffered from the plight of Ramses's schemes for his daughter.

PLACES

Hawote - The hidden Indian land that spans from coast to coast of the U.S. and from Alaska down to Mexico. This land coexists with the U.S., Canada, and Mexico without knowledge from the Outsiders.

Georgia - The normal U.S. state that coexists with the portion of Hawote where Neiko lives.

Geezah - The Pharaoh city located high in the Kilowee Mountains.

Skull Fort - The fortress that is in the Dark Forest that serves as the new place the Pharaohs live. It was built by Anubis the Terrible after Geezah fell.

THE FIVE LANDS

Qari - The land where Neiko's adventure takes place.

Saudi

<u>Occorom</u>

<u>Iduas</u>

<u>Tiawuk</u>

<u>Eht Dnalsi</u> - an island that is part of Iduas where Rip Rat, Darkclaw, and Glacier came from.

<u>Etowah</u> - Island piece of Saudi where the Maximal and Predacon tribes came from. Most of the Attack Pack members are from here.

THE SEVEN TRIBES

<u>Desert Storm Falcons</u> - Neiko's tribe that came from the west to the east thousands of years ago. Present territory is in northeast part of Georgia close to South Carolina and Cherokee territory. Other members include Xartna, Aquila, Nighthawk, and Phoenix.

<u>Scraah Wareagles</u> - Sigma's tribe whose territory is in northwest Georgia. Other members include Puma, Monchiska, Pike, and White Fang.

<u>Chang Battlehawks</u> - Monganata and Windsong's tribe whose territory is next door to Falcon land.

<u>Cheikomaguan Braves</u> - tribe whose land is south of the Scraah. Bear Claw is from this tribe.

<u>Monte Carlo Warriors</u> - tribe whose territory is in central north Georgia.

<u>Scandinavian Vikings</u> - A tough guerilla tribe whose territory is in south central Georgia. Their tactics of fighting are much like the Vikings from Europe but with an Indian twist. They also wear bison horns on both sides of their headdresses.

<u>Mohican-Sparra Wolverines</u> - a conglomerate tribe made up of the Mohicans and Sparras into one tribe several hundred years ago in a pact. In some ways the parent tribes still hold some of their individual traditions and identities, and sometimes it is expressed, but in other times they function as one. This tribe is where Francesco does his espionage for Raven as the chief of this tribe. Their small territory is nearly surrounded by Falcon land in northeast Georgia. Hawk is from the Mohican section of this tribe.

ABOUT THE AUTHOR

A.K. Taylor grew up in the backwoods of Georgia where she learned about nature. She enjoys hunting and fishing, beekeeping, gardening, archery, shooting, hiking, and has various collections.

She also has interest in music, Native American history and heritage, Egyptian history, and the natural sciences. A.K. Taylor has been writing and drawing since the age of 16. A.K. Taylor has graduated from the University of Georgia with a biology degree, and she shares an interest in herpetology with her husband.

FROM THE AUTHOR:

Thank you for reading! If you would be so kind, would you go to your favorite retailer, Goodreads, Booklikes, and leave an honest review? Thank you!

Would you like to get dibs on new releases and behind the scenes action? You also get a free book just for signing up. Join the newsletter today!

ALSO BY AK TAYLOR:

ESCAPE FROM ANCIENT EGYPT
BOOK #2 OF THE NEIKO ADVENTURE SAGA

THE NEWBIE AUTHOR'S SURVIVAL GUIDE

BLOODY KLONDIKE GOLD
(A RANDI BRAVEHEART MYSTERY SHORT STORY)

MANY MORE THINGS TO COME!

TO READ A.K.'S BLOG OR
CONNECT WITH HER ON SOCIAL MEDIA PLEASE VISIT

WWW.BACKWOODSAUTHOR.COM

9 781943 326013